VIRTUAL HERO

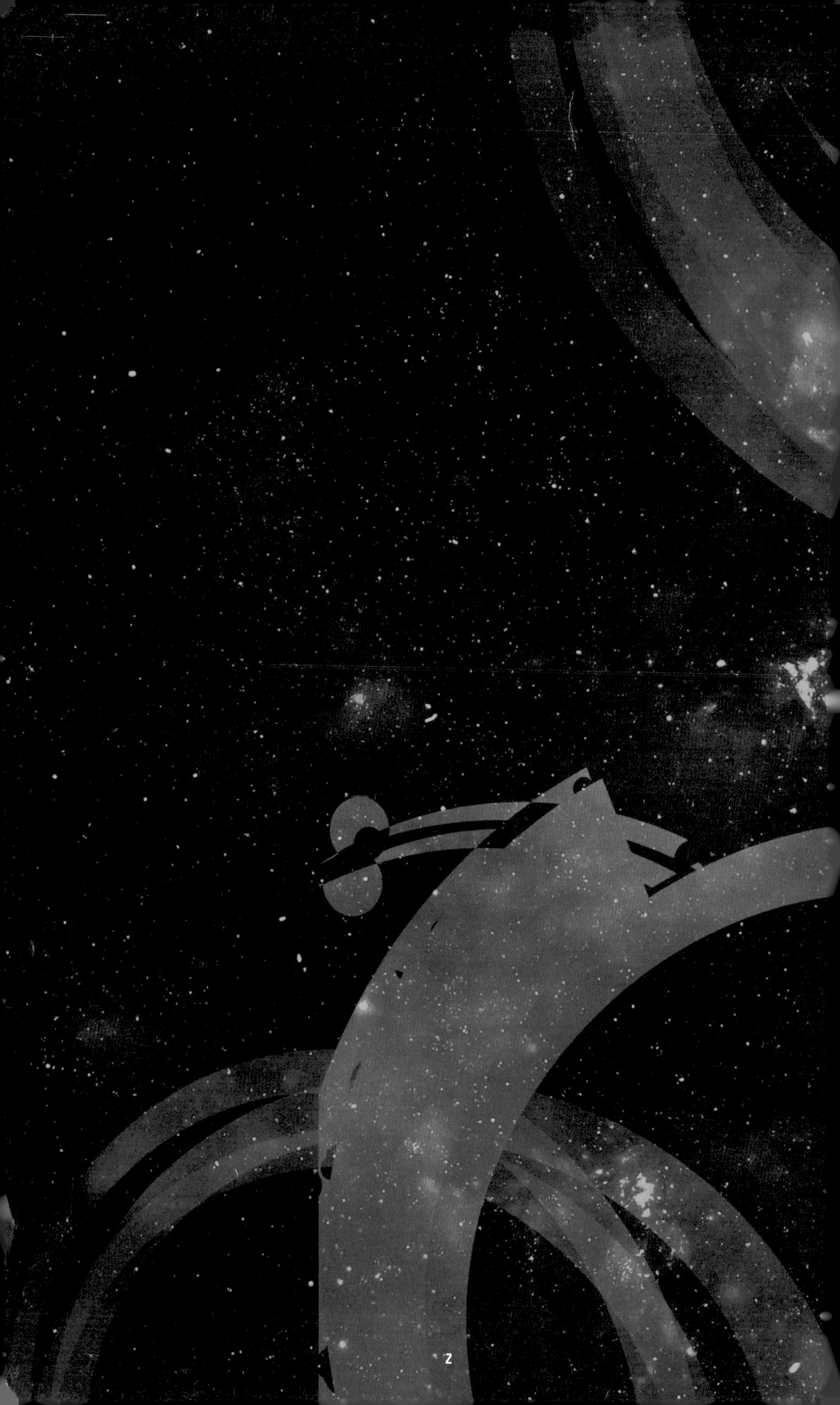

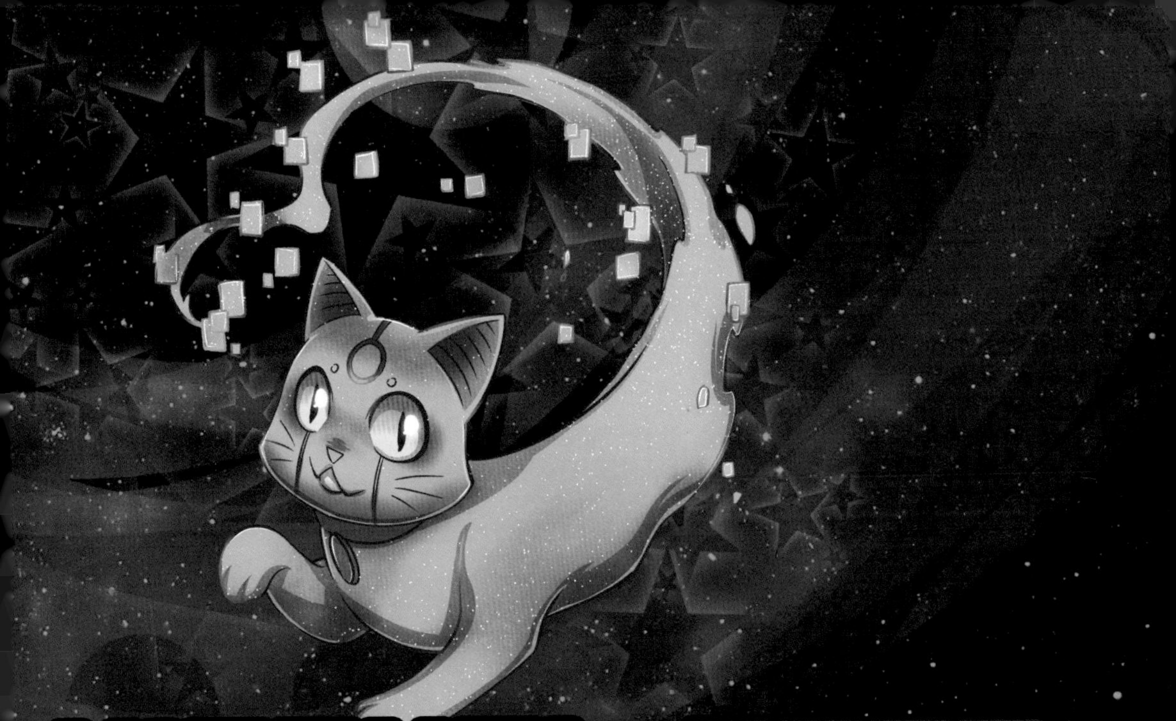

VIRTUAL HERO

AUTHOR: **RUBIUS**

ARTIST: **LOLITA ALDEA**

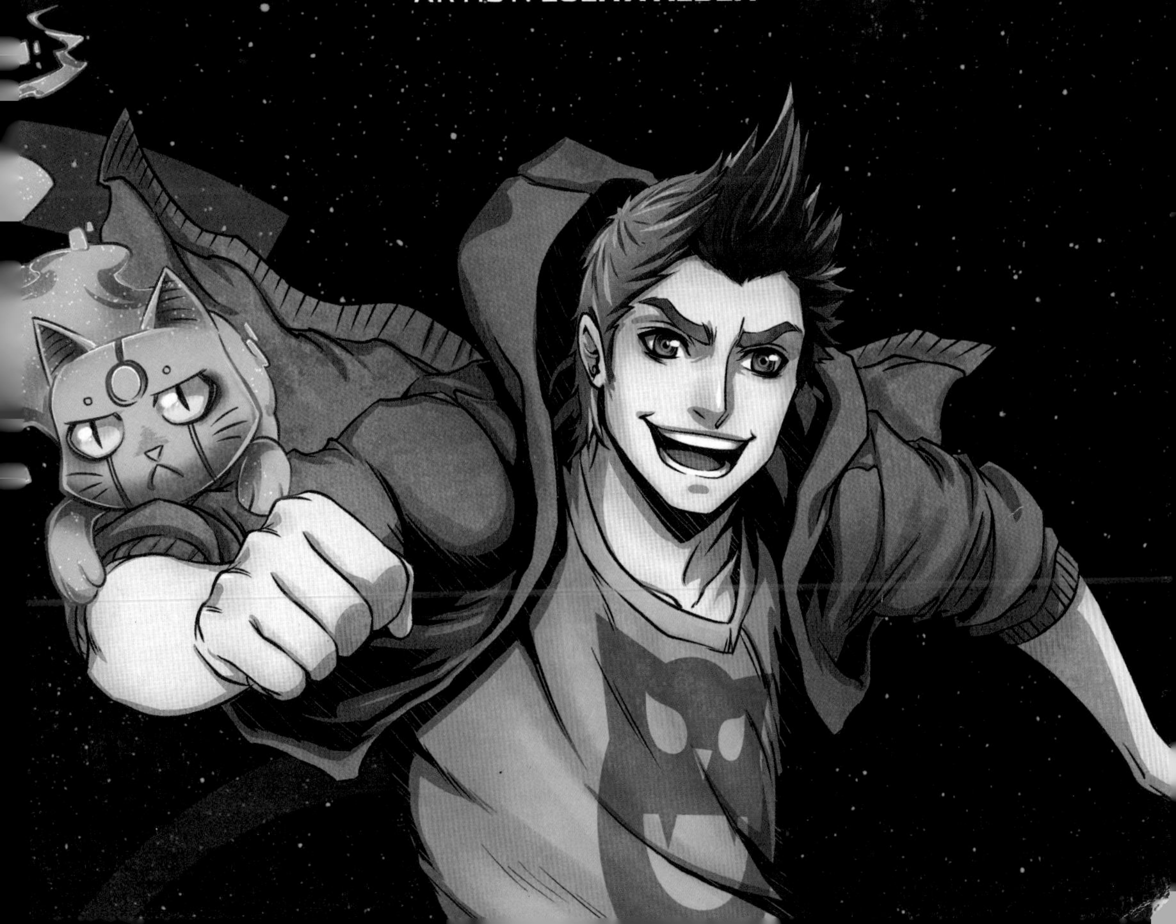

TRANSLATION
IVAN BRANDON

LETTERS
CARLOS MANGUAL

FOR ABLAZE

MANAGING EDITOR
RICH YOUNG

EDITOR
KEVIN KETNER

DESIGNER
RODOLFO MURAGUCHI

Publisher's Cataloging-in-Publication data

Names: Doblas, Rubén, AKA Rubius, author. I Aldea, María Dolores, artist.
Title: Virtual hero / [written by] El Torres; [art by] María Dolores Aldea.
Description: Portland, OR: Ablaze Publishing, 2021.
Identifiers: ISBN: 978-1-950912-38-4
Subjects: LCSH Video games—Comic books, strips, etc. I Virtual reality—Comic books, strips, etc. I Graphic novels. I
Adventure fiction. I BISAC COMICS & GRAPHIC NOVELS / Manga / Action & Adventure
Classification: LCC PQ6654 .02318 V57 2021 I DDC 741.5—dc23

HELLO, GOD'S CREATURES,

This is an epic story, full of action, with traitors, innocents, unexpected encounters, new friends, video game worlds of all kinds and, last but not least, love... a lot of love. (And yes, also some Rubelangel... ahem.)

I invite you to join me in a fantastic adventure that takes place on both sides of the computer screen, full of surprises and with a disturbing ending. Are you ready? If not, nothing happens. I'll wait for you here...

A little longer...

Come on, now. Go!

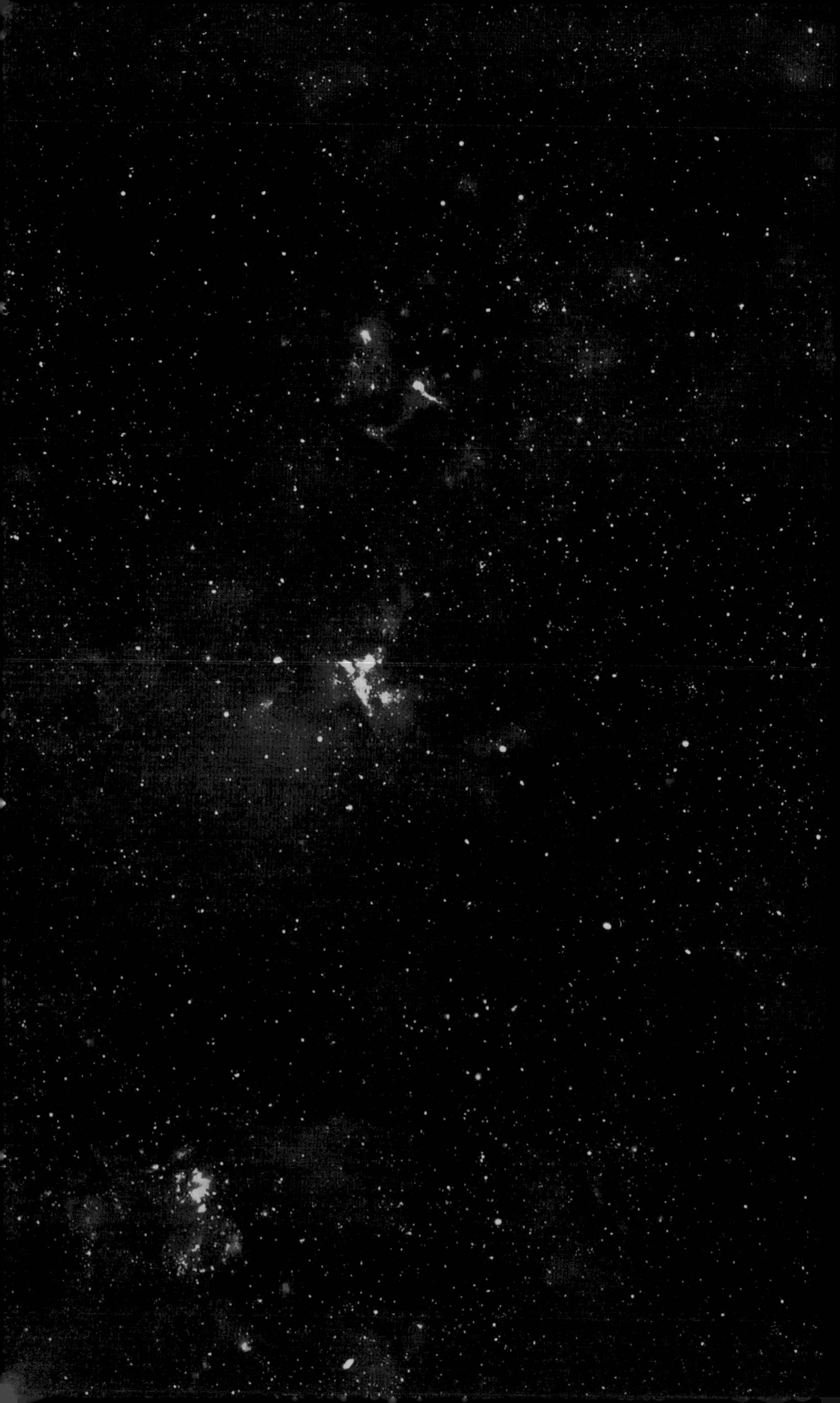

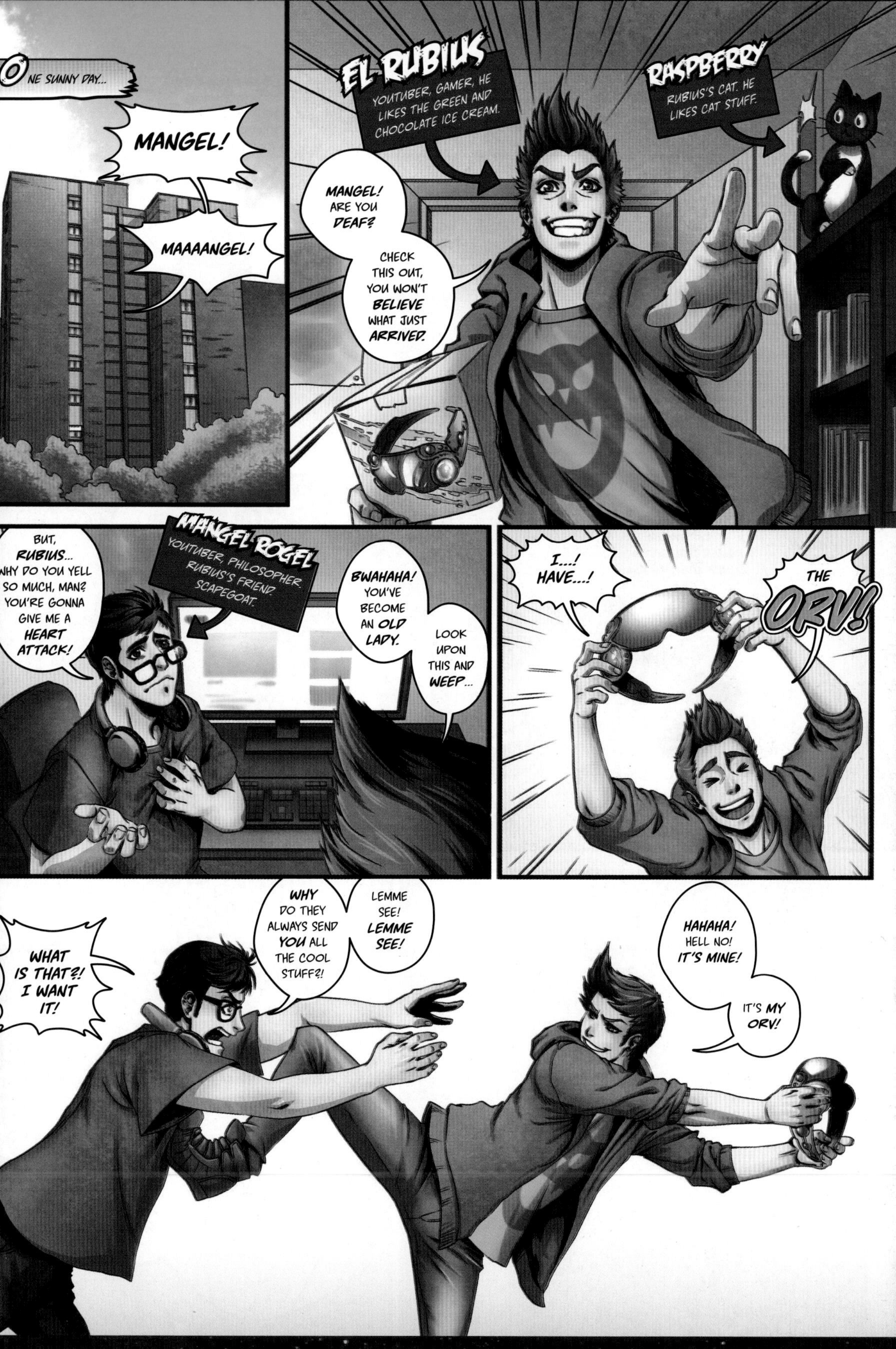
ONE SUNNY DAY...
MANGEL!
MAAAANGEL!
EL RUBIUS
YOUTUBER, GAMER, HE LIKES THE GREEN AND CHOCOLATE ICE CREAM.
RASPBERRY
RUBIUS'S CAT. HE LIKES CAT STUFF.
MANGEL! ARE YOU DEAF?
CHECK THIS OUT, YOU WON'T BELIEVE WHAT JUST ARRIVED.
BUT, RUBIUS... WHY DO YOU YELL SO MUCH, MAN? YOU'RE GONNA GIVE ME A HEART ATTACK!
MANGEL ROGEL
YOUTUBER, PHILOSOPHER. RUBIUS'S FRIEND. SCAPEGOAT.
BWAHAHA! YOU'VE BECOME AN OLD LADY.
LOOK UPON THIS AND WEEP...
I...! HAVE...!
THE ORV!
WHAT IS THAT?! I WANT IT!
WHY DO THEY ALWAYS SEND YOU ALL THE COOL STUFF?!
LEMME SEE! LEMME SEE!
HAHAHA! HELL NO! IT'S MINE!
IT'S MY ORV!

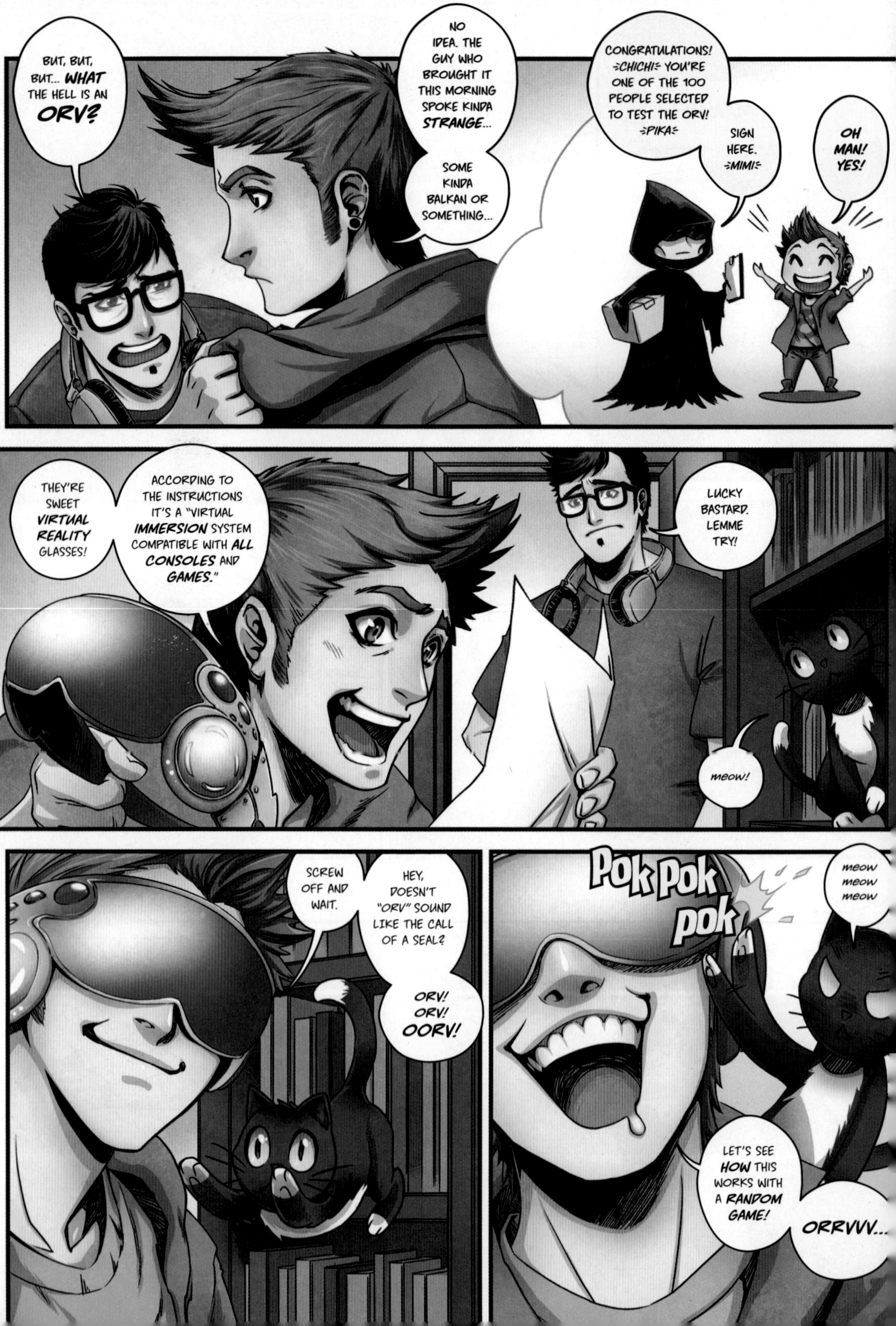
BUT, BUT, BUT... WHAT THE HELL IS AN ORV?
NO IDEA. THE GUY WHO BROUGHT IT THIS MORNING SPOKE KINDA STRANGE...
SOME KINDA BALKAN OR SOMETHING...
CONGRATULATIONS! =CHICHI= YOU'RE ONE OF THE 100 PEOPLE SELECTED TO TEST THE ORV! =PIKA=
SIGN HERE. =MIMI=
OH MAN! YES!
THEY'RE SWEET VIRTUAL REALITY GLASSES!
ACCORDING TO THE INSTRUCTIONS IT'S A "VIRTUAL IMMERSION SYSTEM COMPATIBLE WITH ALL CONSOLES AND GAMES."
LUCKY BASTARD. LEMME TRY!
meow!
SCREW OFF AND WAIT.
HEY, DOESN'T "ORV" SOUND LIKE THE CALL OF A SEAL?
ORV! ORV! OORV!
Pok pok pok
meow meow meow
LET'S SEE HOW THIS WORKS WITH A RANDOM GAME!
ORRVVV...

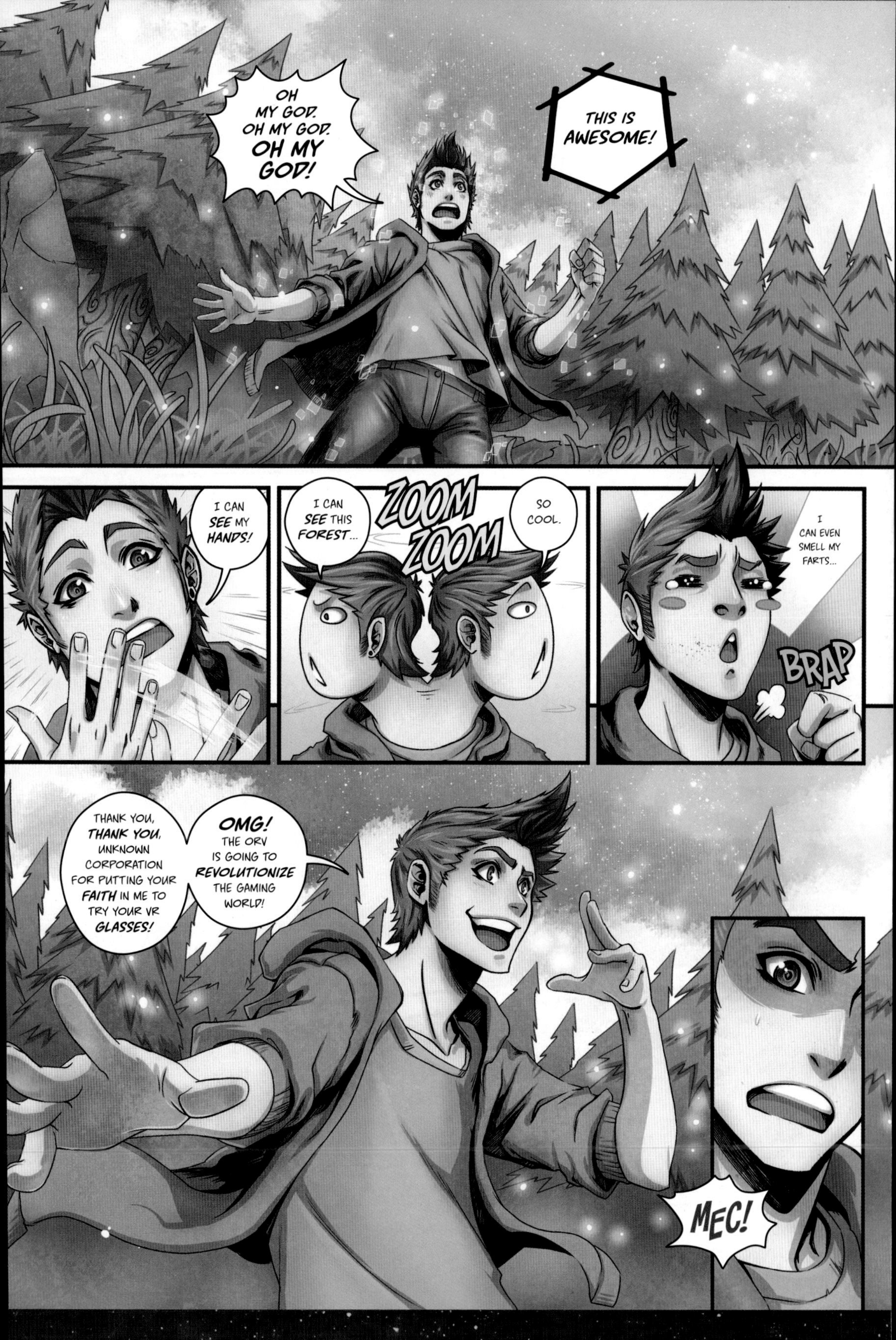
OH MY GOD. OH MY GOD. OH MY GOD!
THIS IS AWESOME!
I CAN SEE MY HANDS!
I CAN SEE THIS FOREST...
ZOOM ZOOM
SO COOL.
I CAN EVEN SMELL MY FARTS...
BRAP
THANK YOU, THANK YOU, UNKNOWN CORPORATION FOR PUTTING YOUR FAITH IN ME TO TRY YOUR VR GLASSES!
OMG! THE ORV IS GOING TO REVOLUTIONIZE THE GAMING WORLD!
MEC!

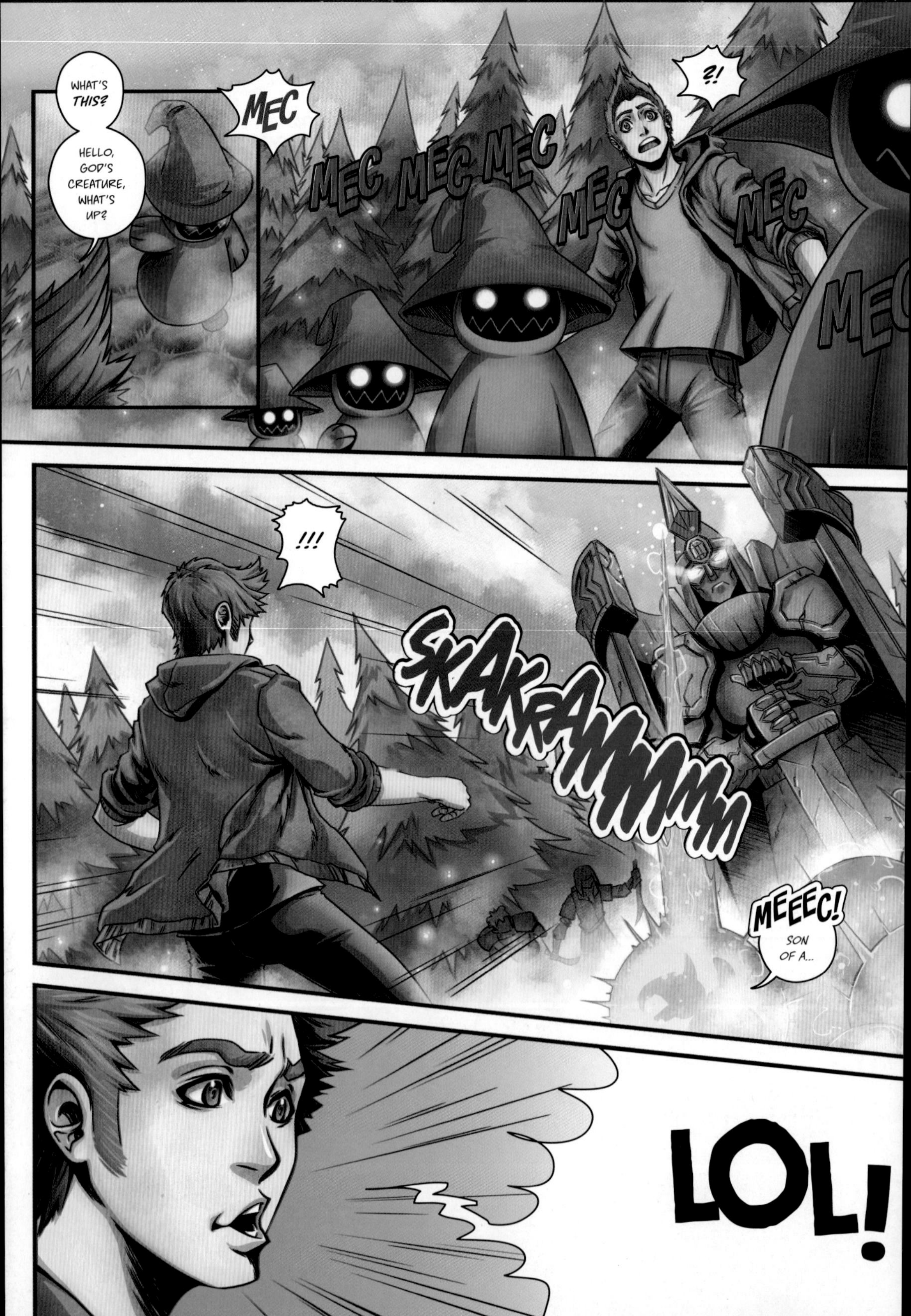

WHAT'S THIS?
HELLO, GOD'S CREATURE, WHAT'S UP?
MEC
?!
MEC MEC MEC
MEC
MEC
MEC
!!!
SKAKRAMMMM
MEEEC!
SON OF A...
LOL!

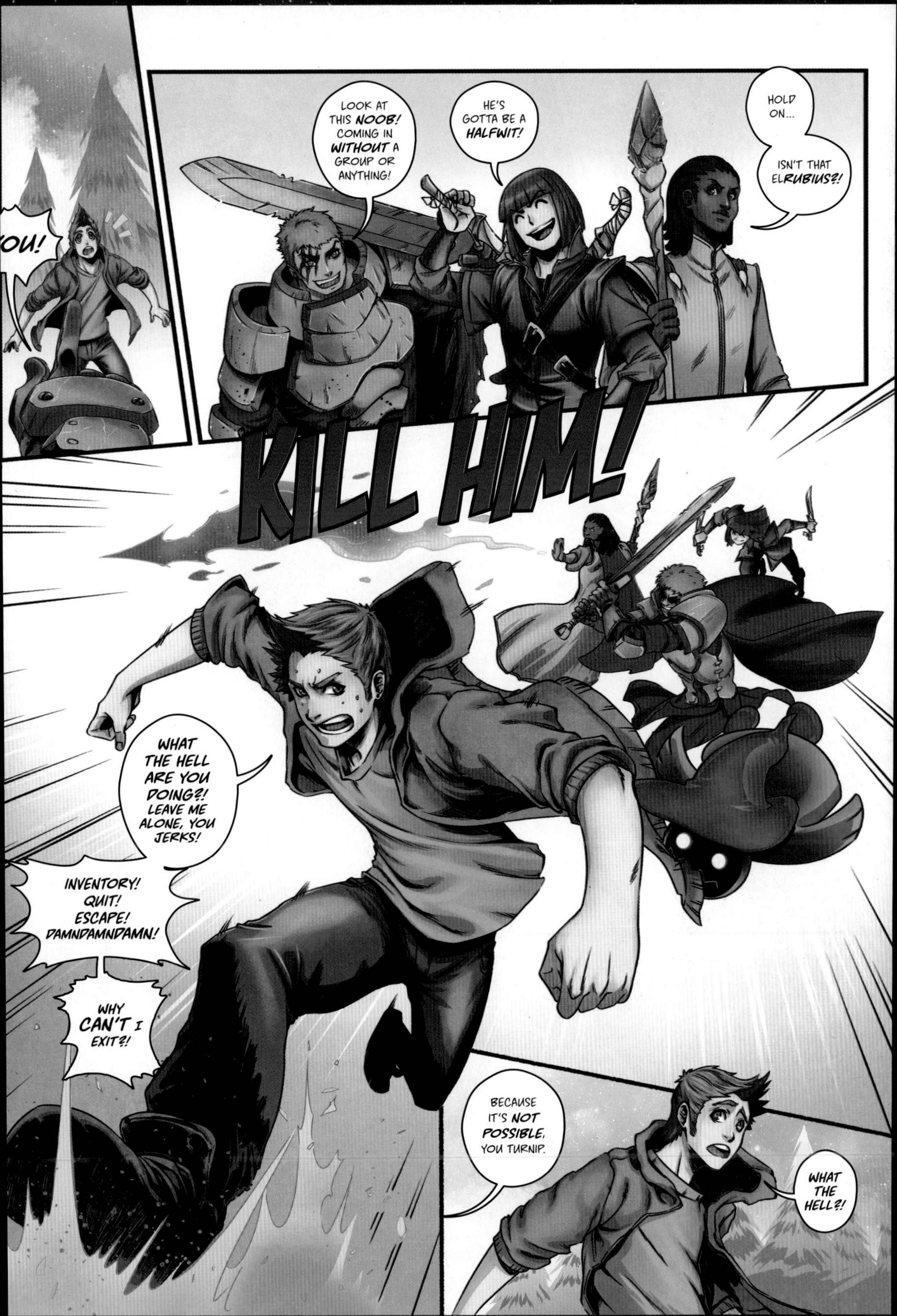

YOU!
LOOK AT THIS NOOB! COMING IN WITHOUT A GROUP OR ANYTHING!
HE'S GOTTA BE A HALFWIT!
HOLD ON...
ISN'T THAT ELRUBIUS?!
KILL HIM!
WHAT THE HELL ARE YOU DOING?! LEAVE ME ALONE, YOU JERKS!
INVENTORY! QUIT! ESCAPE! DAMNDAMNDAMN!
WHY CAN'T I EXIT?!
BECAUSE IT'S NOT POSSIBLE, YOU TURNIP.
WHAT THE HELL?!

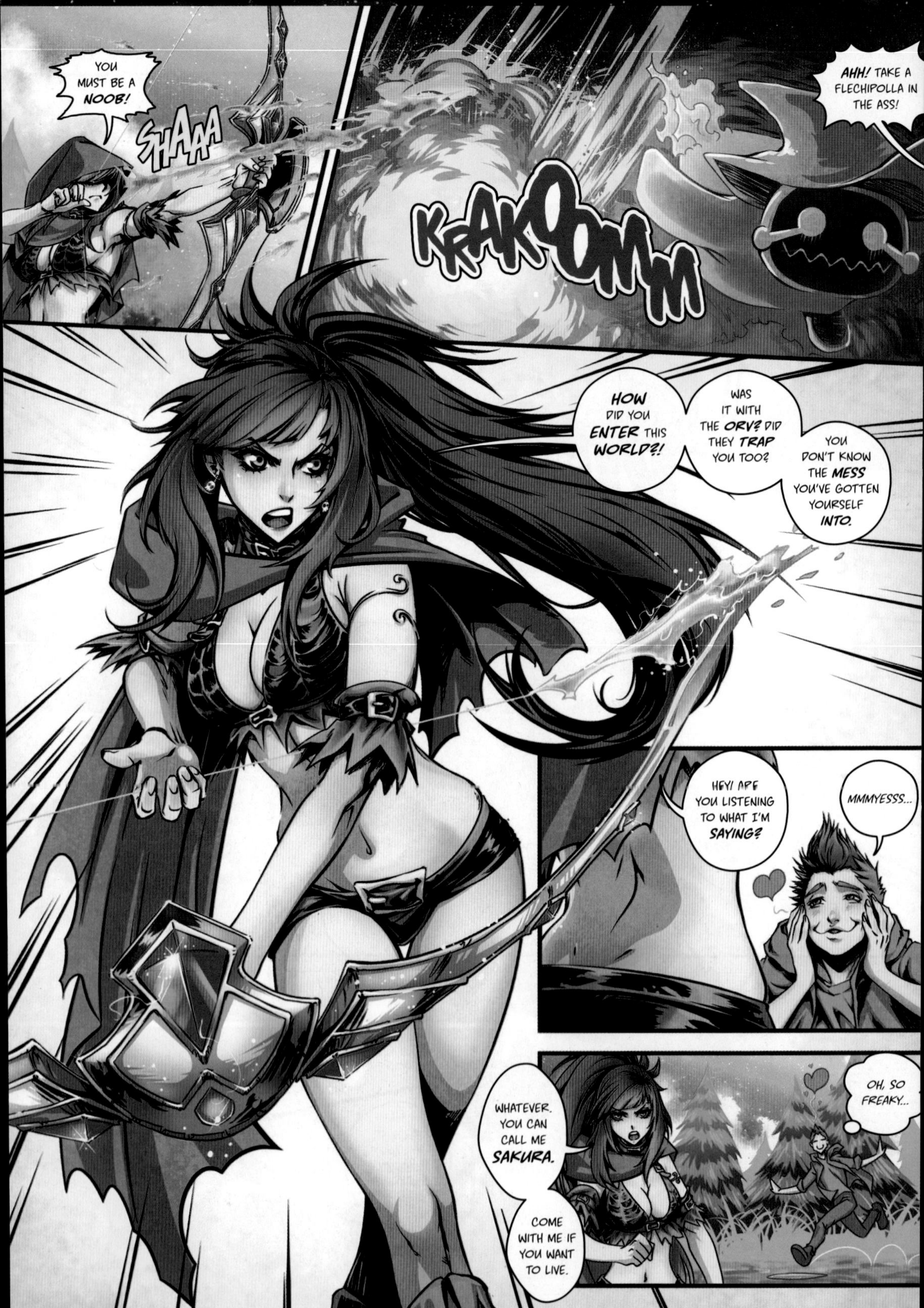
YOU MUST BE A NOOB!
SHAAA
AHH! TAKE A FLECHIPOLLA IN THE ASS!
KRAKOOMM
HOW DID YOU ENTER THIS WORLD?!
WAS IT WITH THE ORV? DID THEY TRAP YOU TOO?
YOU DON'T KNOW THE MESS YOU'VE GOTTEN YOURSELF INTO.
HEY! ARE YOU LISTENING TO WHAT I'M SAYING?
MMMYESSS...
WHATEVER. YOU CAN CALL ME SAKURA.
COME WITH ME IF YOU WANT TO LIVE.
OH, SO FREAKY...

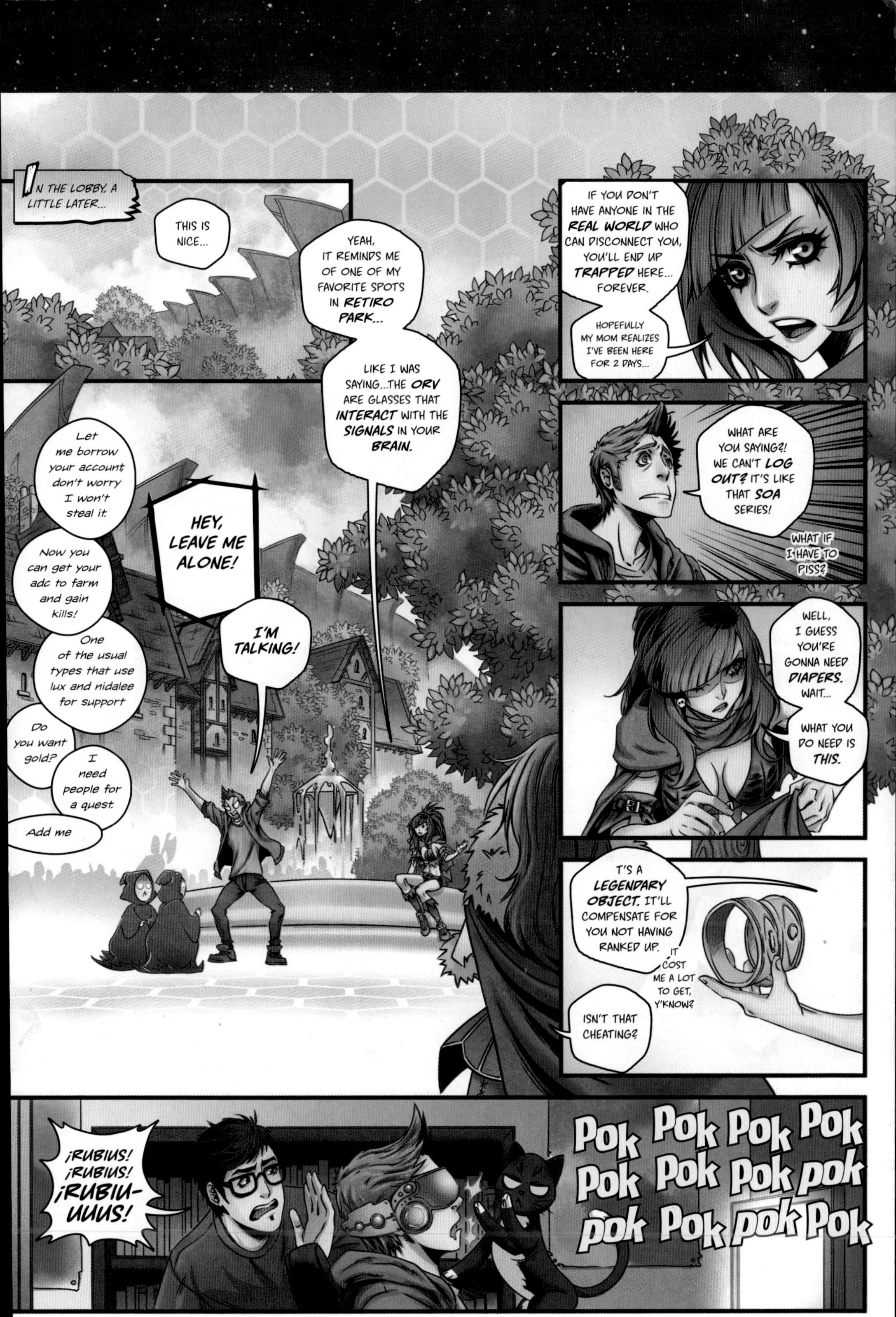
IN THE LOBBY, A LITTLE LATER...
THIS IS NICE...
YEAH, IT REMINDS ME OF ONE OF MY FAVORITE SPOTS IN RETIRO PARK...
LIKE I WAS SAYING...THE ORV ARE GLASSES THAT INTERACT WITH THE SIGNALS IN YOUR BRAIN.
IF YOU DON'T HAVE ANYONE IN THE REAL WORLD WHO CAN DISCONNECT YOU, YOU'LL END UP TRAPPED HERE... FOREVER.
HOPEFULLY MY MOM REALIZES I'VE BEEN HERE FOR 2 DAYS...
Let me borrow your account don't worry I won't steal it.
Now you can get your adc to farm and gain kills!
One of the usual types that use lux and nidalee for support
Do you want gold?
I need people for a quest.
Add me
HEY, LEAVE ME ALONE!
I'M TALKING!
WHAT ARE YOU SAYING?! WE CAN'T LOG OUT? IT'S LIKE THAT SOA SERIES!
WHAT IF I HAVE TO PISS?
WELL, I GUESS YOU'RE GONNA NEED DIAPERS. WAIT...
WHAT YOU DO NEED IS THIS.
T'S A LEGENDARY OBJECT. IT'LL COMPENSATE FOR YOU NOT HAVING RANKED UP.
IT COST ME A LOT TO GET, Y'KNOW?
ISN'T THAT CHEATING?
¡RUBIUS! ¡RUBIUS! ¡RUBIU-UUUS!
Pok Pok Pok Pok Pok Pok Pok pok pok Pok pok Pok

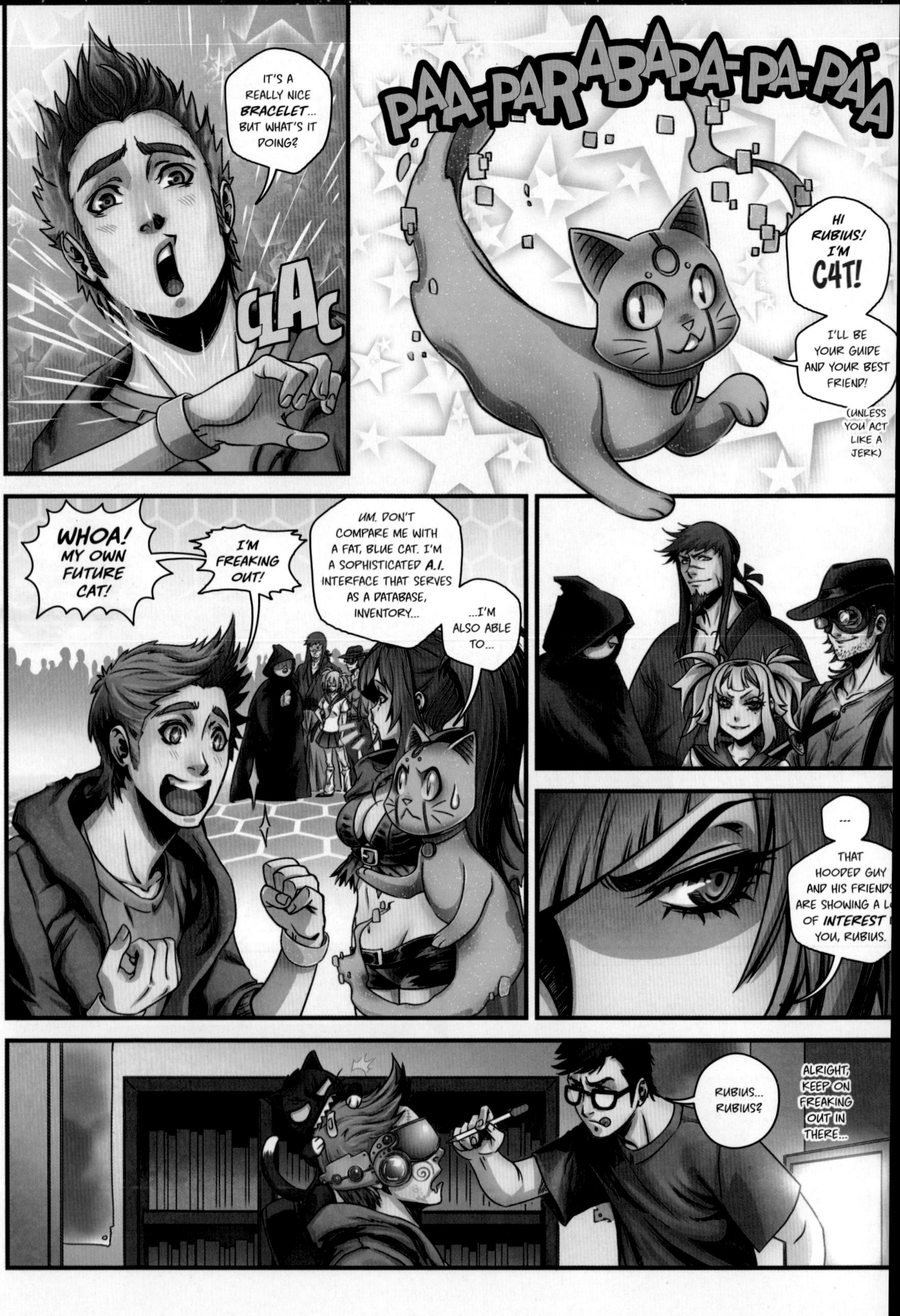
IT'S A REALLY NICE BRACELET... BUT WHAT'S IT DOING?
CLAC
PAA-PARABAPA-PA-PÁA
HI RUBIUS! I'M C4T!
I'LL BE YOUR GUIDE AND YOUR BEST FRIEND!
(UNLESS YOU ACT LIKE A JERK)
WHOA! MY OWN FUTURE CAT!
I'M FREAKING OUT!
UM. DON'T COMPARE ME WITH A FAT, BLUE CAT. I'M A SOPHISTICATED A.I. INTERFACE THAT SERVES AS A DATABASE, INVENTORY...
...I'M ALSO ABLE TO...
...
THAT HOODED GUY AND HIS FRIENDS ARE SHOWING A LO OF INTEREST YOU, RUBIUS.
RUBIUS... RUBIUS?
ALRIGHT, KEEP ON FREAKING OUT IN THERE...

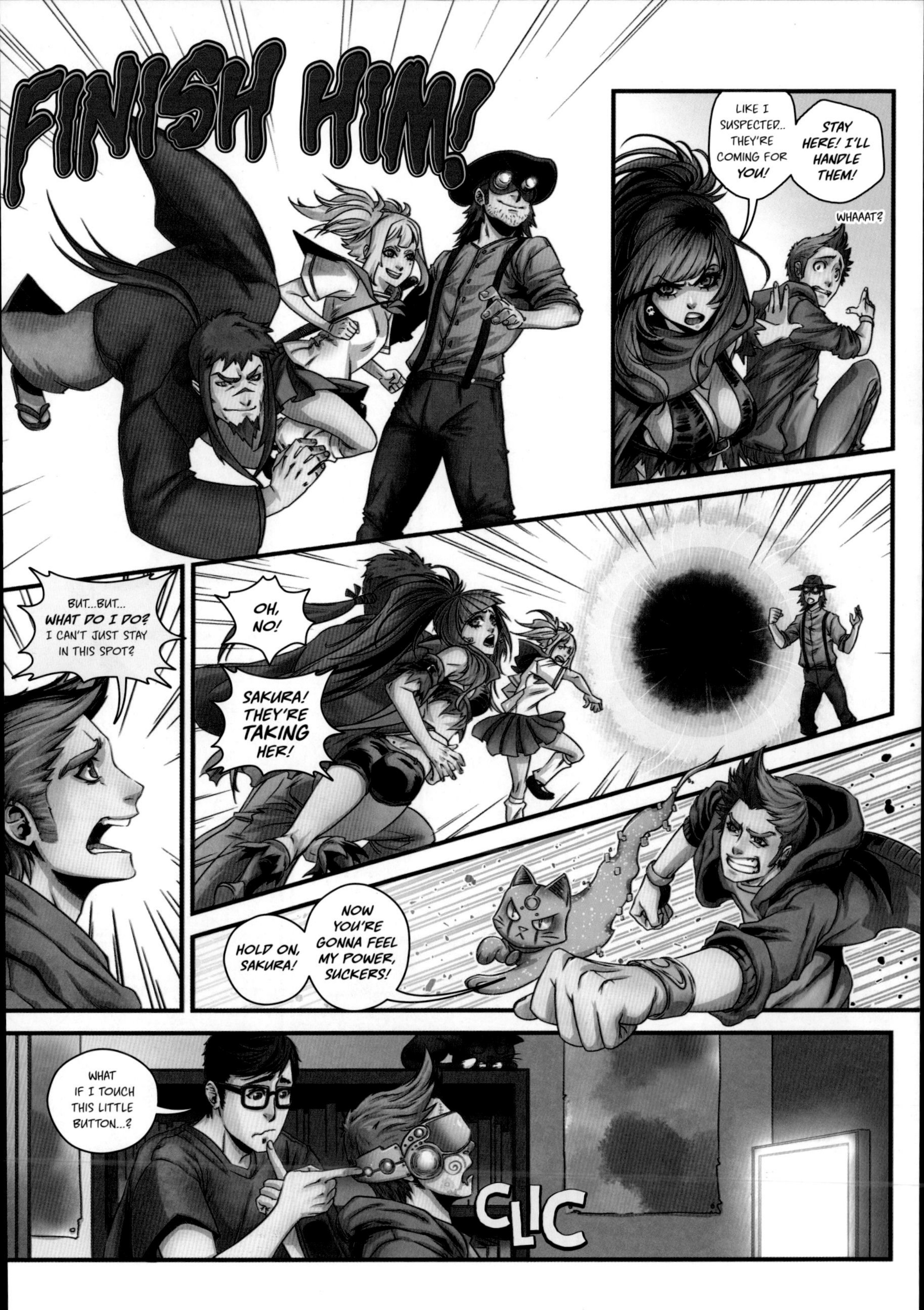
FINISH HIM!
LIKE I SUSPECTED... THEY'RE COMING FOR YOU!
STAY HERE! I'LL HANDLE THEM!
WHAAAT?
BUT...BUT... WHAT DO I DO? I CAN'T JUST STAY IN THIS SPOT?
OH, NO!
SAKURA! THEY'RE TAKING HER!
HOLD ON, SAKURA!
NOW YOU'RE GONNA FEEL MY POWER, SUCKERS!
WHAT IF I TOUCH THIS LITTLE BUTTON...?
CLIC

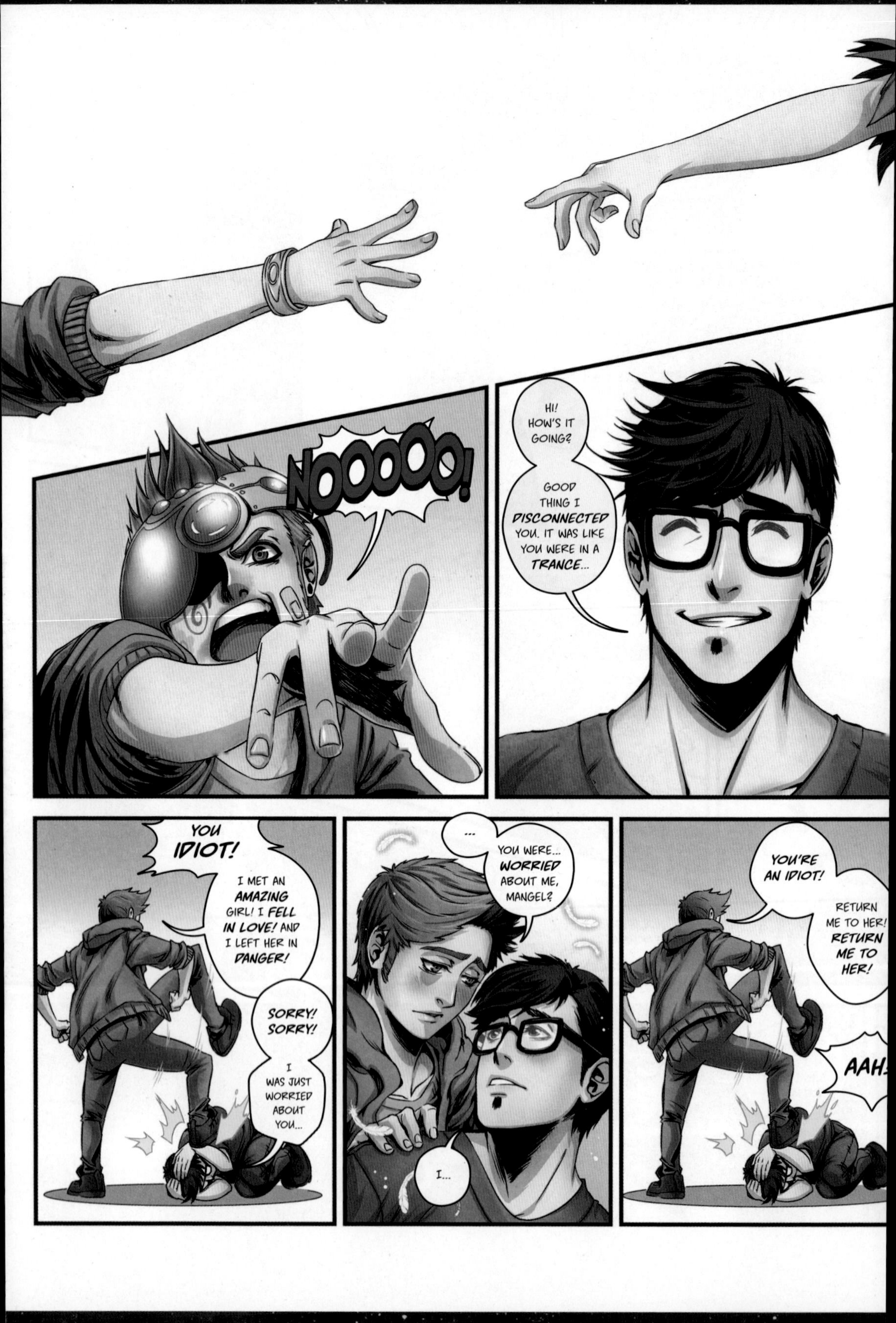
NOOOOO!
HI! HOW'S IT GOING?
GOOD THING I DISCONNECTED YOU. IT WAS LIKE YOU WERE IN A TRANCE...
YOU IDIOT!
I MET AN AMAZING GIRL! I FELL IN LOVE! AND I LEFT HER IN DANGER!
SORRY! SORRY!
I WAS JUST WORRIED ABOUT YOU...
...
YOU WERE... WORRIED ABOUT ME, MANGEL?
I...
YOU'RE AN IDIOT!
RETURN ME TO HER! RETURN ME TO HER!
AAH!

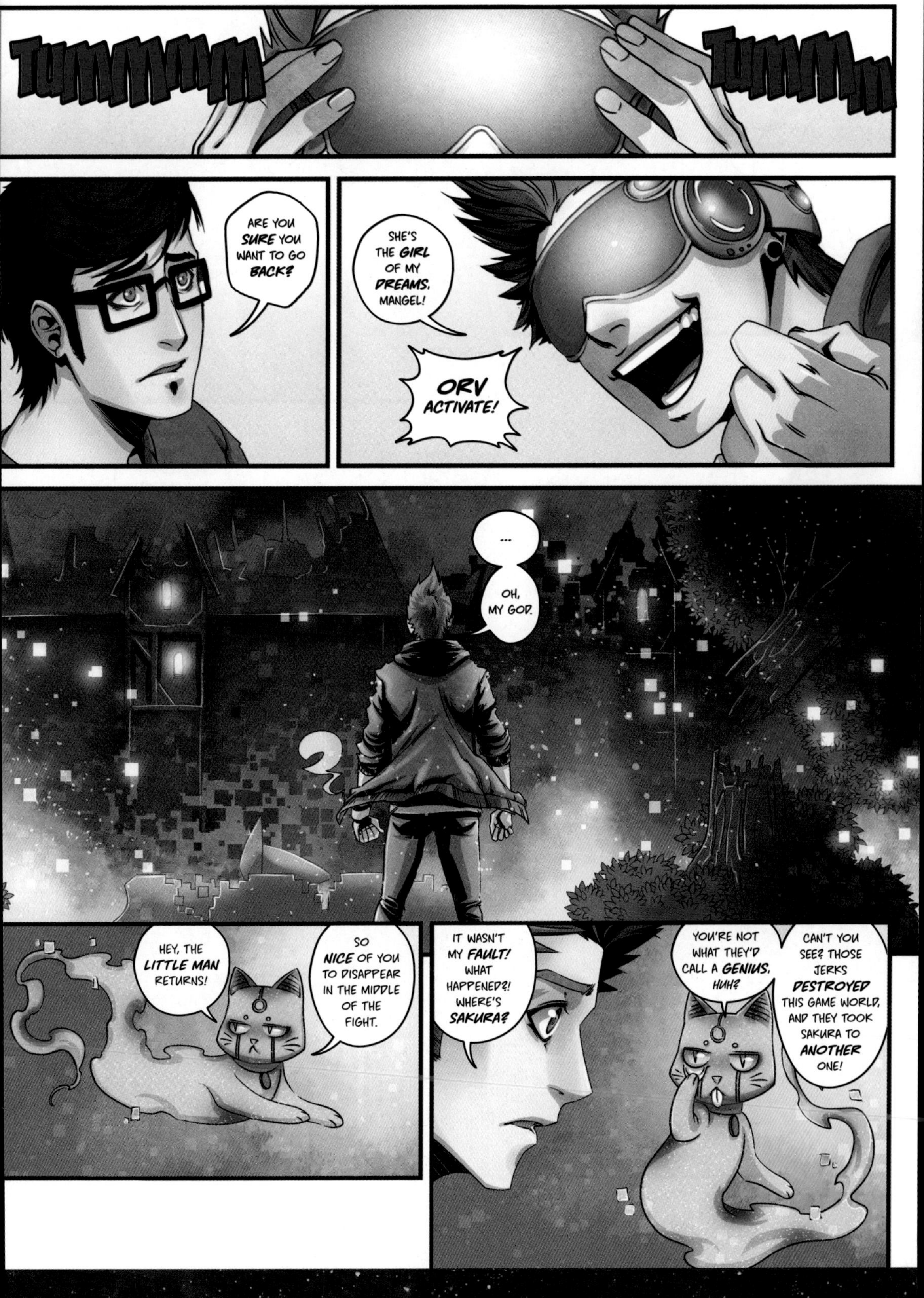
TUMMMM
TUMMMM
ARE YOU SURE YOU WANT TO GO BACK?
SHE'S THE GIRL OF MY DREAMS, MANGEL!
ORV ACTIVATE!
...
OH, MY GOD.
HEY, THE LITTLE MAN RETURNS!
SO NICE OF YOU TO DISAPPEAR IN THE MIDDLE OF THE FIGHT.
IT WASN'T MY FAULT! WHAT HAPPENED?! WHERE'S SAKURA?
YOU'RE NOT WHAT THEY'D CALL A GENIUS, HUH?
CAN'T YOU SEE? THOSE JERKS DESTROYED THIS GAME WORLD, AND THEY TOOK SAKURA TO ANOTHER ONE!

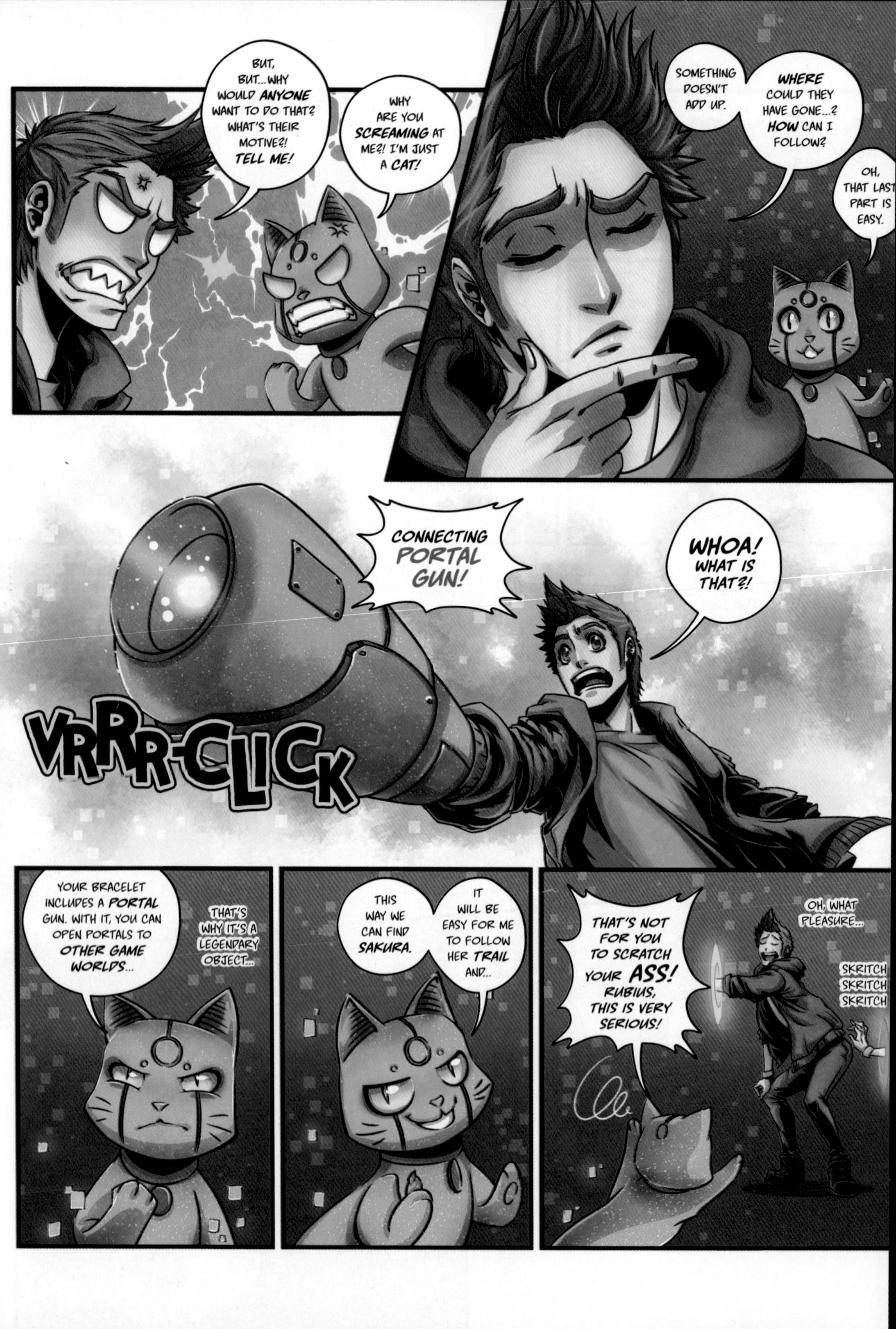
BUT, BUT... WHY WOULD ANYONE WANT TO DO THAT? WHAT'S THEIR MOTIVE?! TELL ME!
WHY ARE YOU SCREAMING AT ME?! I'M JUST A CAT!
SOMETHING DOESN'T ADD UP.
WHERE COULD THEY HAVE GONE...? HOW CAN I FOLLOW?
OH, THAT LAST PART IS EASY.
CONNECTING PORTAL GUN!
WHOA! WHAT IS THAT?!
VRRR-CLICK
YOUR BRACELET INCLUDES A PORTAL GUN. WITH IT, YOU CAN OPEN PORTALS TO OTHER GAME WORLDS...
THAT'S WHY IT'S A LEGENDARY OBJECT...
THIS WAY WE CAN FIND SAKURA.
IT WILL BE EASY FOR ME TO FOLLOW HER TRAIL AND...
THAT'S NOT FOR YOU TO SCRATCH YOUR ASS! RUBIUS, THIS IS VERY SERIOUS!
OH, WHAT PLEASURE...
SKRITCH SKRITCH SKRITCH

WE GO BLINDLY FORWARD...
OBVIOUSLY, BECAUSE YOU **CAN'T SEE SQUAT IN THIS PLACE!**
GOOD THING THE BRACELET HAS A LANTERN...
I'M DETECTING THAT **SAKURA** HAS BEEN THROUGH HERE.
THROUGH... **HERE?**
YOU'RE... SURE?
THIS PLACE IS GIVING ME A REAL **BAD FEELING**...
OF COURSE!
I'LL CHECK WHICH GAME **WORLD** WE'RE IN...
THE THING IS IT'S REMINDING ME OF SOMETHING...

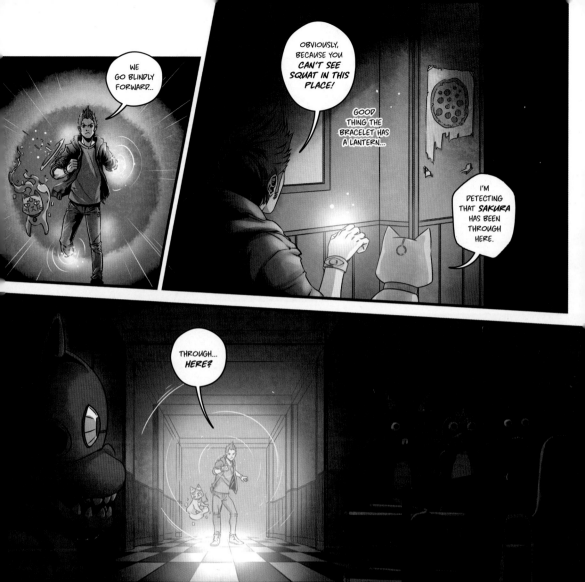

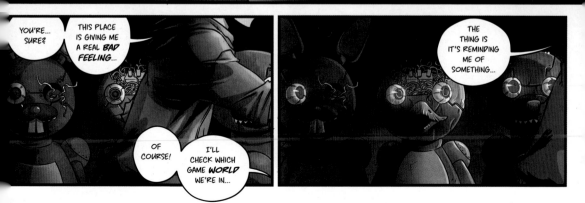

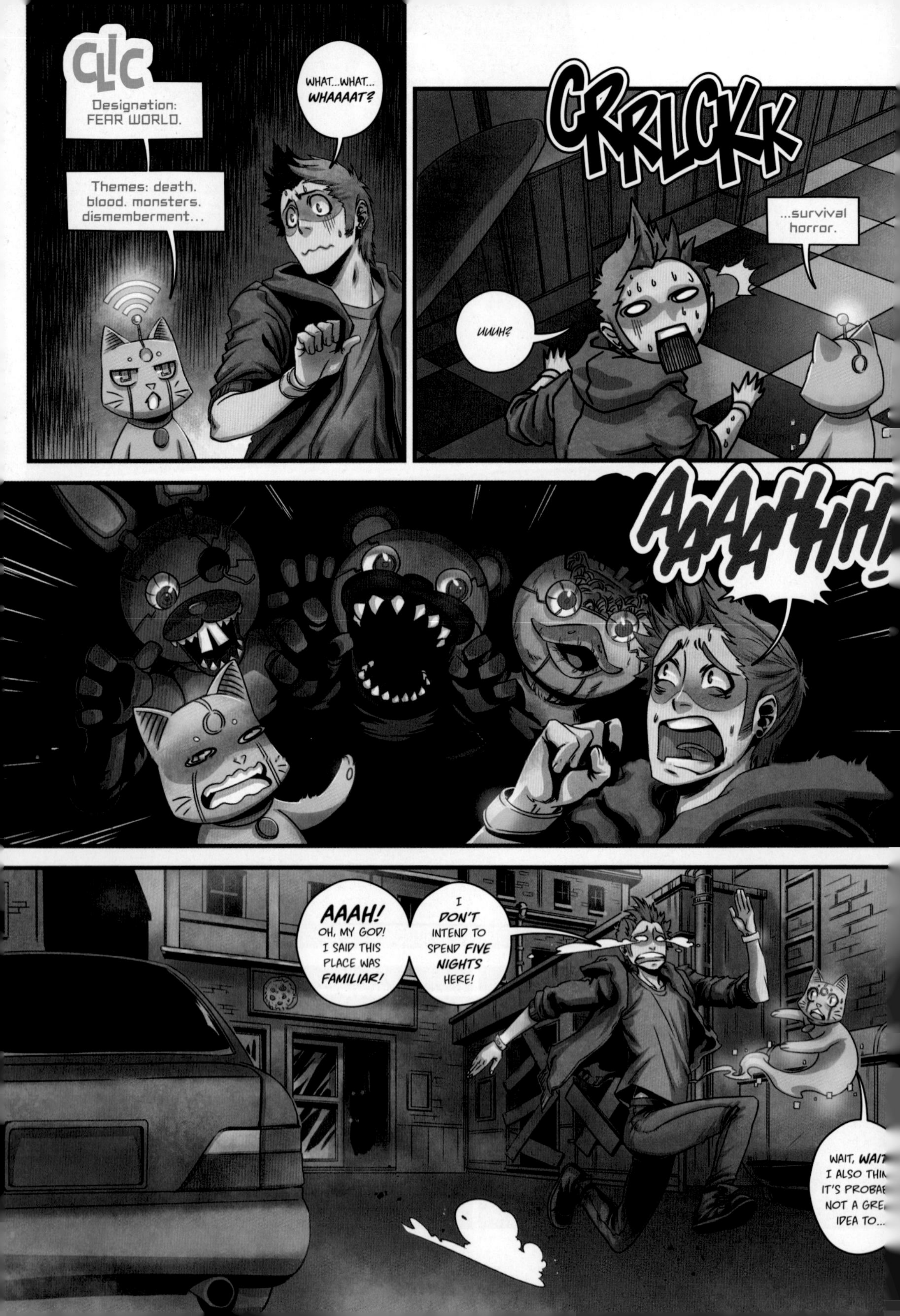
CLIC
Designation: FEAR WORLD.
Themes: death. blood. monsters. dismemberment...
WHAT...WHAT... WHAAAAT?
CRRLCKK
...survival horror.
UUUH?
AAAAHHH!
AAAH! OH, MY GOD! I SAID THIS PLACE WAS FAMILIAR!
I DON'T INTEND TO SPEND FIVE NIGHTS HERE!
WAIT, WAIT I ALSO THIN IT'S PROBAB NOT A GRE IDEA TO...

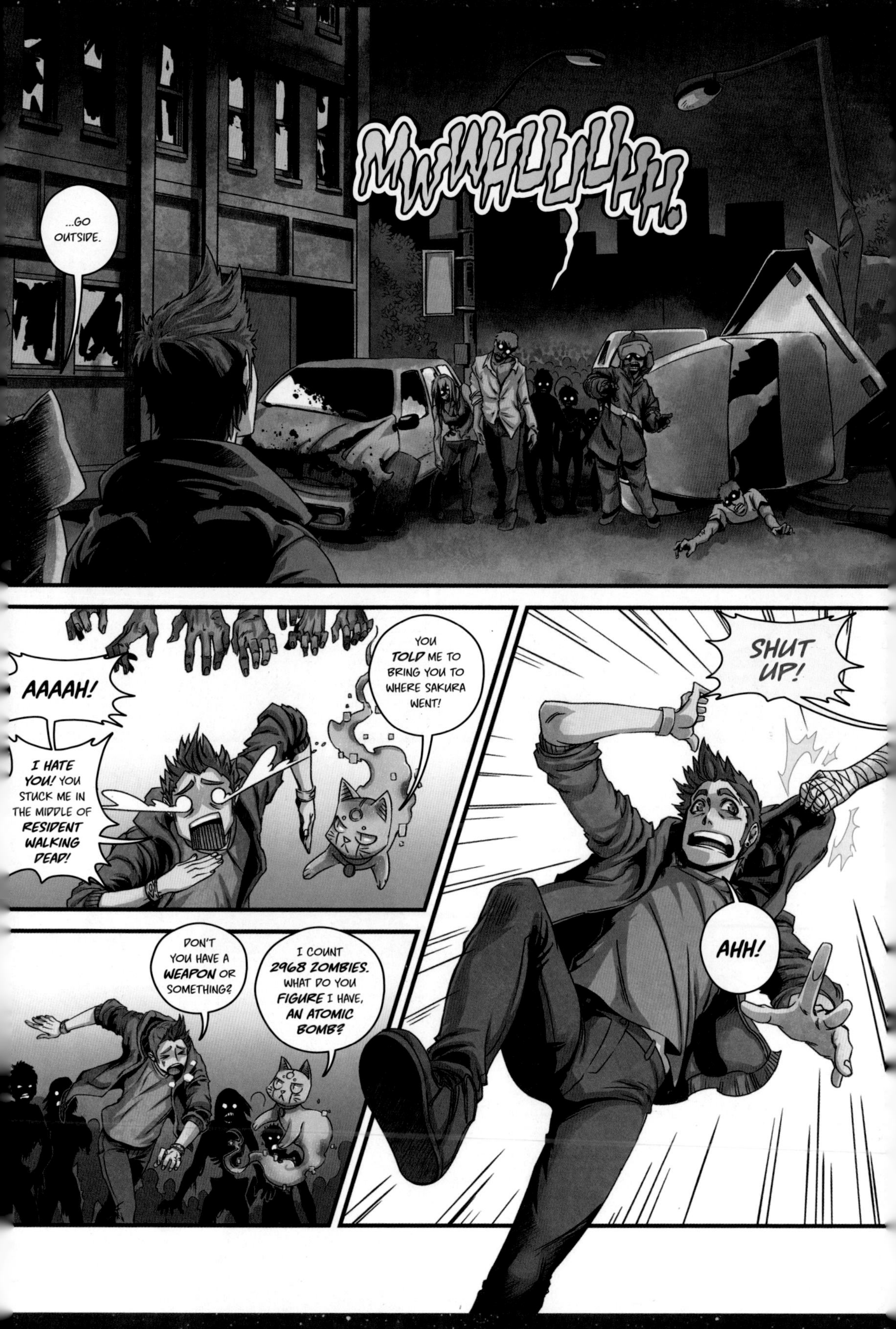

...GO OUTSIDE.
MWWHUUUHH.
AAAAH!
I HATE YOU! YOU STUCK ME IN THE MIDDLE OF RESIDENT WALKING DEAD!
YOU TOLD ME TO BRING YOU TO WHERE SAKURA WENT!
SHUT UP!
AHH!
DON'T YOU HAVE A WEAPON OR SOMETHING?
I COUNT 2968 ZOMBIES. WHAT DO YOU FIGURE I HAVE, AN ATOMIC BOMB?

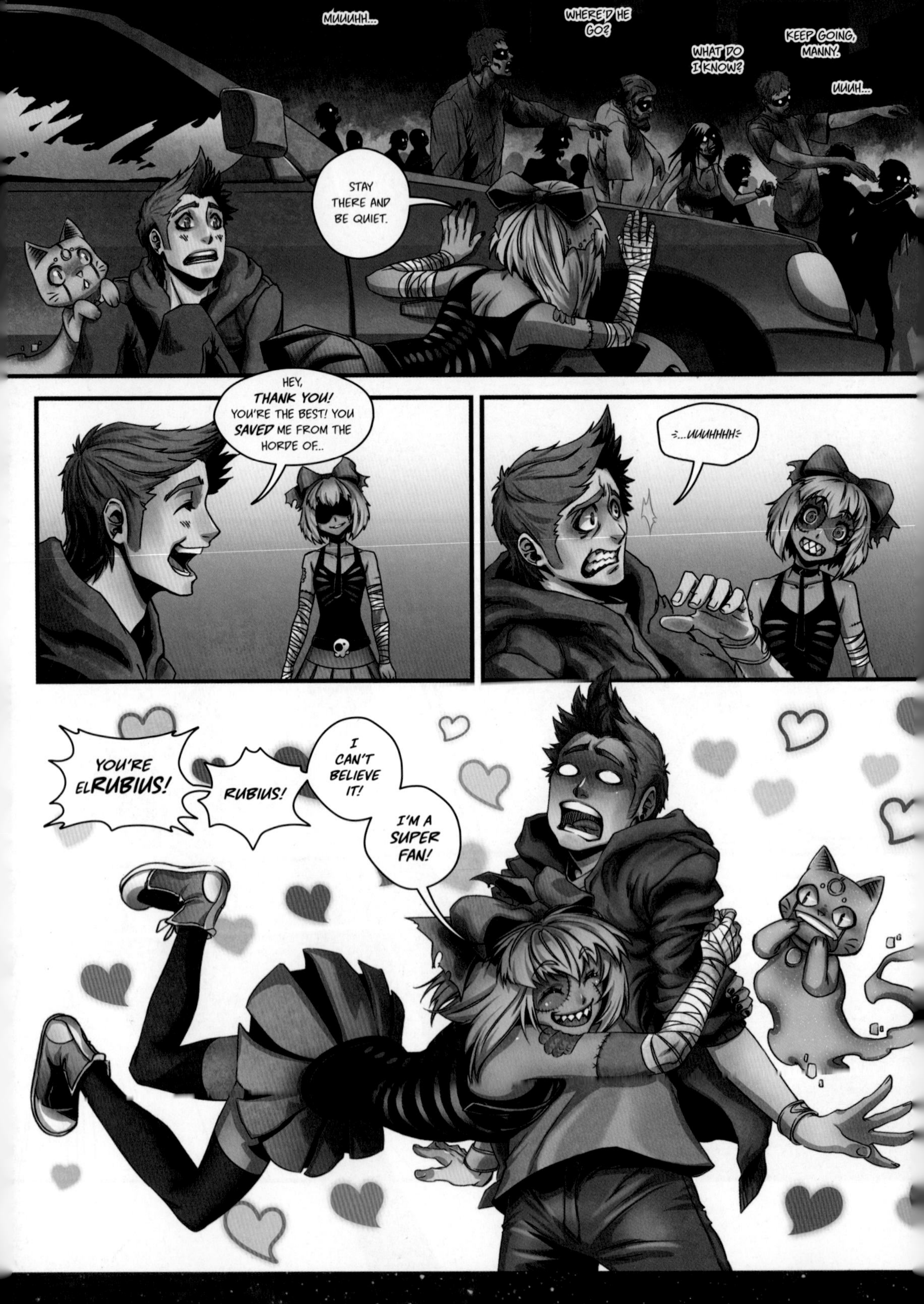

MUUUHH...
WHERE'D HE GO?
WHAT DO I KNOW?
KEEP GOING, MANNY.
UUUH...
STAY THERE AND BE QUIET.
HEY, THANK YOU! YOU'RE THE BEST! YOU SAVED ME FROM THE HORDE OF...
...UUUHHHH
YOU'RE ELRUBIUS!
RUBIUS!
I CAN'T BELIEVE IT!
I'M A SUPER FAN!

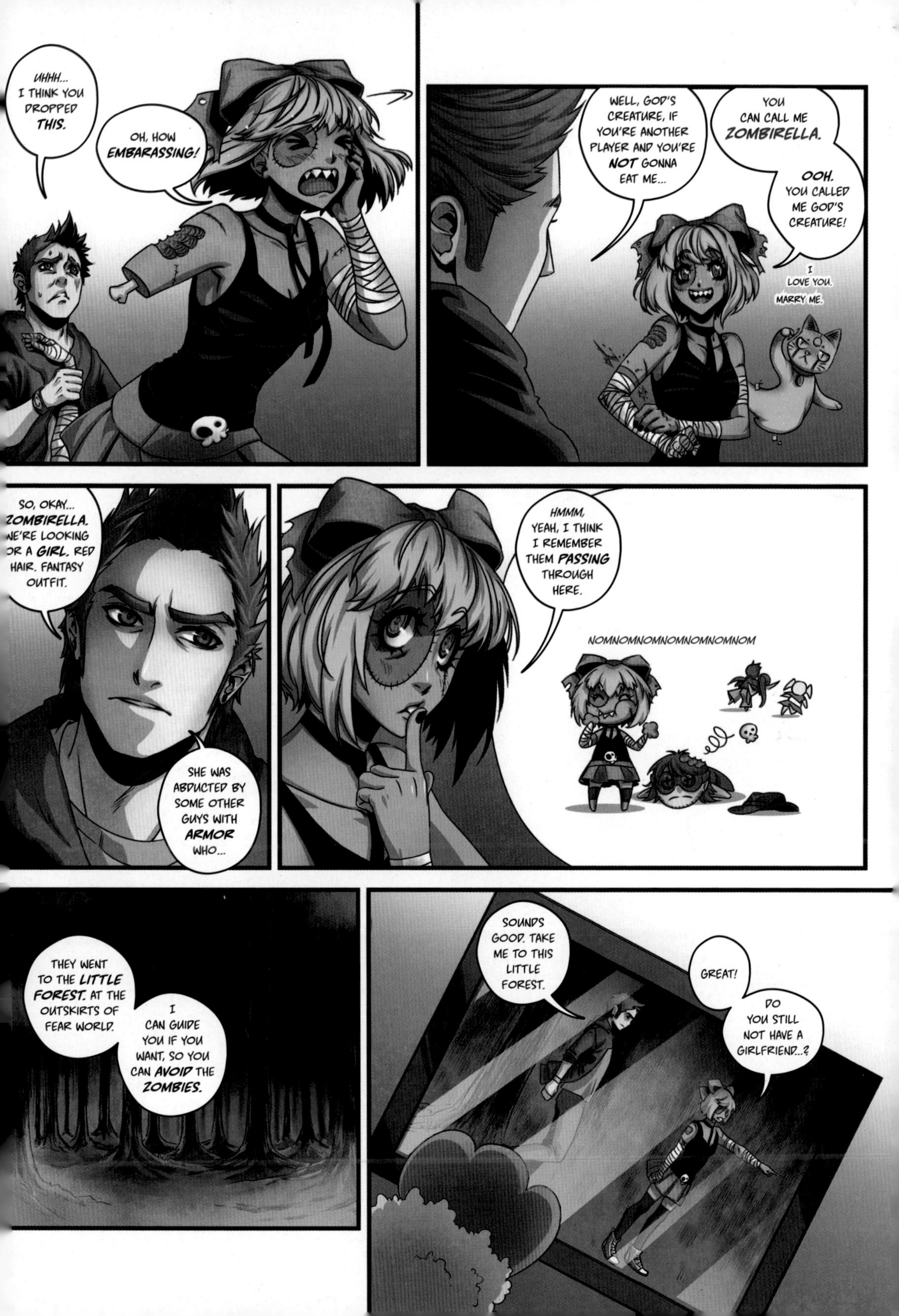

UHHH... I THINK YOU DROPPED THIS.
OH, HOW EMBARASSING!
WELL, GOD'S CREATURE, IF YOU'RE ANOTHER PLAYER AND YOU'RE NOT GONNA EAT ME...
YOU CAN CALL ME ZOMBIRELLA.
OOH. YOU CALLED ME GOD'S CREATURE!
I LOVE YOU. MARRY ME.
SO, OKAY... ZOMBIRELLA. WE'RE LOOKING FOR A GIRL. RED HAIR. FANTASY OUTFIT.
SHE WAS ABDUCTED BY SOME OTHER GUYS WITH ARMOR WHO...
HMMM, YEAH, I THINK I REMEMBER THEM PASSING THROUGH HERE.
NOMNOMNOMNOMNOMNOMNOM
THEY WENT TO THE LITTLE FOREST. AT THE OUTSKIRTS OF FEAR WORLD.
I CAN GUIDE YOU IF YOU WANT, SO YOU CAN AVOID THE ZOMBIES.
SOUNDS GOOD. TAKE ME TO THIS LITTLE FOREST.
GREAT!
DO YOU STILL NOT HAVE A GIRLFRIEND...?

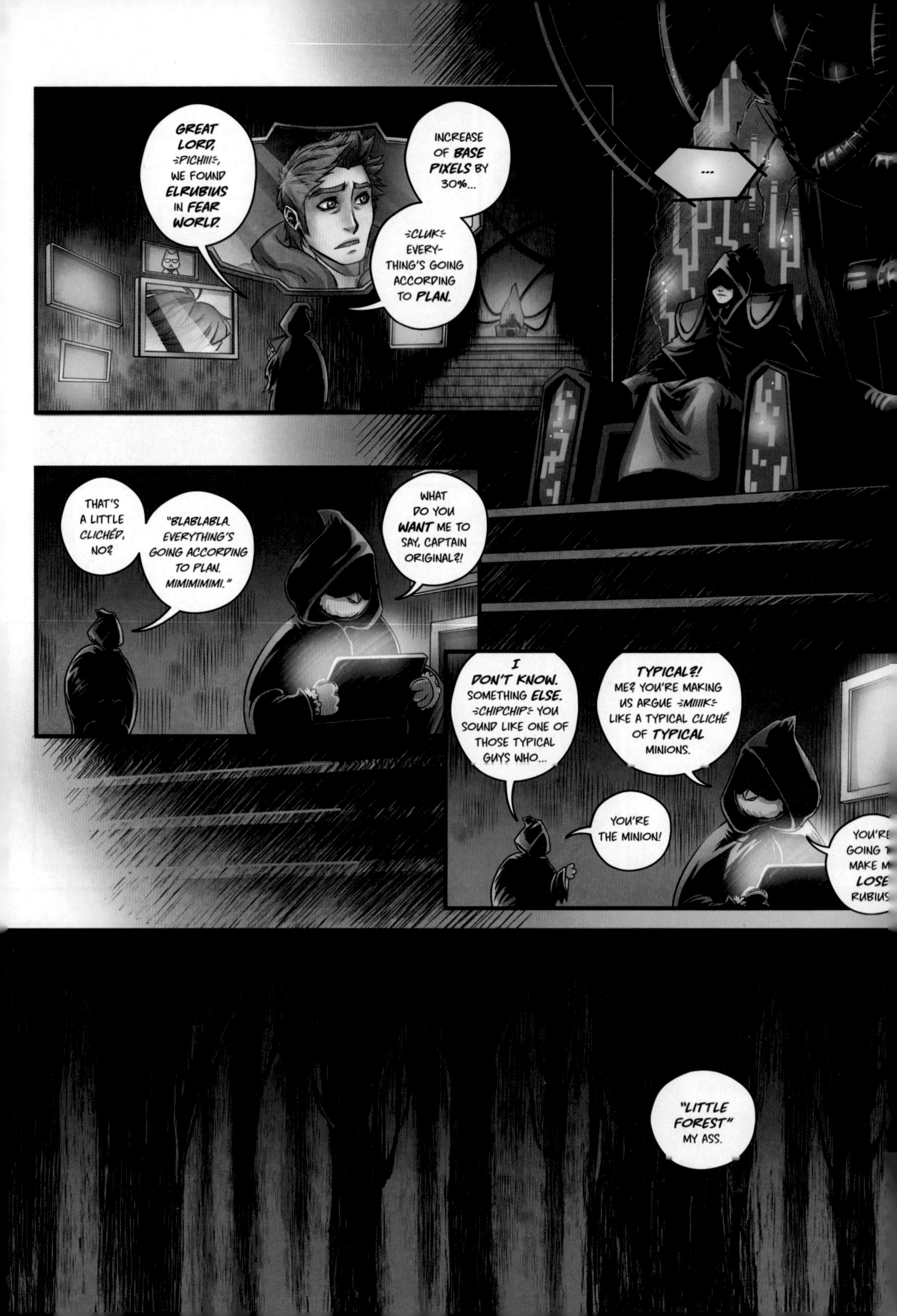
GREAT LORD, =PICHIII=, WE FOUND ELRUBIUS IN FEAR WORLD.
INCREASE OF BASE PIXELS BY 30%...
=CLUK= EVERYTHING'S GOING ACCORDING TO PLAN.
...
THAT'S A LITTLE CLICHÉD, NO?
"BLABLABLA. EVERYTHING'S GOING ACCORDING TO PLAN. MIMIMIMIMI."
WHAT DO YOU WANT ME TO SAY, CAPTAIN ORIGINAL?!
I DON'T KNOW. SOMETHING ELSE. =CHIPCHIP= YOU SOUND LIKE ONE OF THOSE TYPICAL GUYS WHO...
TYPICAL?! ME? YOU'RE MAKING US ARGUE =MIIIIK= LIKE A TYPICAL CLICHÉ OF TYPICAL MINIONS.
YOU'RE THE MINION!
"LITTLE FOREST" MY ASS.

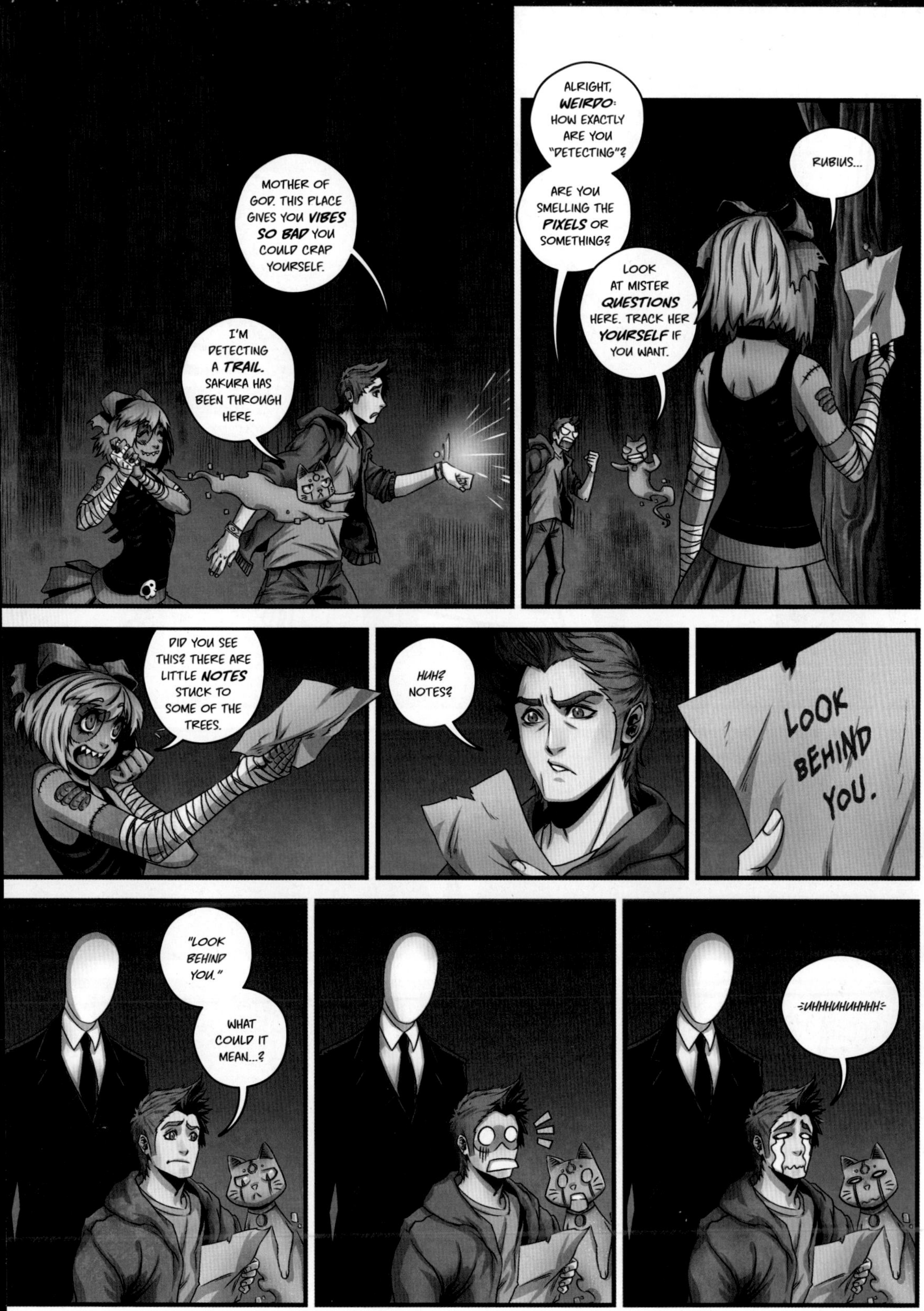
MOTHER OF GOD. THIS PLACE GIVES YOU VIBES SO BAD YOU COULD CRAP YOURSELF.
I'M DETECTING A TRAIL. SAKURA HAS BEEN THROUGH HERE.
ALRIGHT, WEIRDO: HOW EXACTLY ARE YOU "DETECTING"?
ARE YOU SMELLING THE PIXELS OR SOMETHING?
LOOK AT MISTER QUESTIONS HERE. TRACK HER YOURSELF IF YOU WANT.
RUBIUS...
DID YOU SEE THIS? THERE ARE LITTLE NOTES STUCK TO SOME OF THE TREES.
HUH? NOTES?
LOOK BEHIND YOU.
"LOOK BEHIND YOU."
WHAT COULD IT MEAN...?
≈UHHHHUHUHHHH≈

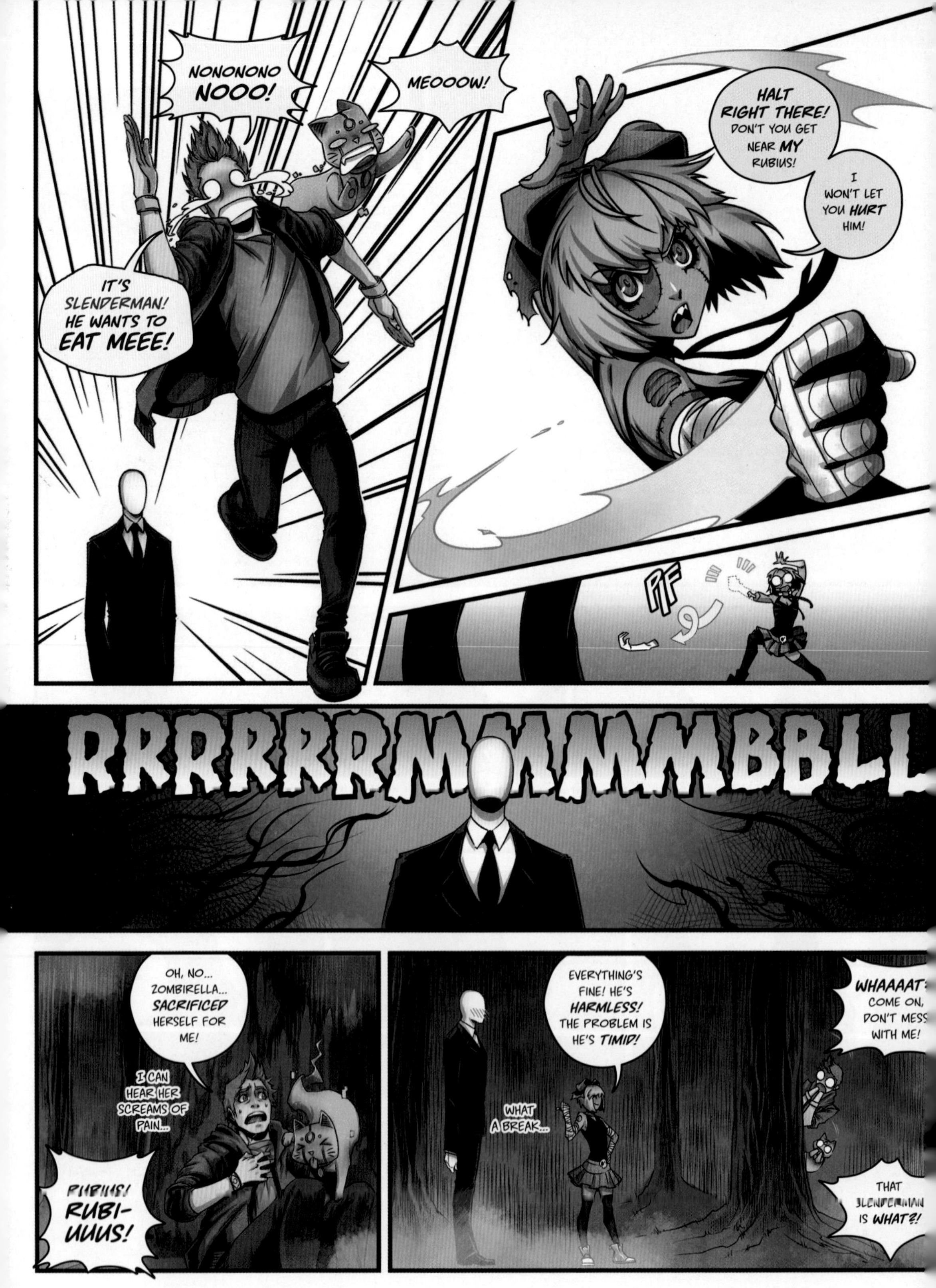
NONONONO NOOO!
MEOOOW!
IT'S SLENDERMAN! HE WANTS TO EAT MEEE!
HALT RIGHT THERE! DON'T YOU GET NEAR MY RUBIUS!
I WON'T LET YOU HURT HIM!
PIF
RRRRRRMMMMMBBLL
OH, NO... ZOMBIRELLA... SACRIFICED HERSELF FOR ME!
I CAN HEAR HER SCREAMS OF PAIN...
RUBIUS! RUBI-UUUS!
EVERYTHING'S FINE! HE'S HARMLESS! THE PROBLEM IS HE'S TIMID!
WHAT A BREAK...
WHAAAAT?! COME ON, DON'T MESS WITH ME!
THAT SLENDERMAN IS WHAT?!

BELIEVE ME, MISTER RUBIUS. THERE IS NOTHING *FURTHER* FROM MY INTENTIONS THAN TO WANT TO SCARE YOU.

I'M DEEPLY PAINED BY *ANY* SHOCK I MIGHT HAVE CAUSED YOU.

I... I JUST HAVE A LOT OF *TROUBLE* MAKING FRIENDS. I LEAVE *NOTES* TO *BREAK* THE ICE...

...BUT THE PEOPLE TEND TO *DIE* FIRST.

NOT SURE WHY.

BLOW MY MIND IN COLOR.

WE'RE LOOKING FOR A *FRIEND!* A GIRL IN *ARMOR!*

MEEEOOOW

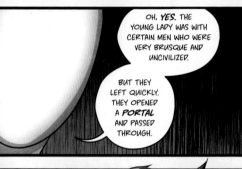

OH, *YES.* THE YOUNG LADY WAS WITH CERTAIN MEN WHO WERE VERY BRUSQUE AND UNCIVILIZED.

BUT THEY LEFT QUICKLY. THEY OPENED A *PORTAL* AND PASSED THROUGH.

CAN YOU TRACK WHERE THEY WENT?

THERE'S A TRAIL OF *SLOTS* IN THE AIR. THEY LEFT THIS WORLD. BUT WE CAN *FOLLOW!*

WELL THEN, *LET'S GO!*

ka-CHUNK

IT CAN'T BE THAT THEY'VE *ESCAPED* US!

I'M COMING FOR YOU, SAKURA!

I HOPE YOU WON'T MIND IF I COME ALONG. I THOROUGHLY ENJOY CONVERSING WITH YOU.

OF COURSE NOT! *WE'LL* ALL GO TOGETHER!

WHEN I CATCH THAT BASIC BITCH SAKURA, I'LL EAT HER BRAINS!

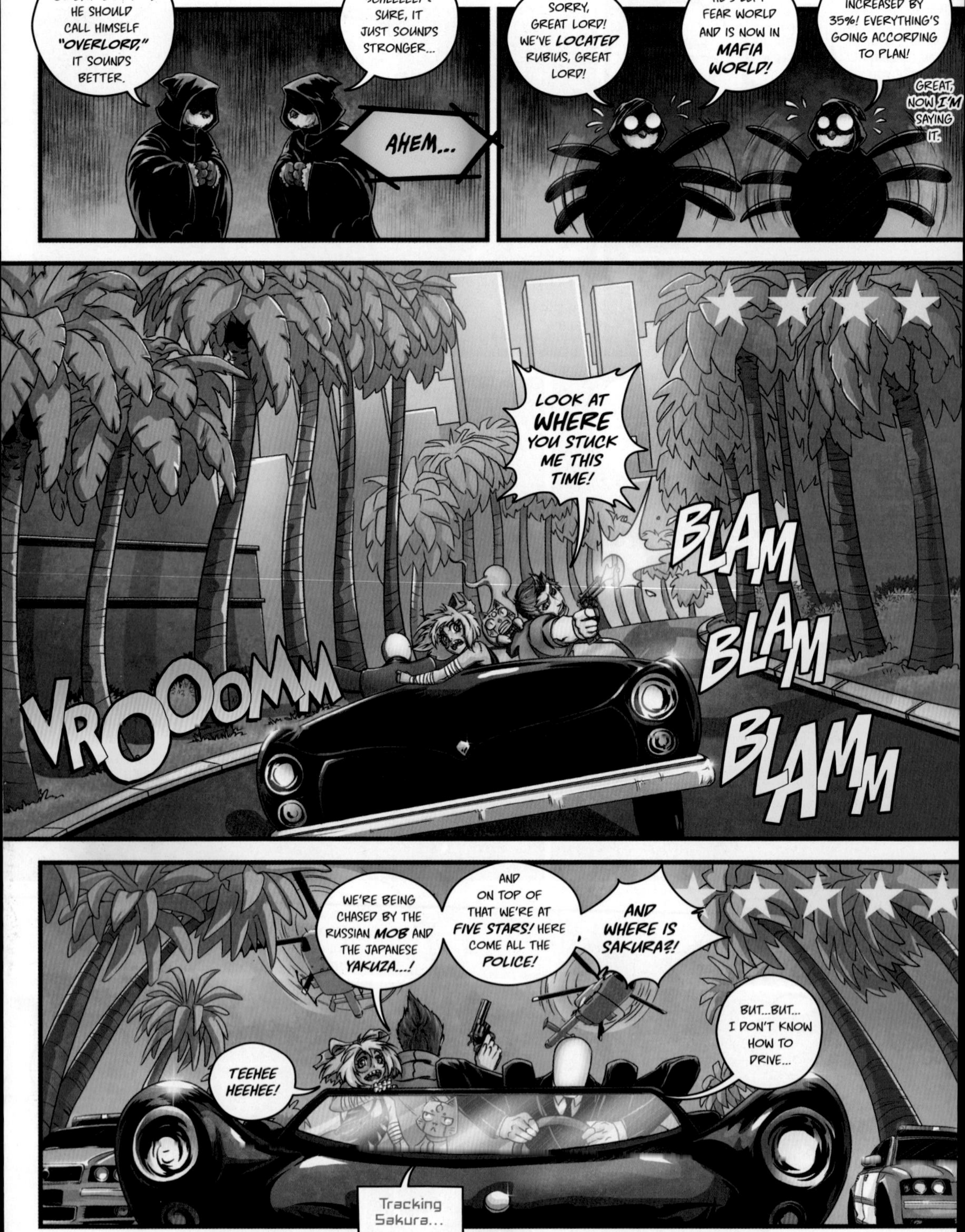
WHY "GREAT LORD"? HE SHOULD CALL HIMSELF "OVERLORD," IT SOUNDS BETTER.
=CHEEEEEP= SURE, IT JUST SOUNDS STRONGER...
AHEM...
SORRY, GREAT LORD! WE'VE LOCATED RUBIUS, GREAT LORD!
HE'S LEFT FEAR WORLD AND IS NOW IN MAFIA WORLD!
BASE PIXELS INCREASED BY 35%! EVERYTHING'S GOING ACCORDING TO PLAN!
GREAT, NOW I'M SAYING IT.
LOOK AT WHERE YOU STUCK ME THIS TIME!
BLAM BLAM BLAMM
VROOOOMM
WE'RE BEING CHASED BY THE RUSSIAN MOB AND THE JAPANESE YAKUZA...!
AND ON TOP OF THAT WE'RE AT FIVE STARS! HERE COME ALL THE POLICE!
AND WHERE IS SAKURA?!
BUT...BUT... I DON'T KNOW HOW TO DRIVE...
TEEHEE HEEHEE!
Tracking Sakura...

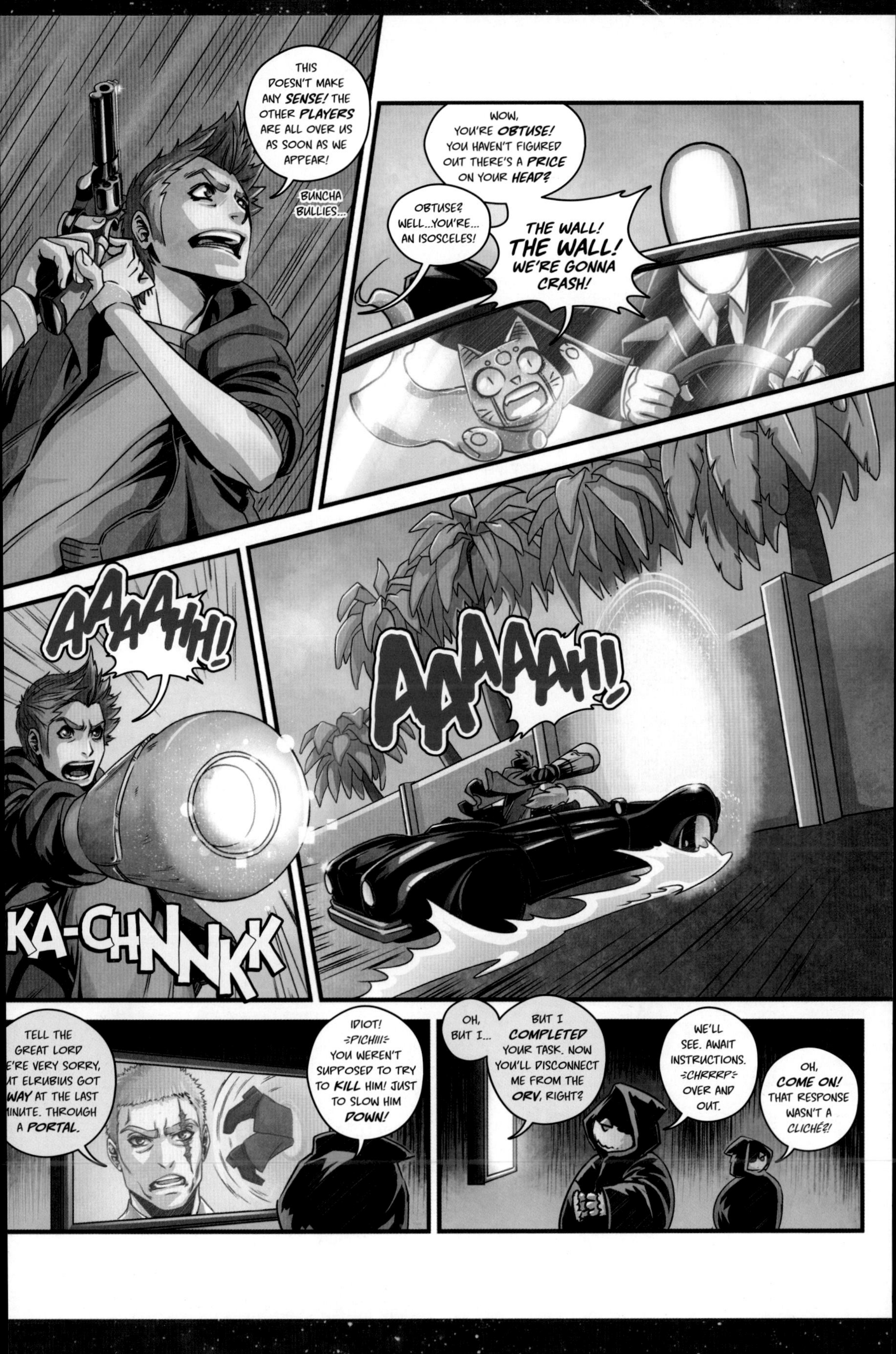

THIS DOESN'T MAKE ANY SENSE! THE OTHER PLAYERS ARE ALL OVER US AS SOON AS WE APPEAR!
BUNCHA BULLIES...
WOW, YOU'RE OBTUSE! YOU HAVEN'T FIGURED OUT THERE'S A PRICE ON YOUR HEAD?
OBTUSE? WELL...YOU'RE... AN ISOSCELES!
THE WALL! THE WALL! WE'RE GONNA CRASH!
AAAAHH!
KA-CHNNKK
AAAAAH!
TELL THE GREAT LORD WE'RE VERY SORRY, THAT ELRUBIUS GOT AWAY AT THE LAST MINUTE. THROUGH A PORTAL.
IDIOT! =PICHIII= YOU WEREN'T SUPPOSED TO TRY TO KILL HIM! JUST TO SLOW HIM DOWN!
OH, BUT I...
BUT I COMPLETED YOUR TASK. NOW YOU'LL DISCONNECT ME FROM THE ORV, RIGHT?
WE'LL SEE. AWAIT INSTRUCTIONS. =CHRRRP= OVER AND OUT.
OH, COME ON! THAT RESPONSE WASN'T A CLICHÉ?!

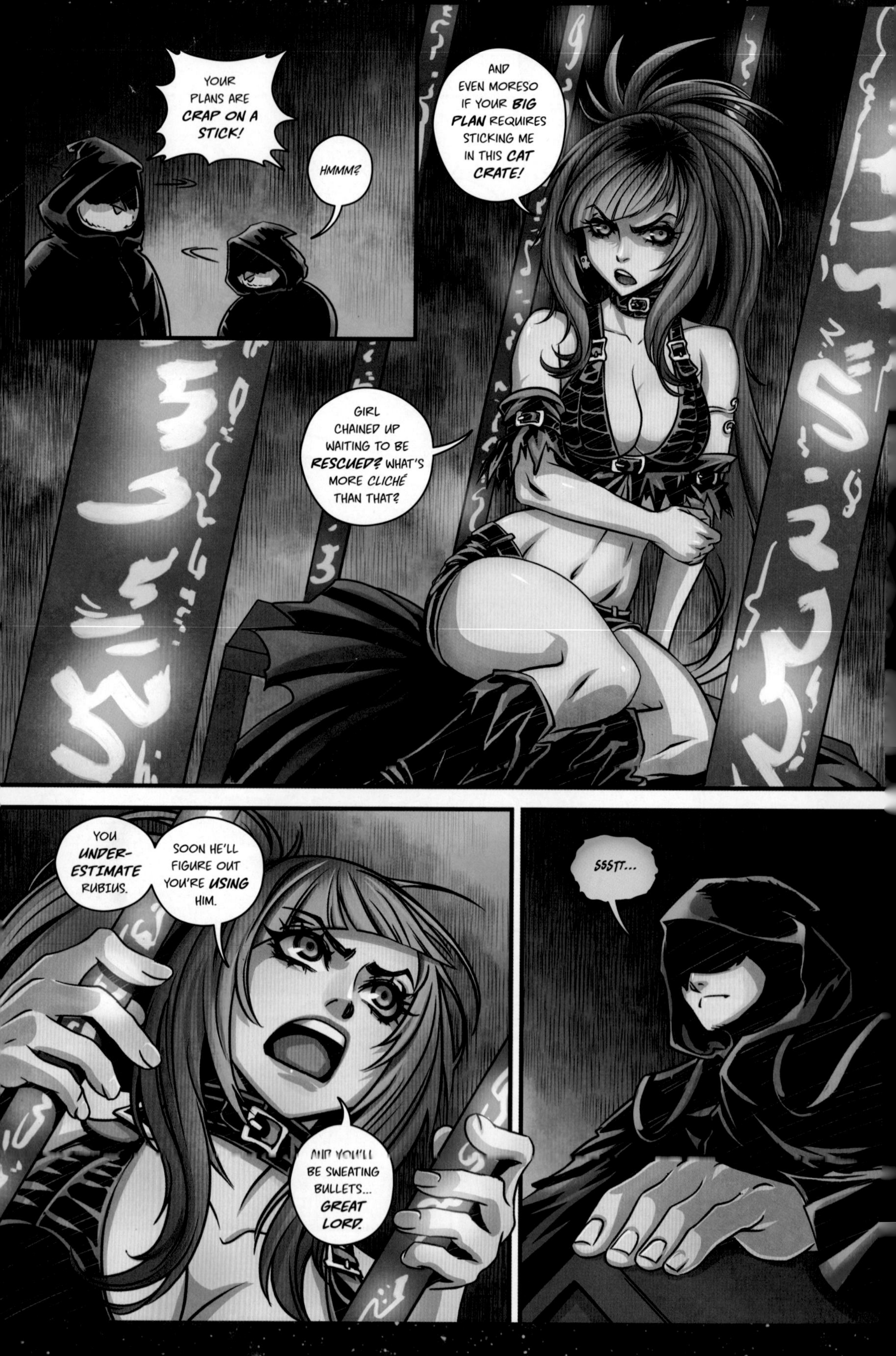
YOUR PLANS ARE CRAP ON A STICK!
HMMM?
AND EVEN MORESO IF YOUR BIG PLAN REQUIRES STICKING ME IN THIS CAT CRATE!
GIRL CHAINED UP WAITING TO BE RESCUED? WHAT'S MORE CLICHÉ THAN THAT?
YOU UNDER-ESTIMATE RUBIUS.
SOON HE'LL FIGURE OUT YOU'RE USING HIM.
AND YOU'LL BE SWEATING BULLETS... GREAT LORD.
SSSTT...

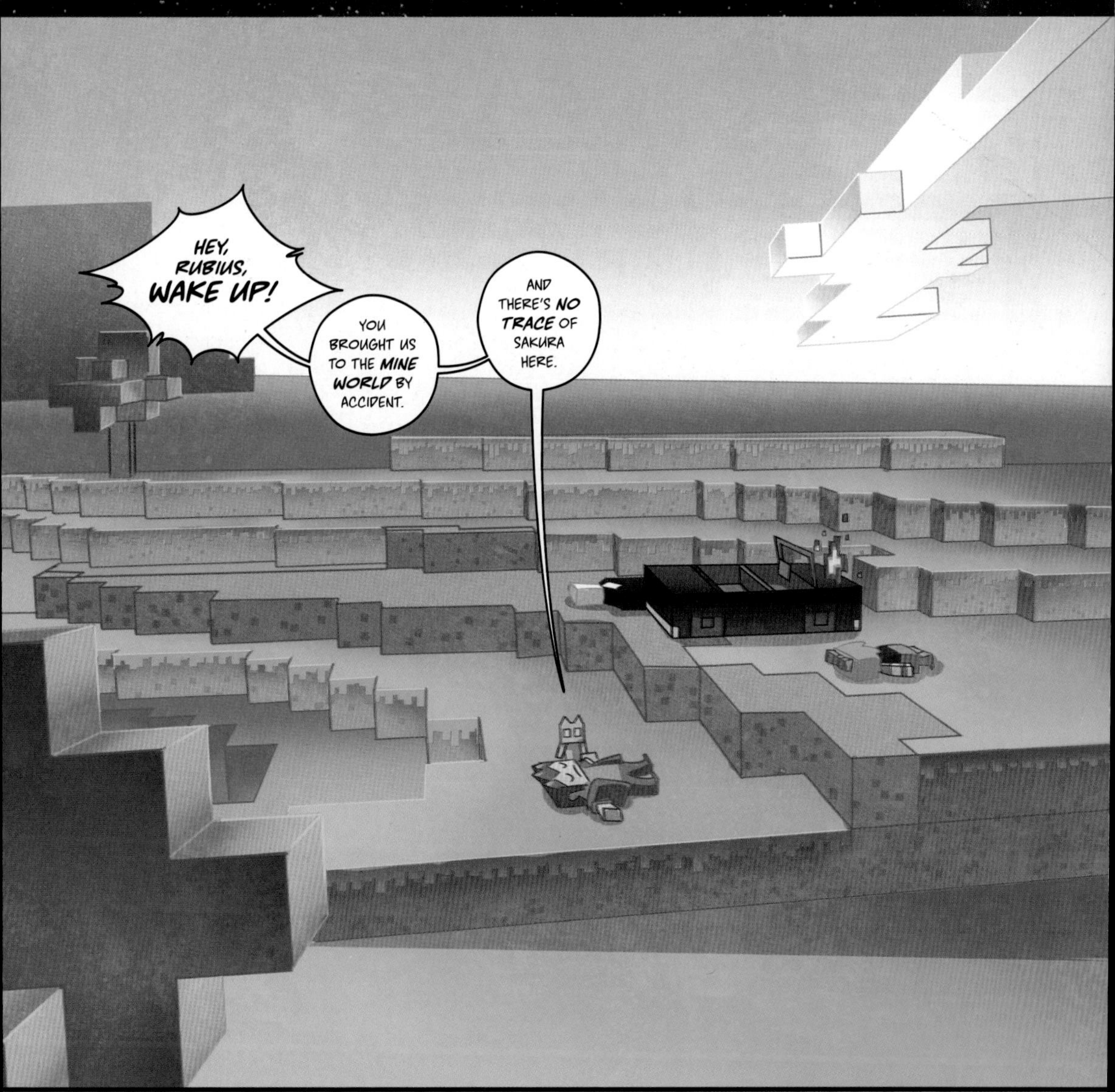
HEY, RUBIUS, WAKE UP!
YOU BROUGHT US TO THE MINE WORLD BY ACCIDENT.
AND THERE'S NO TRACE OF SAKURA HERE.

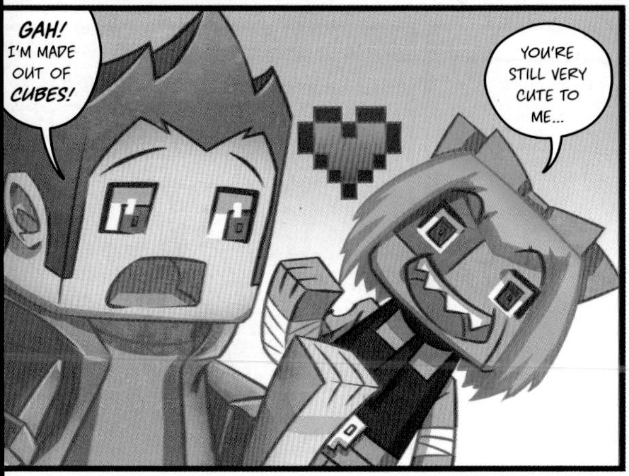
GAH! I'M MADE OUT OF CUBES!
YOU'RE STILL VERY CUTE TO ME...

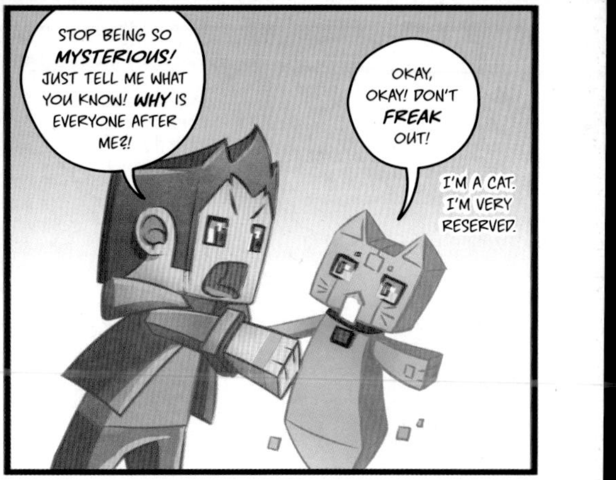
STOP BEING SO MYSTERIOUS! JUST TELL ME WHAT YOU KNOW! WHY IS EVERYONE AFTER ME?!
OKAY, OKAY! DON'T FREAK OUT!
I'M A CAT. I'M VERY RESERVED.

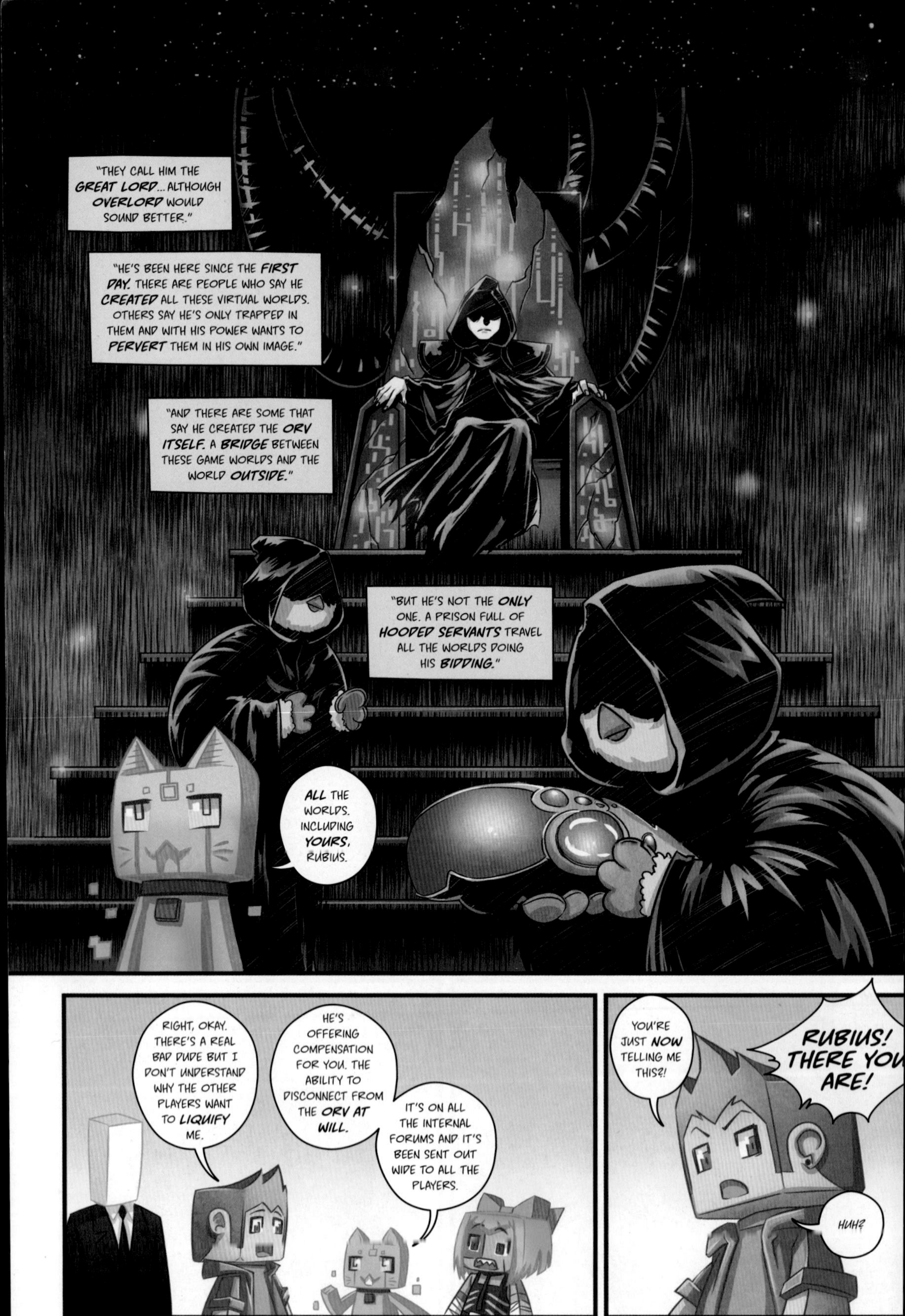
"THEY CALL HIM THE GREAT LORD... ALTHOUGH OVERLORD WOULD SOUND BETTER."
"HE'S BEEN HERE SINCE THE FIRST DAY. THERE ARE PEOPLE WHO SAY HE CREATED ALL THESE VIRTUAL WORLDS. OTHERS SAY HE'S ONLY TRAPPED IN THEM AND WITH HIS POWER WANTS TO PERVERT THEM IN HIS OWN IMAGE."
"AND THERE ARE SOME THAT SAY HE CREATED THE ORV ITSELF. A BRIDGE BETWEEN THESE GAME WORLDS AND THE WORLD OUTSIDE."
"BUT HE'S NOT THE ONLY ONE. A PRISON FULL OF HOODED SERVANTS TRAVEL ALL THE WORLDS DOING HIS BIDDING."
ALL THE WORLDS. INCLUDING YOURS, RUBIUS.
RIGHT, OKAY. THERE'S A REAL BAD DUDE BUT I DON'T UNDERSTAND WHY THE OTHER PLAYERS WANT TO LIQUIFY ME.
HE'S OFFERING COMPENSATION FOR YOU. THE ABILITY TO DISCONNECT FROM THE ORV AT WILL.
IT'S ON ALL THE INTERNAL FORUMS AND IT'S BEEN SENT OUT WIDE TO ALL THE PLAYERS.
YOU'RE JUST NOW TELLING ME THIS?!
RUBIUS! THERE YOU ARE!
HUH?

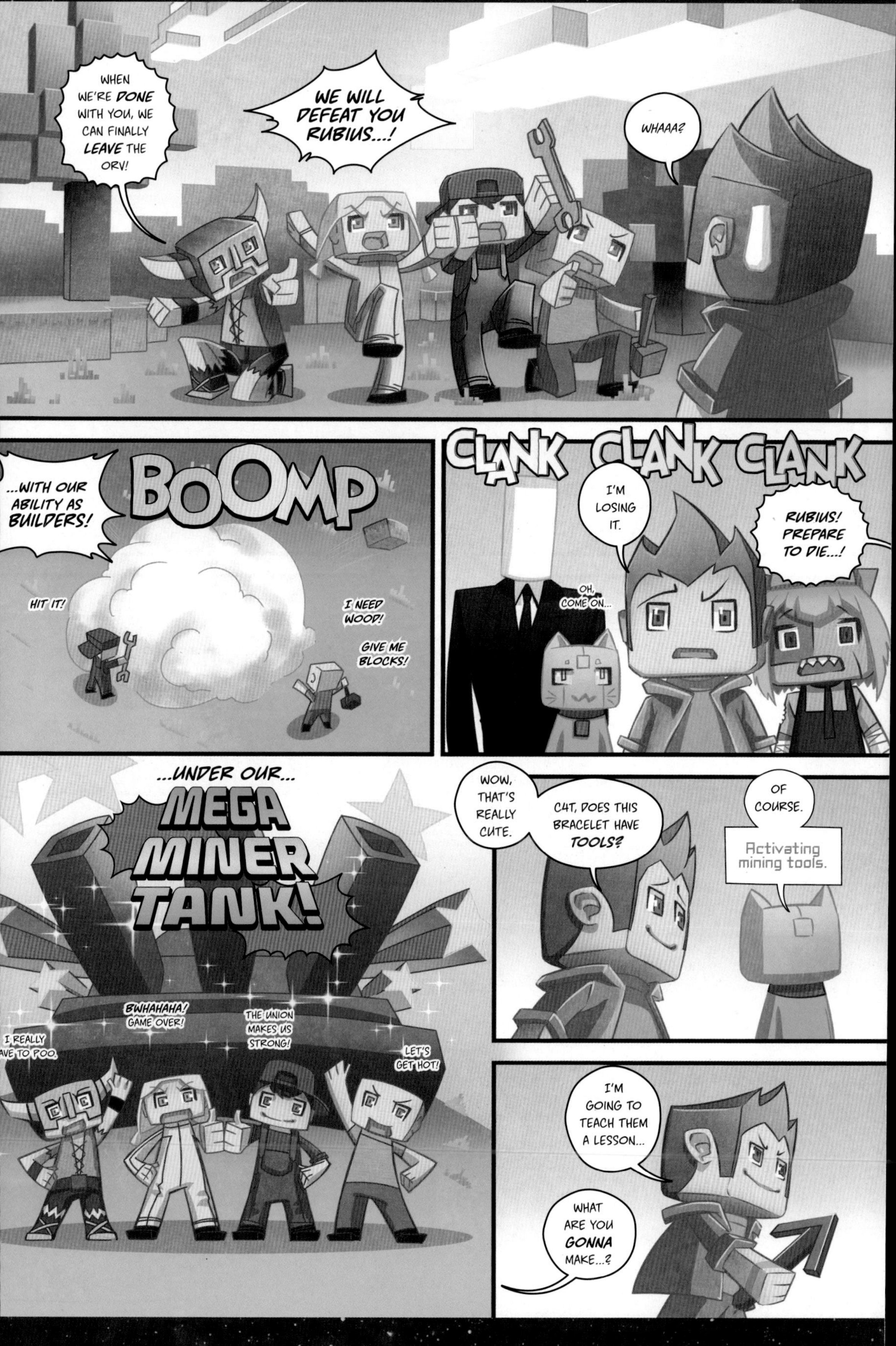

WHEN WE'RE DONE WITH YOU, WE CAN FINALLY LEAVE THE ORV!
WE WILL DEFEAT YOU RUBIUS...!
WHAAA?
...WITH OUR ABILITY AS BUILDERS!
BOOMP
HIT IT!
I NEED WOOD!
GIVE ME BLOCKS!
CLANK CLANK CLANK
I'M LOSING IT.
RUBIUS! PREPARE TO DIE...!
OH, COME ON...
...UNDER OUR...
MEGA MINER TANK!
BWHAHAHA! GAME OVER!
THE UNION MAKES US STRONG!
LET'S GET HOT!
WOW, THAT'S REALLY CUTE.
C4T, DOES THIS BRACELET HAVE TOOLS?
OF COURSE.
Activating mining tools.
I'M GOING TO TEACH THEM A LESSON...
WHAT ARE YOU GONNA MAKE...?

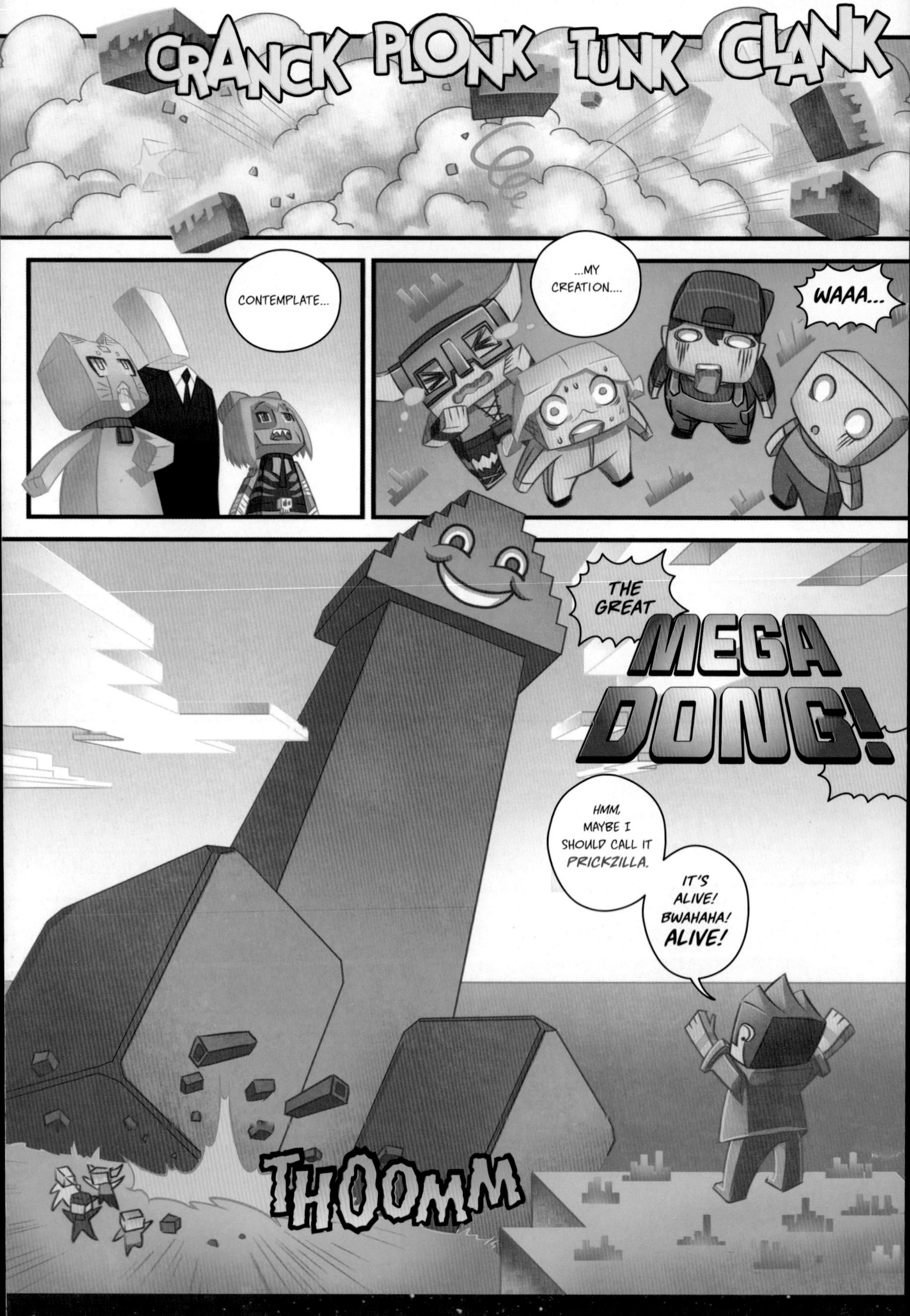
CRANCK PLONK TUNK CLANK
CONTEMPLATE...
...MY CREATION....
WAAA...
THE GREAT
MEGA DONG!
HMM, MAYBE I SHOULD CALL IT PRICKZILLA.
IT'S ALIVE! BWAHAHA! ALIVE!
THOOMM

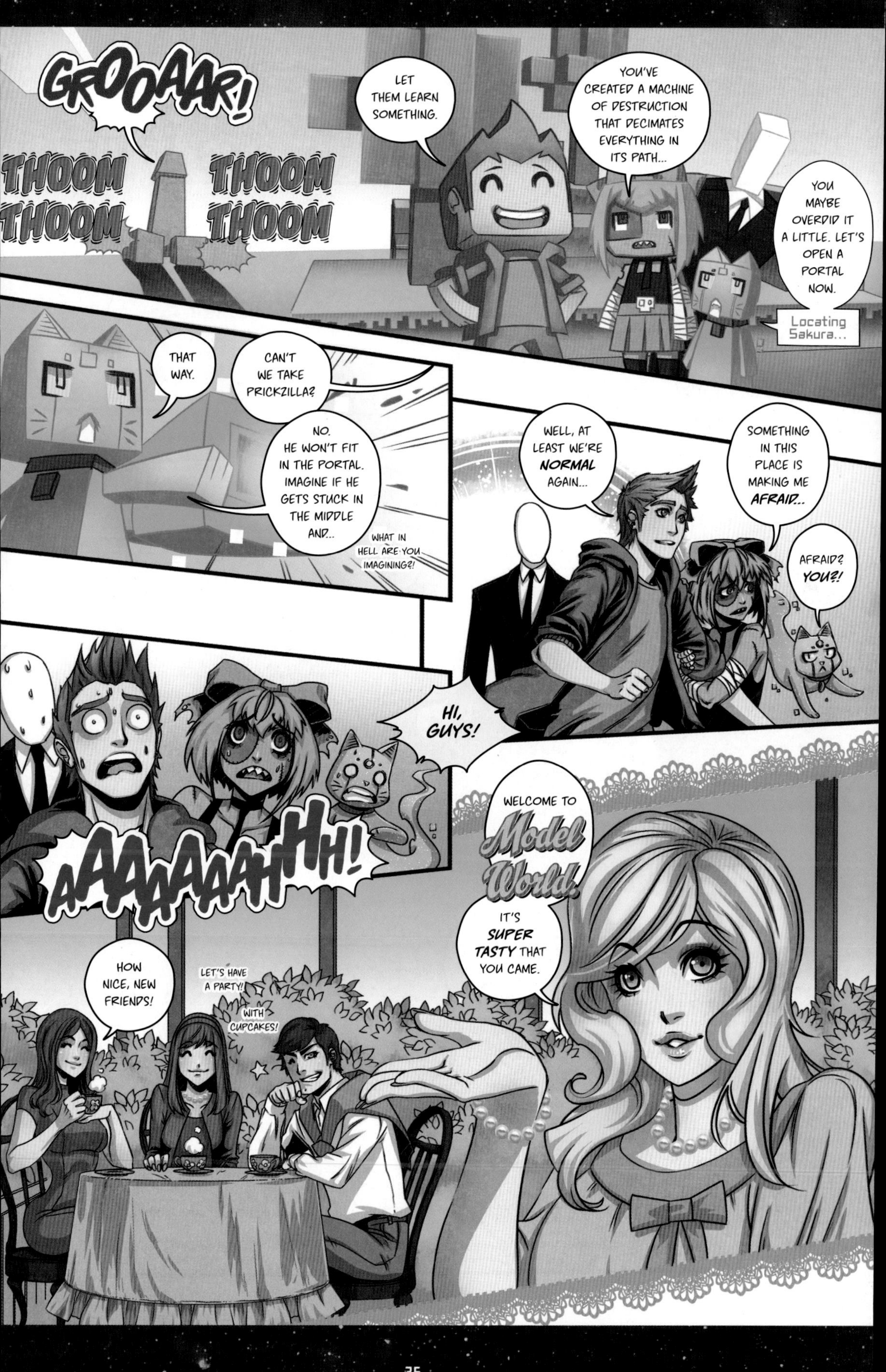
GROOAAR!
THOOM THOOM
THOOM THOOM
LET THEM LEARN SOMETHING.
YOU'VE CREATED A MACHINE OF DESTRUCTION THAT DECIMATES EVERYTHING IN ITS PATH...
YOU MAYBE OVERDID IT A LITTLE. LET'S OPEN A PORTAL NOW.
Locating Sakura...
THAT WAY.
CAN'T WE TAKE PRICKZILLA?
NO. HE WON'T FIT IN THE PORTAL. IMAGINE IF HE GETS STUCK IN THE MIDDLE AND...
WHAT IN HELL ARE YOU IMAGINING?!
WELL, AT LEAST WE'RE NORMAL AGAIN...
SOMETHING IN THIS PLACE IS MAKING ME AFRAID...
AFRAID? YOU?!
HI, GUYS!
AAAAAAAHHH!
WELCOME TO Model World!
IT'S SUPER TASTY THAT YOU CAME.
HOW NICE, NEW FRIENDS!
LET'S HAVE A PARTY!
WITH CUPCAKES!

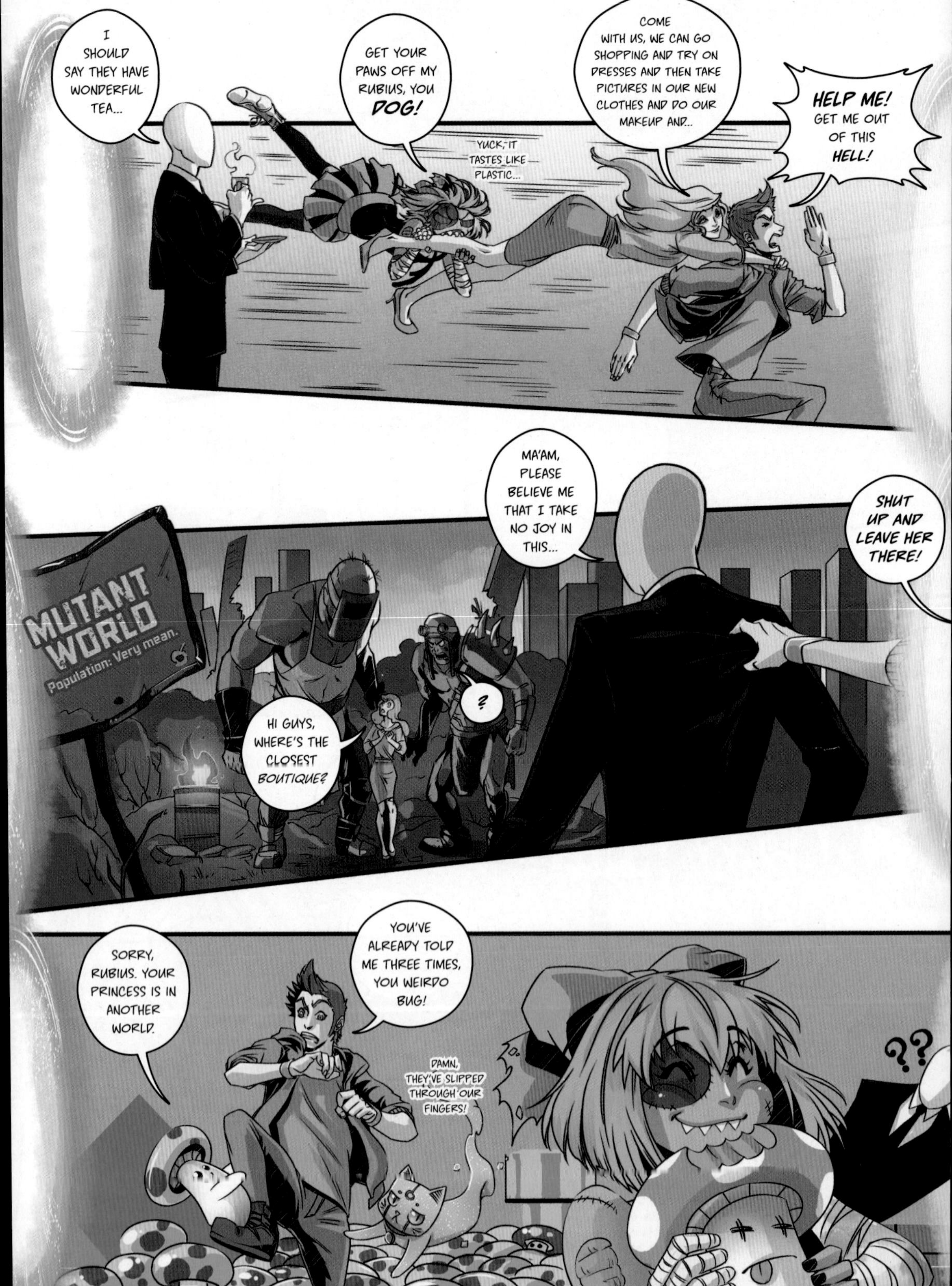
I SHOULD SAY THEY HAVE WONDERFUL TEA...
GET YOUR PAWS OFF MY RUBIUS, YOU DOG!
YUCK, IT TASTES LIKE PLASTIC...
COME WITH US, WE CAN GO SHOPPING AND TRY ON DRESSES AND THEN TAKE PICTURES IN OUR NEW CLOTHES AND DO OUR MAKEUP AND...
HELP ME! GET ME OUT OF THIS HELL!
MUTANT WORLD
Population: Very mean.
MA'AM, PLEASE BELIEVE ME THAT I TAKE NO JOY IN THIS...
SHUT UP AND LEAVE HER THERE!
HI GUYS, WHERE'S THE CLOSEST BOUTIQUE?
?
SORRY, RUBIUS. YOUR PRINCESS IS IN ANOTHER WORLD.
YOU'VE ALREADY TOLD ME THREE TIMES, YOU WEIRDO BUG!
DAMN, THEY'VE SLIPPED THROUGH OUR FINGERS!
??

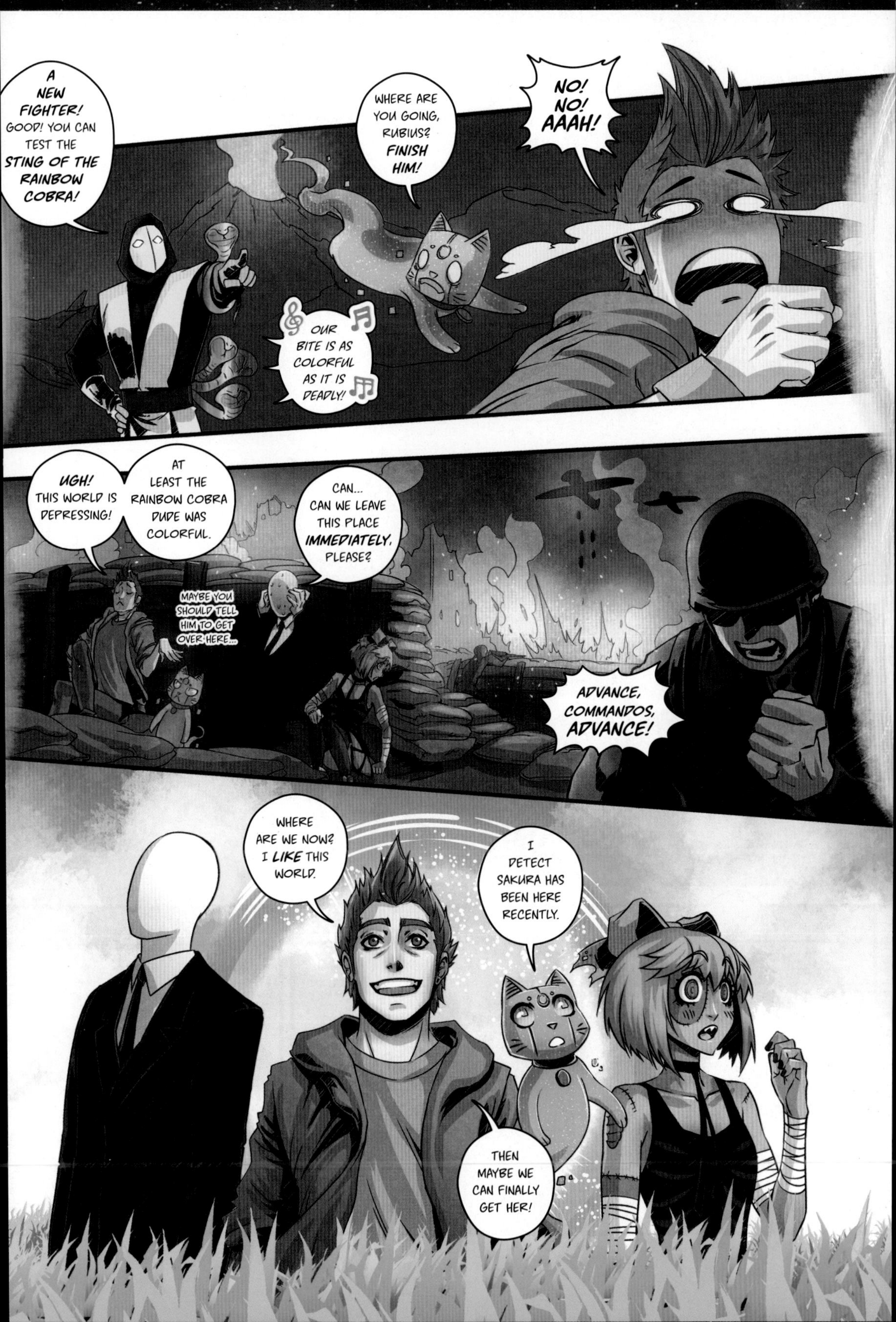
A NEW FIGHTER! GOOD! YOU CAN TEST THE STING OF THE RAINBOW COBRA!
OUR BITE IS AS COLORFUL AS IT IS DEADLY!
WHERE ARE YOU GOING, RUBIUS? FINISH HIM!
NO! NO! AAAH!
UGH! THIS WORLD IS DEPRESSING!
AT LEAST THE RAINBOW COBRA DUDE WAS COLORFUL.
MAYBE YOU SHOULD TELL HIM TO GET OVER HERE...
CAN... CAN WE LEAVE THIS PLACE IMMEDIATELY, PLEASE?
ADVANCE, COMMANDOS, ADVANCE!
WHERE ARE WE NOW? I LIKE THIS WORLD.
I DETECT SAKURA HAS BEEN HERE RECENTLY.
THEN MAYBE WE CAN FINALLY GET HER!

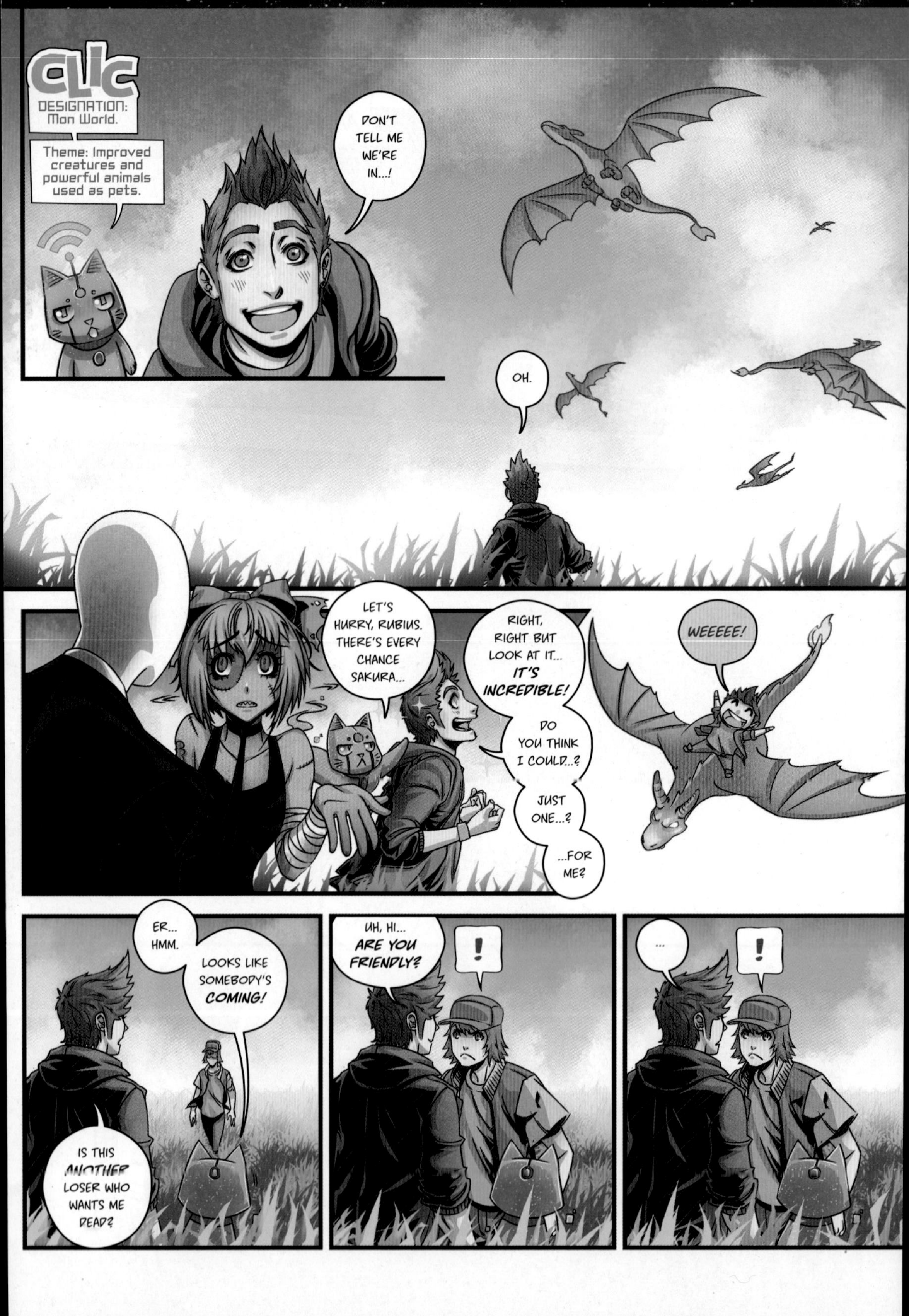
CLIC
DESIGNATION: Mon World.
Theme: Improved creatures and powerful animals used as pets.
DON'T TELL ME WE'RE IN...!
OH.
LET'S HURRY, RUBIUS. THERE'S EVERY CHANCE SAKURA...
RIGHT, RIGHT BUT LOOK AT IT... IT'S INCREDIBLE!
DO YOU THINK I COULD...?
JUST ONE...?
...FOR ME?
WEEEEE!
ER... HMM.
LOOKS LIKE SOMEBODY'S COMING!
IS THIS ANOTHER LOSER WHO WANTS ME DEAD?
UH, HI... ARE YOU FRIENDLY?
!
...
!

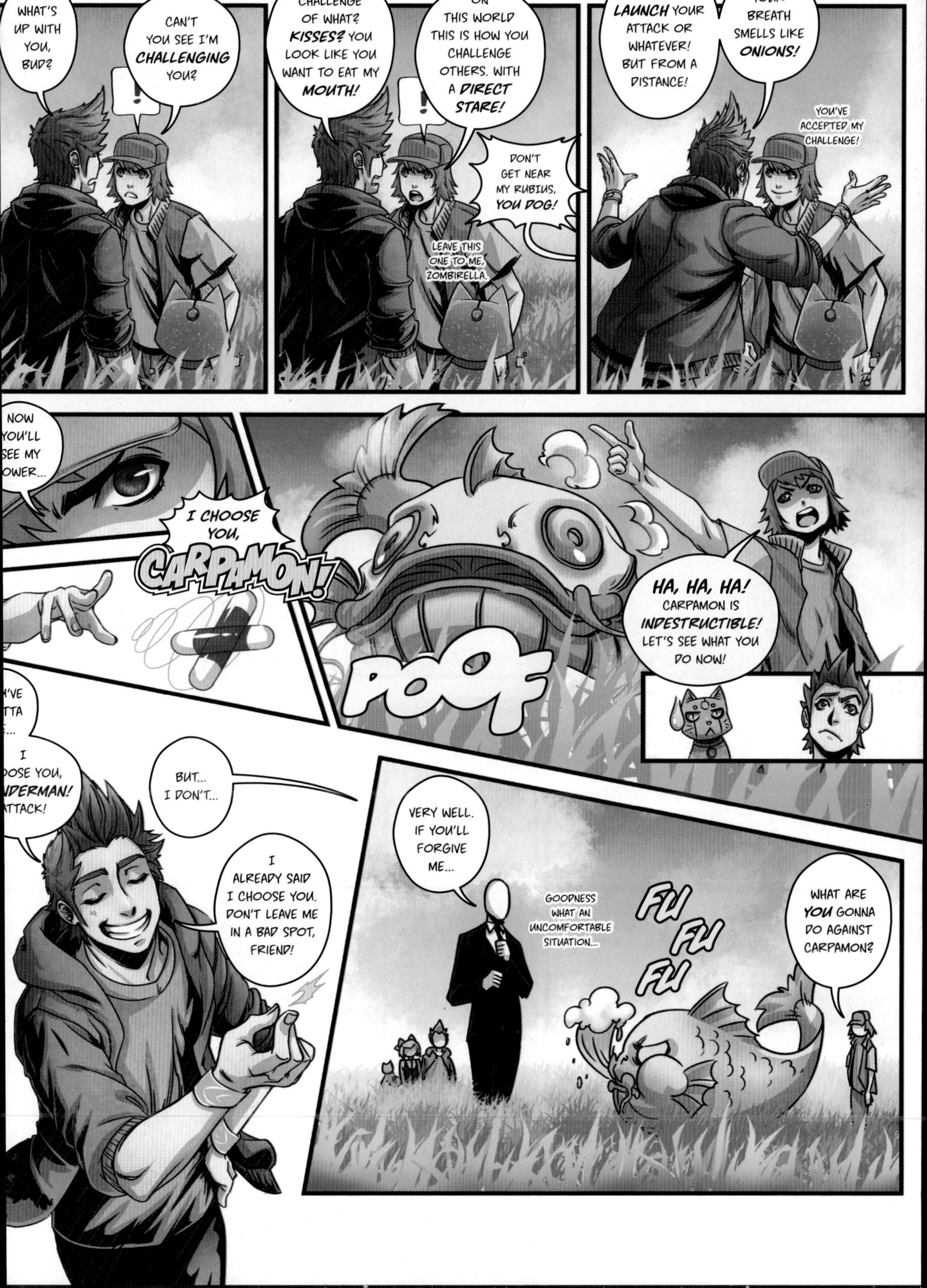
WHAT'S UP WITH YOU, BUD?
CAN'T YOU SEE I'M CHALLENGING YOU?
A CHALLENGE OF WHAT? KISSES? YOU LOOK LIKE YOU WANT TO EAT MY MOUTH!
ON THIS WORLD THIS IS HOW YOU CHALLENGE OTHERS. WITH A DIRECT STARE!
DON'T GET NEAR MY RUBIUS, YOU DOG!
LEAVE THIS ONE TO ME, ZOMBIRELLA.
FINE! LAUNCH YOUR ATTACK OR WHATEVER! BUT FROM A DISTANCE!
YOUR BREATH SMELLS LIKE ONIONS!
YOU'VE ACCEPTED MY CHALLENGE!
NOW YOU'LL SEE MY OWER...
I CHOOSE YOU, CARPAMON!
POOF
HA, HA, HA! CARPAMON IS INDESTRUCTIBLE! LET'S SEE WHAT YOU DO NOW!
I CHOOSE YOU, ATTACK!
BUT... I DON'T...
I ALREADY SAID I CHOOSE YOU. DON'T LEAVE ME IN A BAD SPOT, FRIEND!
VERY WELL. IF YOU'LL FORGIVE ME...
GOODNESS WHAT AN UNCOMFORTABLE SITUATION...
FU FU FU
WHAT ARE YOU GONNA DO AGAINST CARPAMON?

BOO.

DAMN! SLENDERMAN USED HIS "CRAP YOURSELF STARE." VERY EFFECTIVE.

I HOPE I HAVE NOT OVERLY SCARED ANYONE.

RIP

EEEEEHHHH...

NO, NO GOOD...

YOU WERE SO GREAT...

PREEE PREEE PREEEE

YOU THERE! STOP!

THIS IS COMPLETELY NON-COMPLIANT WITH THE RULES OF MON WORLD!

THE MONSTER CHOSEN WAS NOT INDEXED, NOR WAS IT PREVIOUSLY CAPTURED IN A MONCAPSULE. WAS IT EVOLVED? WHAT LEVEL DOES IT HOLD?

AND WHAT TYPE IS IT?

MONS EXTRAORDINARY ARE CHARACTERIZED THROUGH BY THEIR ENORMOUS POWERS ALWAYS HAVE SOME BASE STATS OF 580 MORE (WIT THE EXCEP TION OF POLLA, AT 480 MEMBER EY DARY

LEAVE ME BE, PAL!

HE WON'T SHUT UP AND ON TOP OF IT, I'M GONNA GO DEAF FROM HIS STUPID WHISTLE...!

POF

PAF

CRUNCH

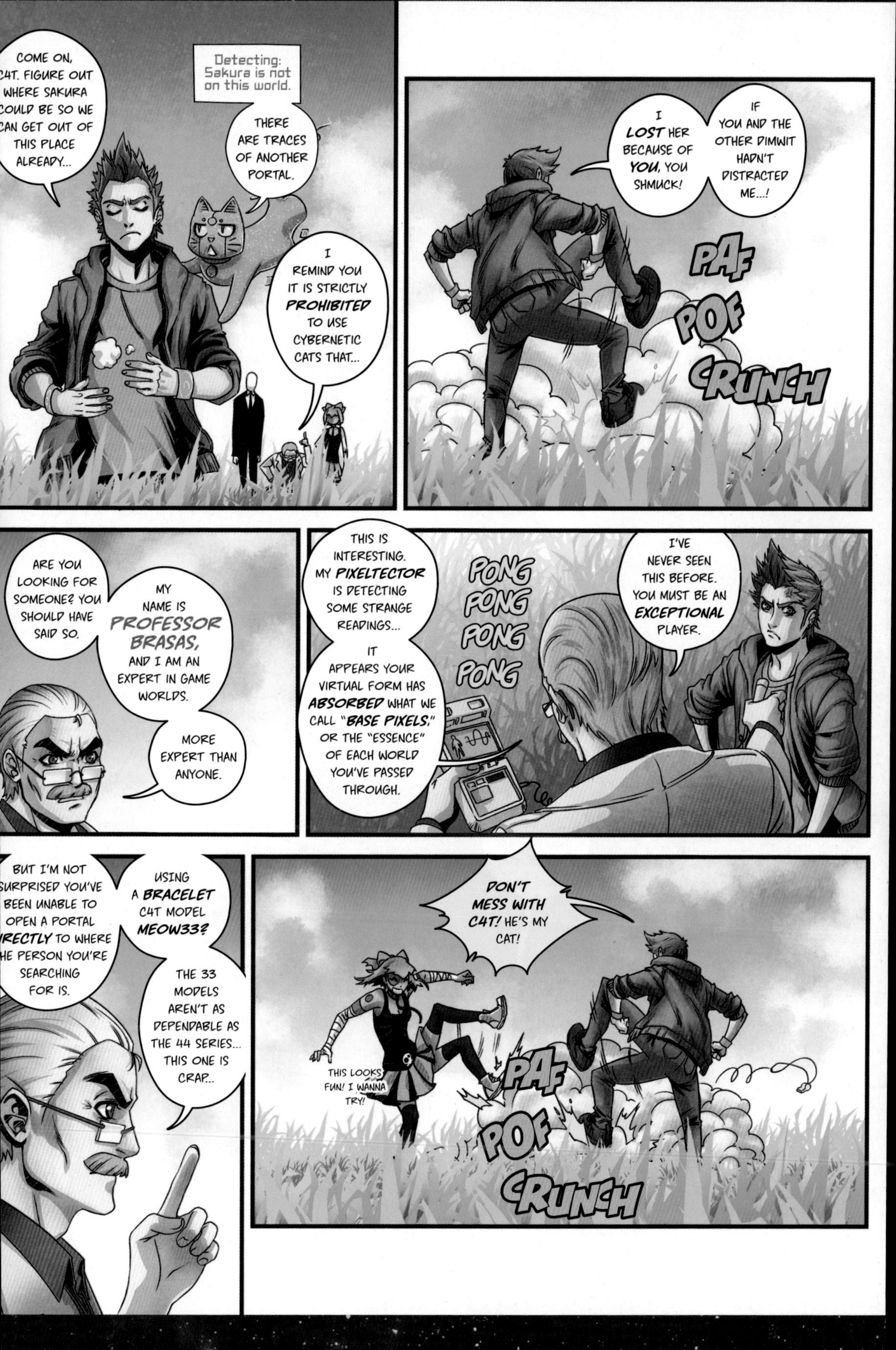

COME ON, C4T. FIGURE OUT WHERE SAKURA COULD BE SO WE CAN GET OUT OF THIS PLACE ALREADY...
Detecting: Sakura is not on this world.
THERE ARE TRACES OF ANOTHER PORTAL.
I REMIND YOU IT IS STRICTLY PROHIBITED TO USE CYBERNETIC CATS THAT...
I LOST HER BECAUSE OF YOU, YOU SHMUCK!
IF YOU AND THE OTHER DIMWIT HADN'T DISTRACTED ME...!
PAF
POF
CRUNCH
ARE YOU LOOKING FOR SOMEONE? YOU SHOULD HAVE SAID SO.
MY NAME IS PROFESSOR BRASAS, AND I AM AN EXPERT IN GAME WORLDS.
MORE EXPERT THAN ANYONE.
THIS IS INTERESTING. MY PIXELTECTOR IS DETECTING SOME STRANGE READINGS...
IT APPEARS YOUR VIRTUAL FORM HAS ABSORBED WHAT WE CALL "BASE PIXELS," OR THE "ESSENCE" OF EACH WORLD YOU'VE PASSED THROUGH.
PONG PONG PONG PONG
I'VE NEVER SEEN THIS BEFORE. YOU MUST BE AN EXCEPTIONAL PLAYER.
BUT I'M NOT SURPRISED YOU'VE BEEN UNABLE TO OPEN A PORTAL DIRECTLY TO WHERE THE PERSON YOU'RE SEARCHING FOR IS.
USING A BRACELET C4T MODEL MEOW33?
THE 33 MODELS AREN'T AS DEPENDABLE AS THE 44 SERIES... THIS ONE IS CRAP...
DON'T MESS WITH C4T! HE'S MY CAT!
THIS LOOKS FUN! I WANNA TRY!
PAF
POF
CRUNCH

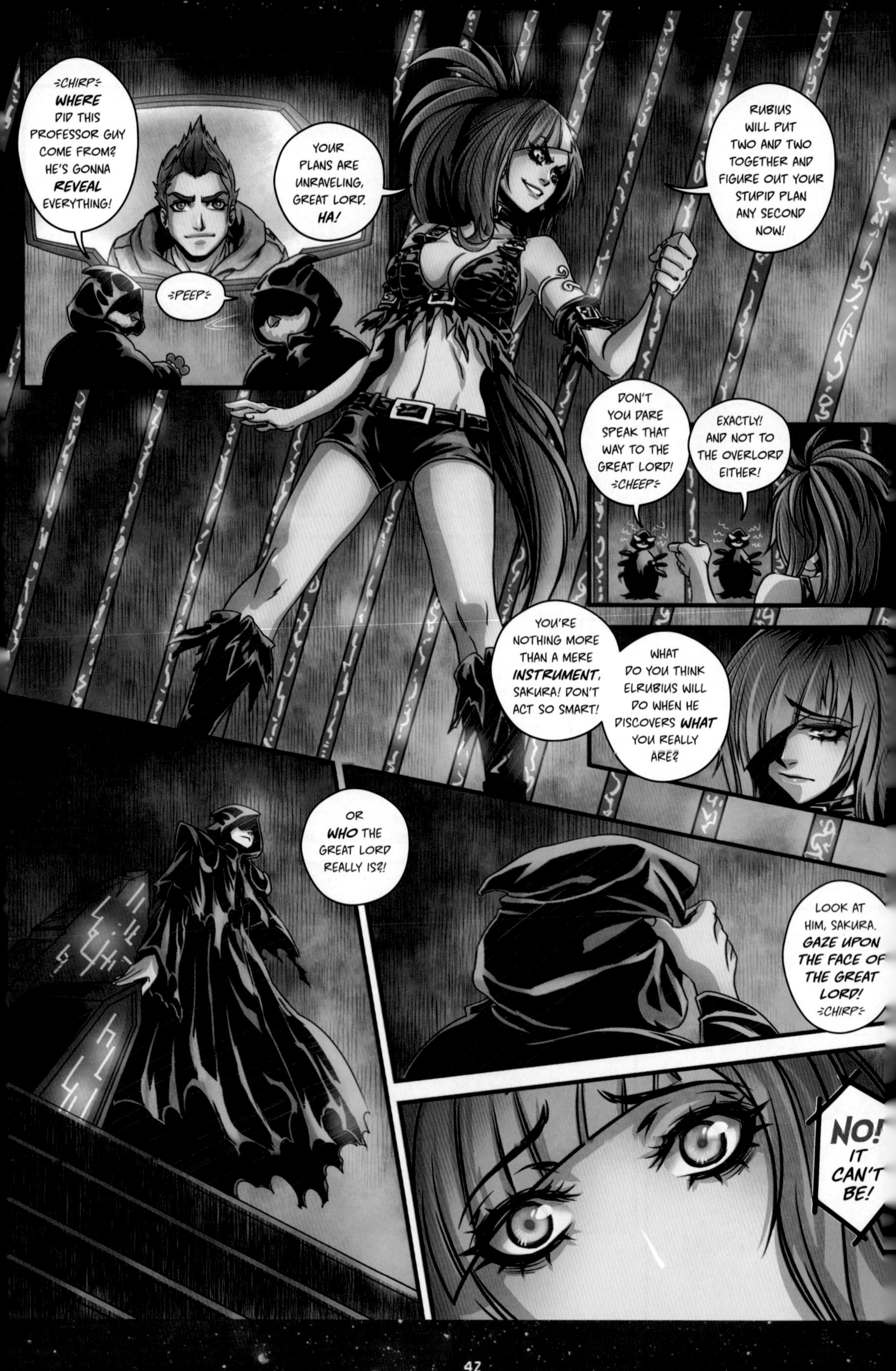

=CHIRP= WHERE DID THIS PROFESSOR GUY COME FROM? HE'S GONNA REVEAL EVERYTHING!
=PEEP=
YOUR PLANS ARE UNRAVELING, GREAT LORD. HA!
RUBIUS WILL PUT TWO AND TWO TOGETHER AND FIGURE OUT YOUR STUPID PLAN ANY SECOND NOW!
DON'T YOU DARE SPEAK THAT WAY TO THE GREAT LORD! =CHEEP=
EXACTLY! AND NOT TO THE OVERLORD EITHER!
YOU'RE NOTHING MORE THAN A MERE INSTRUMENT, SAKURA! DON'T ACT SO SMART!
WHAT DO YOU THINK ELRUBIUS WILL DO WHEN HE DISCOVERS WHAT YOU REALLY ARE?
OR WHO THE GREAT LORD REALLY IS?!
LOOK AT HIM, SAKURA. GAZE UPON THE FACE OF THE GREAT LORD! =CHIRP=
NO! IT CAN'T BE!

NOW IT'S UPDATED.

BRRRPPP

THE *IP* SEARCH SHOULD CONTINUE *AND* THE NEXT PORTAL WILL OPEN WHERE YOUR FRIEND IS.

DON'T THANK ME, IT'S JUST THAT I'M A *GENIUS* AND...

I FEEL MUCH STRONGER.

AND NOW YOU LOOK MUCH MORE HANDSOME, RUBIUS.

WHAT ARE THOSE "BASE PIXELS" YOU WERE TELLING US ABOUT?

BECAUSE ELRUBIUS IS SUCH AN EXCEPTIONAL PLAYER, HE ACTS AS A *MAGNET* FOR *BASE PIXELS*, THE FUNDAMENTAL ESSENCE ALL THE GAME WORLDS ARE *BUILT* ON.

IT'S EASY TO SEE WHOEVER TOOK YOUR FRIEND DID IT SO THAT ELRUBIUS WOULD *JUMP* FROM WORLD TO WORLD AFTER HER AND *ABSORB* BASE PIXELS FROM EACH ONE.

AT THIS MOMENT, RUBIUS IS A TYPE OF HUMAN *REPOSITORY* OF THE GAME WORLDS HE'S PASSED THROUGH. HE HAS AN ENORMOUS QUANTITY OF THE *CONDENSED* ESSENCE OF THE GAMES IN HIS BODY.

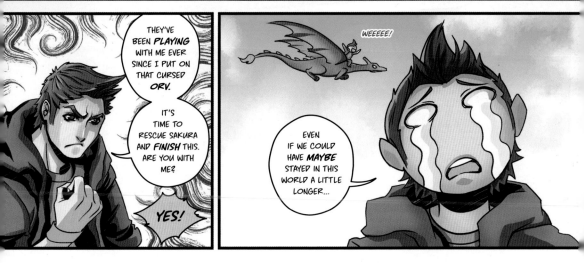

THEY'VE BEEN *PLAYING* WITH ME EVER SINCE I PUT ON THAT CURSED *ORV*.

IT'S TIME TO RESCUE SAKURA AND *FINISH* THIS. ARE YOU WITH ME?

YES!

WEEEEE!

EVEN IF WE COULD HAVE *MAYBE* STAYED IN THIS WORLD A LITTLE LONGER...

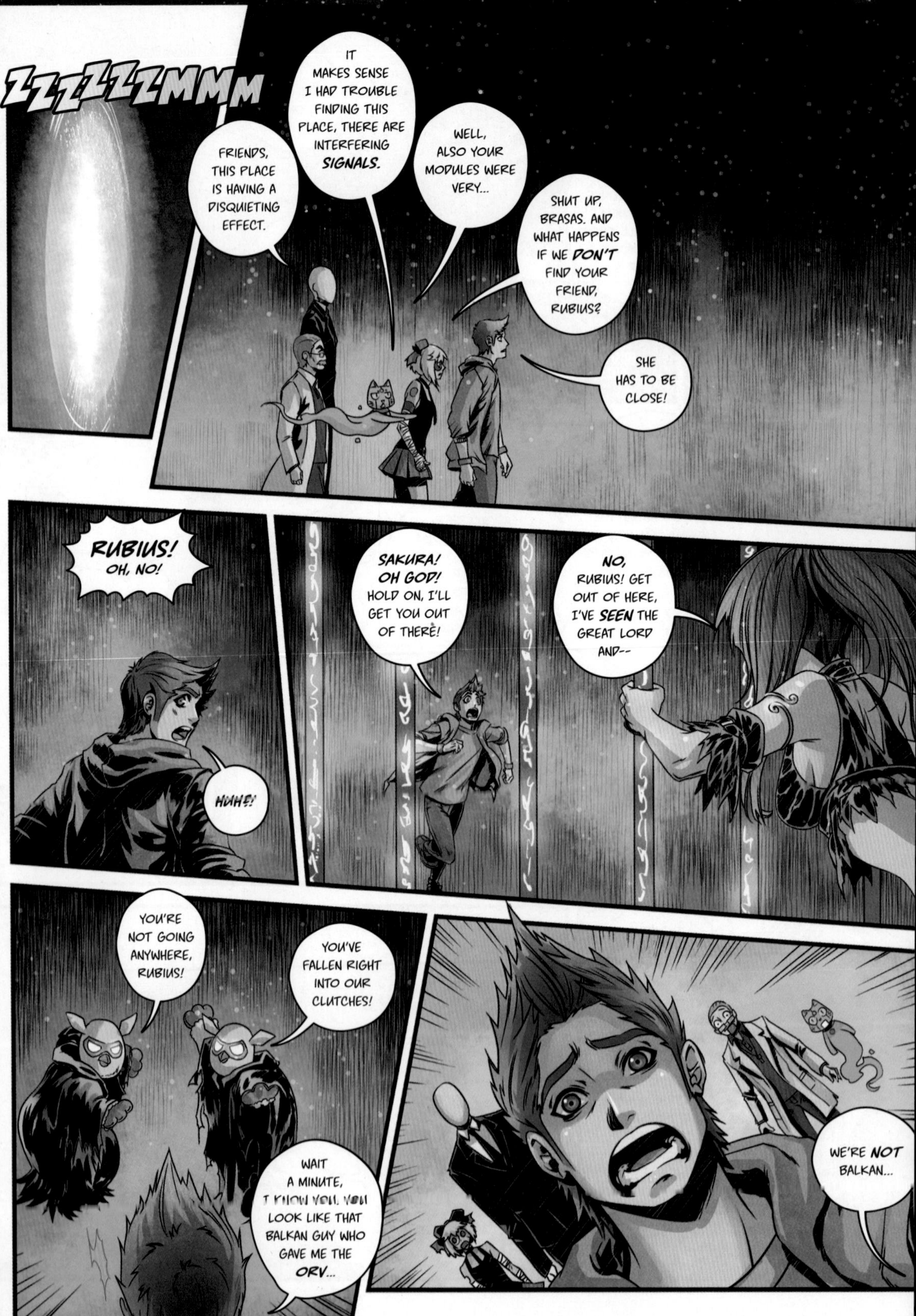
ZZZZZZMMMM
FRIENDS, THIS PLACE IS HAVING A DISQUIETING EFFECT.
IT MAKES SENSE I HAD TROUBLE FINDING THIS PLACE, THERE ARE INTERFERING **SIGNALS.**
WELL, ALSO YOUR MODULES WERE VERY...
SHUT UP, BRASAS. AND WHAT HAPPENS IF WE **DON'T** FIND YOUR FRIEND, RUBIUS?
SHE HAS TO BE CLOSE!
RUBIUS! OH, NO!
HUH?!
SAKURA! OH GOD! HOLD ON, I'LL GET YOU OUT OF THERE!
NO, RUBIUS! GET OUT OF HERE, I'VE **SEEN** THE GREAT LORD AND--
YOU'RE NOT GOING ANYWHERE, RUBIUS!
YOU'VE FALLEN RIGHT INTO OUR CLUTCHES!
WAIT A MINUTE, I KNOW YOU. YOU LOOK LIKE THAT BALKAN GUY WHO GAVE ME THE **ORV...**
WE'RE **NOT** BALKAN...

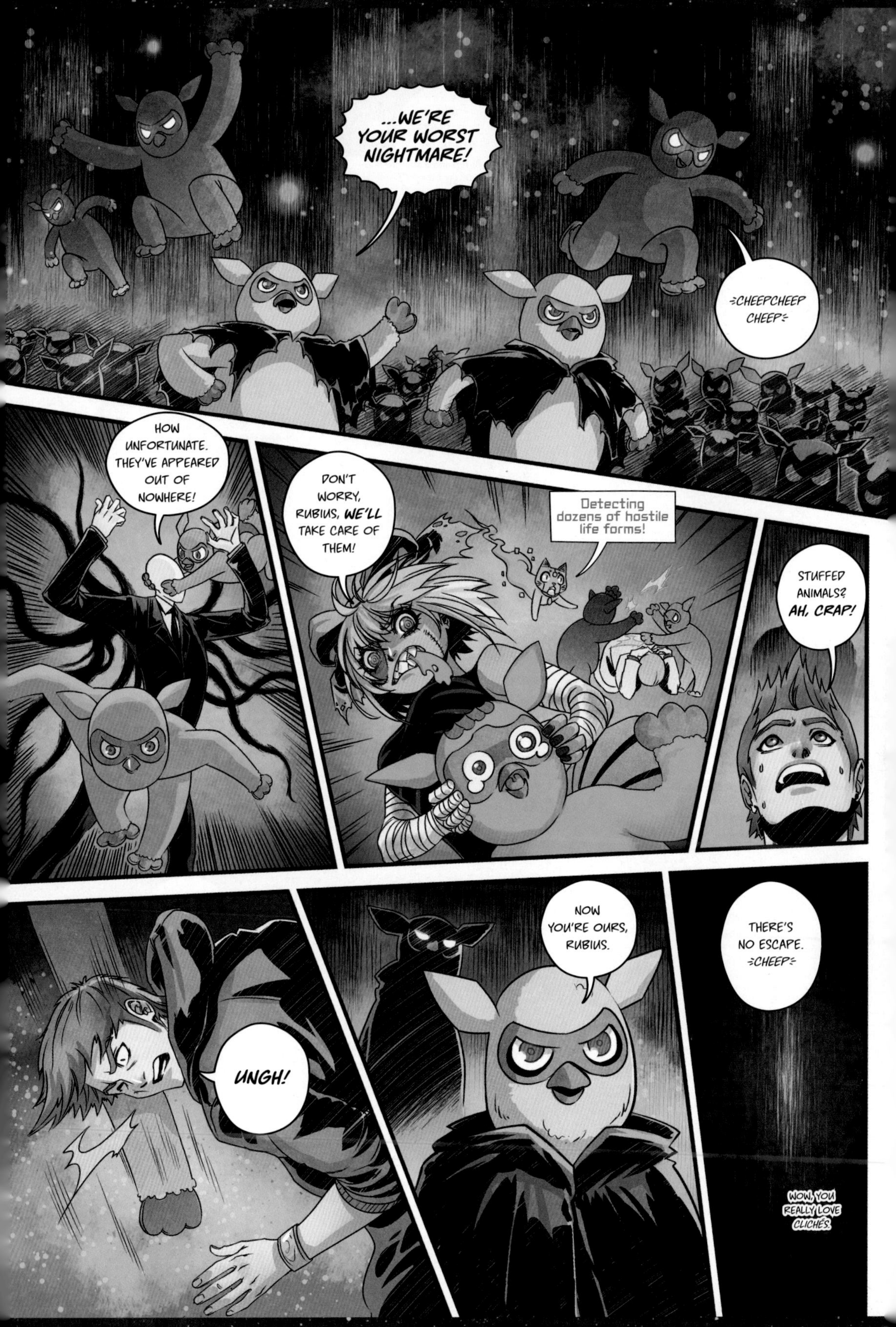
...WE'RE YOUR WORST NIGHTMARE!
=CHEEPCHEEP CHEEP=
HOW UNFORTUNATE. THEY'VE APPEARED OUT OF NOWHERE!
DON'T WORRY, RUBIUS, WE'LL TAKE CARE OF THEM!
Detecting dozens of hostile life forms!
STUFFED ANIMALS? AH, CRAP!
UNGH!
NOW YOU'RE OURS, RUBIUS.
THERE'S NO ESCAPE. =CHEEP=
WOW, YOU REALLY LOVE CLICHÉS.

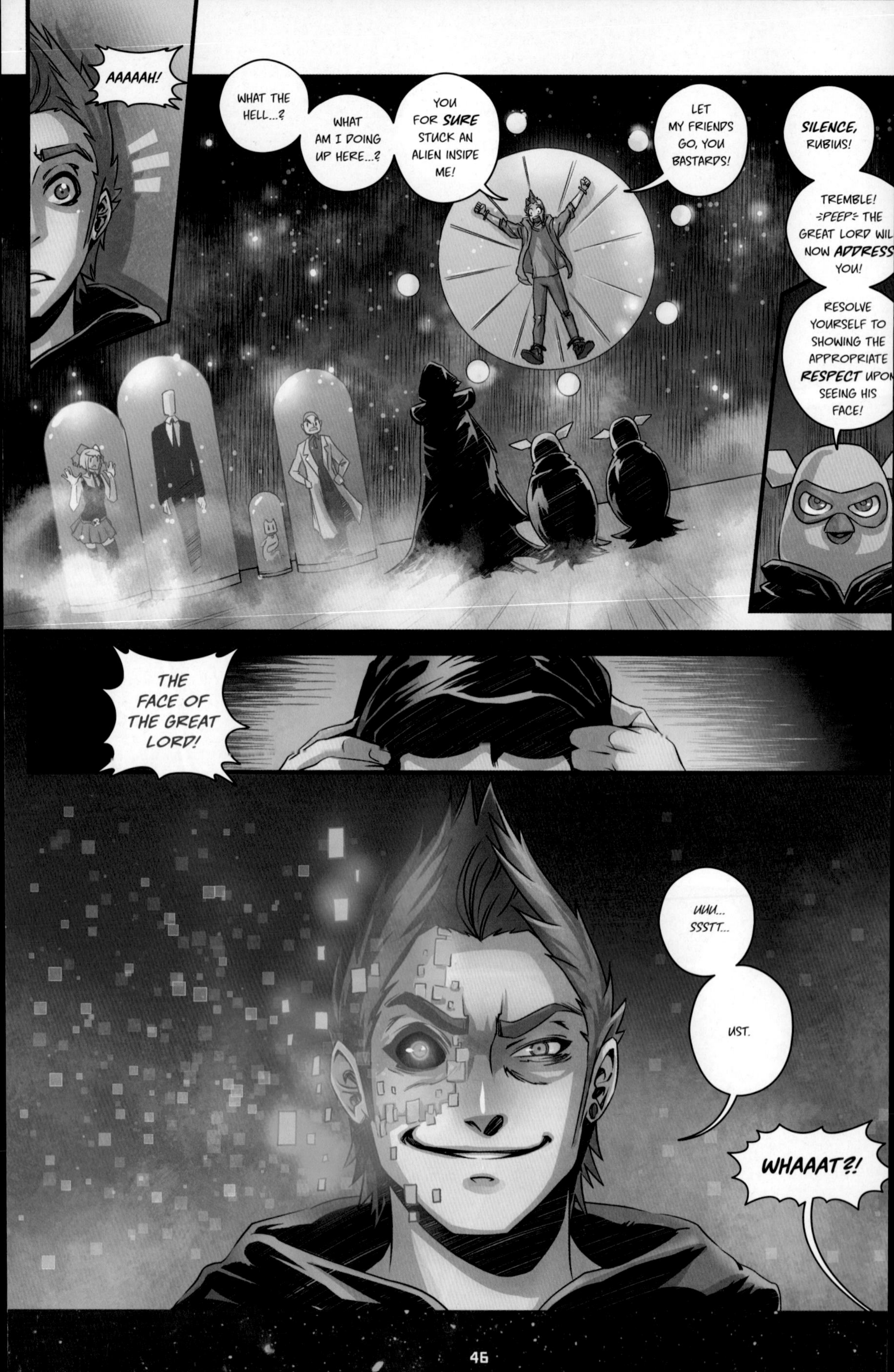

AAAAAH!
WHAT THE HELL...?
WHAT AM I DOING UP HERE...?
YOU FOR SURE STUCK AN ALIEN INSIDE ME!
LET MY FRIENDS GO, YOU BASTARDS!
SILENCE, RUBIUS!
TREMBLE! =PEEP= THE GREAT LORD WIL NOW ADDRESS YOU!
RESOLVE YOURSELF TO SHOWING THE APPROPRIATE RESPECT UPON SEEING HIS FACE!
THE FACE OF THE GREAT LORD!
UUU... SSSTT...
UST.
WHAAAT?!

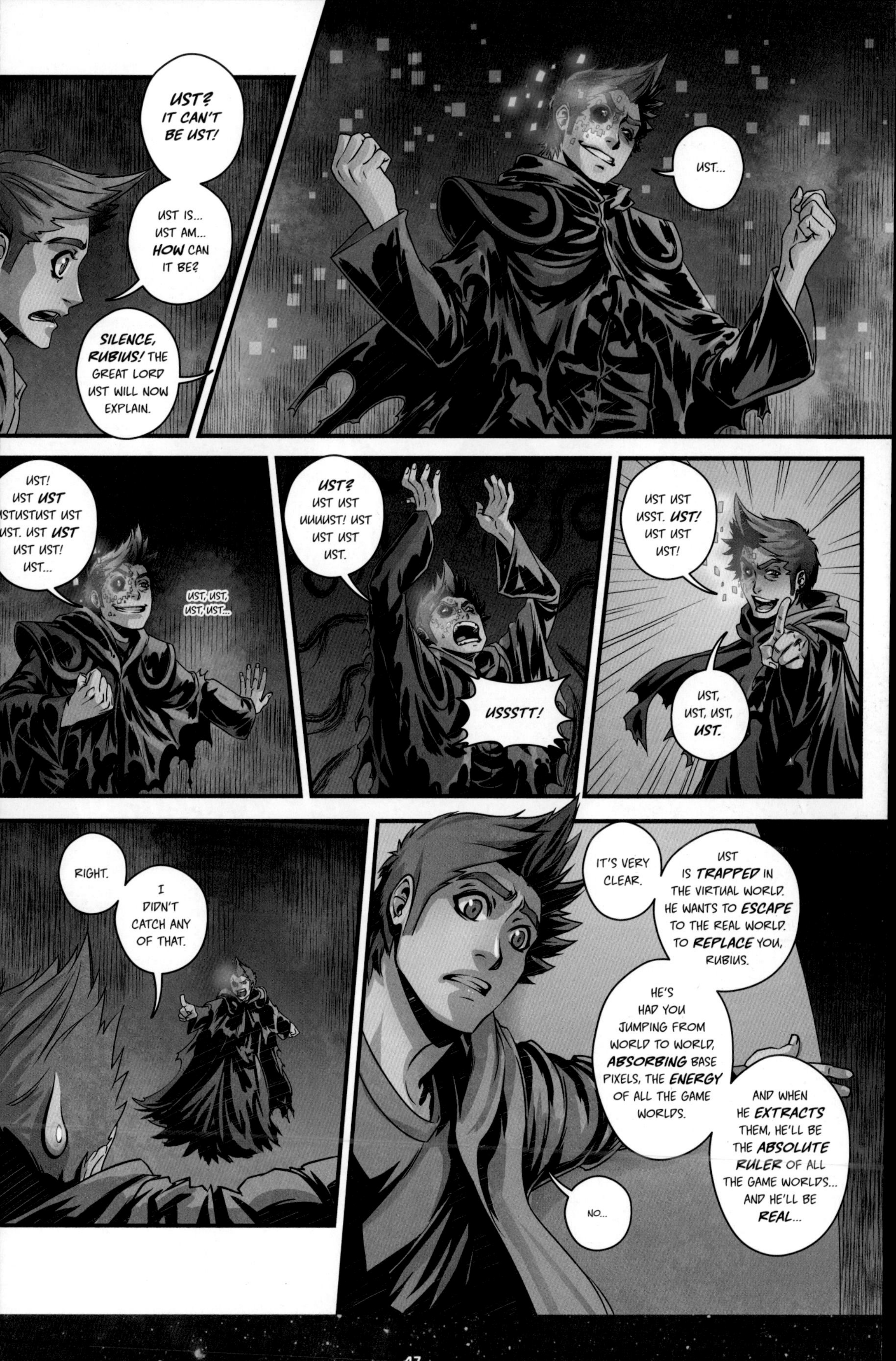
UST? IT CAN'T BE UST!
UST IS... UST AM... HOW CAN IT BE?
SILENCE, RUBIUS! THE GREAT LORD UST WILL NOW EXPLAIN.
UST...
UST! UST UST STUSTUST UST UST. UST UST UST UST! UST...
UST, UST, UST, UST...
UST? UST UST UUUUST! UST UST UST UST.
USSSTT!
UST UST USST. UST! UST UST UST!
UST, UST, UST, UST.
RIGHT.
I DIDN'T CATCH ANY OF THAT.
IT'S VERY CLEAR.
UST IS TRAPPED IN THE VIRTUAL WORLD. HE WANTS TO ESCAPE TO THE REAL WORLD. TO REPLACE YOU, RUBIUS.
HE'S HAD YOU JUMPING FROM WORLD TO WORLD, ABSORBING BASE PIXELS, THE ENERGY OF ALL THE GAME WORLDS.
NO...
AND WHEN HE EXTRACTS THEM, HE'LL BE THE ABSOLUTE RULER OF ALL THE GAME WORLDS... AND HE'LL BE REAL...

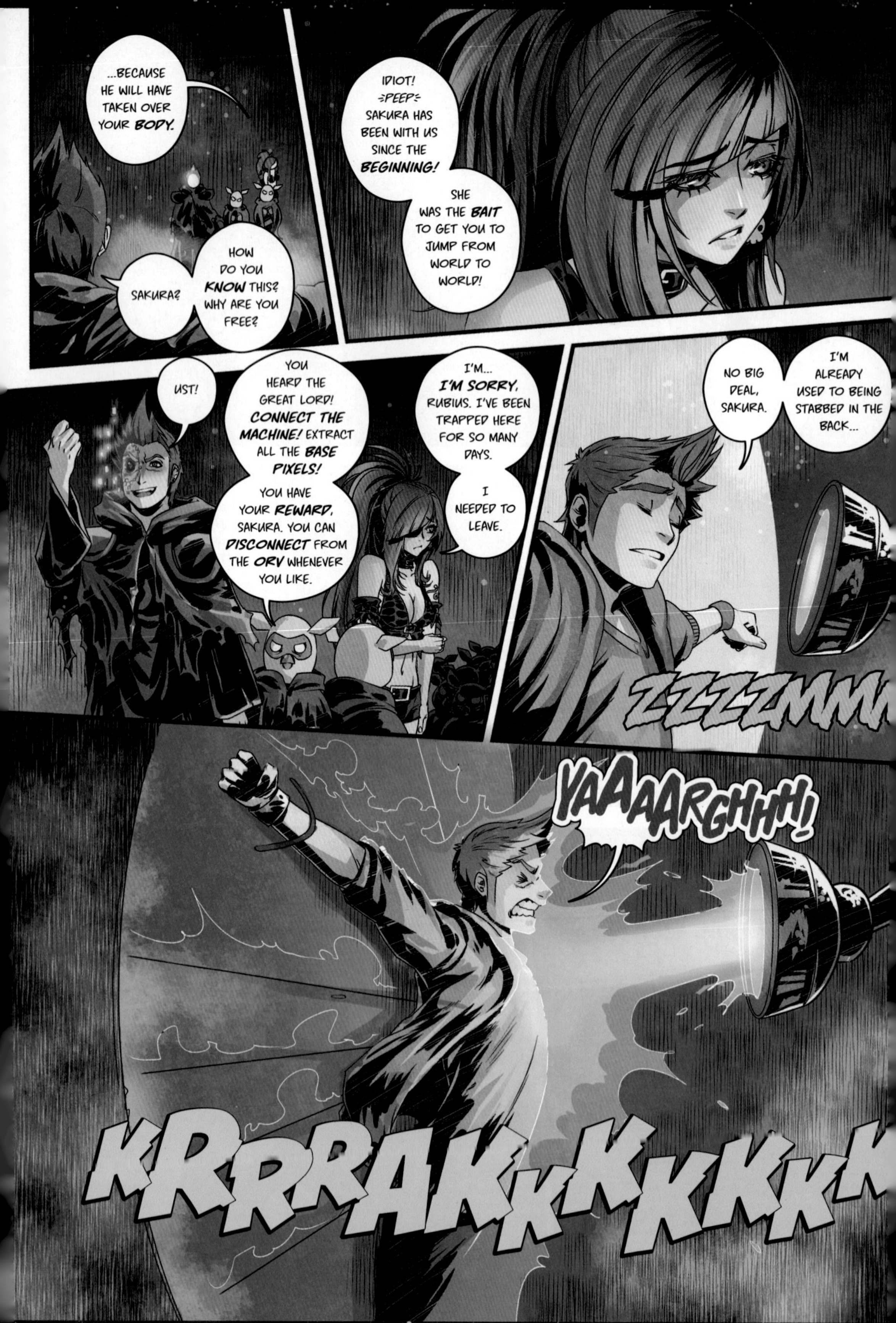

...BECAUSE HE WILL HAVE TAKEN OVER YOUR BODY.
SAKURA?
HOW DO YOU KNOW THIS? WHY ARE YOU FREE?
IDIOT! =PEEP= SAKURA HAS BEEN WITH US SINCE THE BEGINNING!
SHE WAS THE BAIT TO GET YOU TO JUMP FROM WORLD TO WORLD!
UST!
YOU HEARD THE GREAT LORD! CONNECT THE MACHINE! EXTRACT ALL THE BASE PIXELS!
YOU HAVE YOUR REWARD, SAKURA. YOU CAN DISCONNECT FROM THE ORV WHENEVER YOU LIKE.
I'M... I'M SORRY, RUBIUS. I'VE BEEN TRAPPED HERE FOR SO MANY DAYS.
I NEEDED TO LEAVE.
NO BIG DEAL, SAKURA.
I'M ALREADY USED TO BEING STABBED IN THE BACK...
ZZZZMMM
YAAAARGHHH!
KRRRAKKKKKKK

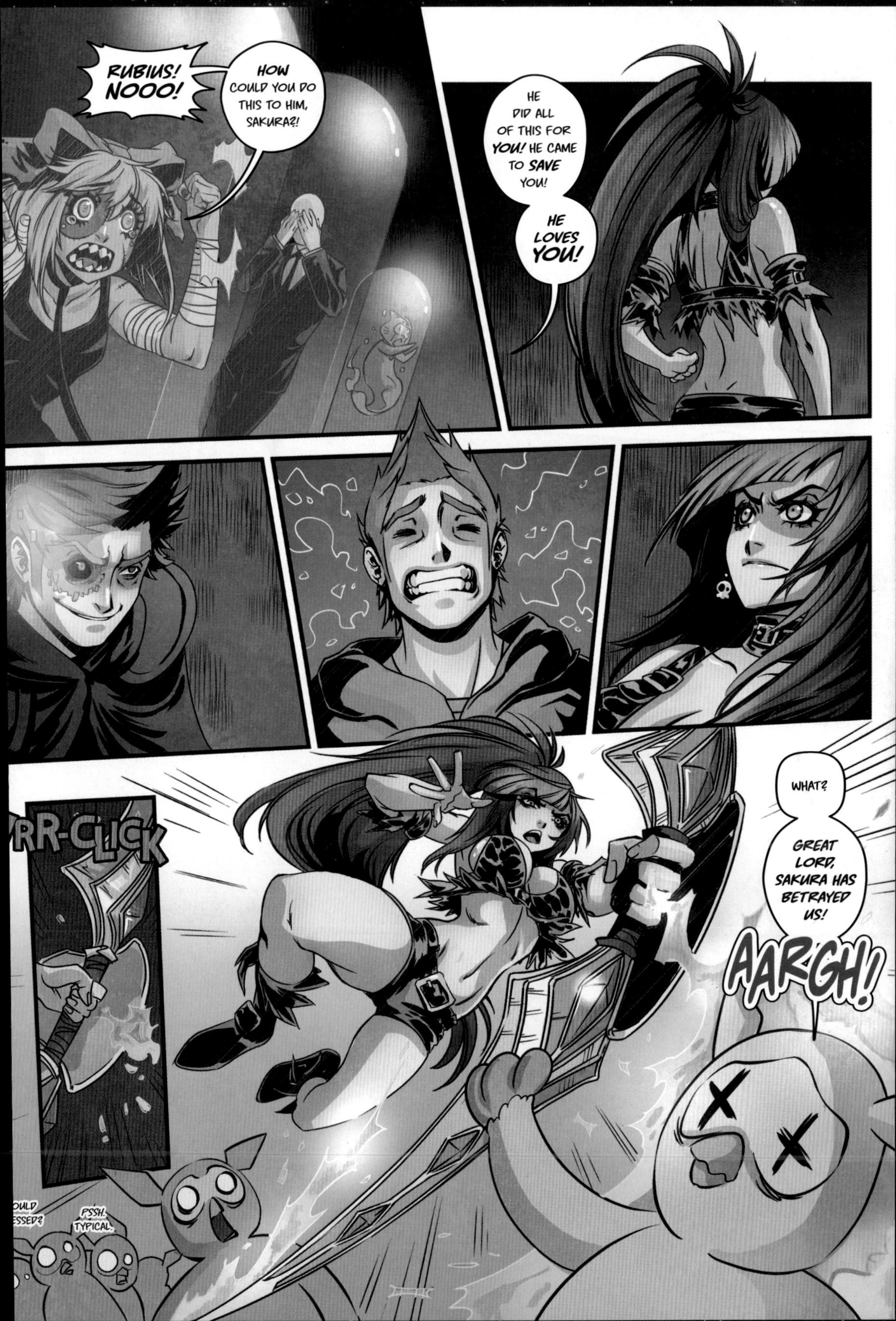
RUBIUS! NOOO!
HOW COULD YOU DO THIS TO HIM, SAKURA?!
HE DID ALL OF THIS FOR YOU! HE CAME TO SAVE YOU!
HE LOVES YOU!
RR-CLICK
WHAT?
GREAT LORD, SAKURA HAS BETRAYED US!
AARGH!
PSSH. TYPICAL.

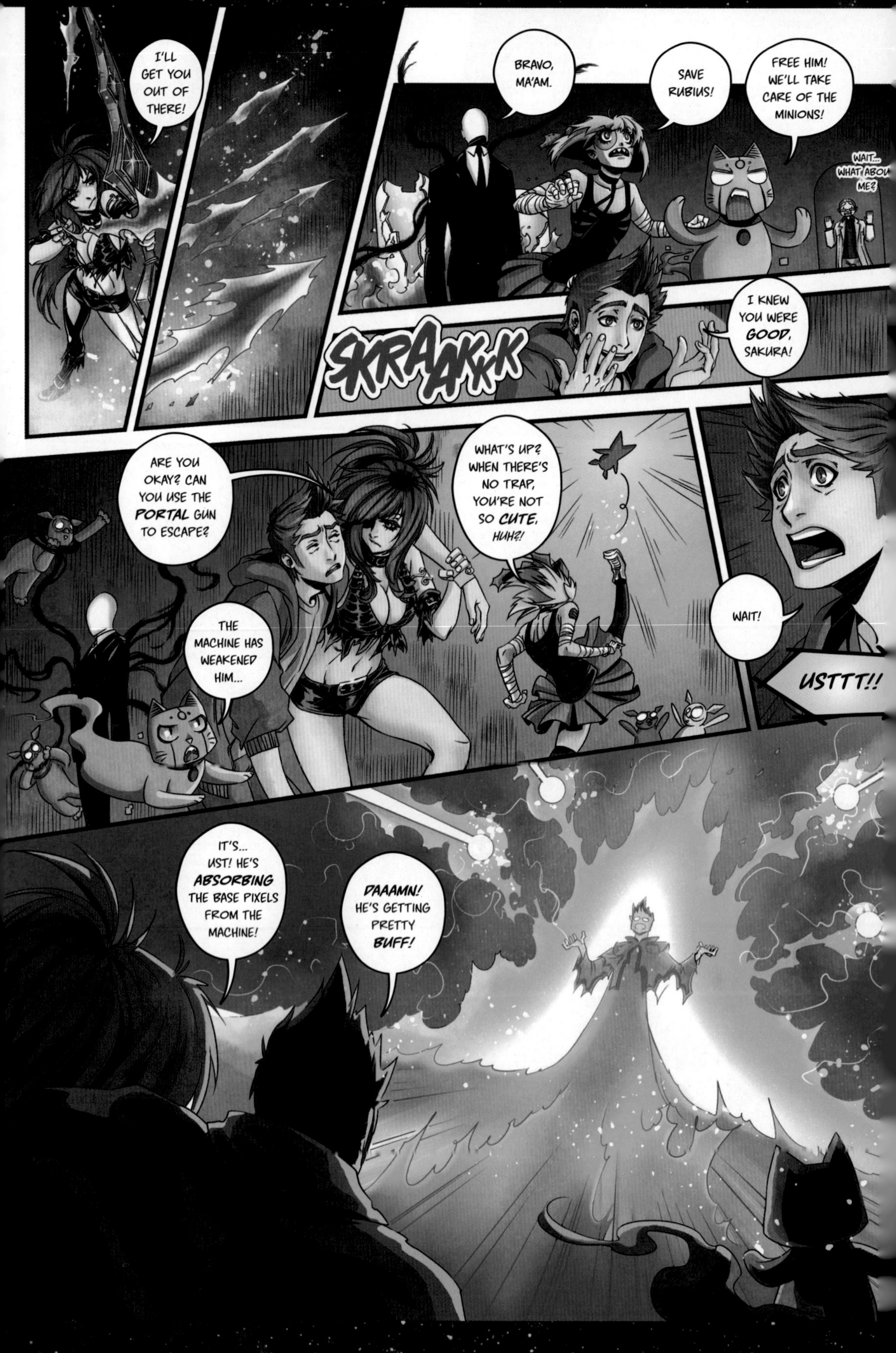
I'LL GET YOU OUT OF THERE!
BRAVO, MA'AM.
SAVE RUBIUS!
FREE HIM! WE'LL TAKE CARE OF THE MINIONS!
WAIT... WHAT ABOUT ME?
SKRAAKKK
I KNEW YOU WERE GOOD, SAKURA!
ARE YOU OKAY? CAN YOU USE THE PORTAL GUN TO ESCAPE?
WHAT'S UP? WHEN THERE'S NO TRAP, YOU'RE NOT SO CUTE, HUH?!
THE MACHINE HAS WEAKENED HIM...
WAIT!
USTTT!!
IT'S... UST! HE'S ABSORBING THE BASE PIXELS FROM THE MACHINE!
DAAAMN! HE'S GETTING PRETTY BUFF!

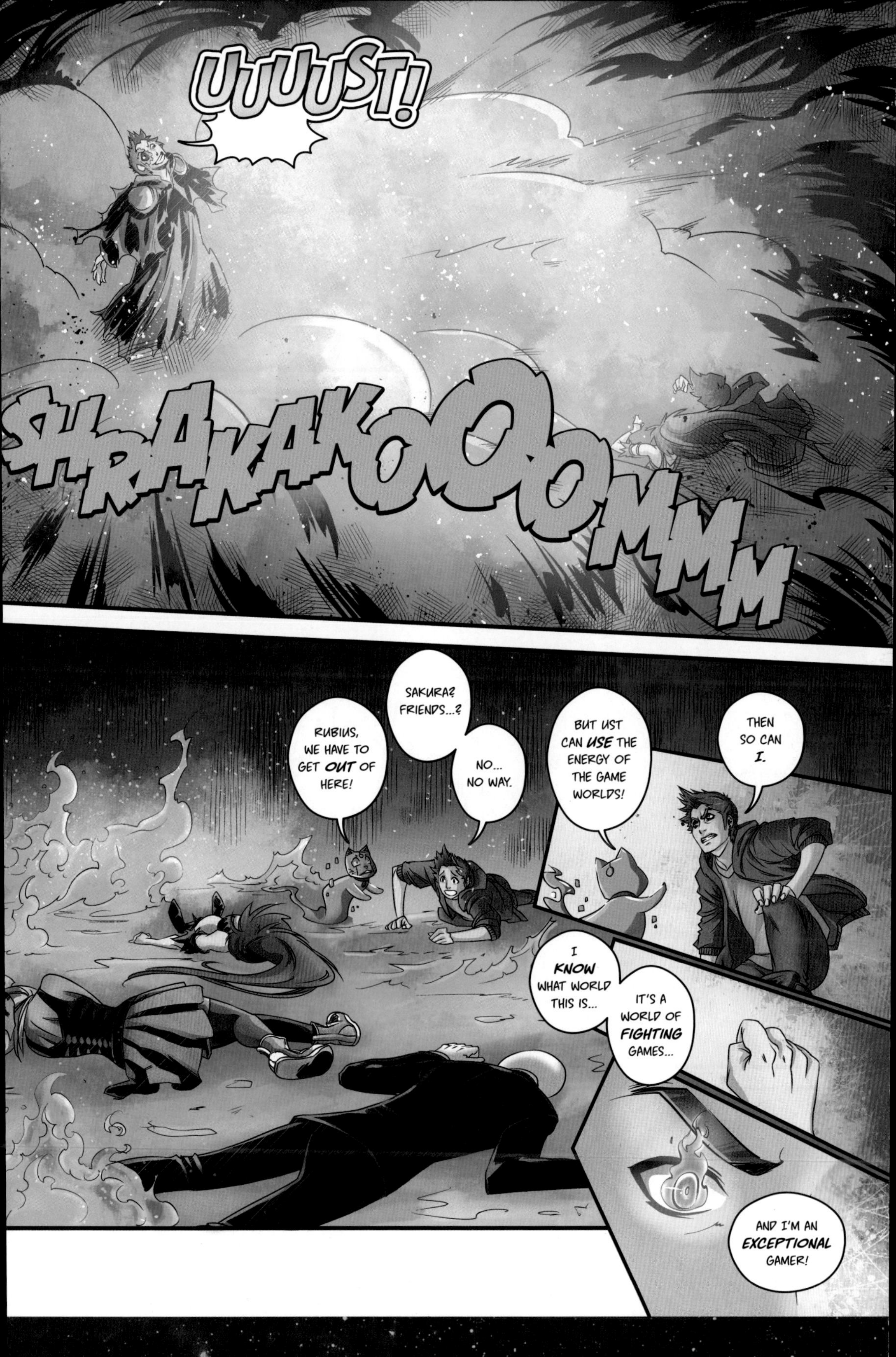
UUUUST!
SHRAKAKOOOOOMMMM
RUBIUS, WE HAVE TO GET OUT OF HERE!
SAKURA? FRIENDS...?
NO... NO WAY.
BUT UST CAN USE THE ENERGY OF THE GAME WORLDS!
THEN SO CAN I.
I KNOW WHAT WORLD THIS IS...
IT'S A WORLD OF FIGHTING GAMES...
AND I'M AN EXCEPTIONAL GAMER!

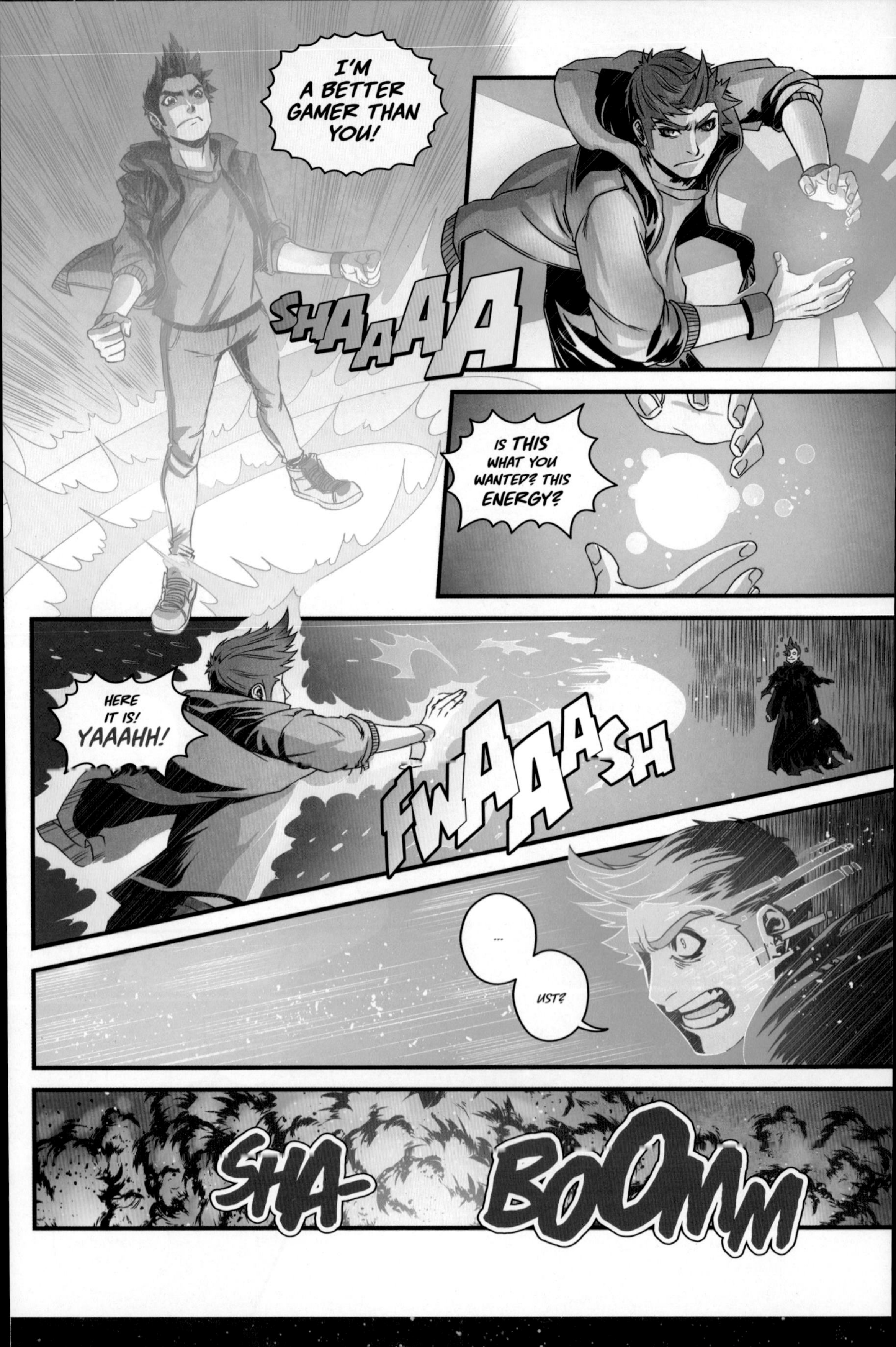
I'M A BETTER GAMER THAN YOU!
SHAAAAA
IS THIS WHAT YOU WANTED? THIS ENERGY?
HERE IT IS! YAAAHH!
FWAAAASH
...
UST?
SHA-BOOMM

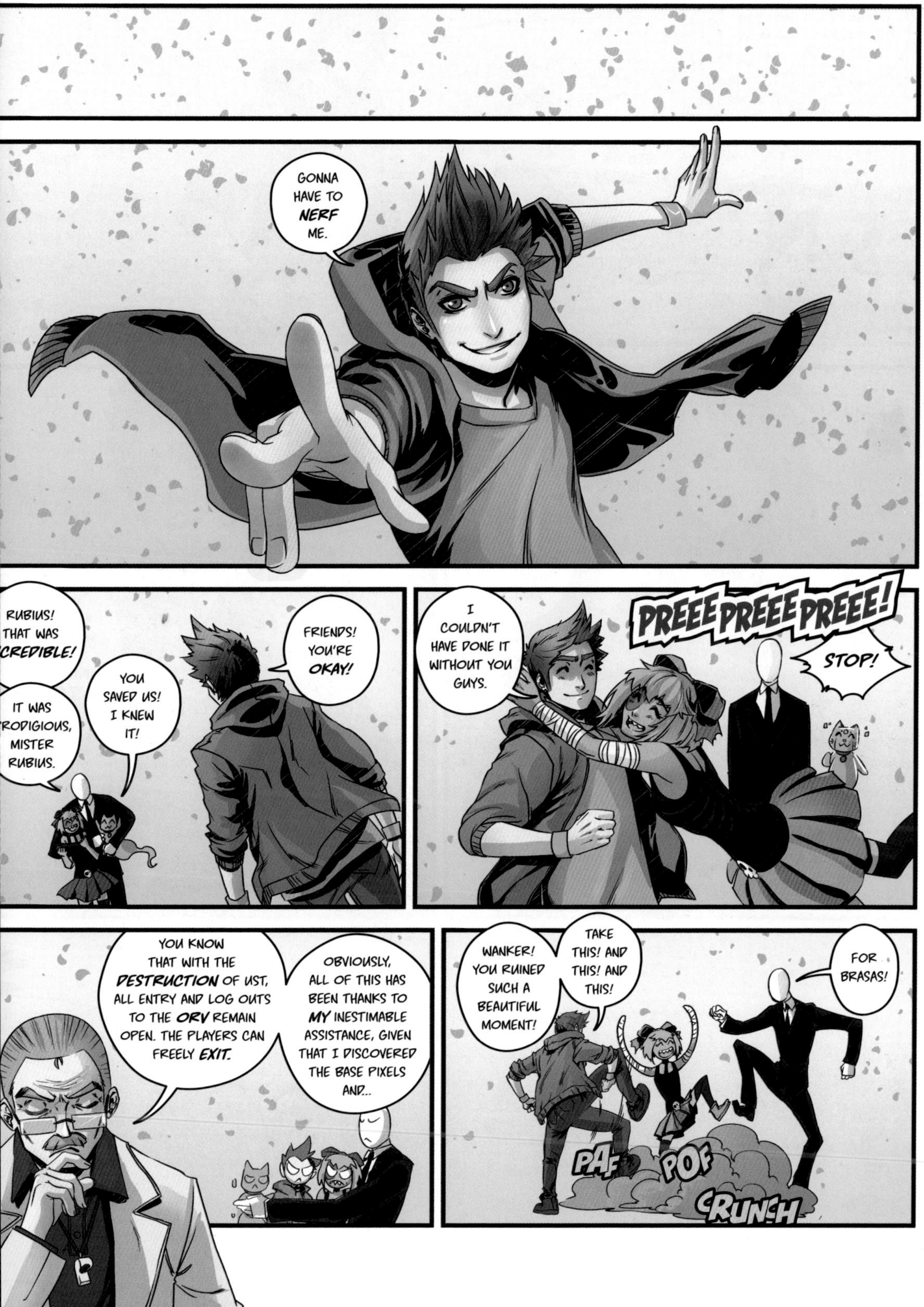
GONNA HAVE TO NERF ME.
RUBIUS! THAT WAS CREDIBLE!
IT WAS RODIGIOUS, MISTER RUBIUS.
YOU SAVED US! I KNEW IT!
FRIENDS! YOU'RE OKAY!
I COULDN'T HAVE DONE IT WITHOUT YOU GUYS.
PREEE PREEE PREEE!
STOP!
YOU KNOW THAT WITH THE DESTRUCTION OF UST, ALL ENTRY AND LOG OUTS TO THE ORV REMAIN OPEN. THE PLAYERS CAN FREELY EXIT.
OBVIOUSLY, ALL OF THIS HAS BEEN THANKS TO MY INESTIMABLE ASSISTANCE, GIVEN THAT I DISCOVERED THE BASE PIXELS AND...
WANKER! YOU RUINED SUCH A BEAUTIFUL MOMENT!
TAKE THIS! AND THIS! AND THIS!
FOR BRASAS!
PAF
POF
CRUNCH

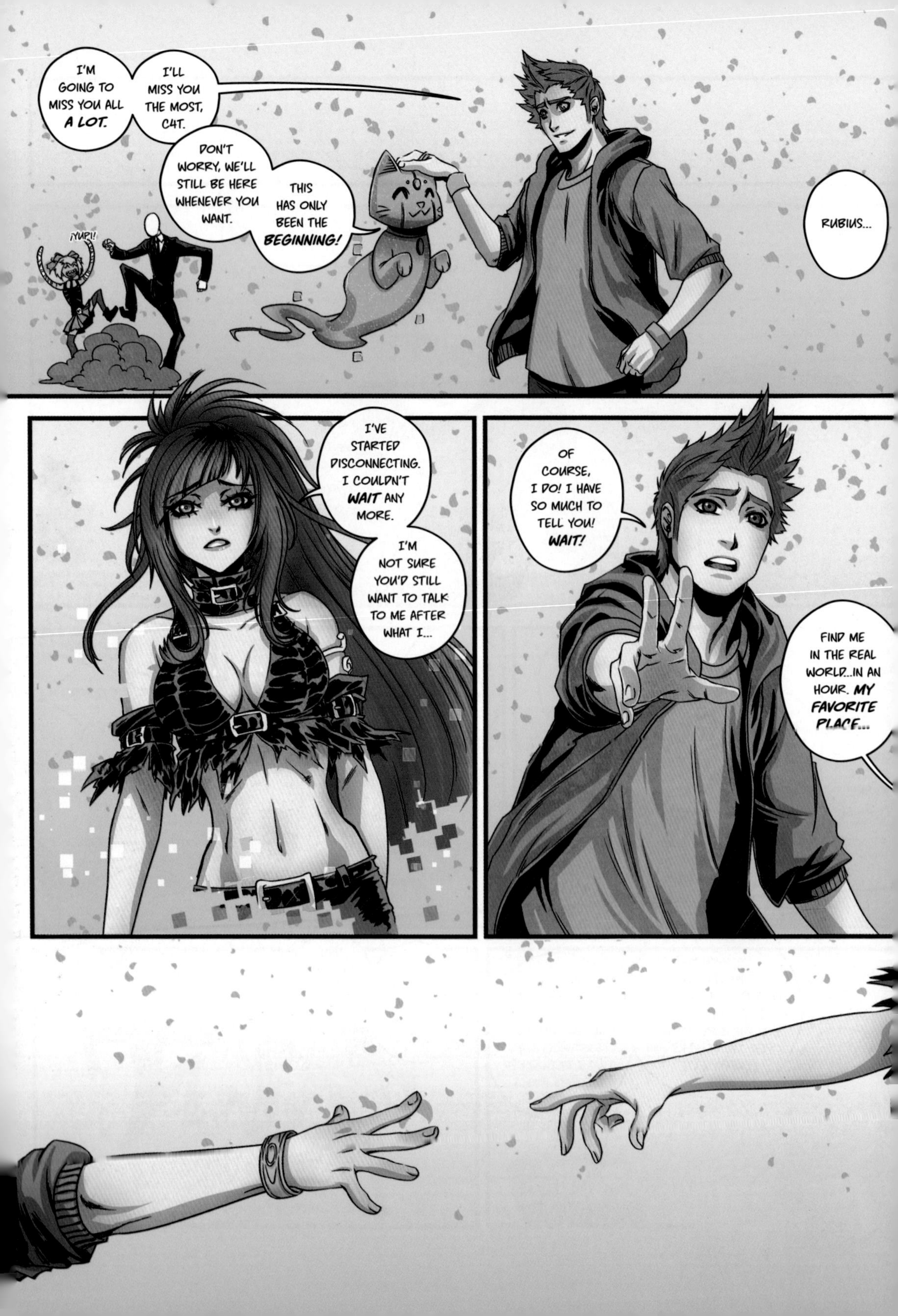

I'M GOING TO MISS YOU ALL A LOT.
I'LL MISS YOU THE MOST, C4T.
DON'T WORRY, WE'LL STILL BE HERE WHENEVER YOU WANT.
THIS HAS ONLY BEEN THE BEGINNING!
¡YUPI!
RUBIUS...
I'VE STARTED DISCONNECTING. I COULDN'T WAIT ANY MORE.
I'M NOT SURE YOU'D STILL WANT TO TALK TO ME AFTER WHAT I...
OF COURSE, I DO! I HAVE SO MUCH TO TELL YOU! WAIT!
FIND ME IN THE REAL WORLD...IN AN HOUR. MY FAVORITE PLACE...

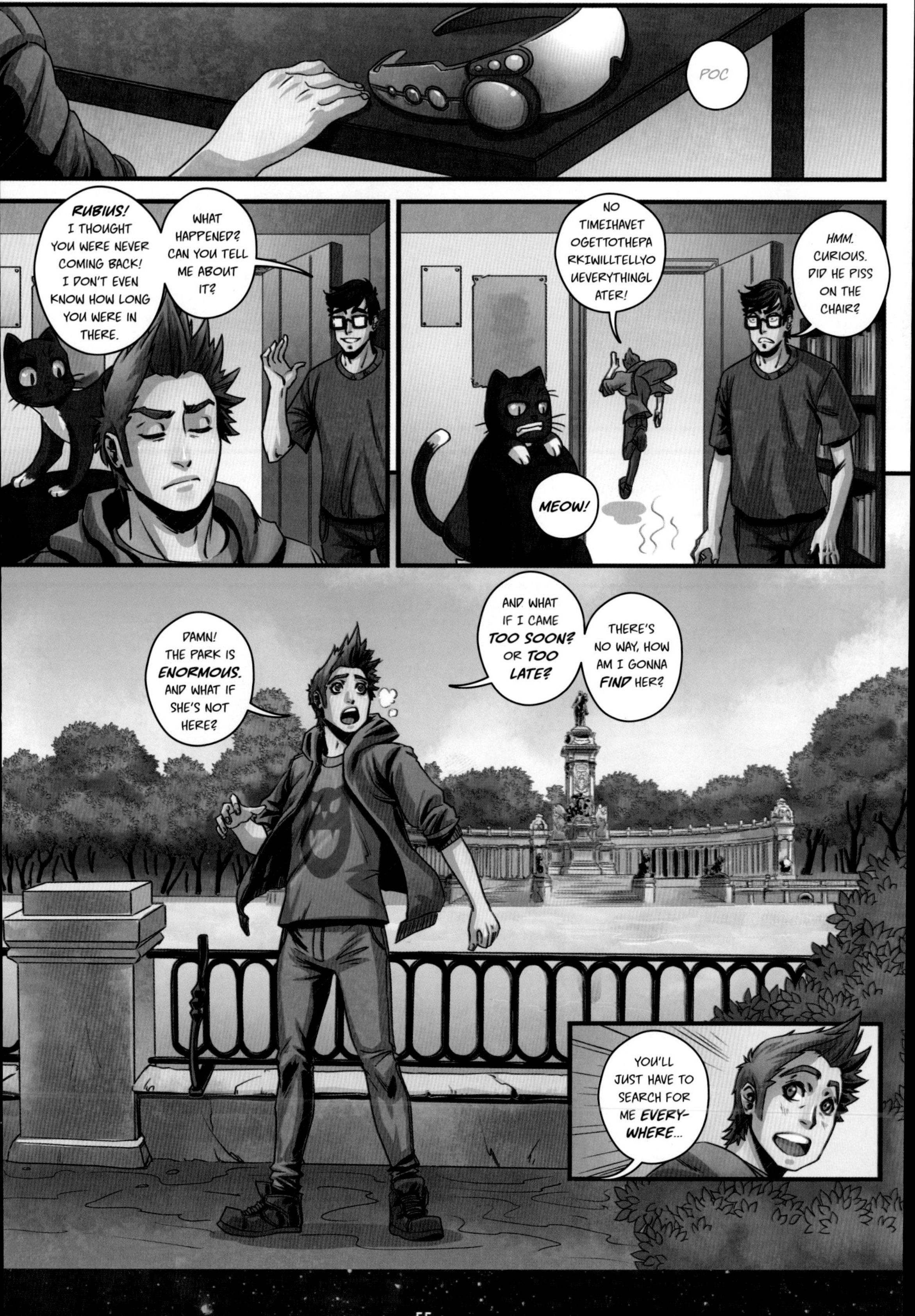
POC
RUBIUS! I THOUGHT YOU WERE NEVER COMING BACK! I DON'T EVEN KNOW HOW LONG YOU WERE IN THERE.
WHAT HAPPENED? CAN YOU TELL ME ABOUT IT?
NO TIMEIHAVET OGETTOTHEPA RKIWILLTELLYO UEVERYTHINGL ATER!
HMM. CURIOUS. DID HE PISS ON THE CHAIR?
MEOW!
DAMN! THE PARK IS ENORMOUS. AND WHAT IF SHE'S NOT HERE?
AND WHAT IF I CAME TOO SOON? OR TOO LATE?
THERE'S NO WAY, HOW AM I GONNA FIND HER?
YOU'LL JUST HAVE TO SEARCH FOR ME EVERY-WHERE...

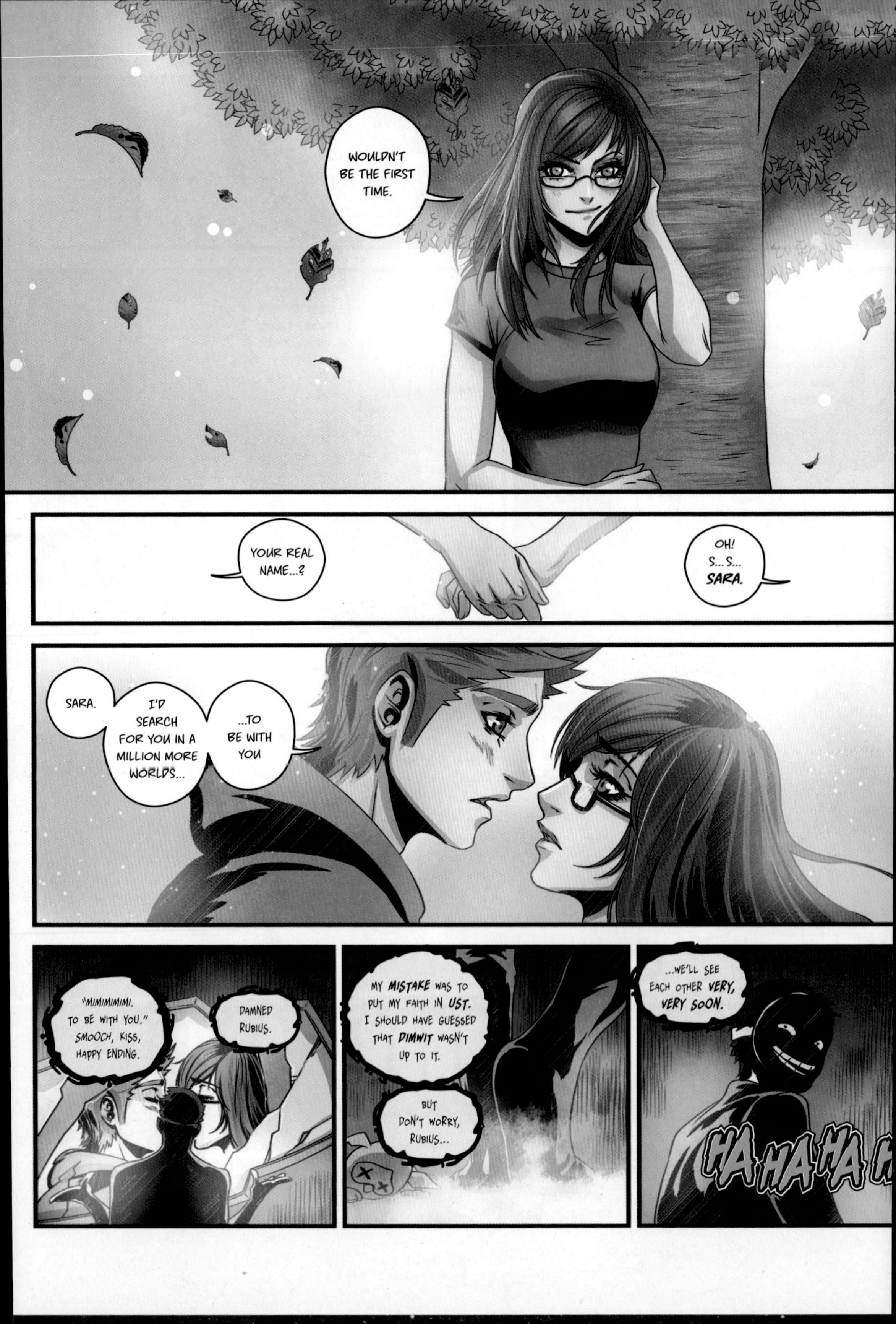
WOULDN'T BE THE FIRST TIME.
YOUR REAL NAME...?
OH! S... S... SARA.
SARA.
I'D SEARCH FOR YOU IN A MILLION MORE WORLDS...
...TO BE WITH YOU
"MIMIMIMIMI. TO BE WITH YOU." SMOOCH, KISS, HAPPY ENDING.
DAMNED RUBIUS.
MY MISTAKE WAS TO PUT MY FAITH IN UST. I SHOULD HAVE GUESSED THAT DIMWIT WASN'T UP TO IT.
BUT DON'T WORRY, RUBIUS...
...WE'LL SEE EACH OTHER VERY, VERY SOON.
HA HA HA

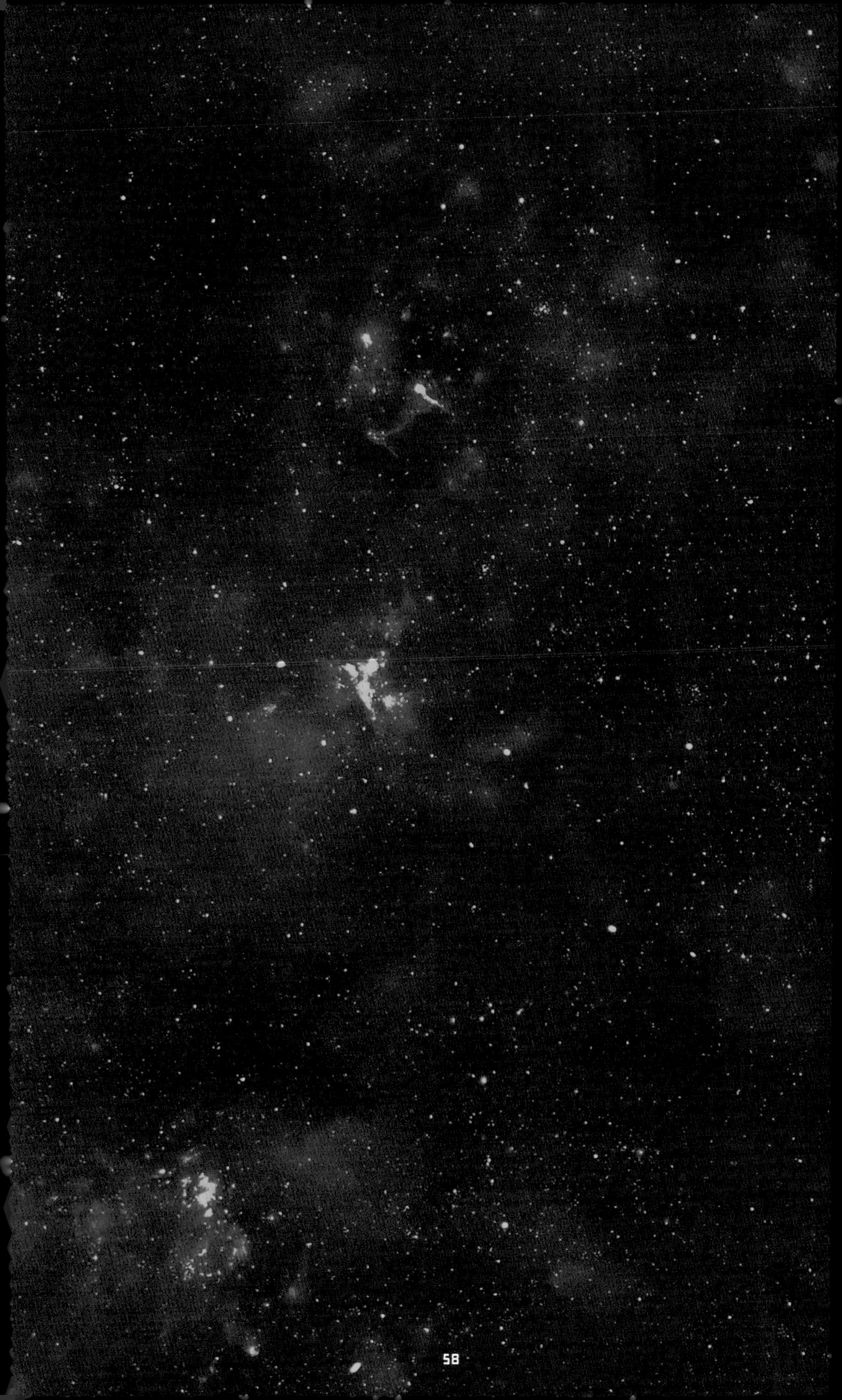

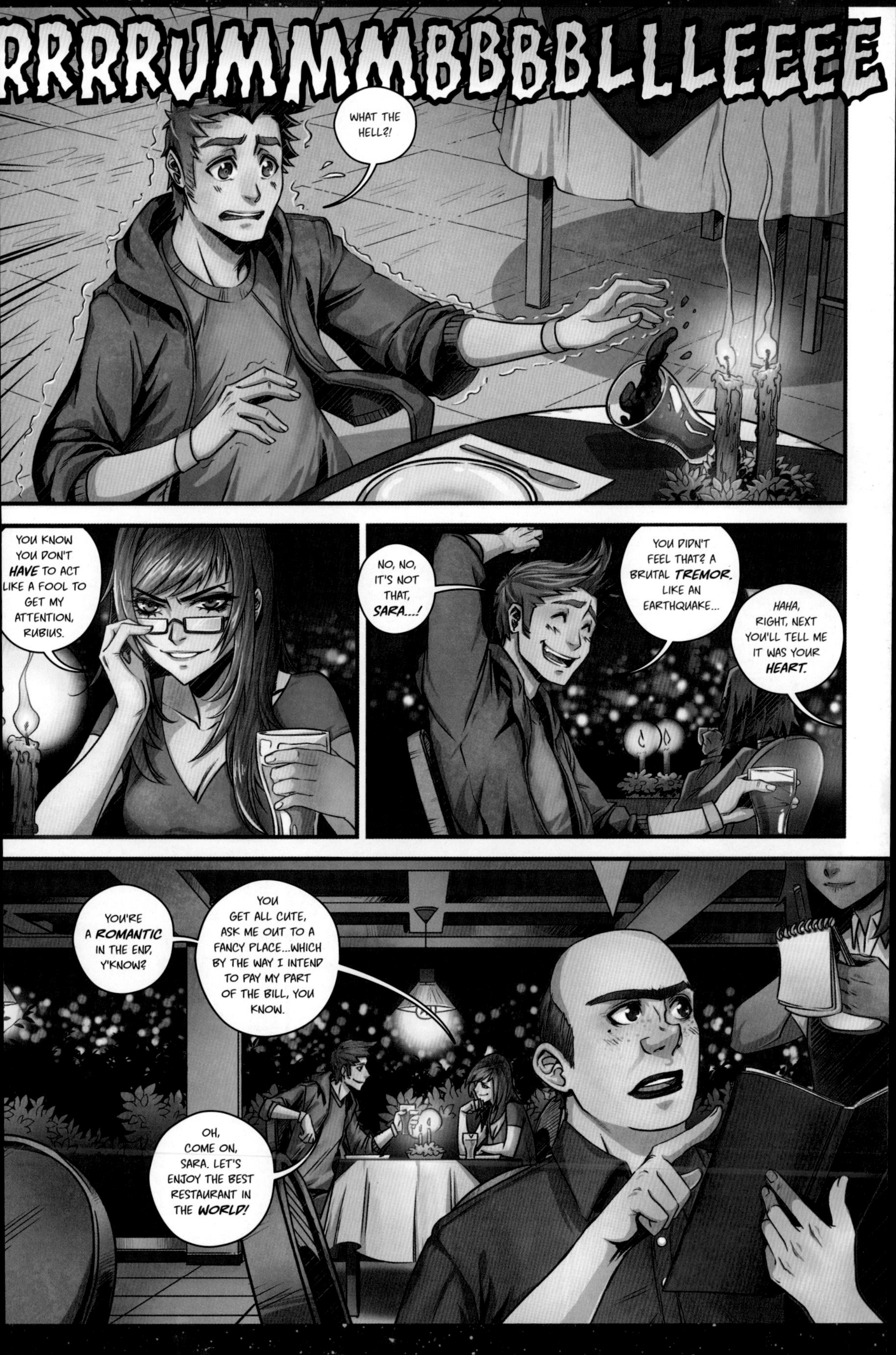
RRRRUMMMBBBBLLLEEEE
WHAT THE HELL?!
YOU KNOW YOU DON'T HAVE TO ACT LIKE A FOOL TO GET MY ATTENTION, RUBIUS.
NO, NO, IT'S NOT THAT, SARA...!
YOU DIDN'T FEEL THAT? A BRUTAL TREMOR. LIKE AN EARTHQUAKE...
HAHA, RIGHT, NEXT YOU'LL TELL ME IT WAS YOUR HEART.
YOU'RE A ROMANTIC IN THE END, Y'KNOW?
YOU GET ALL CUTE, ASK ME OUT TO A FANCY PLACE...WHICH BY THE WAY I INTEND TO PAY MY PART OF THE BILL, YOU KNOW.
OH, COME ON, SARA. LET'S ENJOY THE BEST RESTAURANT IN THE WORLD!

YOU THOUGHT WE'D GET A BURGER ON OUR *FIRST DATE?!*

I WANT EVERYTHING TO BE PERFEC--

--OOOOF!

BUMP

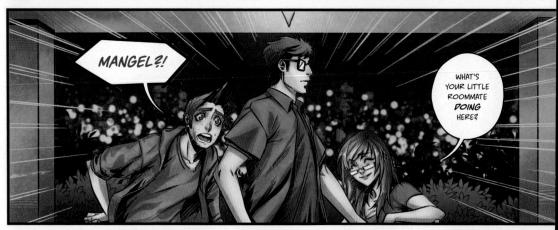

MANGEL?!

WHAT'S YOUR LITTLE ROOMMATE *DOING* HERE?

BUT...BUT... MANGEL?

WHAT THE HELL ARE YOU DOING...?

TOMP

TOMP

...

CHOOGA CHOO CHOO!

MANGEEEL...

BOOM BOO POW!

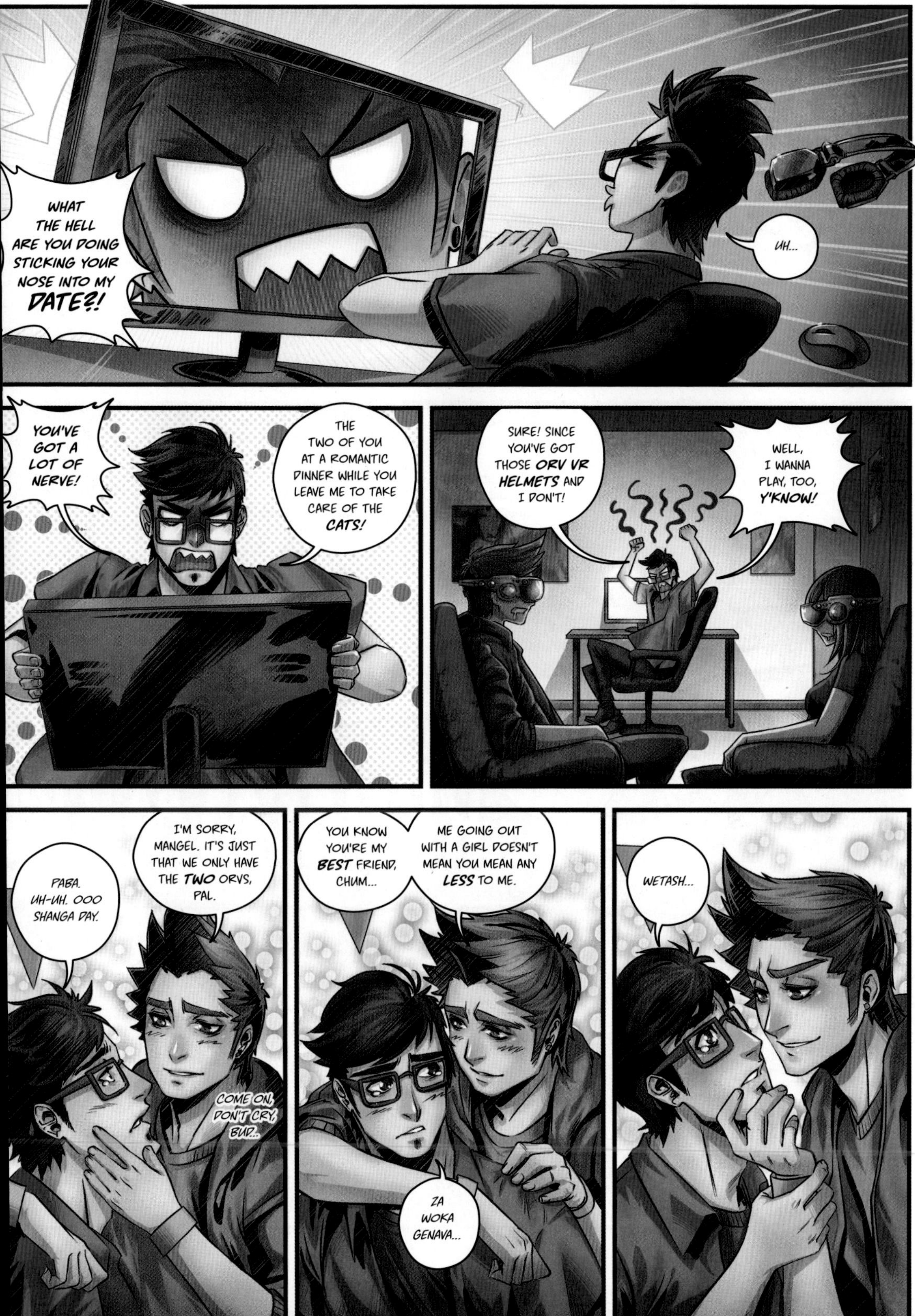
WHAT THE HELL ARE YOU DOING STICKING YOUR NOSE INTO MY DATE?!
UH...
YOU'VE GOT A LOT OF NERVE!
THE TWO OF YOU AT A ROMANTIC DINNER WHILE YOU LEAVE ME TO TAKE CARE OF THE CATS!
SURE! SINCE YOU'VE GOT THOSE ORV VR HELMETS AND I DON'T!
WELL, I WANNA PLAY, TOO, Y'KNOW!
PABA. UH-UH. OOO SHANGA DAY.
I'M SORRY, MANGEL. IT'S JUST THAT WE ONLY HAVE THE TWO ORVS, PAL.
COME ON, DON'T CRY, BUD...
YOU KNOW YOU'RE MY BEST FRIEND, CHUM...
ME GOING OUT WITH A GIRL DOESN'T MEAN YOU MEAN ANY LESS TO ME.
ZA WOKA GENAVA...
WETASH...

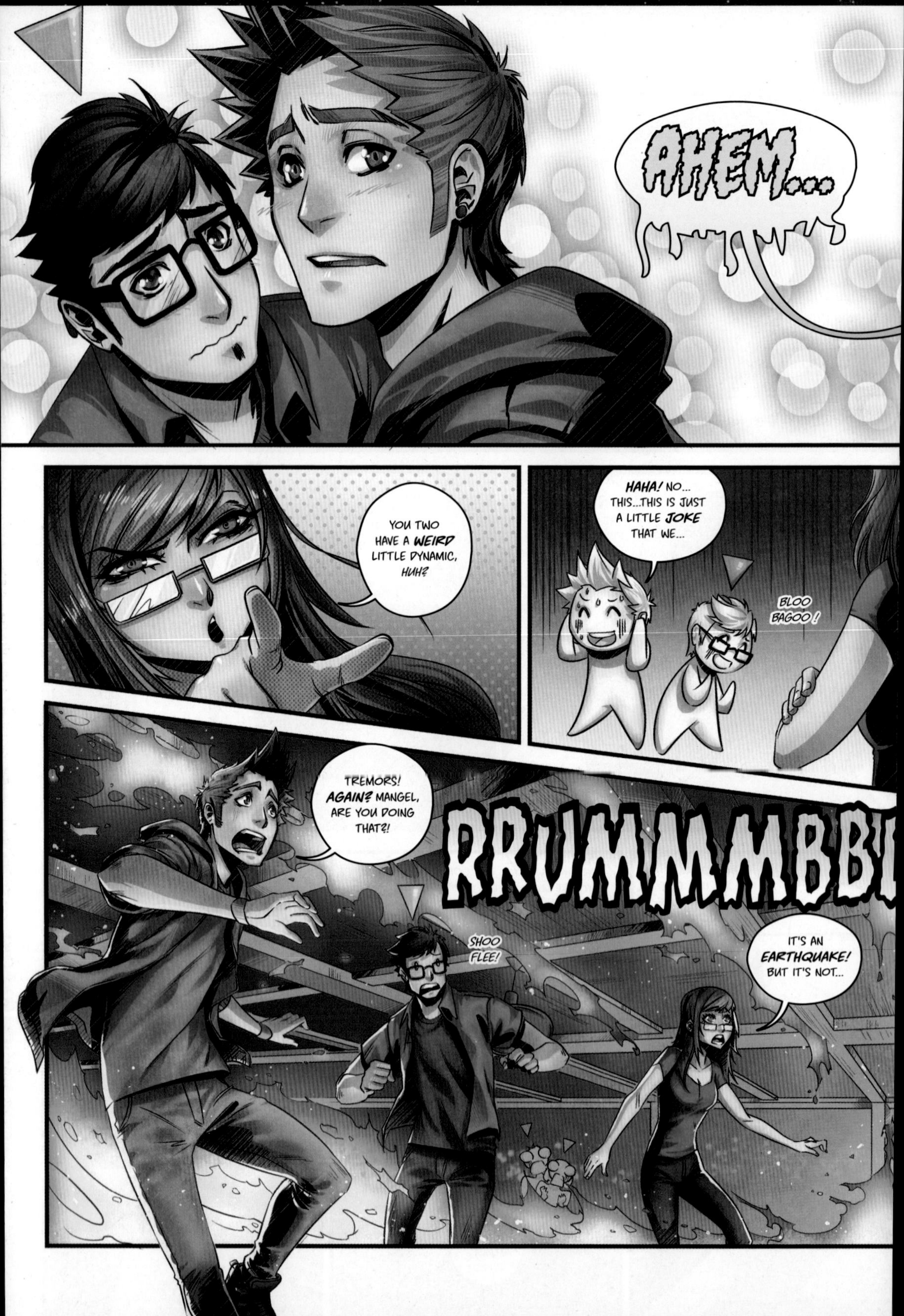
AHEM...
YOU TWO HAVE A WEIRD LITTLE DYNAMIC, HUH?
HAHA! NO... THIS...THIS IS JUST A LITTLE JOKE THAT WE...
BLOO BAGOO!
TREMORS! AGAIN? MANGEL, ARE YOU DOING THAT?!
RRUMMMBBL
SHOO FLEE!
IT'S AN EARTHQUAKE! BUT IT'S NOT...

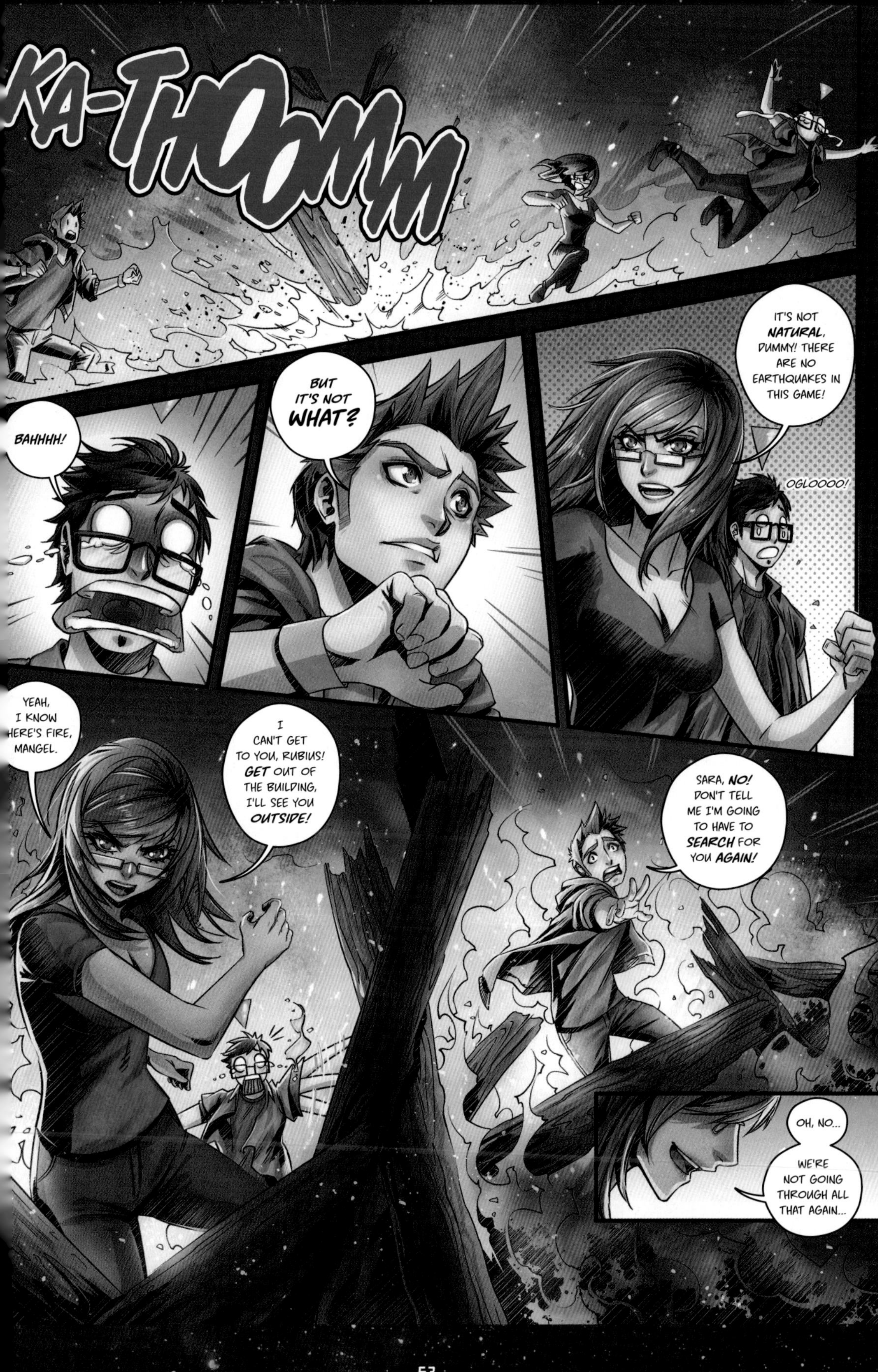
KA-THOOMM
BAHHHH!
BUT IT'S NOT WHAT?
IT'S NOT NATURAL, DUMMY! THERE ARE NO EARTHQUAKES IN THIS GAME!
OGLOOOO!
YEAH, I KNOW HERE'S FIRE, MANGEL.
I CAN'T GET TO YOU, RUBIUS! GET OUT OF THE BUILDING, I'LL SEE YOU OUTSIDE!
SARA, NO! DON'T TELL ME I'M GOING TO HAVE TO SEARCH FOR YOU AGAIN!
OH, NO...
WE'RE NOT GOING THROUGH ALL THAT AGAIN...

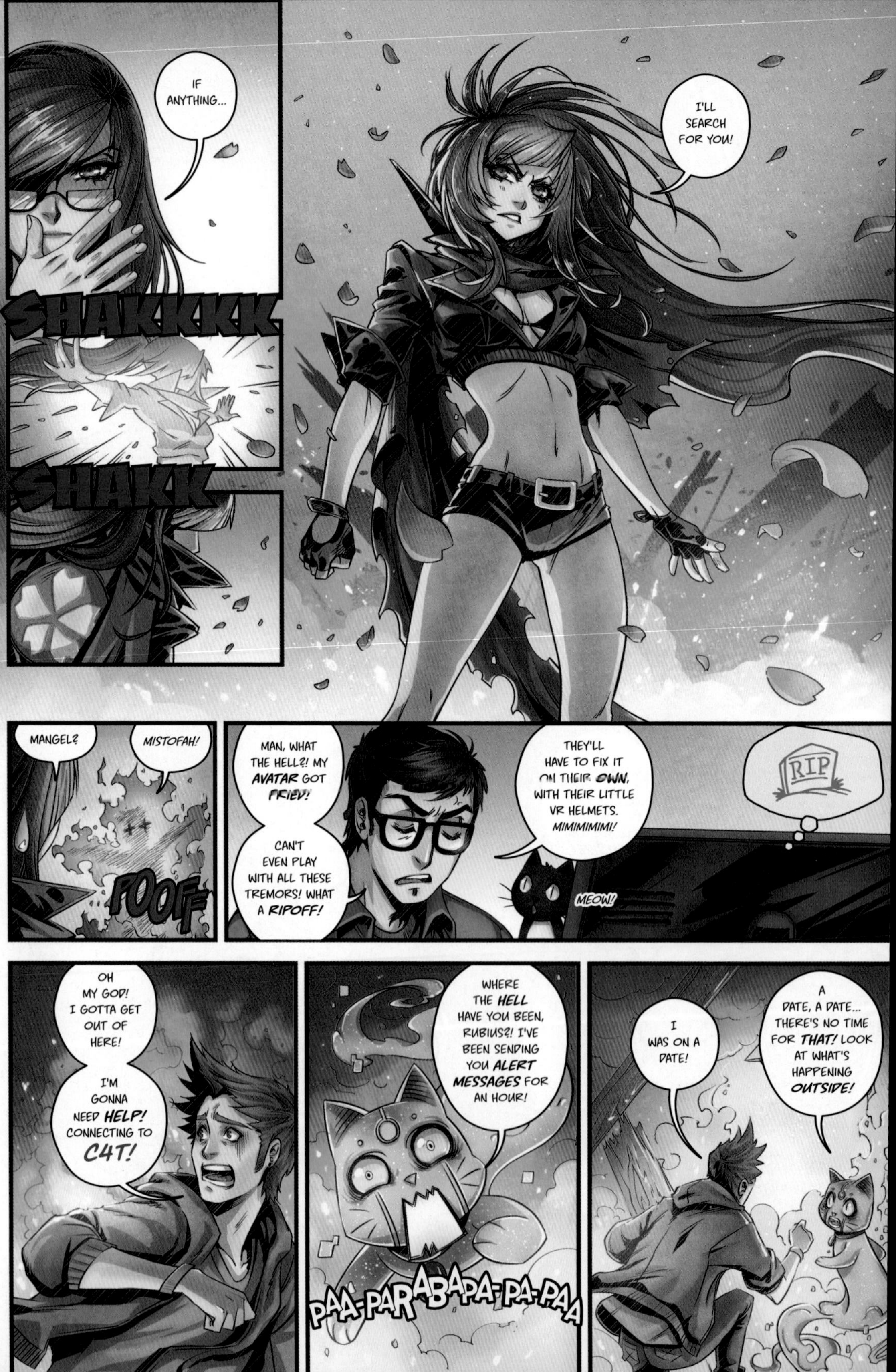
IF ANYTHING...
I'LL SEARCH FOR YOU!
SHAKKKK
SHAKK
MANGEL?
MISTOFAH!
POOFF
MAN, WHAT THE HELL?! MY AVATAR GOT FRIED!
CAN'T EVEN PLAY WITH ALL THESE TREMORS! WHAT A RIPOFF!
THEY'LL HAVE TO FIX IT ON THEIR OWN, WITH THEIR LITTLE VR HELMETS. MIMIMIMIMI!
MEOW!
RIP
OH MY GOD! I GOTTA GET OUT OF HERE!
I'M GONNA NEED HELP! CONNECTING TO C4T!
WHERE THE HELL HAVE YOU BEEN, RUBIUS?! I'VE BEEN SENDING YOU ALERT MESSAGES FOR AN HOUR!
PAA-PARABAPA-PA-PAA
I WAS ON A DATE!
A DATE, A DATE... THERE'S NO TIME FOR THAT! LOOK AT WHAT'S HAPPENING OUTSIDE!

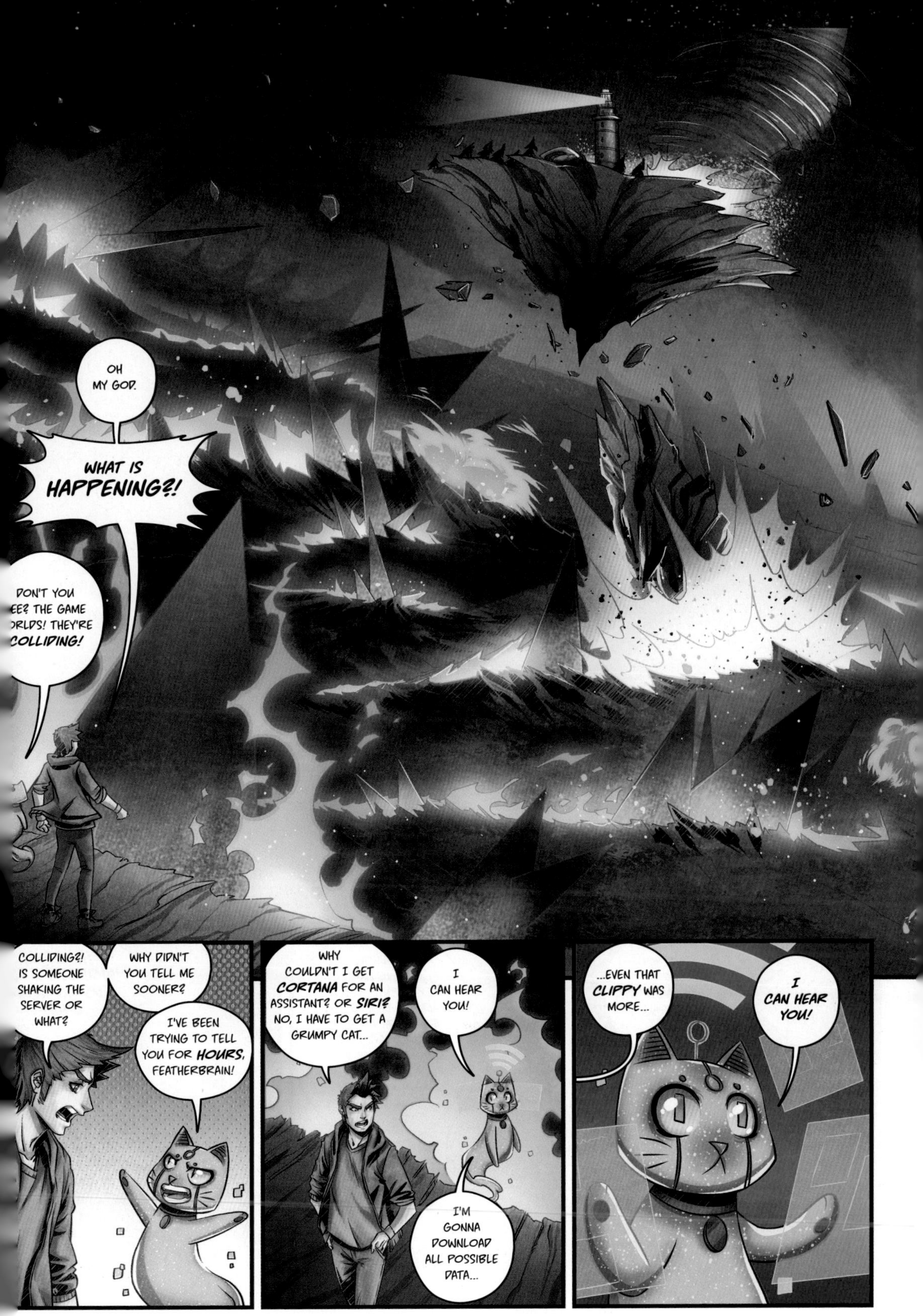
OH MY GOD.
WHAT IS HAPPENING?!
DON'T YOU EE? THE GAME ORLDS! THEY'RE COLLIDING!
COLLIDING?! IS SOMEONE SHAKING THE SERVER OR WHAT?
WHY DIDN'T YOU TELL ME SOONER?
I'VE BEEN TRYING TO TELL YOU FOR HOURS, FEATHERBRAIN!
WHY COULDN'T I GET CORTANA FOR AN ASSISTANT? OR SIRI? NO, I HAVE TO GET A GRUMPY CAT...
I CAN HEAR YOU!
I'M GONNA DOWNLOAD ALL POSSIBLE DATA...
...EVEN THAT CLIPPY WAS MORE...
I CAN HEAR YOU!

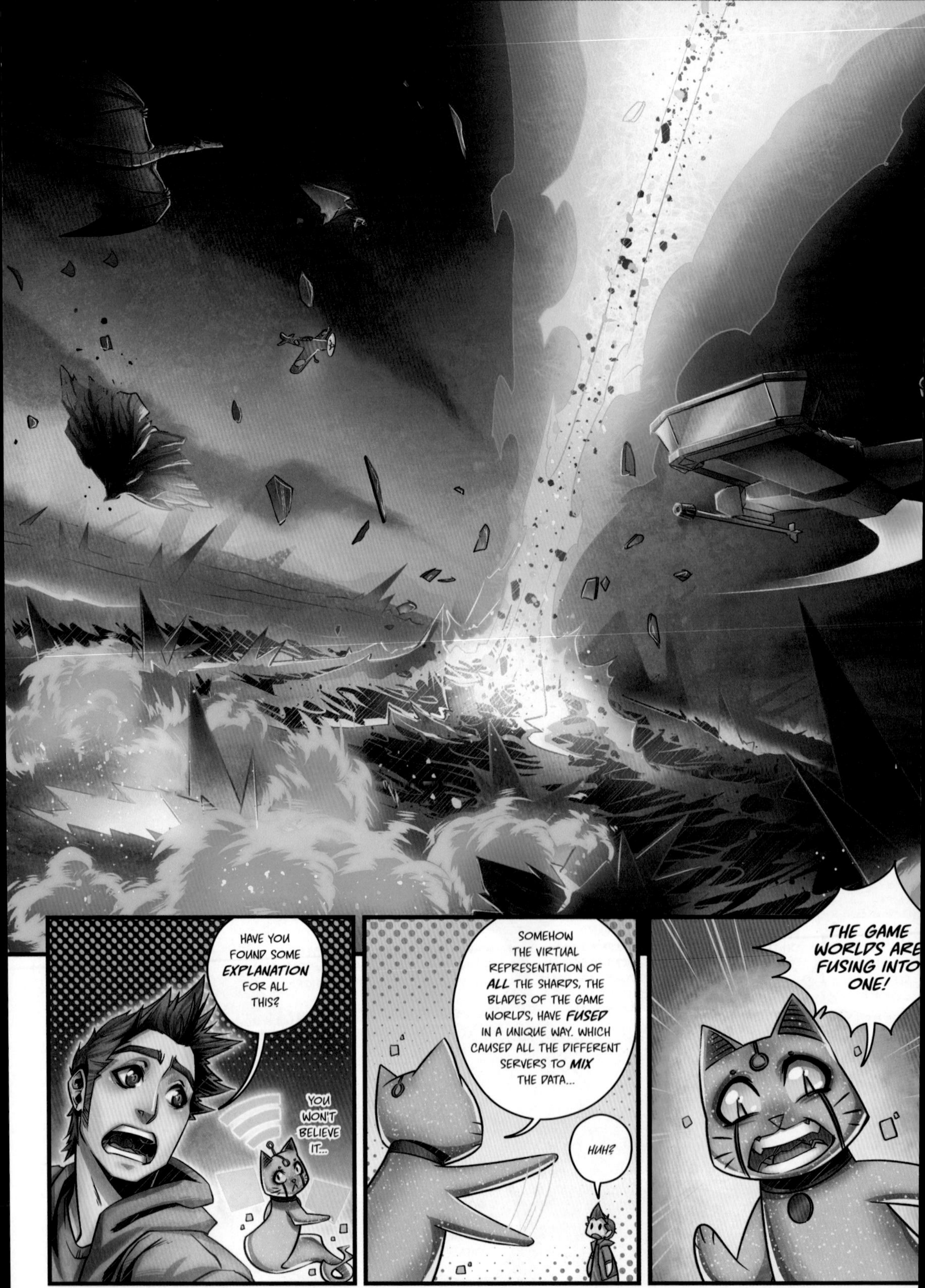
HAVE YOU FOUND SOME EXPLANATION FOR ALL THIS?
YOU WON'T BELIEVE IT...
SOMEHOW THE VIRTUAL REPRESENTATION OF ALL THE SHARDS, THE BLADES OF THE GAME WORLDS, HAVE FUSED IN A UNIQUE WAY. WHICH CAUSED ALL THE DIFFERENT SERVERS TO MIX THE DATA...
HUH?
THE GAME WORLDS ARE FUSING INTO ONE!

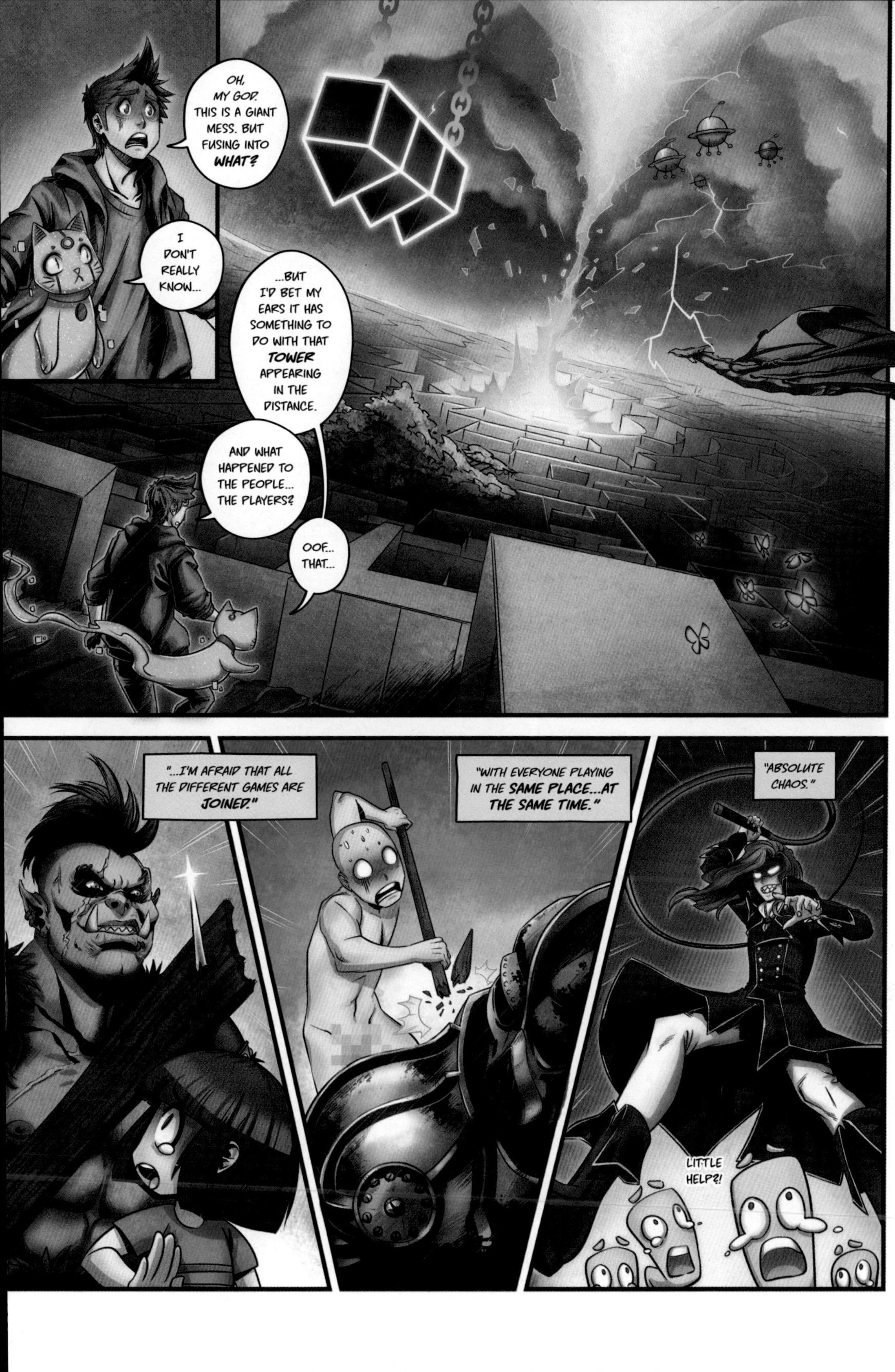
OH, MY GOD. THIS IS A GIANT MESS. BUT FUSING INTO WHAT?
I DON'T REALLY KNOW...
...BUT I'D BET MY EARS IT HAS SOMETHING TO DO WITH THAT TOWER APPEARING IN THE DISTANCE.
AND WHAT HAPPENED TO THE PEOPLE... THE PLAYERS?
OOF... THAT...
"...I'M AFRAID THAT ALL THE DIFFERENT GAMES ARE JOINED."
"WITH EVERYONE PLAYING IN THE SAME PLACE...AT THE SAME TIME."
"ABSOLUTE CHAOS."
LITTLE HELP?!

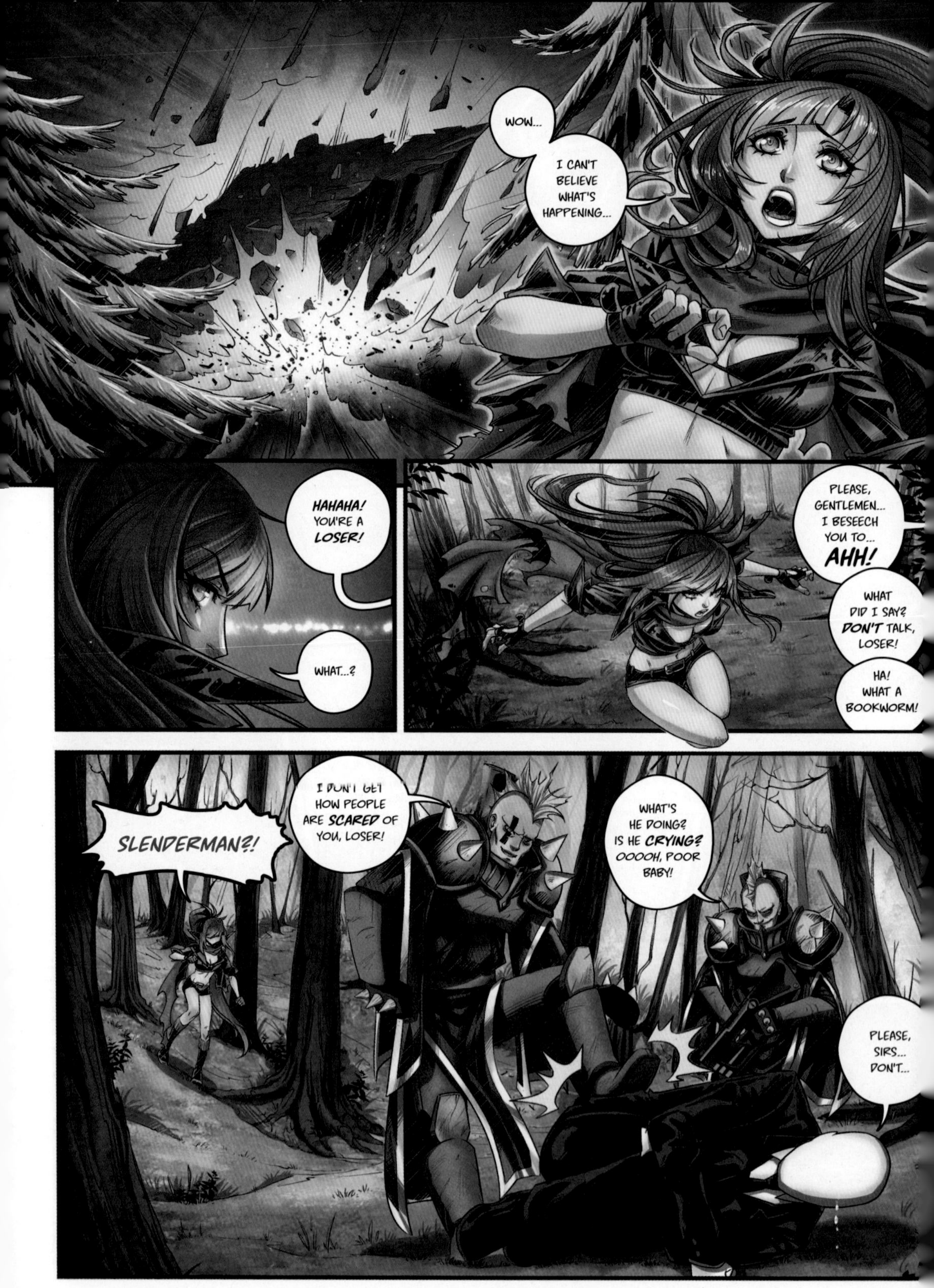
WOW...
I CAN'T BELIEVE WHAT'S HAPPENING...
HAHAHA! YOU'RE A LOSER!
WHAT...?
PLEASE, GENTLEMEN... I BESEECH YOU TO... AHH!
WHAT DID I SAY? DON'T TALK, LOSER!
HA! WHAT A BOOKWORM!
SLENDERMAN?!
I DON'T GET HOW PEOPLE ARE SCARED OF YOU, LOSER!
WHAT'S HE DOING? IS HE CRYING? OOOOH, POOR BABY!
PLEASE, SIRS... DON'T...

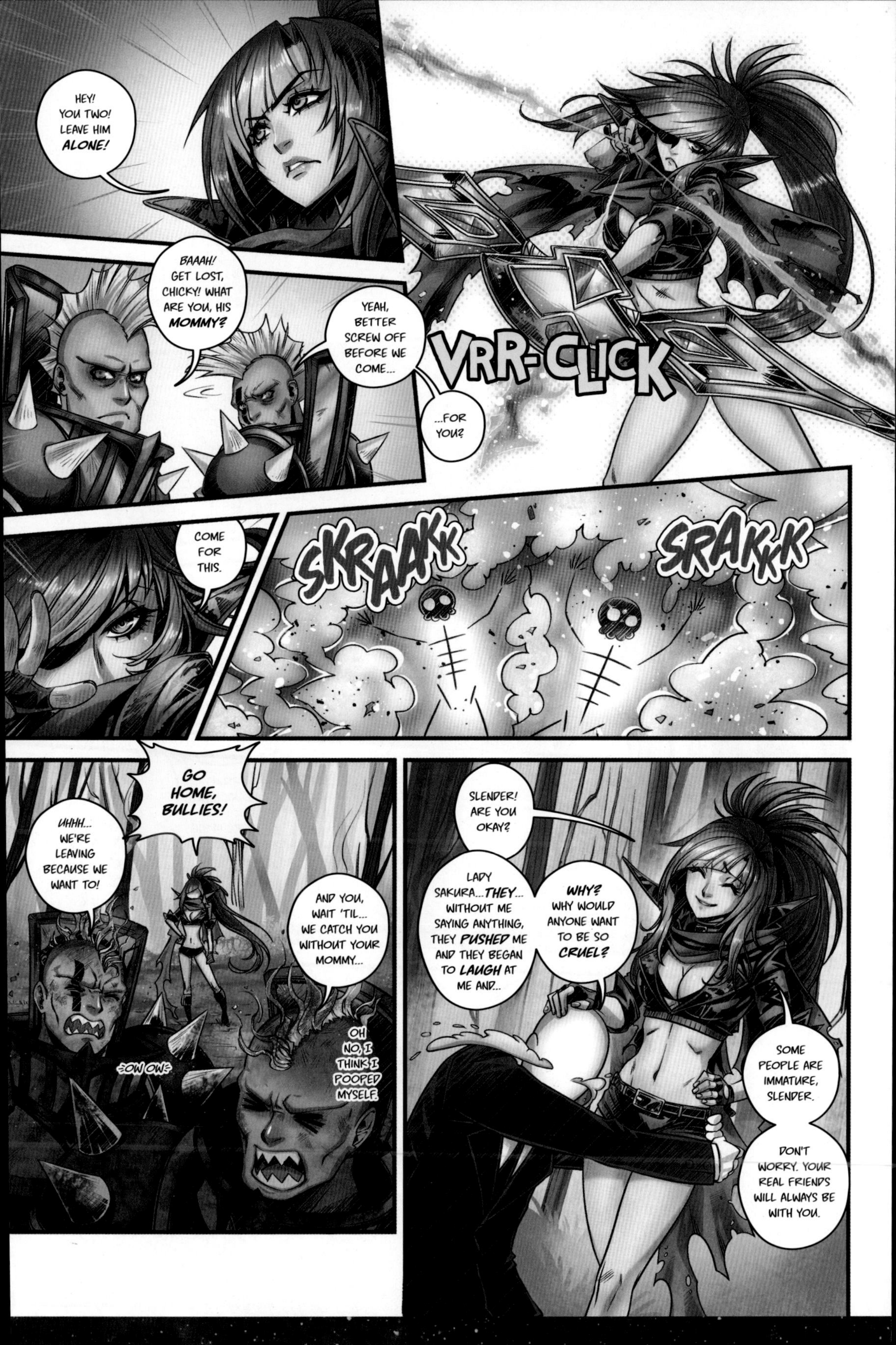
HEY! YOU TWO! LEAVE HIM ALONE!
BAAAH! GET LOST, CHICKY! WHAT ARE YOU, HIS MOMMY?
YEAH, BETTER SCREW OFF BEFORE WE COME...
...FOR YOU?
VRR-CLICK
COME FOR THIS.
SKRAAKK
SRAKKK
GO HOME, BULLIES!
UHHH... WE'RE LEAVING BECAUSE WE WANT TO!
AND YOU, WAIT 'TIL... WE CATCH YOU WITHOUT YOUR MOMMY...
OW OW
OH NO, I THINK I POOPED MYSELF.
SLENDER! ARE YOU OKAY?
LADY SAKURA...THEY... WITHOUT ME SAYING ANYTHING, THEY PUSHED ME AND THEY BEGAN TO LAUGH AT ME AND...
WHY? WHY WOULD ANYONE WANT TO BE SO CRUEL?
SOME PEOPLE ARE IMMATURE, SLENDER.
DON'T WORRY. YOUR REAL FRIENDS WILL ALWAYS BE WITH YOU.

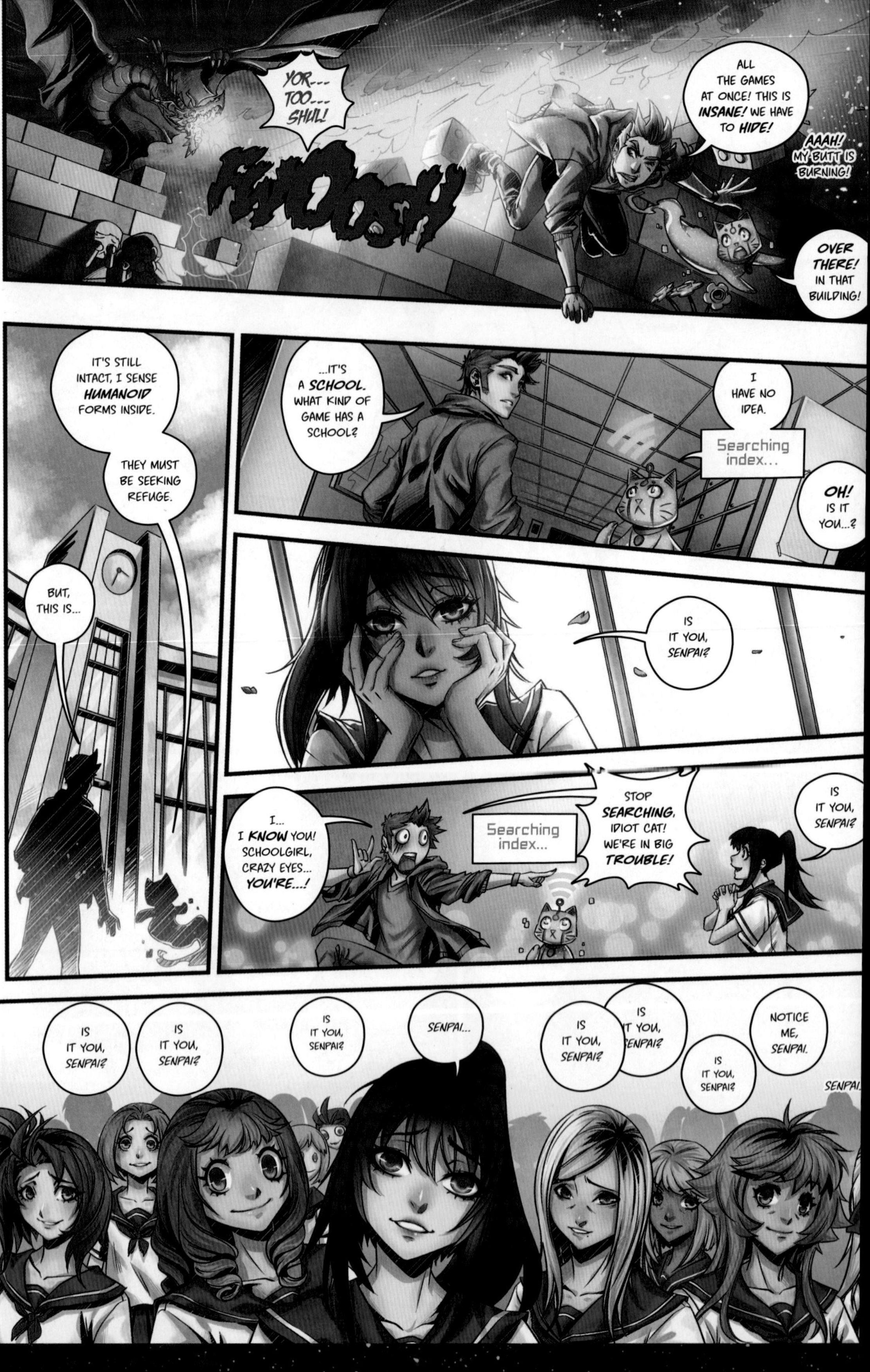

YOR--- TOO--- SHUL!
FWOOSH
ALL THE GAMES AT ONCE! THIS IS INSANE! WE HAVE TO HIDE!
AAAH! MY BUTT IS BURNING!
OVER THERE! IN THAT BUILDING!
IT'S STILL INTACT, I SENSE HUMANOID FORMS INSIDE.
THEY MUST BE SEEKING REFUGE.
BUT, THIS IS...
...IT'S A SCHOOL. WHAT KIND OF GAME HAS A SCHOOL?
I HAVE NO IDEA.
Searching index...
OH! IS IT YOU...?
IS IT YOU, SENPAI?
I... I KNOW YOU! SCHOOLGIRL, CRAZY EYES... YOU'RE...!
Searching index...
STOP SEARCHING, IDIOT CAT! WE'RE IN BIG TROUBLE!
IS IT YOU, SENPAI?
IS IT YOU, SENPAI?
IS IT YOU, SENPAI?
IS IT YOU, SENPAI?
SENPAI...
IS IT YOU, SENPAI?
IS IT YOU, SENPAI?
IS IT YOU, SENPAI?
NOTICE ME, SENPAI.
SENPAI

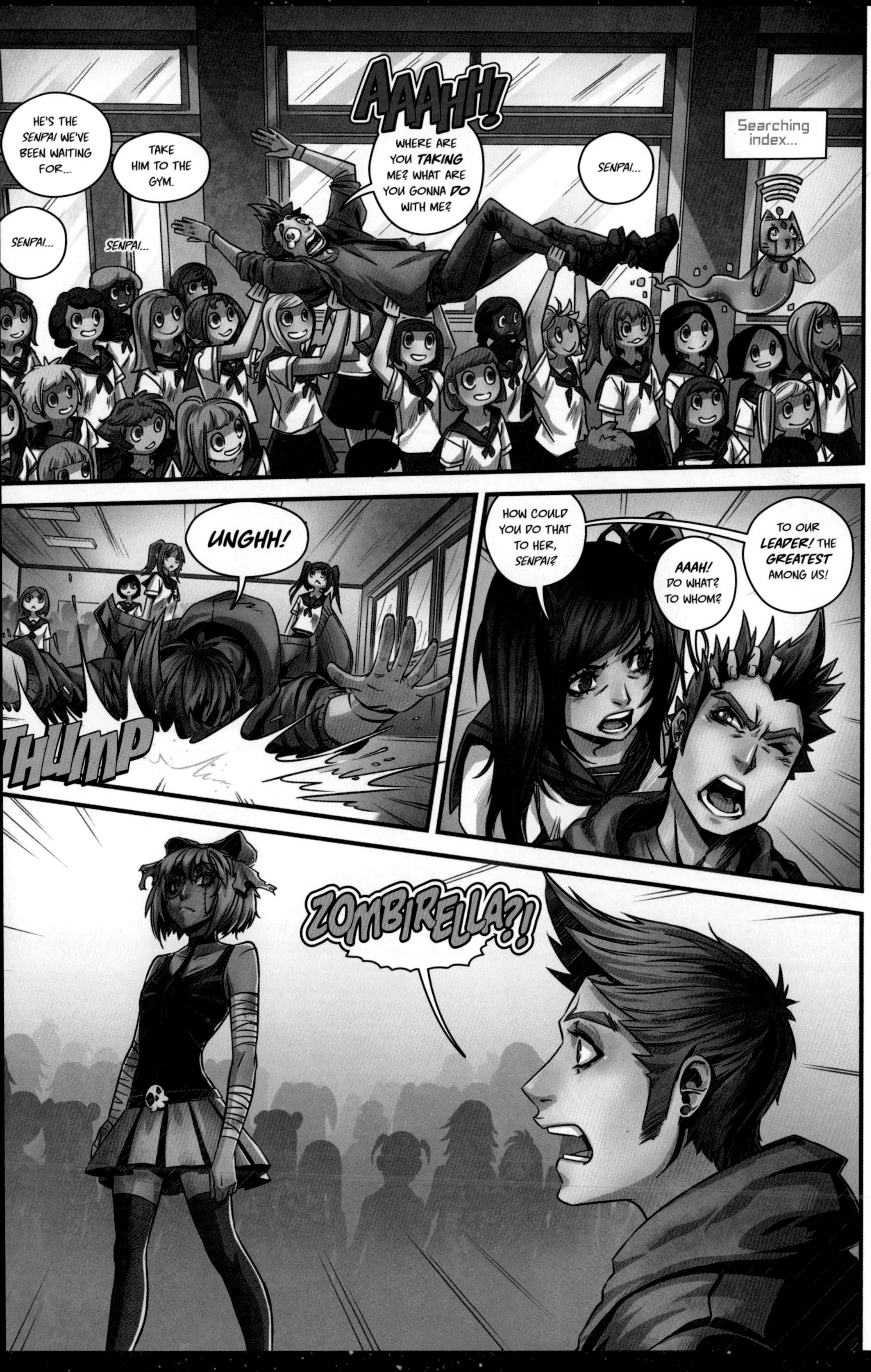
HE'S THE SENPAI WE'VE BEEN WAITING FOR...
TAKE HIM TO THE GYM.
SENPAI...
SENPAI...
AAAHH!
WHERE ARE YOU TAKING ME? WHAT ARE YOU GONNA DO WITH ME?
SENPAI...
Searching index...
UNGHH!
THUMP
HOW COULD YOU DO THAT TO HER, SENPAI?
AAAH! DO WHAT? TO WHOM?
TO OUR LEADER! THE GREATEST AMONG US!
ZOMBIRELLA?!

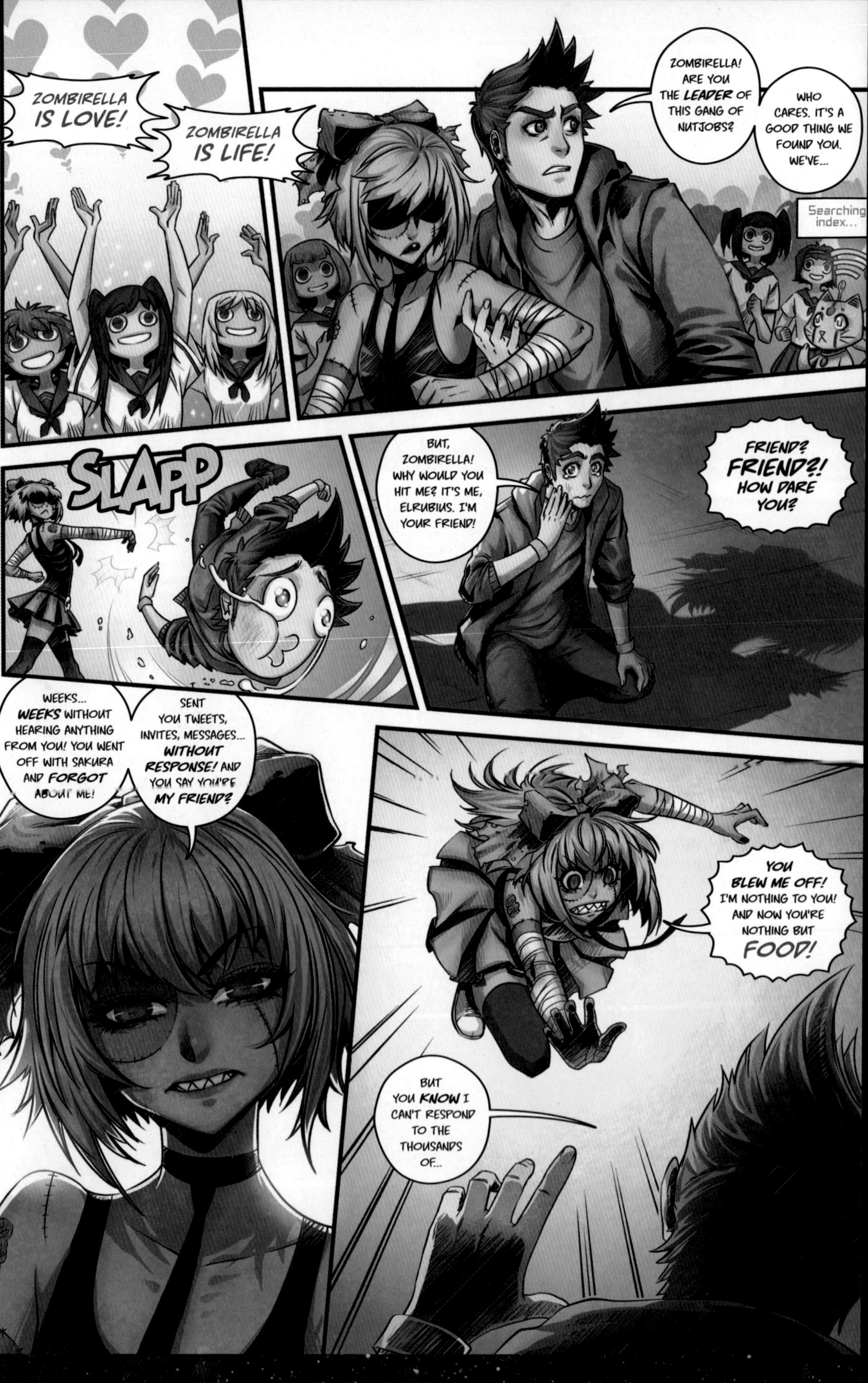
ZOMBIRELLA IS LOVE!
ZOMBIRELLA IS LIFE!
ZOMBIRELLA! ARE YOU THE LEADER OF THIS GANG OF NUTJOBS?
WHO CARES. IT'S A GOOD THING WE FOUND YOU. WE'VE...
Searching index...
SLAPP
BUT, ZOMBIRELLA! WHY WOULD YOU HIT ME? IT'S ME, ELRUBIUS. I'M YOUR FRIEND!
FRIEND? FRIEND?! HOW DARE YOU?
WEEKS... WEEKS WITHOUT HEARING ANYTHING FROM YOU! YOU WENT OFF WITH SAKURA AND FORGOT ABOUT ME!
SENT YOU TWEETS, INVITES, MESSAGES... WITHOUT RESPONSE! AND YOU SAY YOU'RE MY FRIEND?
YOU BLEW ME OFF! I'M NOTHING TO YOU! AND NOW YOU'RE NOTHING BUT FOOD!
BUT YOU KNOW I CAN'T RESPOND TO THE THOUSANDS OF...

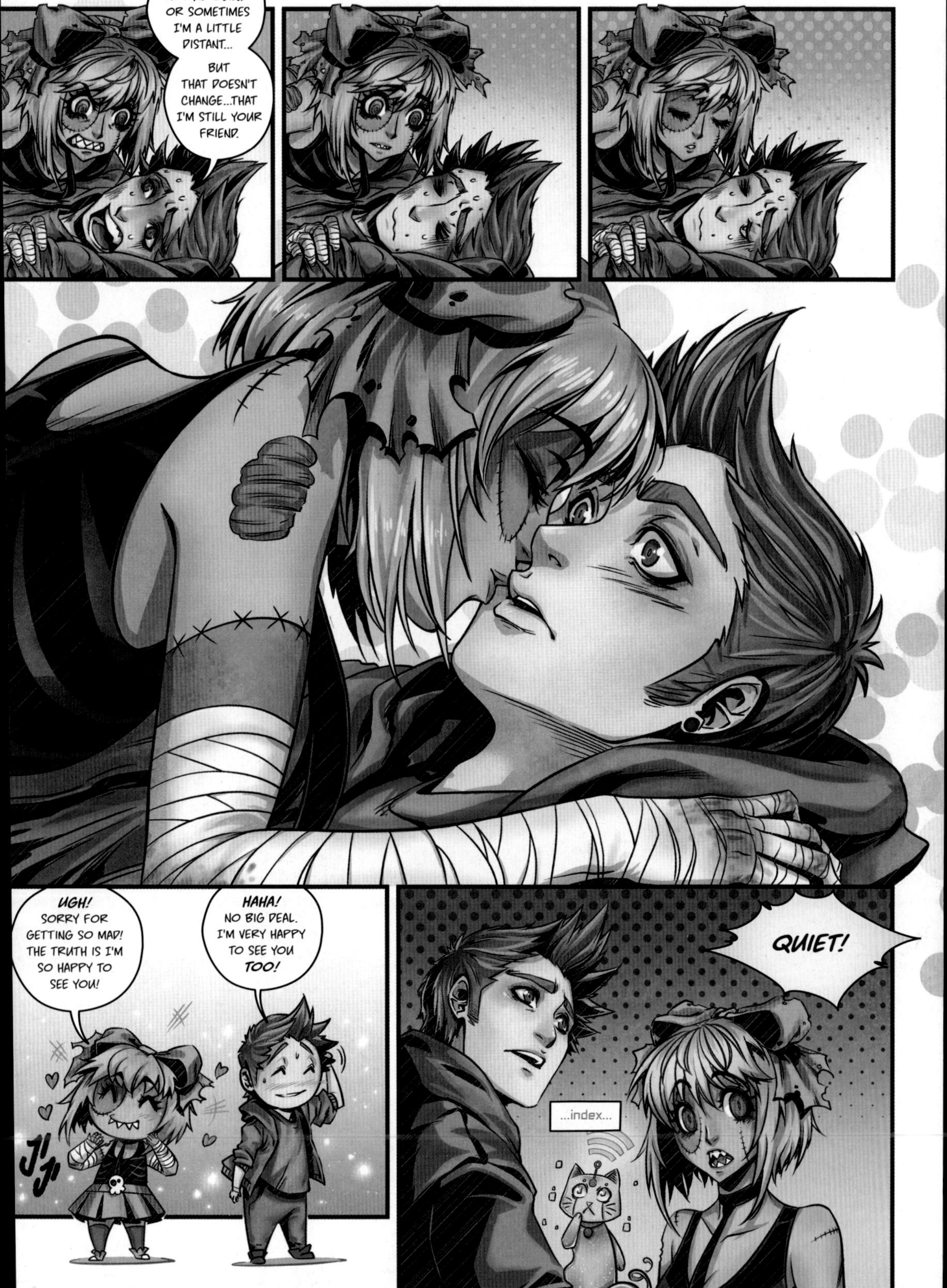
MAYBE I'M... NOT AROUND OR SOMETIMES I'M A LITTLE DISTANT...
BUT THAT DOESN'T CHANGE...THAT I'M STILL YOUR FRIEND.
UGH! SORRY FOR GETTING SO MAD! THE TRUTH IS I'M SO HAPPY TO SEE YOU!
HAHA! NO BIG DEAL. I'M VERY HAPPY TO SEE YOU TOO!
QUIET!
...index...

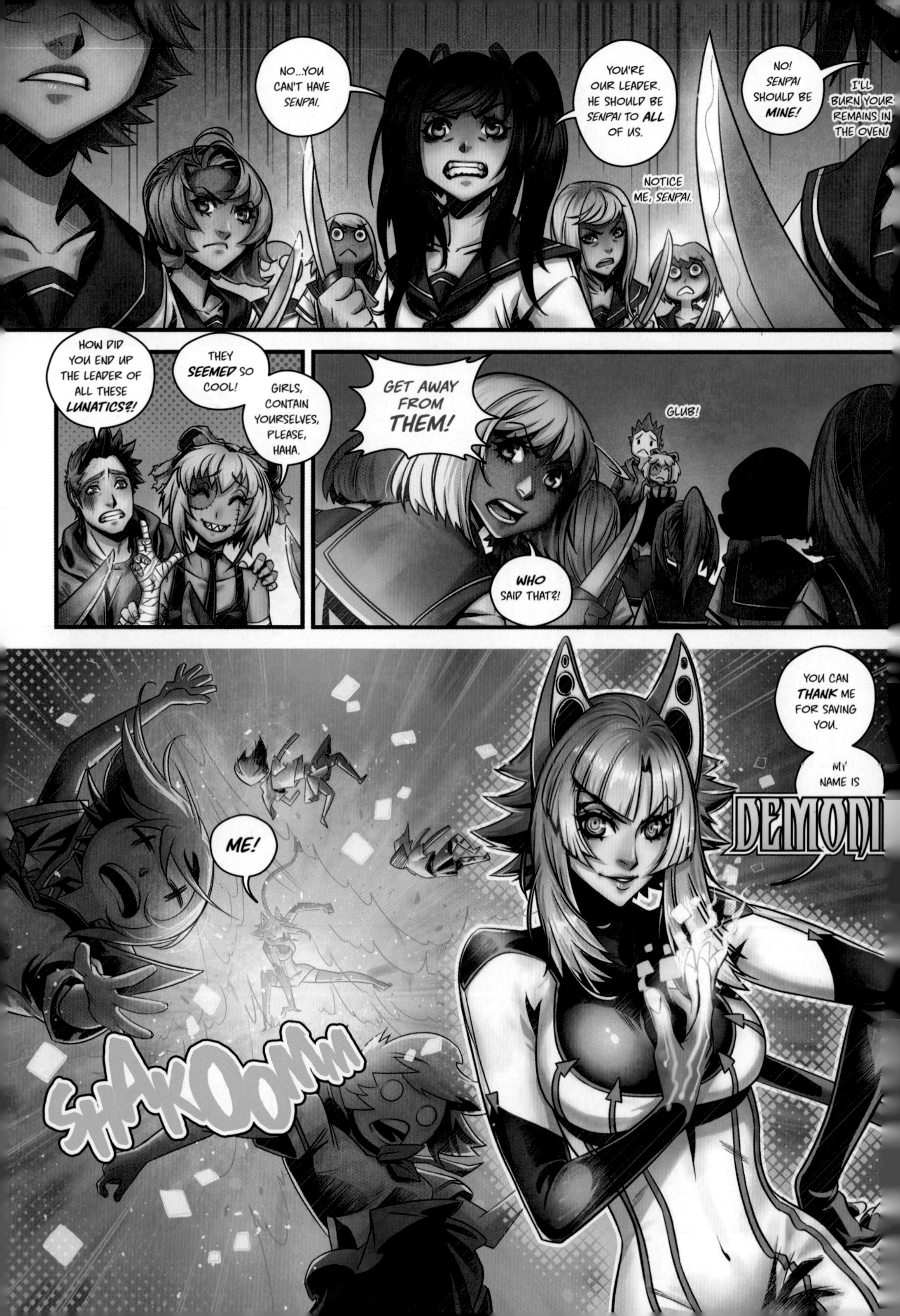
NO...YOU CAN'T HAVE SENPAI.
YOU'RE OUR LEADER. HE SHOULD BE SENPAI TO ALL OF US.
NOTICE ME, SENPAI.
NO! SENPAI SHOULD BE MINE!
I'LL BURN YOUR REMAINS IN THE OVEN!
HOW DID YOU END UP THE LEADER OF ALL THESE LUNATICS?!
THEY SEEMED SO COOL!
GIRLS, CONTAIN YOURSELVES, PLEASE, HAHA.
GET AWAY FROM THEM!
GLUB!
WHO SAID THAT?!
ME!
SHAKOOMM
YOU CAN THANK ME FOR SAVING YOU.
MI' NAME IS
DEMONI

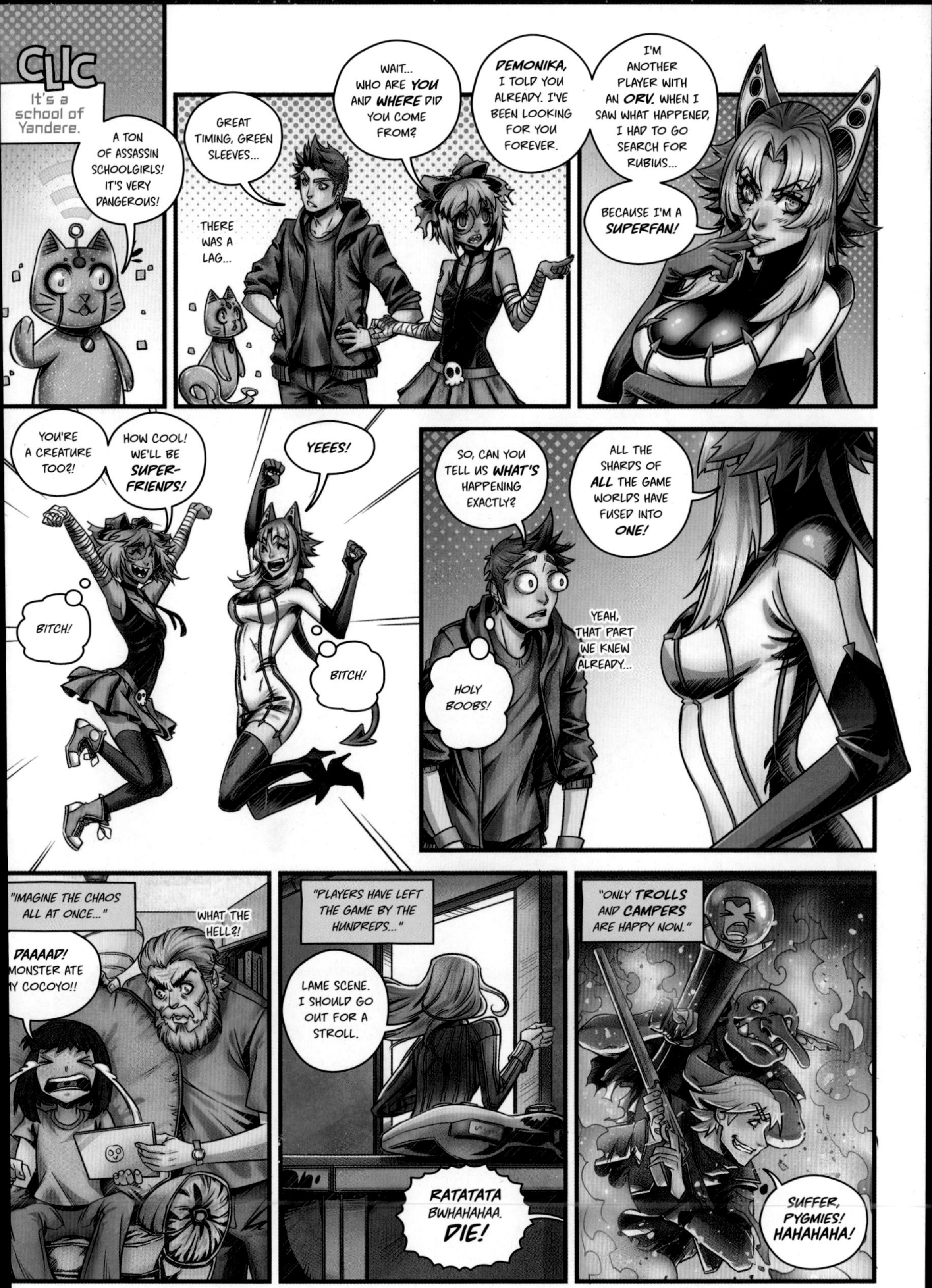

CLIC
It's a school of Yandere.
A TON OF ASSASSIN SCHOOLGIRLS! IT'S VERY DANGEROUS!
GREAT TIMING, GREEN SLEEVES...
THERE WAS A LAG...
WAIT... WHO ARE YOU AND WHERE DID YOU COME FROM?
DEMONIKA, I TOLD YOU ALREADY. I'VE BEEN LOOKING FOR YOU FOREVER.
I'M ANOTHER PLAYER WITH AN ORV. WHEN I SAW WHAT HAPPENED, I HAD TO GO SEARCH FOR RUBIUS...
BECAUSE I'M A SUPERFAN!
YOU'RE A CREATURE TOO?!
HOW COOL! WE'LL BE SUPER-FRIENDS!
YEEES!
BITCH!
BITCH!
SO, CAN YOU TELL US WHAT'S HAPPENING EXACTLY?
ALL THE SHARDS OF ALL THE GAME WORLDS HAVE FUSED INTO ONE!
HOLY BOOBS!
YEAH, THAT PART WE KNEW ALREADY...
"IMAGINE THE CHAOS ALL AT ONCE..."
WHAT THE HELL?!
DAAAAD! MONSTER ATE MY COCOYO!!
"PLAYERS HAVE LEFT THE GAME BY THE HUNDREDS..."
LAME SCENE. I SHOULD GO OUT FOR A STROLL.
RATATATA BWHAHAHAA. DIE!
"ONLY TROLLS AND CAMPERS ARE HAPPY NOW."
SUFFER, PYGMIES! HAHAHAHA!

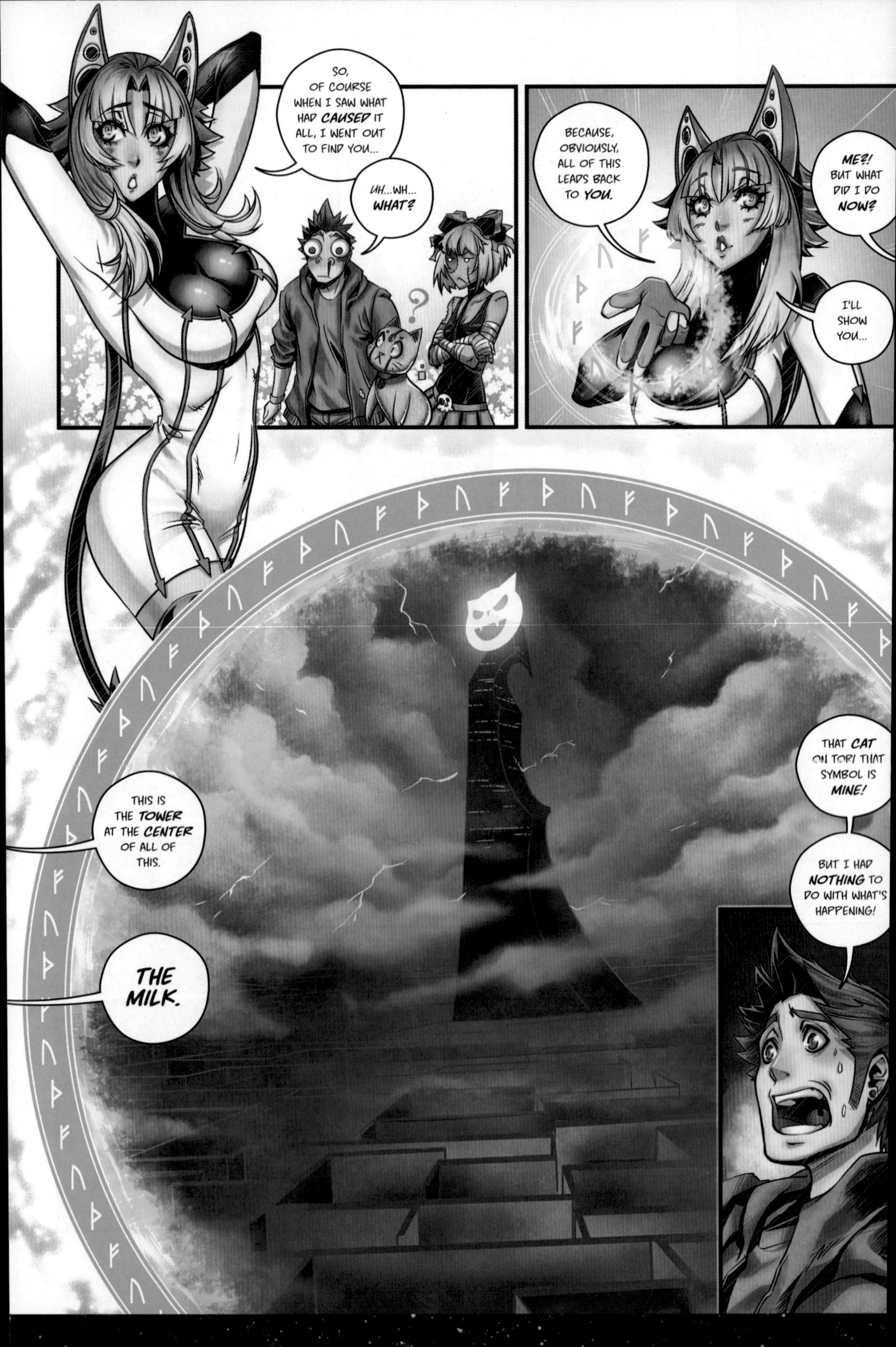
SO, OF COURSE WHEN I SAW WHAT HAD **CAUSED** IT ALL, I WENT OUT TO FIND YOU...
UH...WH... **WHAT?**
?
BECAUSE, OBVIOUSLY, ALL OF THIS LEADS BACK TO **YOU.**
ME?! BUT WHAT DID I DO **NOW?**
I'LL SHOW YOU...
THIS IS THE **TOWER** AT THE **CENTER** OF ALL OF THIS.
THE MILK.
THAT **CAT** ON TOP! THAT SYMBOL IS **MINE!**
BUT I HAD **NOTHING** TO DO WITH WHAT'S HAPPENING!

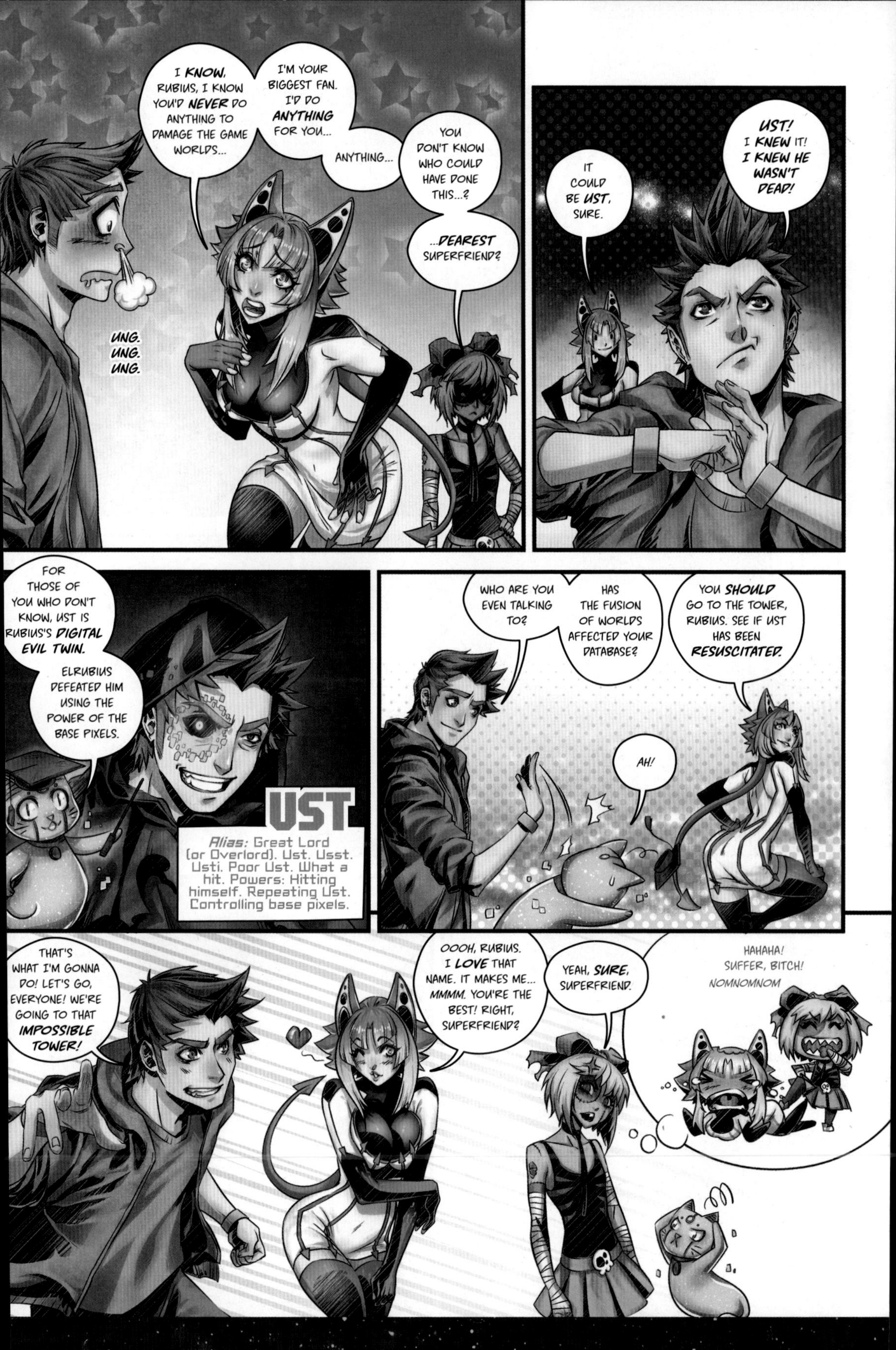
I KNOW, RUBIUS, I KNOW YOU'D NEVER DO ANYTHING TO DAMAGE THE GAME WORLDS...
I'M YOUR BIGGEST FAN. I'D DO ANYTHING FOR YOU...
ANYTHING...
YOU DON'T KNOW WHO COULD HAVE DONE THIS...?
...DEAREST SUPERFRIEND?
UNG. UNG. UNG.
IT COULD BE UST, SURE.
UST! I KNEW IT! I KNEW HE WASN'T DEAD!
FOR THOSE OF YOU WHO DON'T KNOW, UST IS RUBIUS'S DIGITAL EVIL TWIN.
ELRUBIUS DEFEATED HIM USING THE POWER OF THE BASE PIXELS.
UST
Alias: Great Lord (or Overlord). Ust. Usst. Usti. Poor Ust. What a hit. Powers: Hitting himself. Repeating Ust. Controlling base pixels.
WHO ARE YOU EVEN TALKING TO?
HAS THE FUSION OF WORLDS AFFECTED YOUR DATABASE?
YOU SHOULD GO TO THE TOWER, RUBIUS. SEE IF UST HAS BEEN RESUSCITATED.
AH!
THAT'S WHAT I'M GONNA DO! LET'S GO, EVERYONE! WE'RE GOING TO THAT IMPOSSIBLE TOWER!
OOOH, RUBIUS. I LOVE THAT NAME. IT MAKES ME... MMMM. YOU'RE THE BEST! RIGHT, SUPERFRIEND?
YEAH, SURE, SUPERFRIEND.
HAHAHA! SUFFER, BITCH!
NOMNOMNOM

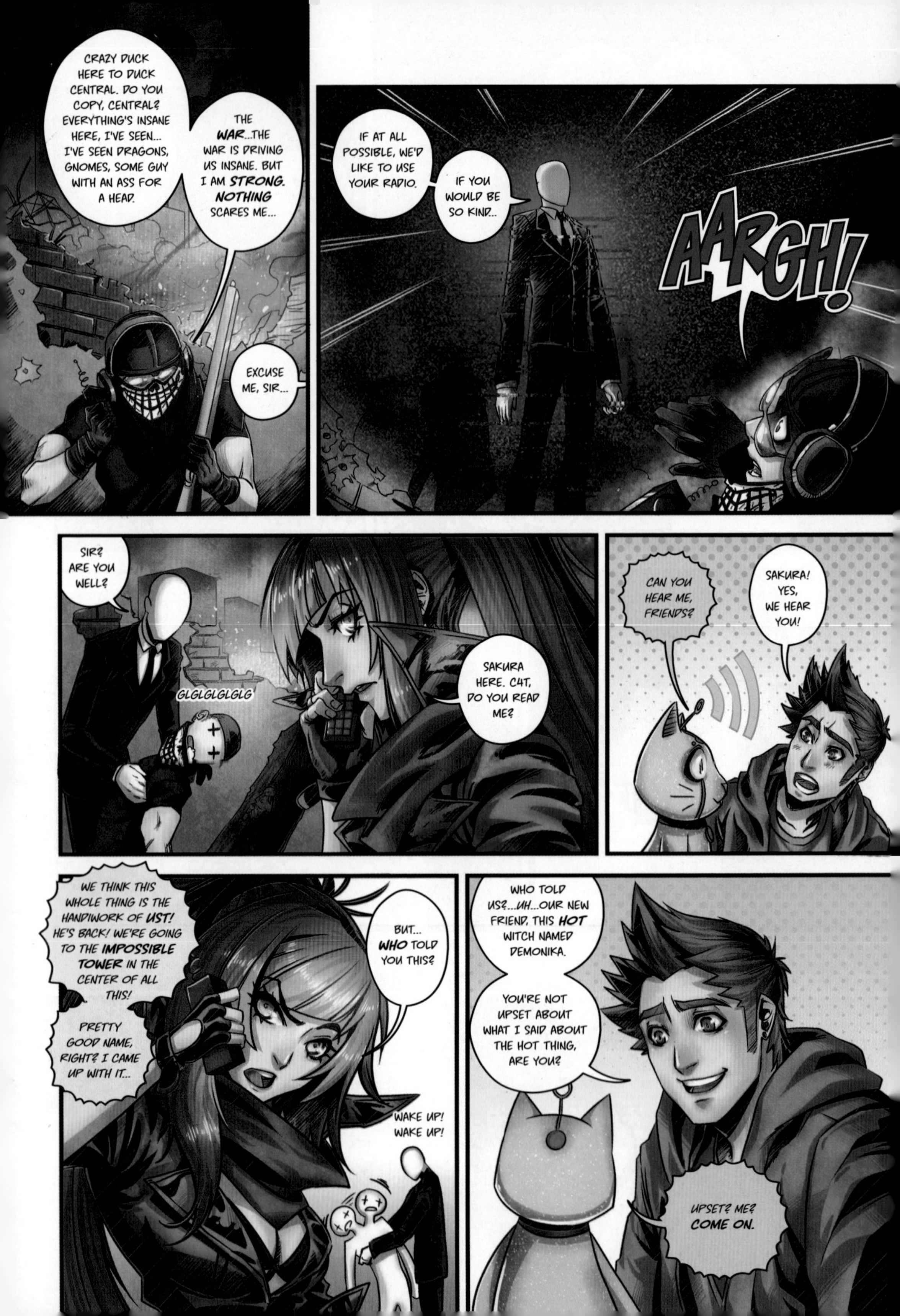
CRAZY DUCK HERE TO DUCK CENTRAL. DO YOU COPY, CENTRAL? EVERYTHING'S INSANE HERE, I'VE SEEN... I'VE SEEN DRAGONS, GNOMES, SOME GUY WITH AN ASS FOR A HEAD.
THE WAR...THE WAR IS DRIVING US INSANE. BUT I AM STRONG. NOTHING SCARES ME...
EXCUSE ME, SIR...
IF AT ALL POSSIBLE, WE'D LIKE TO USE YOUR RADIO.
IF YOU WOULD BE SO KIND...
AARGH!
SIR? ARE YOU WELL?
GLGLGLGLGLG
SAKURA HERE. C4T, DO YOU READ ME?
CAN YOU HEAR ME, FRIENDS?
SAKURA! YES, WE HEAR YOU!
WE THINK THIS WHOLE THING IS THE HANDIWORK OF UST! HE'S BACK! WE'RE GOING TO THE IMPOSSIBLE TOWER IN THE CENTER OF ALL THIS!
PRETTY GOOD NAME, RIGHT? I CAME UP WITH IT...
BUT... WHO TOLD YOU THIS?
WAKE UP! WAKE UP!
WHO TOLD US?...UH...OUR NEW FRIEND, THIS HOT WITCH NAMED DEMONIKA.
YOU'RE NOT UPSET ABOUT WHAT I SAID ABOUT THE HOT THING, ARE YOU?
UPSET? ME? COME ON.

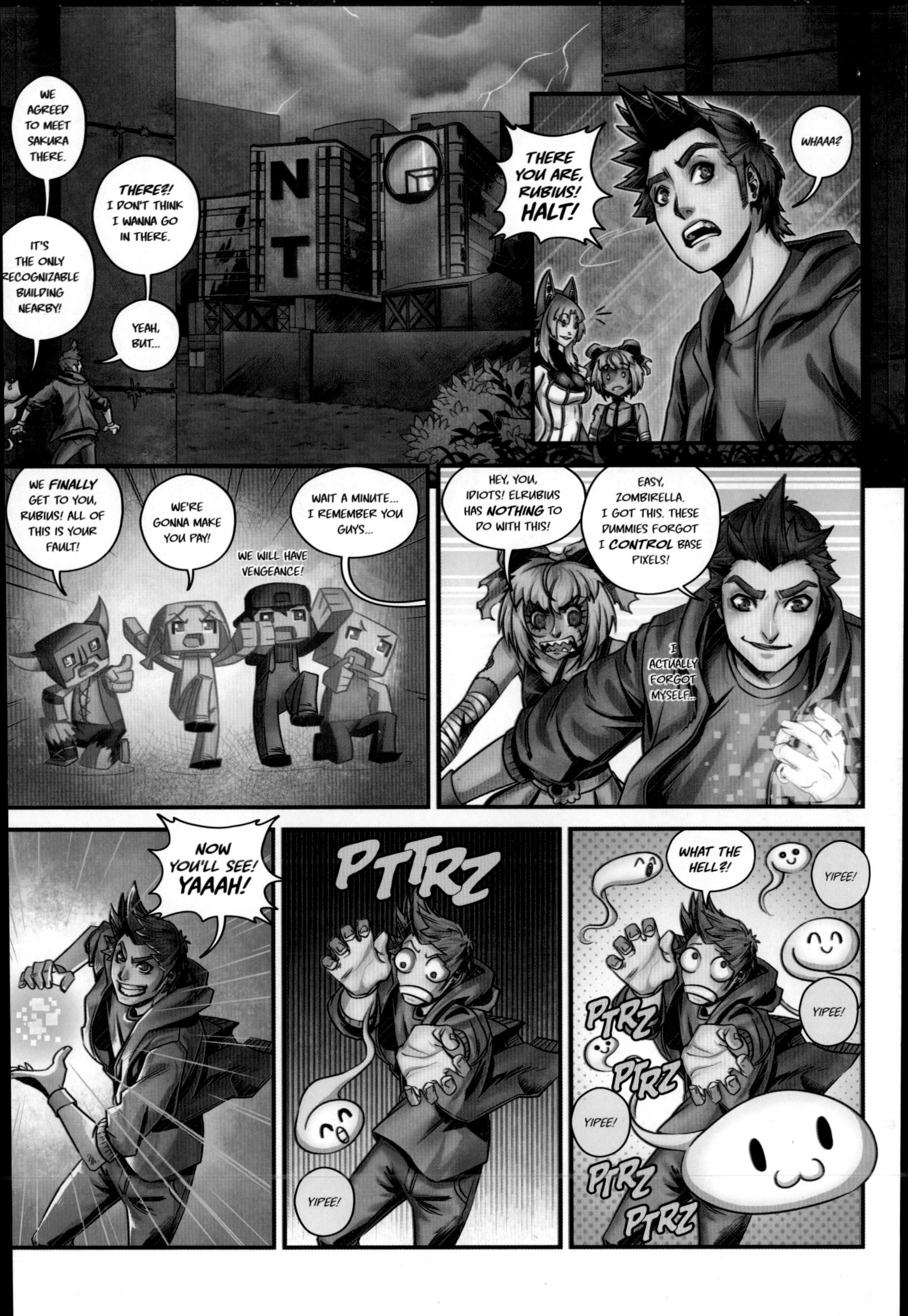

WE AGREED TO MEET SAKURA THERE.
THERE?! I DON'T THINK I WANNA GO IN THERE.
IT'S THE ONLY RECOGNIZABLE BUILDING NEARBY!
YEAH, BUT...
THERE YOU ARE, RUBIUS! HALT!
WHAAA?
WE FINALLY GET TO YOU, RUBIUS! ALL OF THIS IS YOUR FAULT!
WE'RE GONNA MAKE YOU PAY!
WE WILL HAVE VENGEANCE!
WAIT A MINUTE... I REMEMBER YOU GUYS...
HEY, YOU, IDIOTS! ELRUBIUS HAS NOTHING TO DO WITH THIS!
EASY, ZOMBIRELLA. I GOT THIS. THESE DUMMIES FORGOT I CONTROL BASE PIXELS!
I ACTUALLY FORGOT MYSELF...
NOW YOU'LL SEE! YAAAH!
PTTRZ
YIPEE!
WHAT THE HELL?!
YIPEE!
YIPEE!
PTRZ
PTRZ
YIPEE!
PTRZ
PTRZ

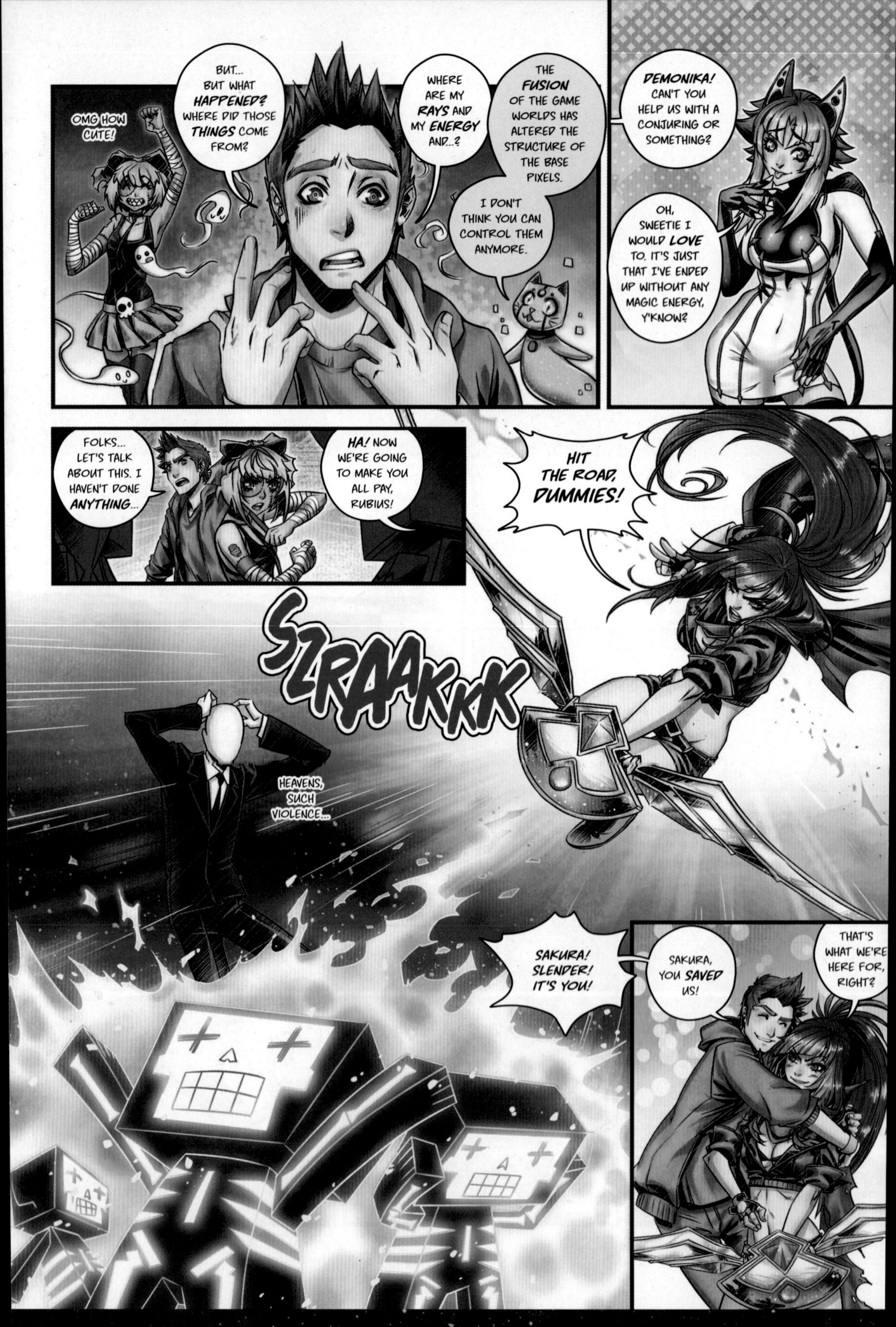
OMG HOW CUTE!
BUT... BUT WHAT HAPPENED? WHERE DID THOSE THINGS COME FROM?
WHERE ARE MY RAYS AND MY ENERGY AND...?
THE FUSION OF THE GAME WORLDS HAS ALTERED THE STRUCTURE OF THE BASE PIXELS.
I DON'T THINK YOU CAN CONTROL THEM ANYMORE.
DEMONIKA! CAN'T YOU HELP US WITH A CONJURING OR SOMETHING?
OH, SWEETIE I WOULD LOVE TO. IT'S JUST THAT I'VE ENDED UP WITHOUT ANY MAGIC ENERGY, Y'KNOW?
FOLKS... LET'S TALK ABOUT THIS. I HAVEN'T DONE ANYTHING...
HA! NOW WE'RE GOING TO MAKE YOU ALL PAY, RUBIUS!
HIT THE ROAD, DUMMIES!
SZRAAKKK
HEAVENS, SUCH VIOLENCE...
SAKURA! SLENDER! IT'S YOU!
SAKURA, YOU SAVED US!
THAT'S WHAT WE'RE HERE FOR, RIGHT?

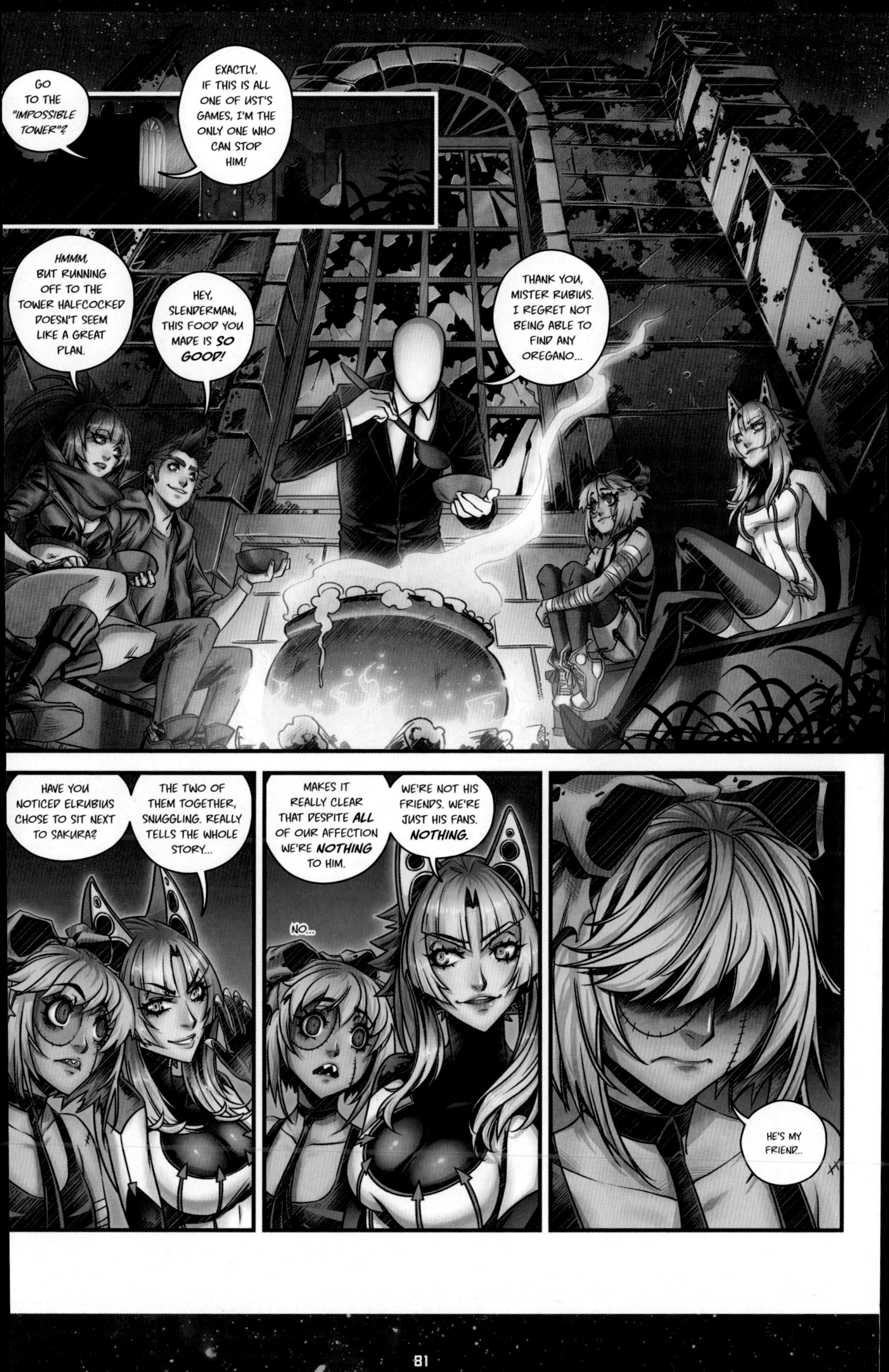
GO TO THE "IMPOSSIBLE TOWER"?
EXACTLY. IF THIS IS ALL ONE OF UST'S GAMES, I'M THE ONLY ONE WHO CAN STOP HIM!
HMMM, BUT RUNNING OFF TO THE TOWER HALFCOCKED DOESN'T SEEM LIKE A GREAT PLAN.
HEY, SLENDERMAN, THIS FOOD YOU MADE IS SO GOOD!
THANK YOU, MISTER RUBIUS. I REGRET NOT BEING ABLE TO FIND ANY OREGANO...
HAVE YOU NOTICED ELRUBIUS CHOSE TO SIT NEXT TO SAKURA?
THE TWO OF THEM TOGETHER, SNUGGLING. REALLY TELLS THE WHOLE STORY...
MAKES IT REALLY CLEAR THAT DESPITE ALL OF OUR AFFECTION WE'RE NOTHING TO HIM.
WE'RE NOT HIS FRIENDS. WE'RE JUST HIS FANS. NOTHING.
NO...
HE'S MY FRIEND...

HEY, SLENDERMAN!

YES, MR. RUBIUS?

SAKURA TOLD ME ABOUT THOSE BULLIES. HAS THAT HAPPENED BEFORE OR WAS THAT THE FIRST TIME?

OH, MR. RUBIUS, I...WELL...

SOME TIME AGO, TWO PLAYERS APPEARED IN THE FOREST WHERE I LIVE...

I GREETED THEM PLEASANTLY BECAUSE THEY SEEMED AFRAID...

...AND SINCE THEN...

WHY DIDN'T YOU SAY ANYTHING BEFORE?

IT...IT MADE ME REALLY EMBARRASSED.

SLENDER, I KNOW IT'S HARD...

BUT YOU CAN'T BE QUIET WITH BULLIES.

NOT WHEN THEY'[RE] BULLYING YO[U] OR SOMEO[NE] ELSE.

BULLIES TAKE REFUGE IN THE SILENCE OF OTHERS. IN NOTHING HAPPENING TO THEM. YOU'RE NOT TO BLAME, THEY ARE.

AND WE'LL ALWAYS BE THERE TO SUPPORT YOU, SLENDERMAN.

THAT'S WHAT FRIENDS ARE FOR.

MY FRIENDS...

THANK YOU, MISTER RUBIUS. THANK YOU SO MUCH.

LAAAME...

THIS HAS BEEN INCREDIBLE, RUBIUS.

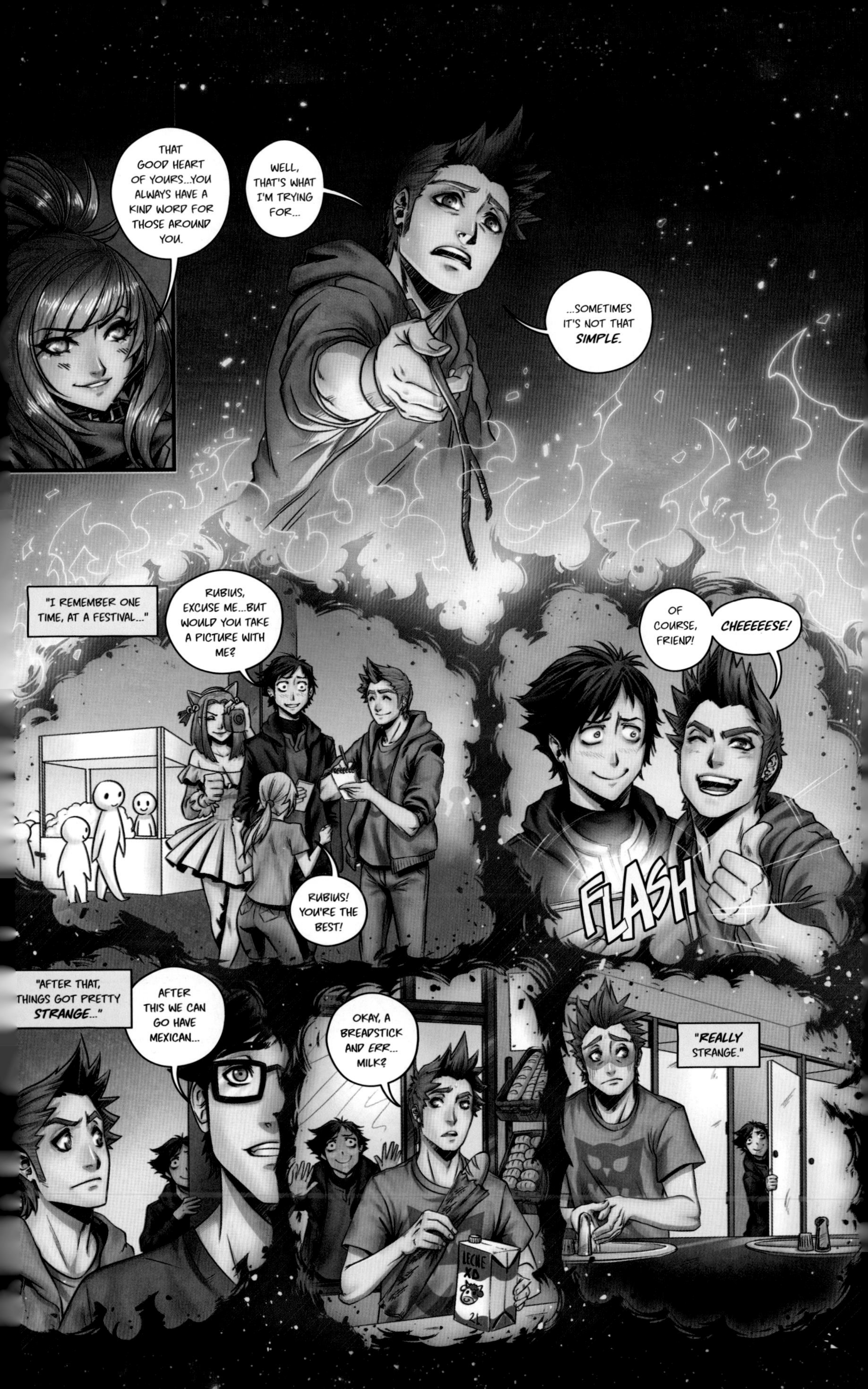
THAT GOOD HEART OF YOURS...YOU ALWAYS HAVE A KIND WORD FOR THOSE AROUND YOU.
WELL, THAT'S WHAT I'M TRYING FOR...
...SOMETIMES IT'S NOT THAT SIMPLE.
"I REMEMBER ONE TIME, AT A FESTIVAL..."
RUBIUS, EXCUSE ME...BUT WOULD YOU TAKE A PICTURE WITH ME?
RUBIUS! YOU'RE THE BEST!
OF COURSE, FRIEND!
CHEEEEESE!
FLASH
"AFTER THAT, THINGS GOT PRETTY STRANGE..."
AFTER THIS WE CAN GO HAVE MEXICAN...
OKAY, A BREADSTICK AND ERR... MILK?
LECHE XD
"REALLY STRANGE."

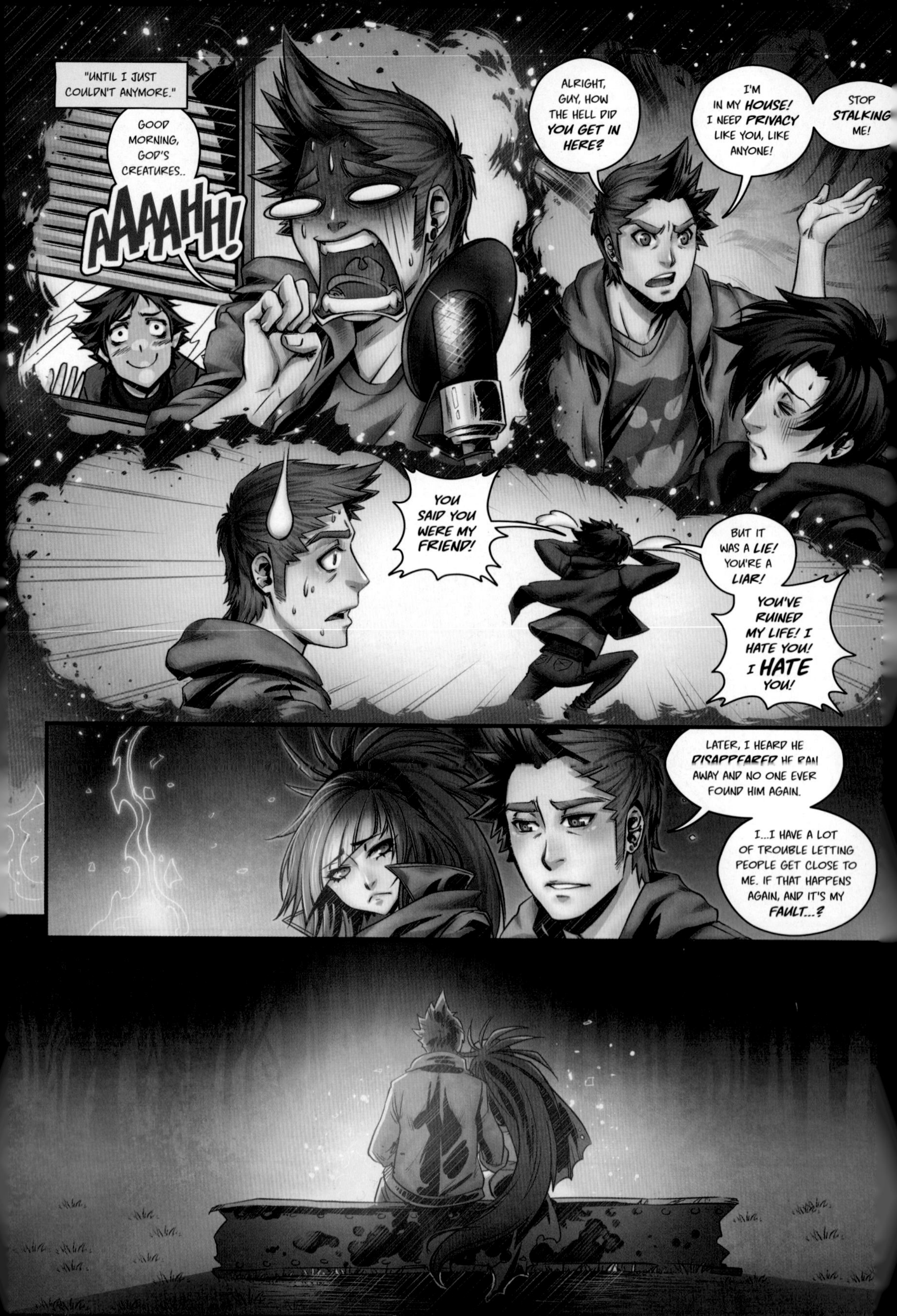
"UNTIL I JUST COULDN'T ANYMORE."
GOOD MORNING, GOD'S CREATURES..
AAAAHH!
ALRIGHT, GUY, HOW THE HELL DID YOU GET IN HERE?
I'M IN MY HOUSE! I NEED PRIVACY LIKE YOU, LIKE ANYONE!
STOP STALKING ME!
YOU SAID YOU WERE MY FRIEND!
BUT IT WAS A LIE! YOU'RE A LIAR!
YOU'VE RUINED MY LIFE! I HATE YOU! I HATE YOU!
LATER, I HEARD HE DISAPPEARED HE RAN AWAY AND NO ONE EVER FOUND HIM AGAIN.
I...I HAVE A LOT OF TROUBLE LETTING PEOPLE GET CLOSE TO ME. IF THAT HAPPENS AGAIN, AND IT'S MY FAULT...?

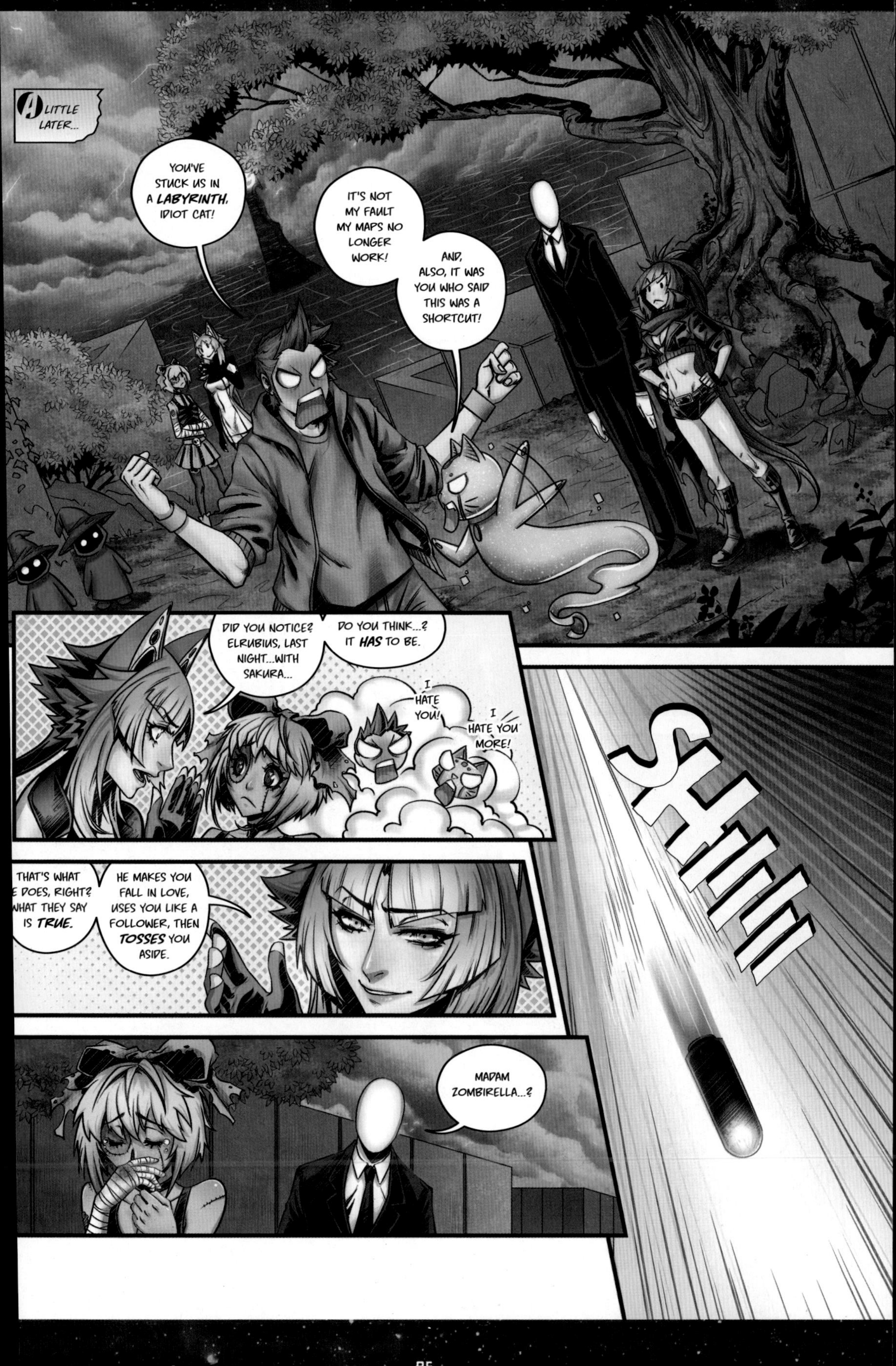
A LITTLE LATER...
YOU'VE STUCK US IN A LABYRINTH, IDIOT CAT!
IT'S NOT MY FAULT MY MAPS NO LONGER WORK!
AND, ALSO, IT WAS YOU WHO SAID THIS WAS A SHORTCUT!
DID YOU NOTICE? ELRUBIUS, LAST NIGHT...WITH SAKURA...
DO YOU THINK...? IT HAS TO BE.
I HATE YOU!
I HATE YOU MORE!
SHIIIII
THAT'S WHAT E DOES, RIGHT? WHAT THEY SAY IS TRUE.
HE MAKES YOU FALL IN LOVE, USES YOU LIKE A FOLLOWER, THEN TOSSES YOU ASIDE.
MADAM ZOMBIRELLA...?

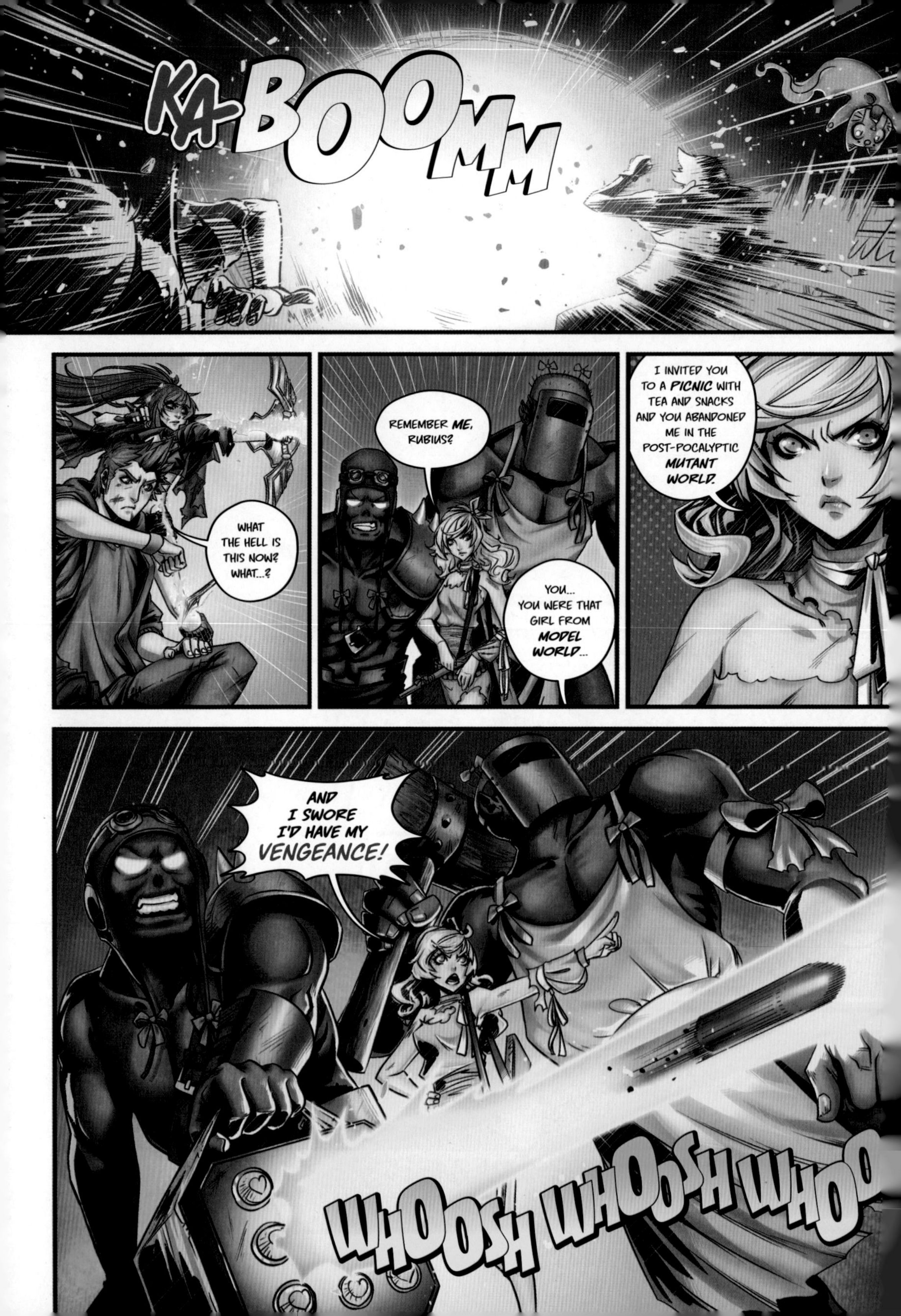
KA-BOOMMM
WHAT THE HELL IS THIS NOW? WHAT...?
REMEMBER ME, RUBIUS?
YOU... YOU WERE THAT GIRL FROM MODEL WORLD...
I INVITED YOU TO A PICNIC WITH TEA AND SNACKS AND YOU ABANDONED ME IN THE POST-POCALYPTIC MUTANT WORLD.
AND I SWORE I'D HAVE MY VENGEANCE!
WHOOSH WHOOSH WHOO

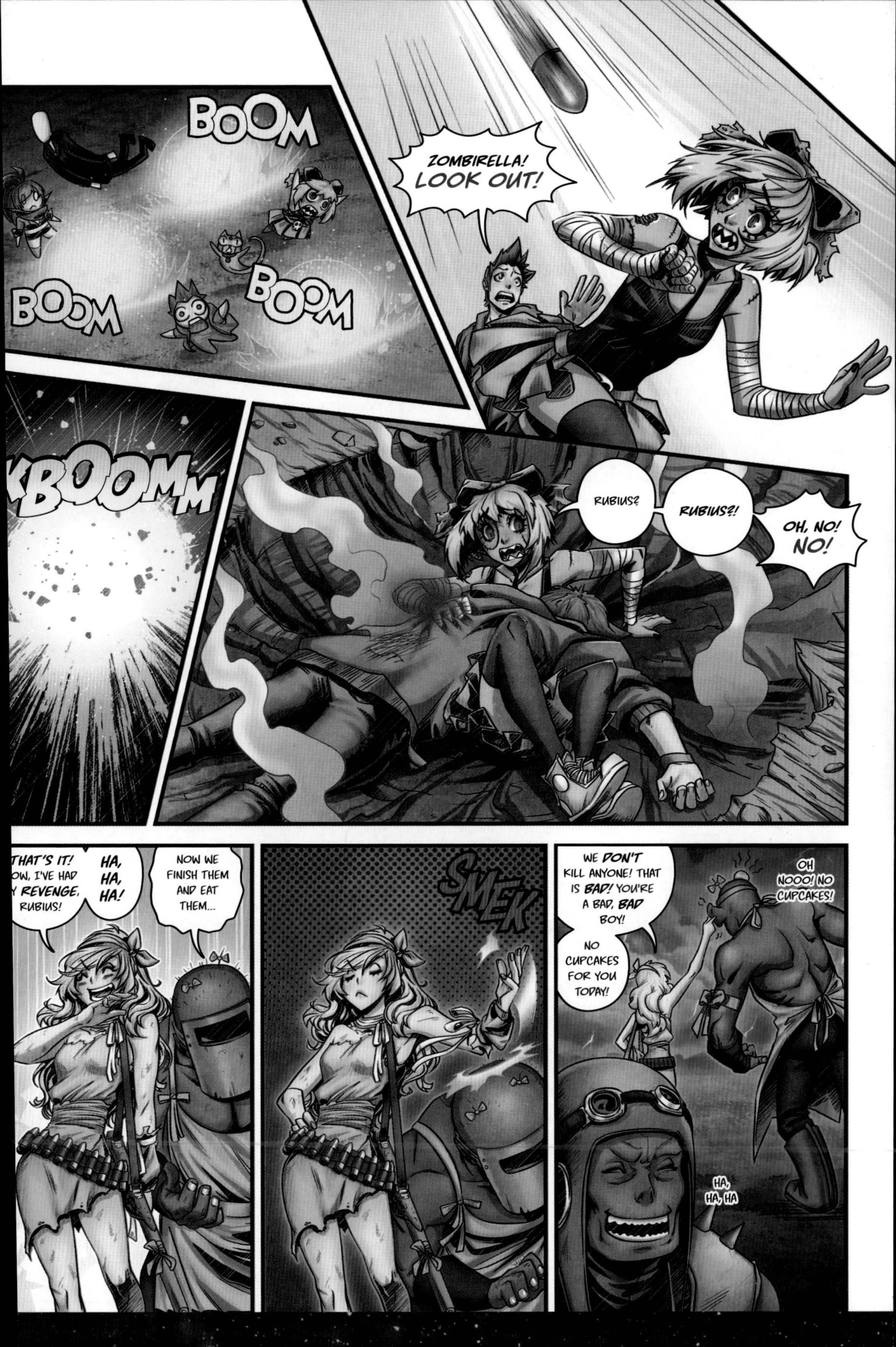
BOOM
BOOM
BOOM
ZOMBIRELLA! LOOK OUT!
KBOOMM
RUBIUS?
RUBIUS?!
OH, NO! NO!
THAT'S IT! OW, I'VE HAD Y REVENGE, RUBIUS!
HA, HA, HA!
NOW WE FINISH THEM AND EAT THEM...
SMEK
WE DON'T KILL ANYONE! THAT IS BAD! YOU'RE A BAD, BAD BOY!
NO CUPCAKES FOR YOU TODAY!
OH NOOO! NO CUPCAKES!
HA, HA, HA

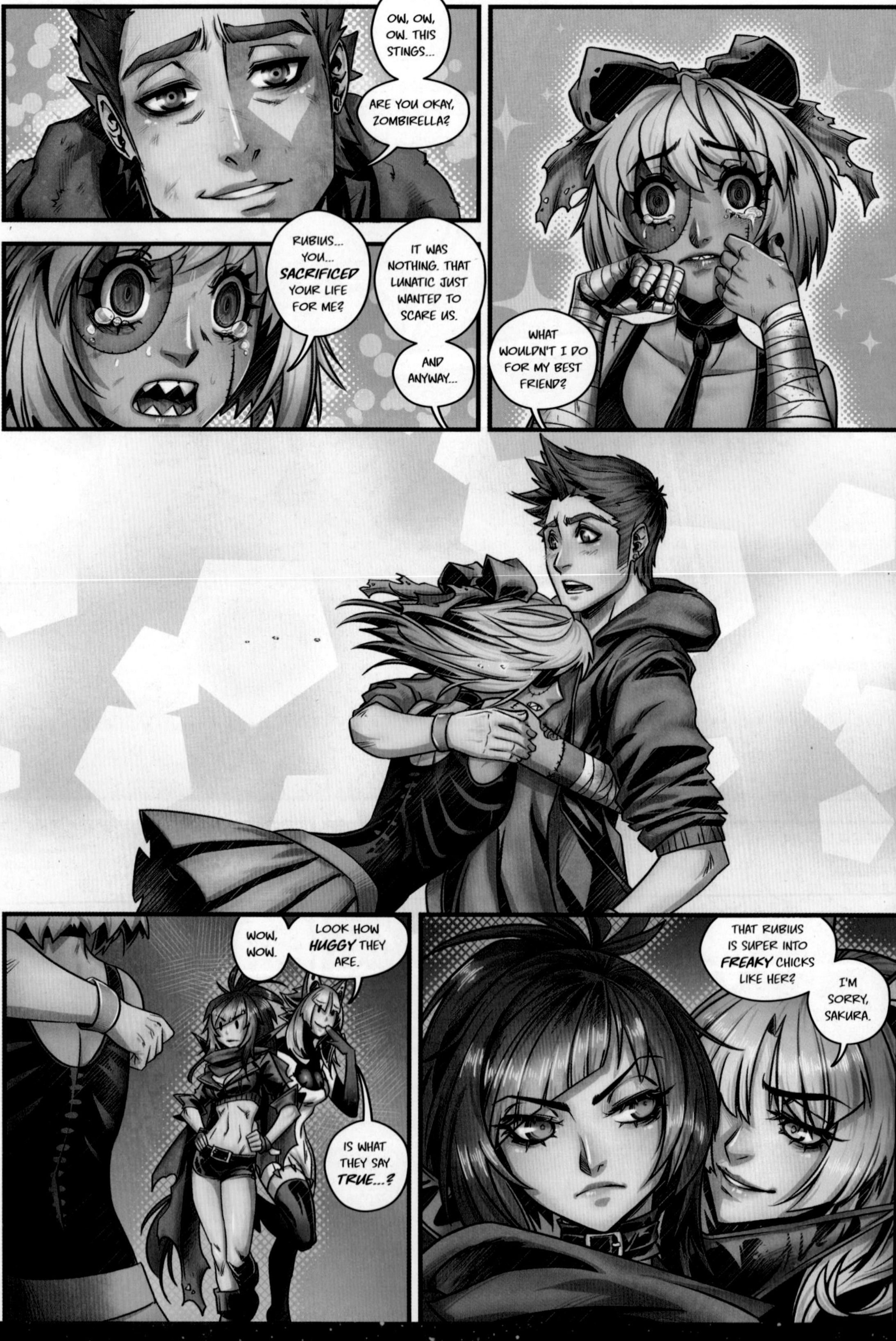
OW, OW, OW. THIS STINGS...
ARE YOU OKAY, ZOMBIRELLA?
RUBIUS... YOU... SACRIFICED YOUR LIFE FOR ME?
IT WAS NOTHING. THAT LUNATIC JUST WANTED TO SCARE US.
AND ANYWAY...
WHAT WOULDN'T I DO FOR MY BEST FRIEND?
WOW, WOW.
LOOK HOW HUGGY THEY ARE.
IS WHAT THEY SAY TRUE...?
THAT RUBIUS IS SUPER INTO FREAKY CHICKS LIKE HER?
I'M SORRY, SAKURA.

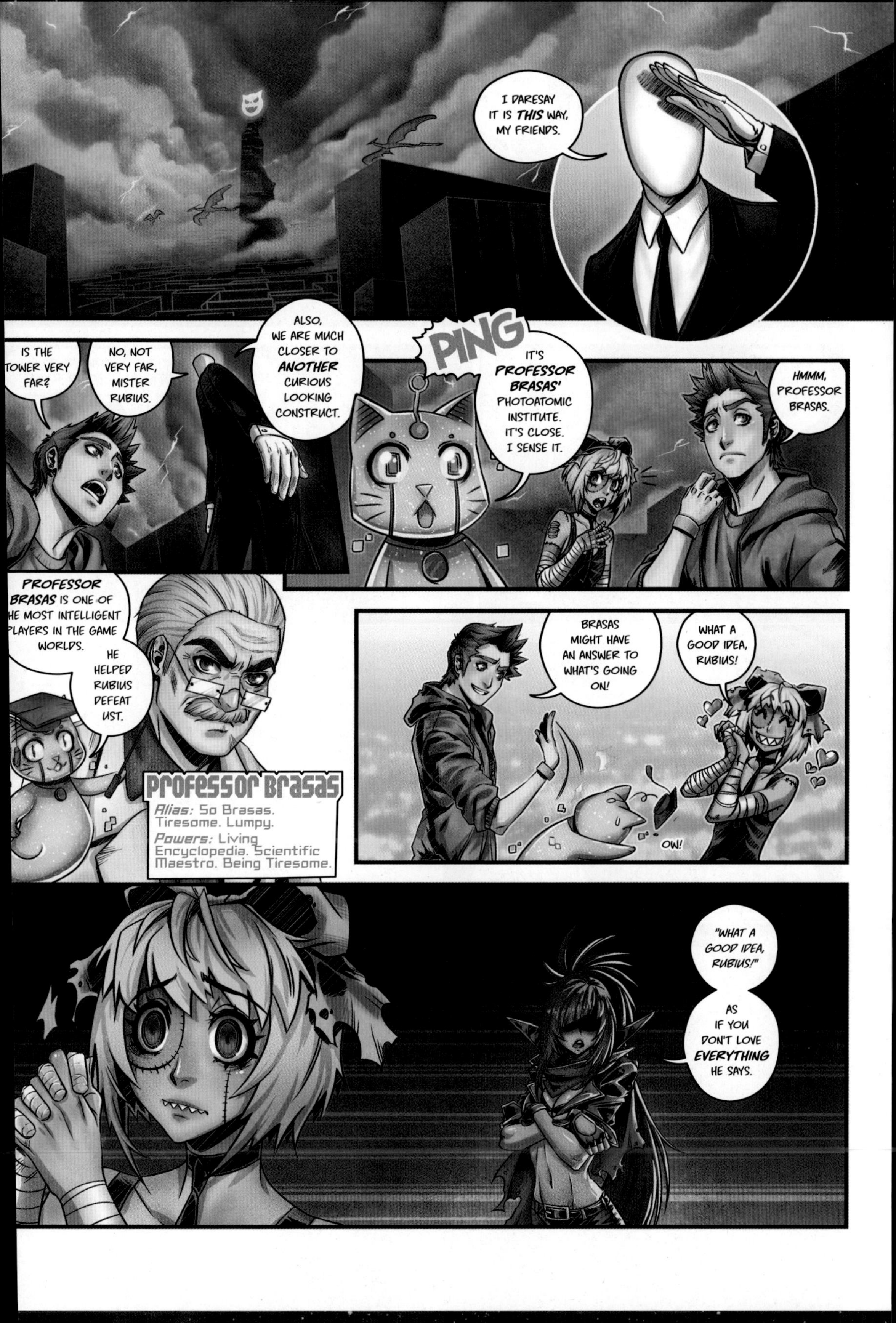

I DARESAY IT IS THIS WAY, MY FRIENDS.
IS THE TOWER VERY FAR?
NO, NOT VERY FAR, MISTER RUBIUS.
ALSO, WE ARE MUCH CLOSER TO ANOTHER CURIOUS LOOKING CONSTRUCT.
PING
IT'S PROFESSOR BRASAS' PHOTOATOMIC INSTITUTE. IT'S CLOSE. I SENSE IT.
HMMM, PROFESSOR BRASAS.
PROFESSOR BRASAS IS ONE OF HE MOST INTELLIGENT PLAYERS IN THE GAME WORLDS.
HE HELPED RUBIUS DEFEAT UST.
Professor Brasas
Alias: So Brasas. Tiresome. Lumpy.
Powers: Living Encyclopedia. Scientific Maestro. Being Tiresome.
BRASAS MIGHT HAVE AN ANSWER TO WHAT'S GOING ON!
WHAT A GOOD IDEA, RUBIUS!
OW!
"WHAT A GOOD IDEA, RUBIUS!"
AS IF YOU DON'T LOVE EVERYTHING HE SAYS.

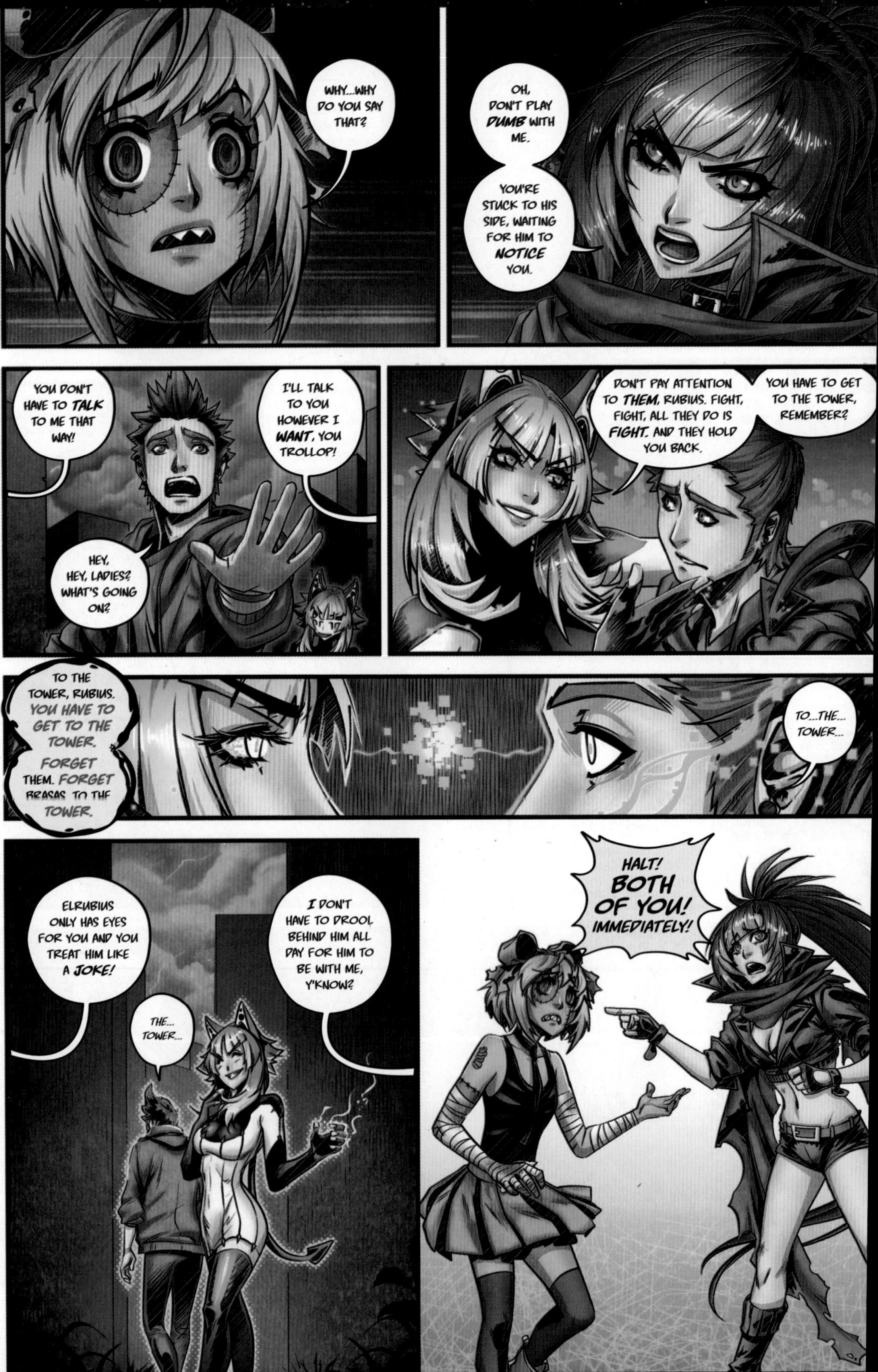
WHY...WHY DO YOU SAY THAT?
OH, DON'T PLAY DUMB WITH ME.
YOU'RE STUCK TO HIS SIDE, WAITING FOR HIM TO NOTICE YOU.
YOU DON'T HAVE TO TALK TO ME THAT WAY!
I'LL TALK TO YOU HOWEVER I WANT, YOU TROLLOP!
HEY, HEY, LADIES? WHAT'S GOING ON?
DON'T PAY ATTENTION TO THEM, RUBIUS. FIGHT, FIGHT, ALL THEY DO IS FIGHT. AND THEY HOLD YOU BACK.
YOU HAVE TO GET TO THE TOWER, REMEMBER?
TO THE TOWER, RUBIUS. YOU HAVE TO GET TO THE TOWER. FORGET THEM. FORGET BRASAS. TO THE TOWER.
TO...THE... TOWER...
ELRUBIUS ONLY HAS EYES FOR YOU AND YOU TREAT HIM LIKE A JOKE!
THE... TOWER...
I DON'T HAVE TO DROOL BEHIND HIM ALL DAY FOR HIM TO BE WITH ME, Y'KNOW?
HALT! BOTH OF YOU! IMMEDIATELY!

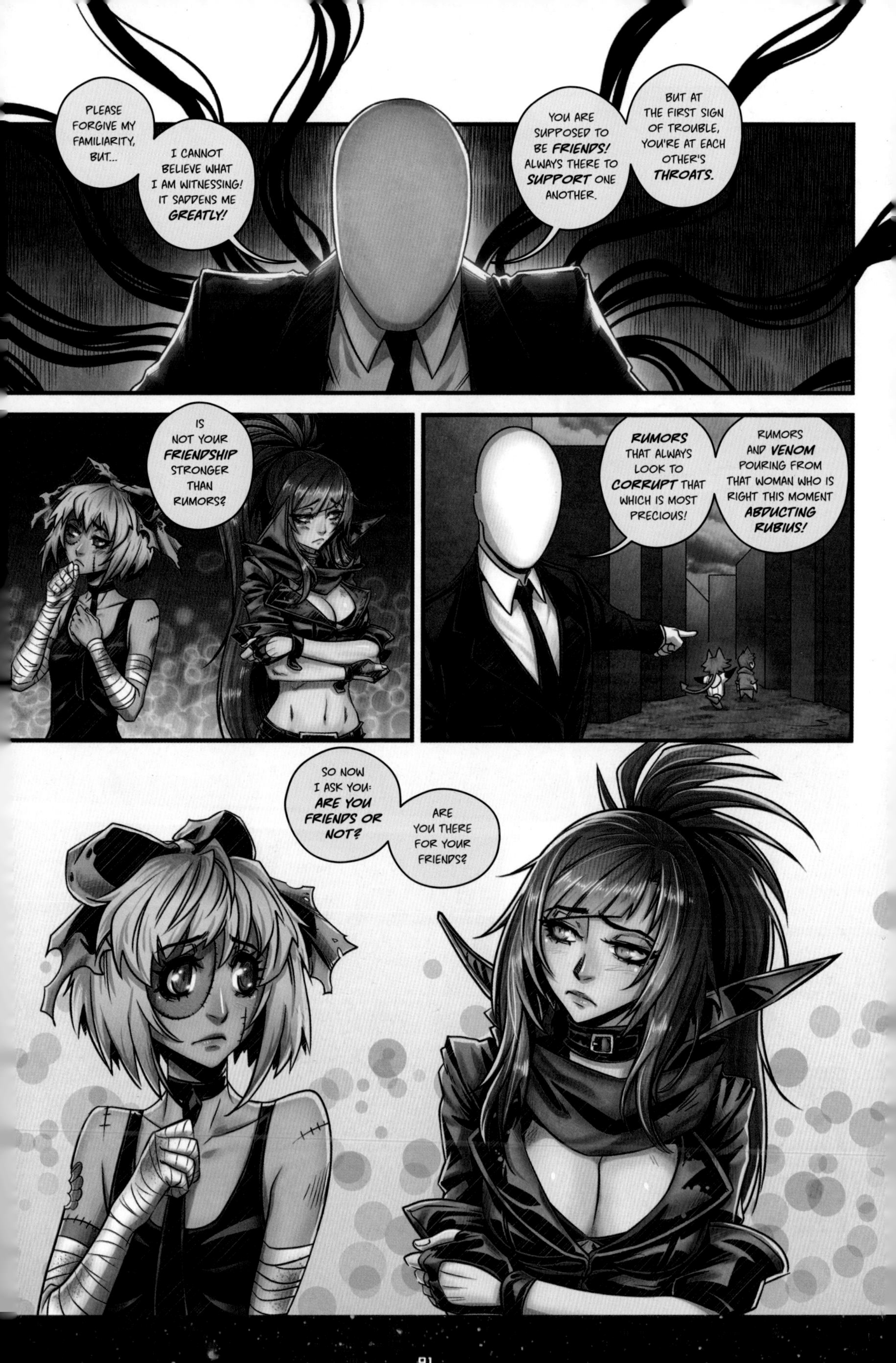
PLEASE FORGIVE MY FAMILIARITY, BUT...
I CANNOT BELIEVE WHAT I AM WITNESSING! IT SADDENS ME **GREATLY!**
YOU ARE SUPPOSED TO BE **FRIENDS!** ALWAYS THERE TO **SUPPORT** ONE ANOTHER.
BUT AT THE FIRST SIGN OF TROUBLE, YOU'RE AT EACH OTHER'S **THROATS.**
IS NOT YOUR **FRIENDSHIP** STRONGER THAN RUMORS?
RUMORS THAT ALWAYS LOOK TO **CORRUPT** THAT WHICH IS MOST PRECIOUS!
RUMORS AND **VENOM** POURING FROM THAT WOMAN WHO IS RIGHT THIS MOMENT **ABDUCTING RUBIUS!**
SO NOW I ASK YOU: **ARE YOU FRIENDS OR NOT?**
ARE YOU THERE FOR YOUR FRIENDS?

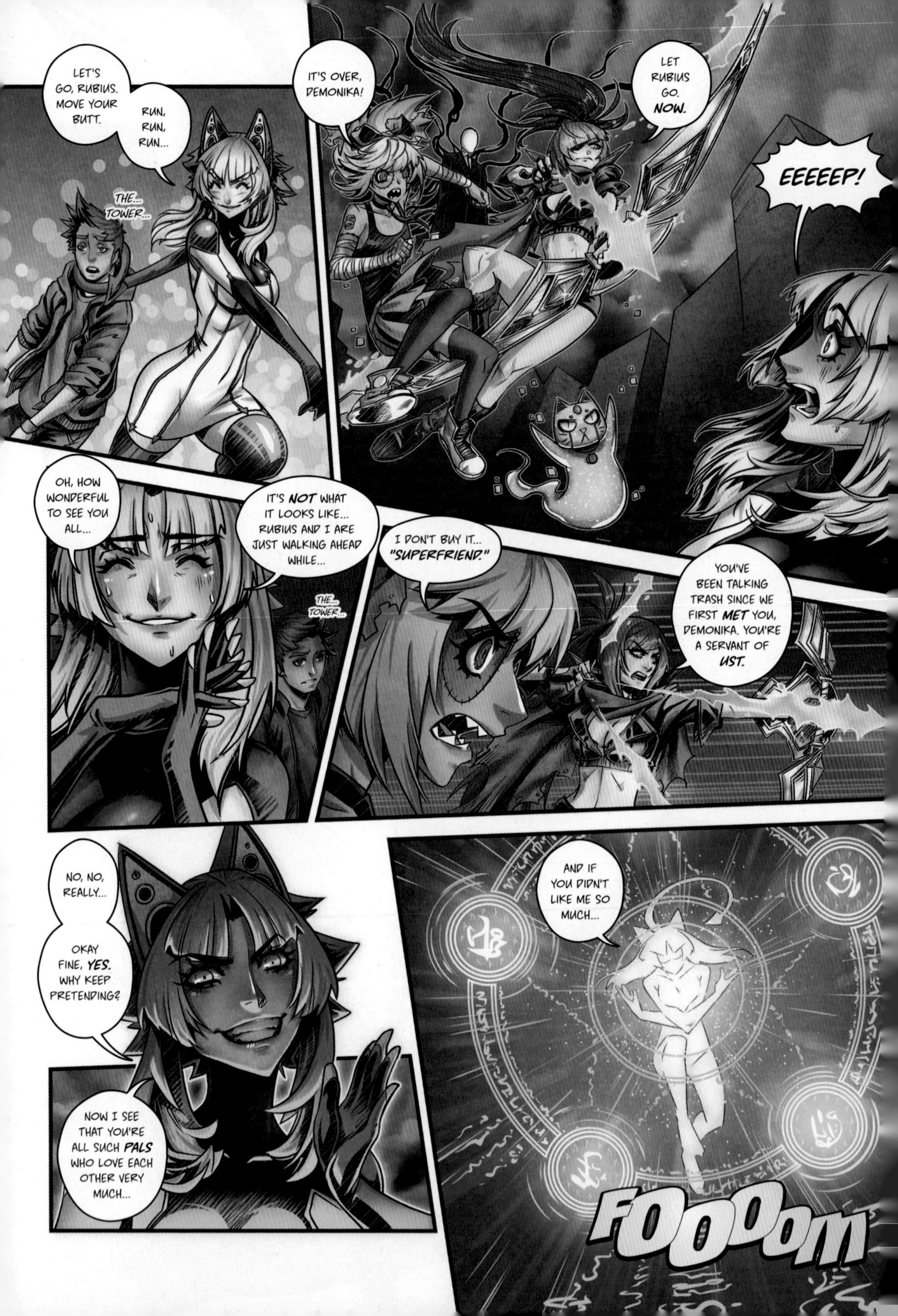
LET'S GO, RUBIUS. MOVE YOUR BUTT.
RUN, RUN, RUN...
THE... TOWER...
IT'S OVER, DEMONIKA!
LET RUBIUS GO. NOW.
EEEEEP!
OH, HOW WONDERFUL TO SEE YOU ALL...
IT'S NOT WHAT IT LOOKS LIKE... RUBIUS AND I ARE JUST WALKING AHEAD WHILE...
THE... TOWER...
I DON'T BUY IT... "SUPERFRIEND."
YOU'VE BEEN TALKING TRASH SINCE WE FIRST MET YOU, DEMONIKA. YOU'RE A SERVANT OF UST.
NO, NO, REALLY...
OKAY FINE, YES. WHY KEEP PRETENDING?
NOW I SEE THAT YOU'RE ALL SUCH PALS WHO LOVE EACH OTHER VERY MUCH...
AND IF YOU DIDN'T LIKE ME SO MUCH...
FOOOOM

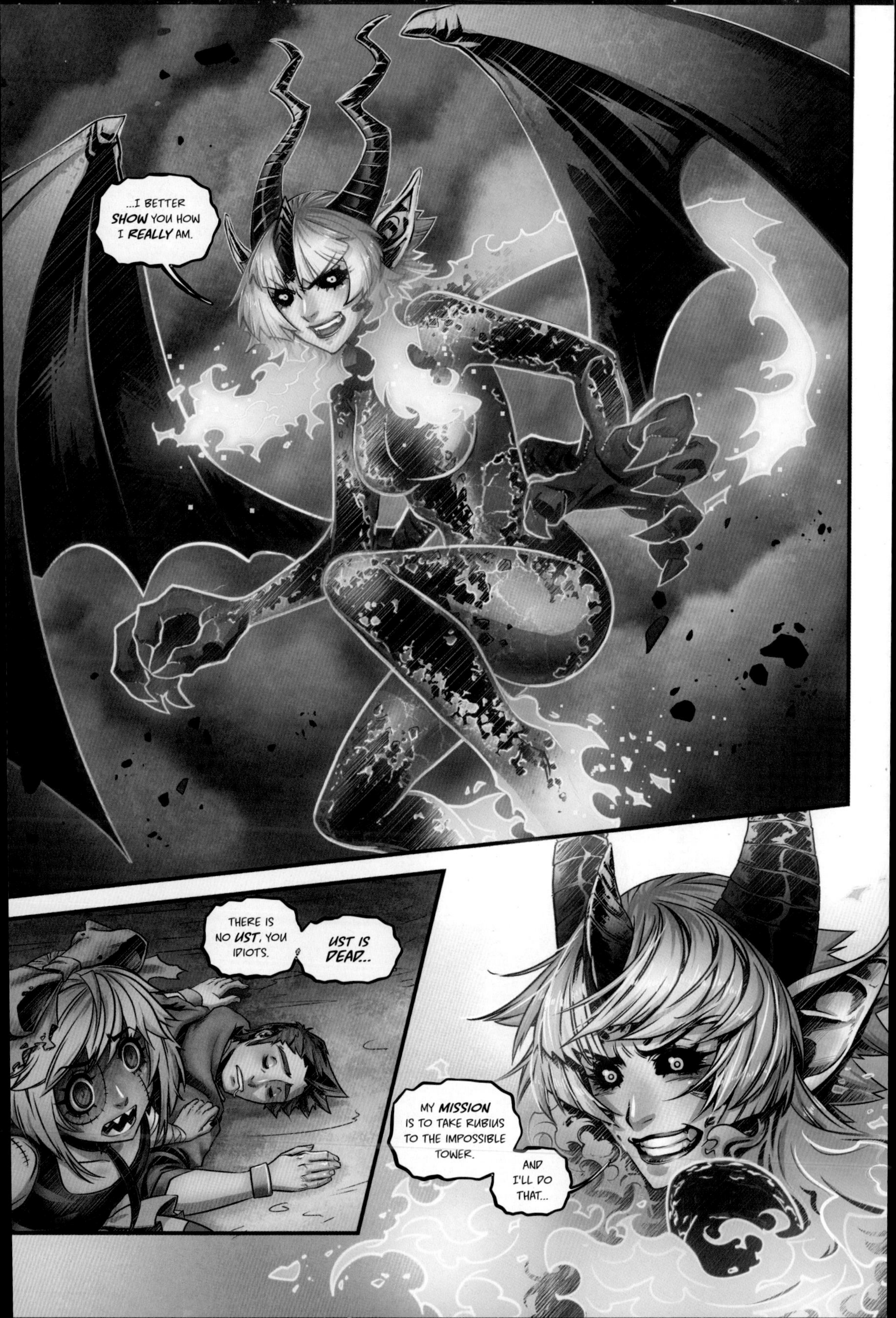
...I BETTER SHOW YOU HOW I REALLY AM.
THERE IS NO UST, YOU IDIOTS.
UST IS DEAD...
MY MISSION IS TO TAKE RUBIUS TO THE IMPOSSIBLE TOWER.
AND I'LL DO THAT...

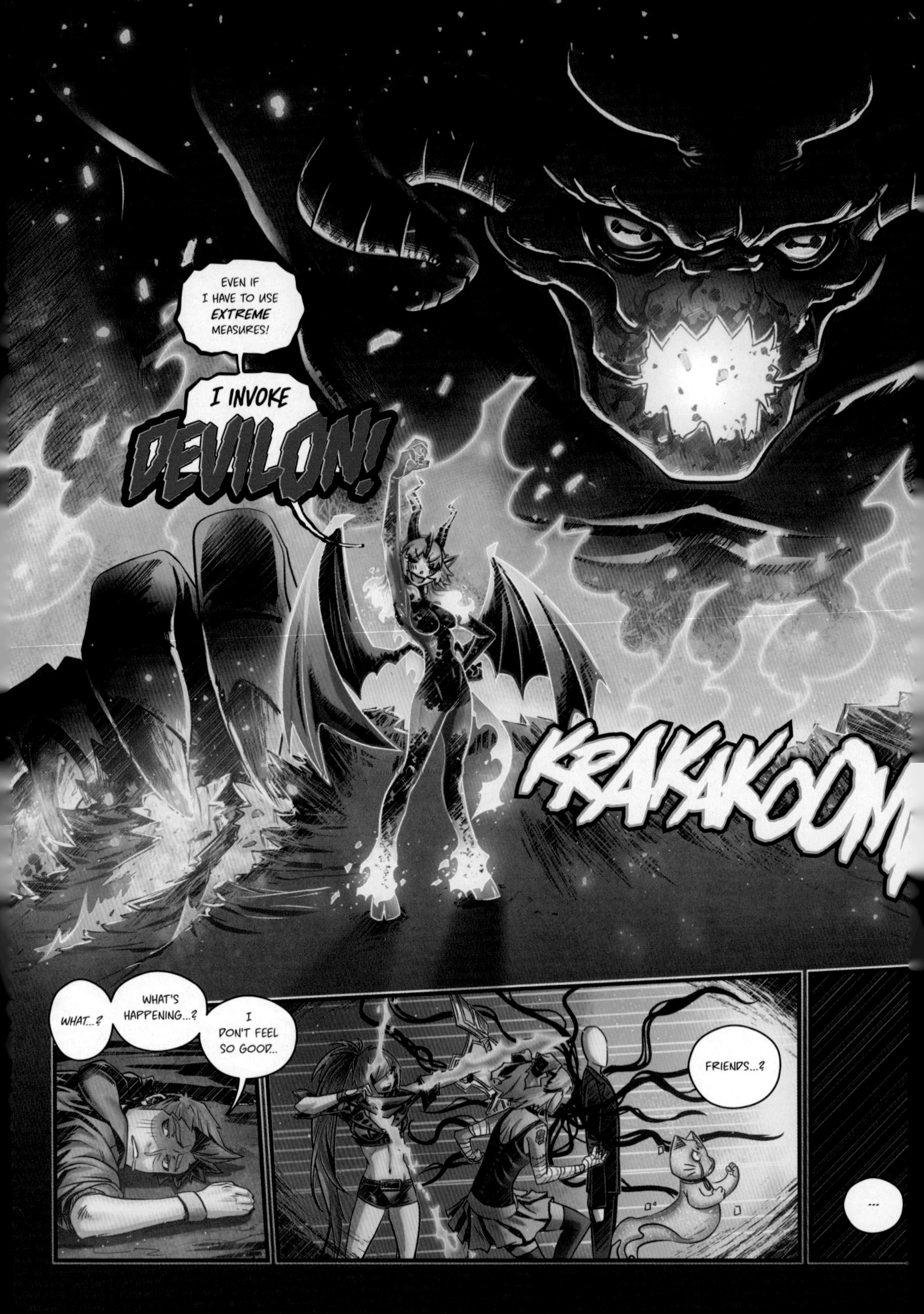
EVEN IF I HAVE TO USE EXTREME MEASURES!
I INVOKE
DEVILON!
KRAKAKOOM
WHAT...?
WHAT'S HAPPENING...?
I DON'T FEEL SO GOOD...
FRIENDS...?
...

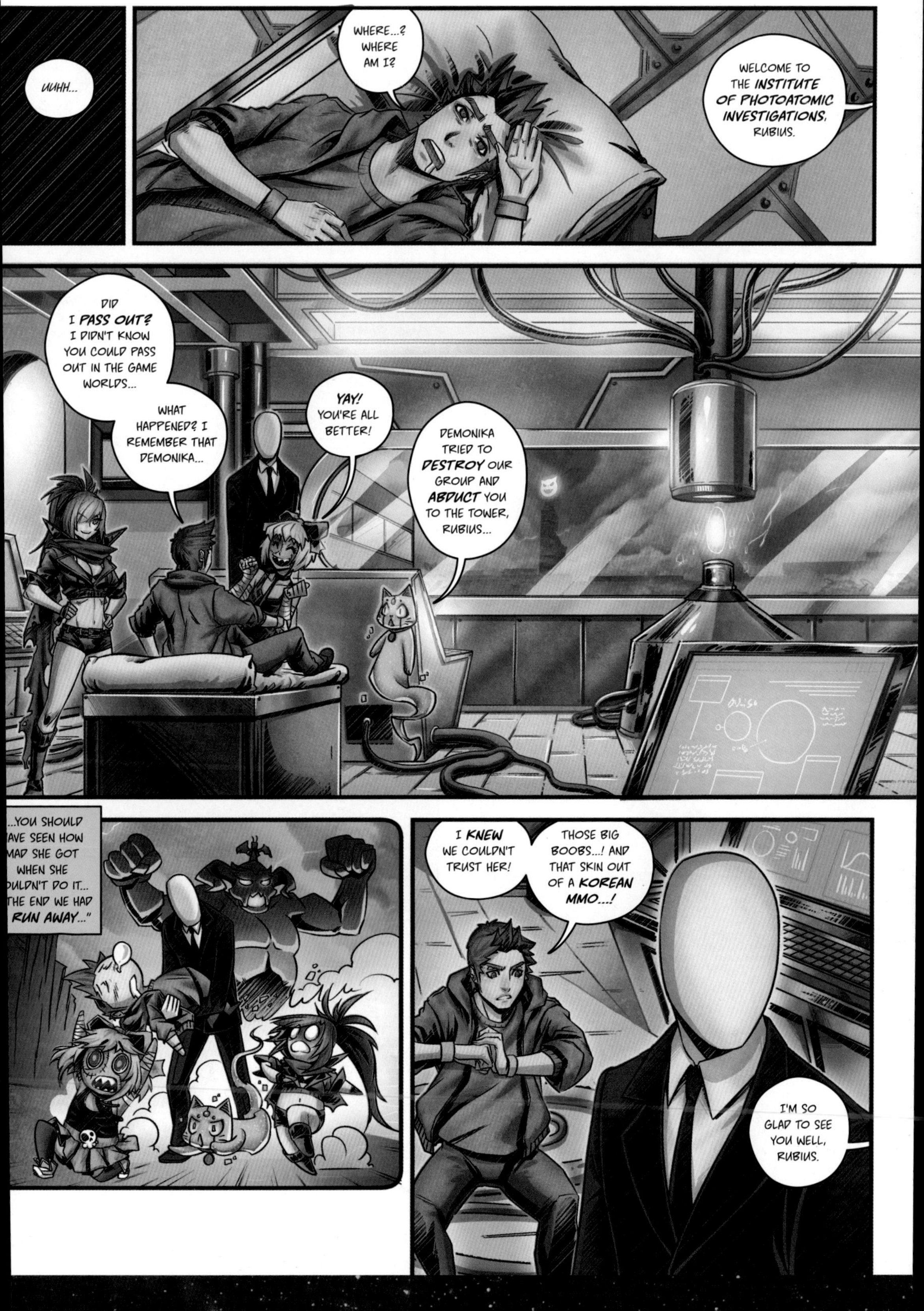

UUHH...
WHERE...? WHERE AM I?
WELCOME TO THE INSTITUTE OF PHOTOATOMIC INVESTIGATIONS, RUBIUS.
DID I PASS OUT? I DIDN'T KNOW YOU COULD PASS OUT IN THE GAME WORLDS...
WHAT HAPPENED? I REMEMBER THAT DEMONIKA...
YAY! YOU'RE ALL BETTER!
DEMONIKA TRIED TO DESTROY OUR GROUP AND ABDUCT YOU TO THE TOWER, RUBIUS...
...YOU SHOULD AVE SEEN HOW MAD SHE GOT WHEN SHE OULDN'T DO IT... THE END WE HAD RUN AWAY..."
I KNEW WE COULDN'T TRUST HER!
THOSE BIG BOOBS...! AND THAT SKIN OUT OF A KOREAN MMO...!
I'M SO GLAD TO SEE YOU WELL, RUBIUS.

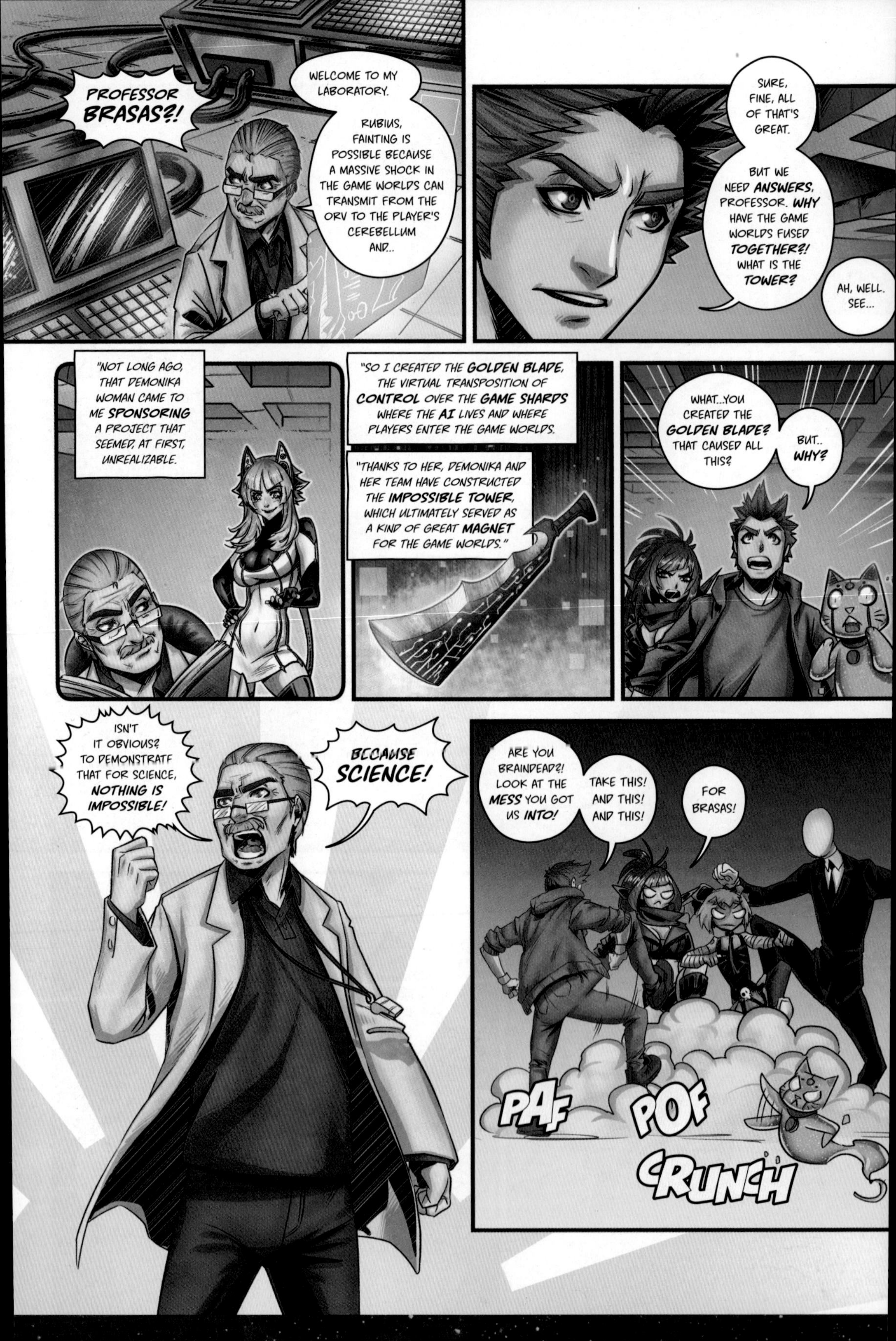
PROFESSOR BRASAS?!
WELCOME TO MY LABORATORY.
RUBIUS, FAINTING IS POSSIBLE BECAUSE A MASSIVE SHOCK IN THE GAME WORLDS CAN TRANSMIT FROM THE ORV TO THE PLAYER'S CEREBELLUM AND...
SURE, FINE, ALL OF THAT'S GREAT.
BUT WE NEED ANSWERS, PROFESSOR. WHY HAVE THE GAME WORLDS FUSED TOGETHER?! WHAT IS THE TOWER?
AH, WELL. SEE...
"NOT LONG AGO, THAT DEMONIKA WOMAN CAME TO ME SPONSORING A PROJECT THAT SEEMED, AT FIRST, UNREALIZABLE.
"SO I CREATED THE GOLDEN BLADE, THE VIRTUAL TRANSPOSITION OF CONTROL OVER THE GAME SHARDS WHERE THE AI LIVES AND WHERE PLAYERS ENTER THE GAME WORLDS.
"THANKS TO HER, DEMONIKA AND HER TEAM HAVE CONSTRUCTED THE IMPOSSIBLE TOWER, WHICH ULTIMATELY SERVED AS A KIND OF GREAT MAGNET FOR THE GAME WORLDS."
WHAT...YOU CREATED THE GOLDEN BLADE? THAT CAUSED ALL THIS?
BUT.. WHY?
ISN'T IT OBVIOUS? TO DEMONSTRATE THAT FOR SCIENCE, NOTHING IS IMPOSSIBLE!
BECAUSE SCIENCE!
ARE YOU BRAINDEAD?! LOOK AT THE MESS YOU GOT US INTO!
TAKE THIS! AND THIS! AND THIS!
FOR BRASAS!
PAF
POF
CRUNCH

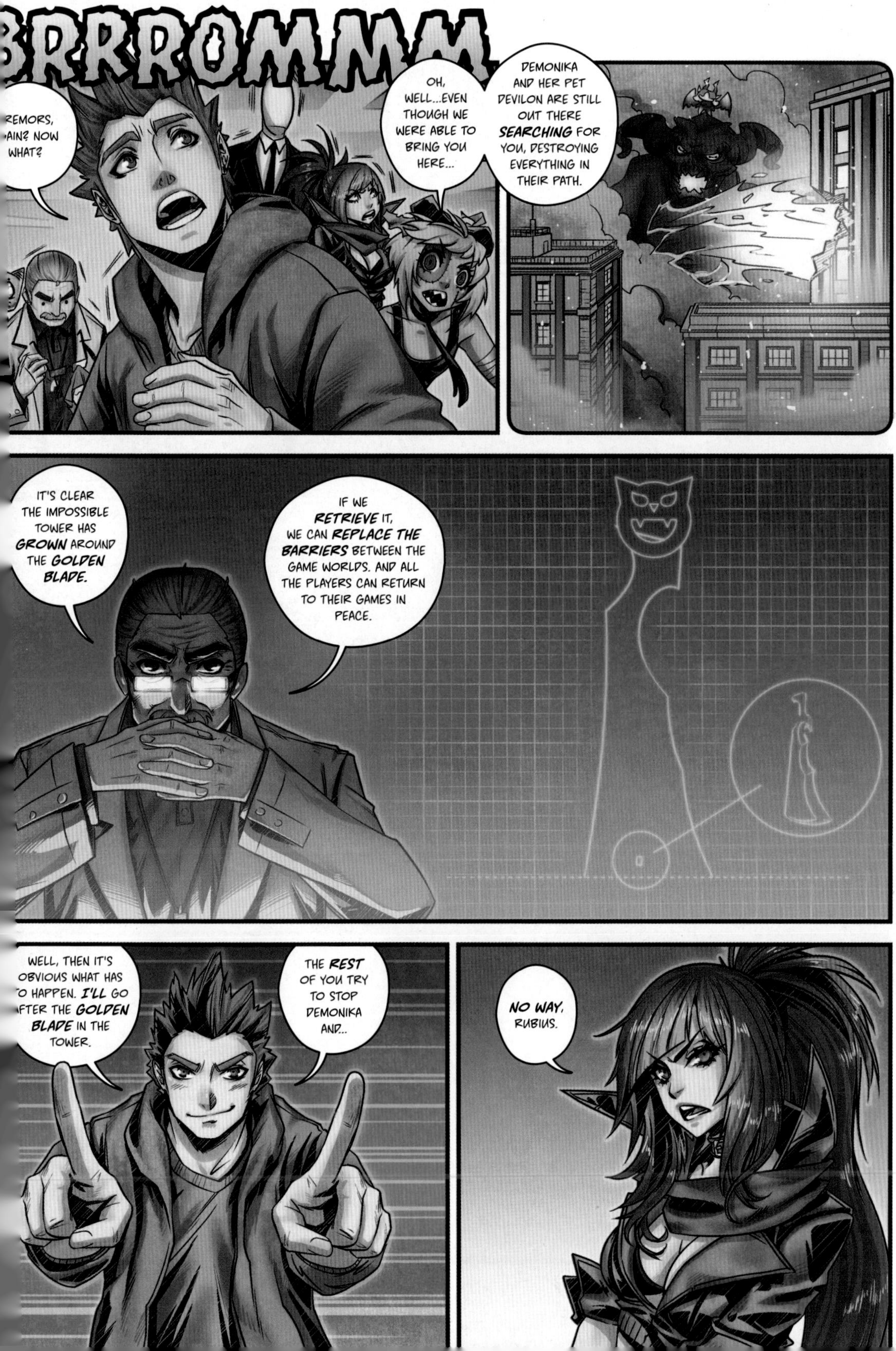
BRRROMMM
REMORS, AIN? NOW WHAT?
OH, WELL...EVEN THOUGH WE WERE ABLE TO BRING YOU HERE...
DEMONIKA AND HER PET DEVILON ARE STILL OUT THERE SEARCHING FOR YOU, DESTROYING EVERYTHING IN THEIR PATH.
IT'S CLEAR THE IMPOSSIBLE TOWER HAS GROWN AROUND THE GOLDEN BLADE.
IF WE RETRIEVE IT, WE CAN REPLACE THE BARRIERS BETWEEN THE GAME WORLDS. AND ALL THE PLAYERS CAN RETURN TO THEIR GAMES IN PEACE.
WELL, THEN IT'S OBVIOUS WHAT HAS O HAPPEN. I'LL GO FTER THE GOLDEN BLADE IN THE TOWER.
THE REST OF YOU TRY TO STOP DEMONIKA AND...
NO WAY, RUBIUS.

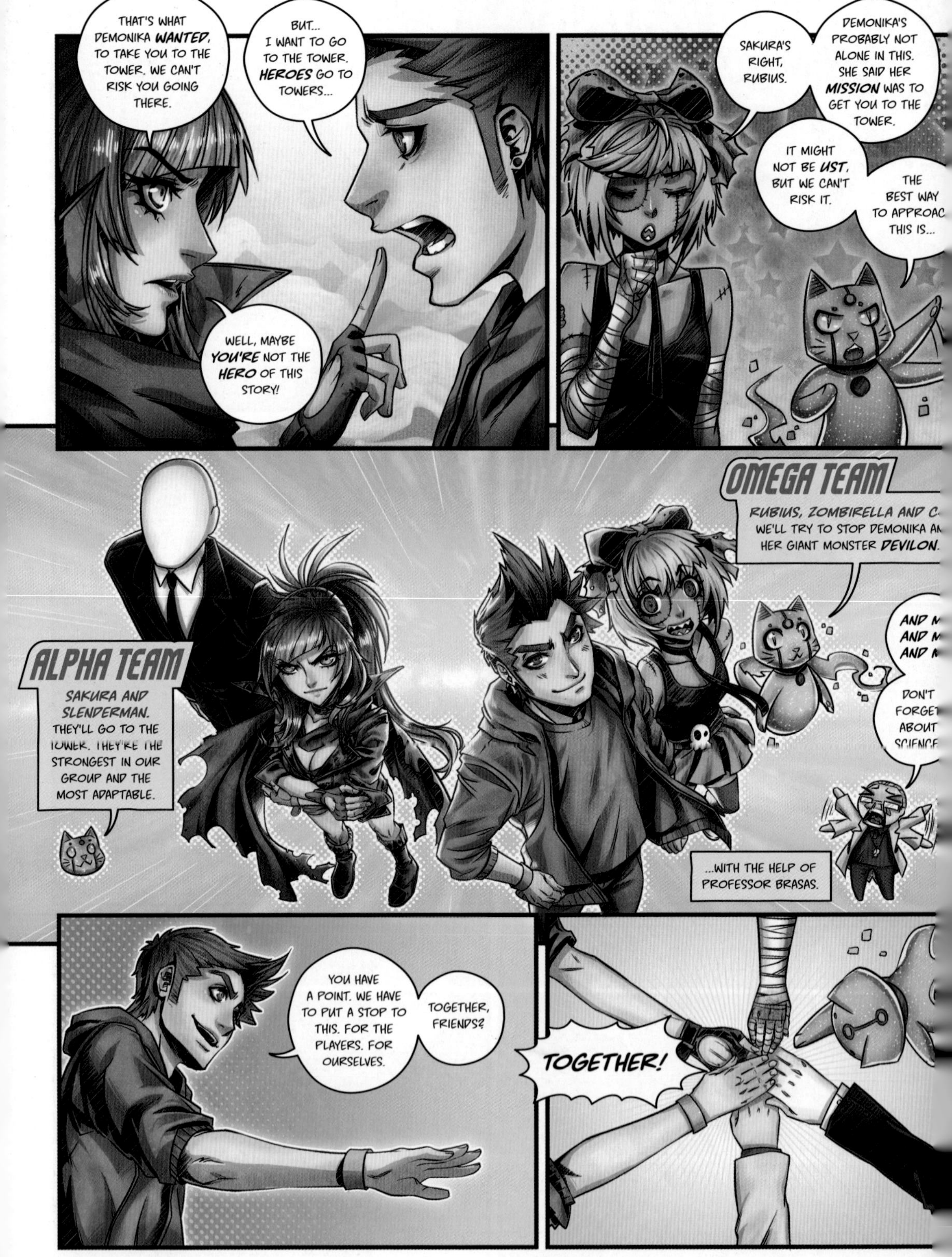
THAT'S WHAT DEMONIKA **WANTED**, TO TAKE YOU TO THE TOWER. WE CAN'T RISK YOU GOING THERE.
BUT... I WANT TO GO TO THE TOWER. **HEROES** GO TO TOWERS...
WELL, MAYBE **YOU'RE** NOT THE **HERO** OF THIS STORY!
SAKURA'S RIGHT, RUBIUS.
DEMONIKA'S PROBABLY NOT ALONE IN THIS. SHE SAID HER **MISSION** WAS TO GET YOU TO THE TOWER.
IT MIGHT NOT BE **UST**, BUT WE CAN'T RISK IT.
THE BEST WAY TO APPROAC THIS IS...
ALPHA TEAM
SAKURA AND SLENDERMAN. THEY'LL GO TO THE TOWER. THEY'RE THE STRONGEST IN OUR GROUP AND THE MOST ADAPTABLE.
OMEGA TEAM
RUBIUS, ZOMBIRELLA AND C WE'LL TRY TO STOP DEMONIKA AN HER GIANT MONSTER **DEVILON**.
AND M AND M AND M
DON'T FORGE ABOUT SCIENCE
...WITH THE HELP OF PROFESSOR BRASAS.
YOU HAVE A POINT. WE HAVE TO PUT A STOP TO THIS. FOR THE PLAYERS. FOR OURSELVES.
TOGETHER, FRIENDS?
TOGETHER!

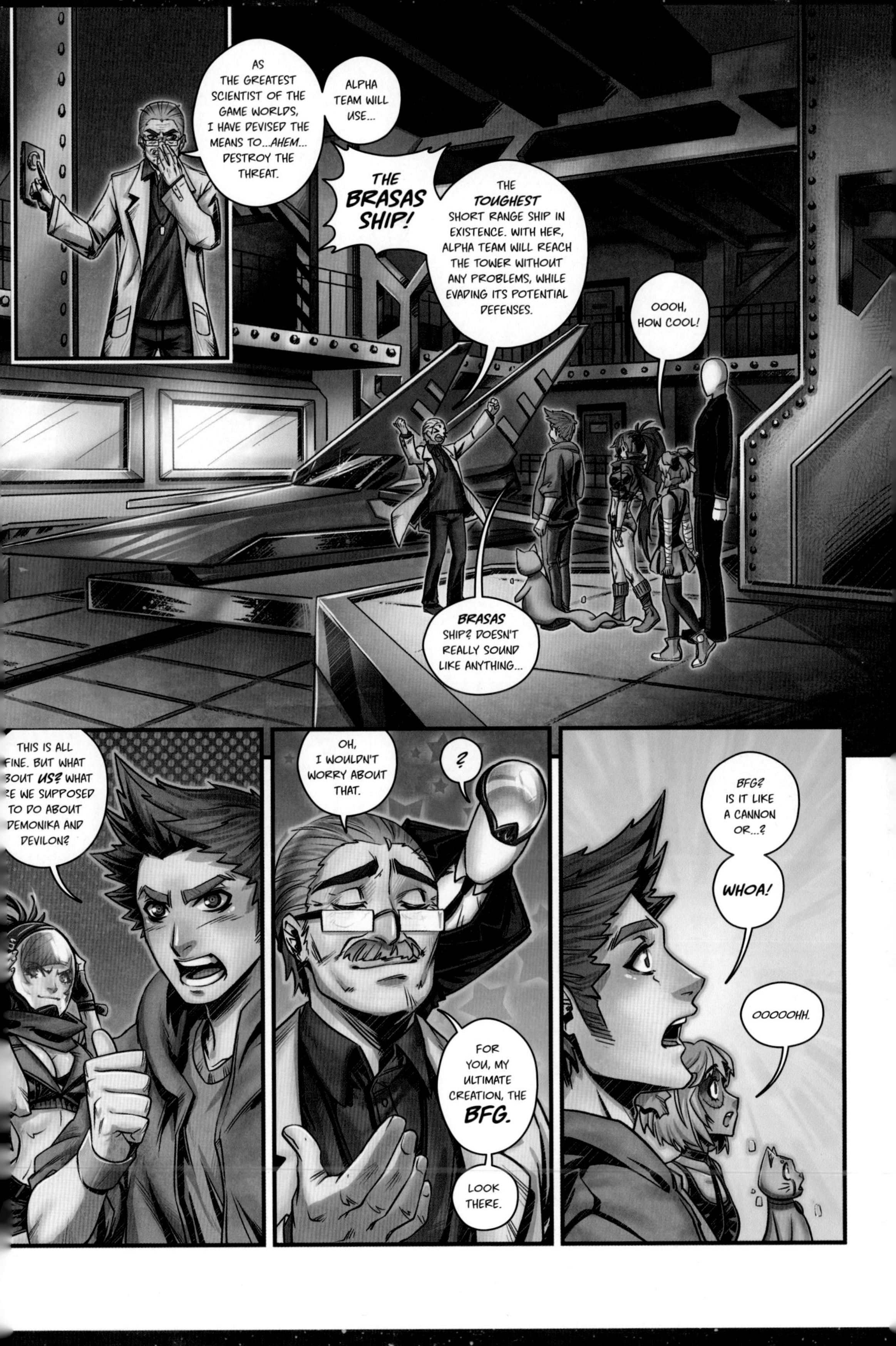
AS THE GREATEST SCIENTIST OF THE GAME WORLDS, I HAVE DEVISED THE MEANS TO...AHEM... DESTROY THE THREAT.
ALPHA TEAM WILL USE...
THE BRASAS SHIP!
THE TOUGHEST SHORT RANGE SHIP IN EXISTENCE. WITH HER, ALPHA TEAM WILL REACH THE TOWER WITHOUT ANY PROBLEMS, WHILE EVADING ITS POTENTIAL DEFENSES.
OOOH, HOW COOL!
BRASAS SHIP? DOESN'T REALLY SOUND LIKE ANYTHING...
THIS IS ALL FINE. BUT WHAT ABOUT US? WHAT ARE WE SUPPOSED TO DO ABOUT DEMONIKA AND DEVILON?
OH, I WOULDN'T WORRY ABOUT THAT.
?
FOR YOU, MY ULTIMATE CREATION, THE BFG.
LOOK THERE.
BFG? IS IT LIKE A CANNON OR...?
WHOA!
OOOOOHH.

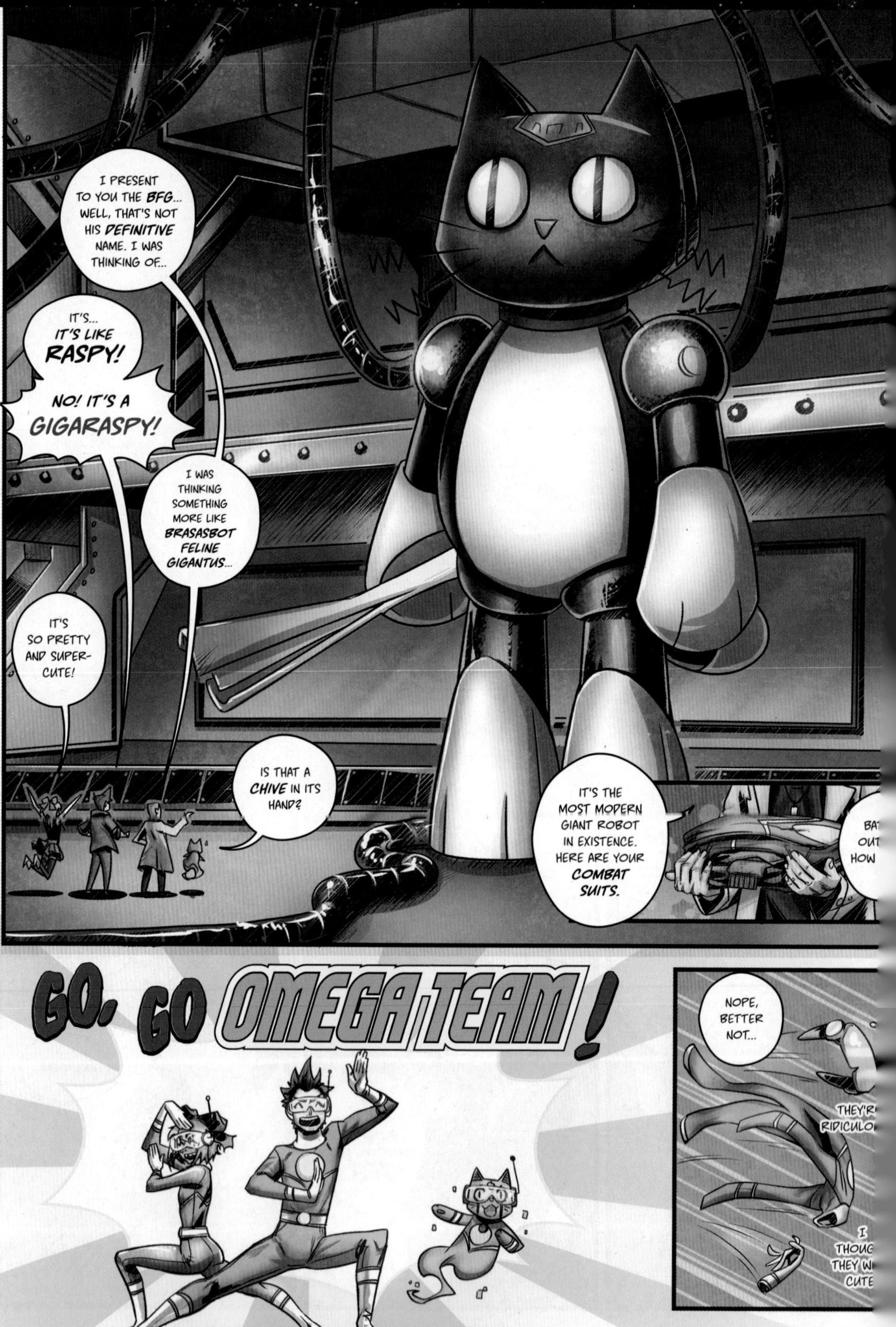
I PRESENT TO YOU THE BFG... WELL, THAT'S NOT HIS DEFINITIVE NAME. I WAS THINKING OF...
IT'S... IT'S LIKE RASPY!
NO! IT'S A GIGARASPY!
I WAS THINKING SOMETHING MORE LIKE BRASASBOT FELINE GIGANTUS...
IT'S SO PRETTY AND SUPER-CUTE!
IS THAT A CHIVE IN ITS HAND?
IT'S THE MOST MODERN GIANT ROBOT IN EXISTENCE. HERE ARE YOUR COMBAT SUITS.
GO, GO OMEGA TEAM!
NOPE, BETTER NOT...

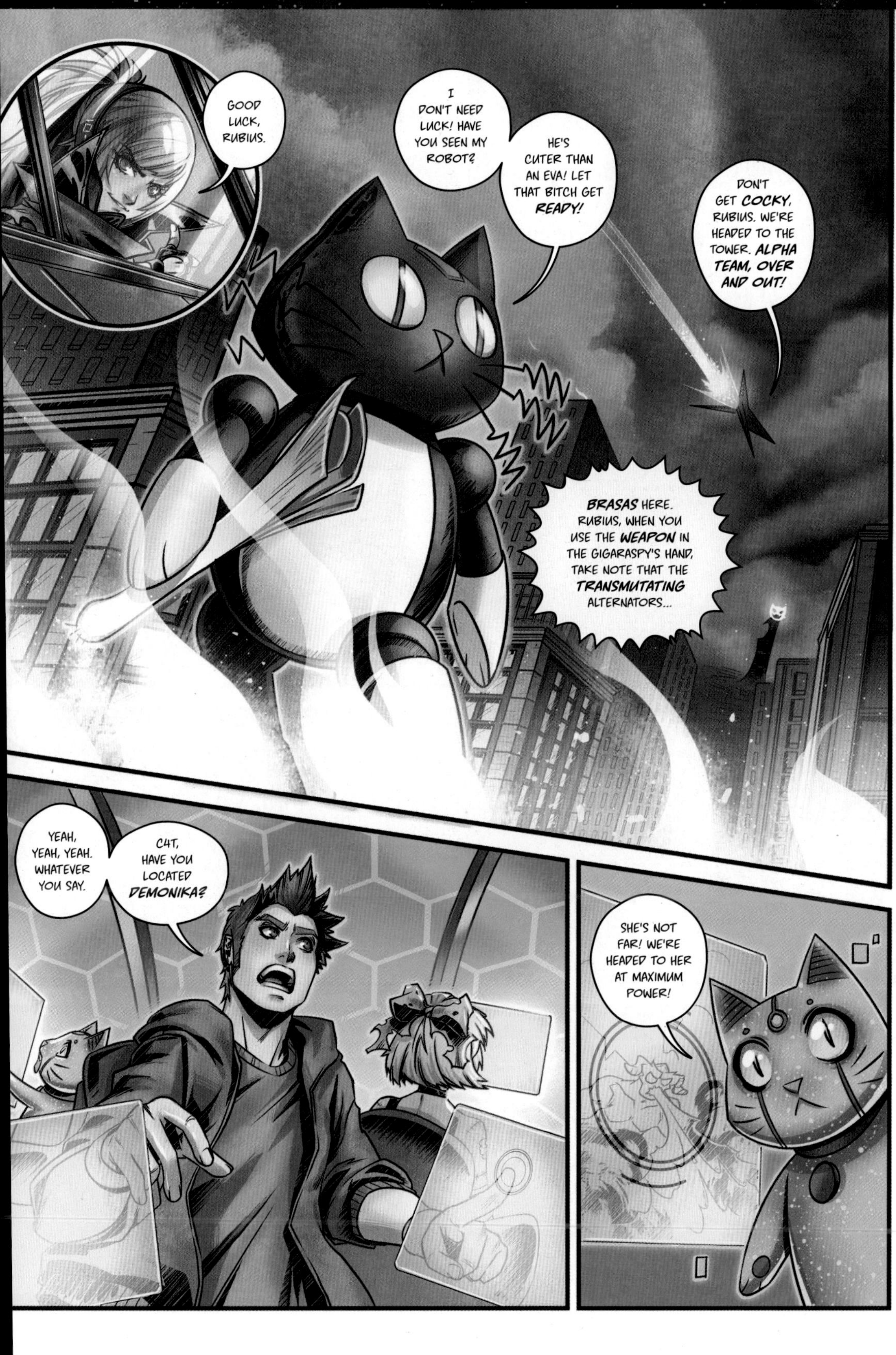
GOOD LUCK, RUBIUS.
I DON'T NEED LUCK! HAVE YOU SEEN MY ROBOT?
HE'S CUTER THAN AN EVA! LET THAT BITCH GET READY!
DON'T GET COCKY, RUBIUS. WE'RE HEADED TO THE TOWER. ALPHA TEAM, OVER AND OUT!
BRASAS HERE. RUBIUS, WHEN YOU USE THE WEAPON IN THE GIGARASPY'S HAND, TAKE NOTE THAT THE TRANSMUTATING ALTERNATORS...
YEAH, YEAH, YEAH. WHATEVER YOU SAY.
C4T, HAVE YOU LOCATED DEMONIKA?
SHE'S NOT FAR! WE'RE HEADED TO HER AT MAXIMUM POWER!

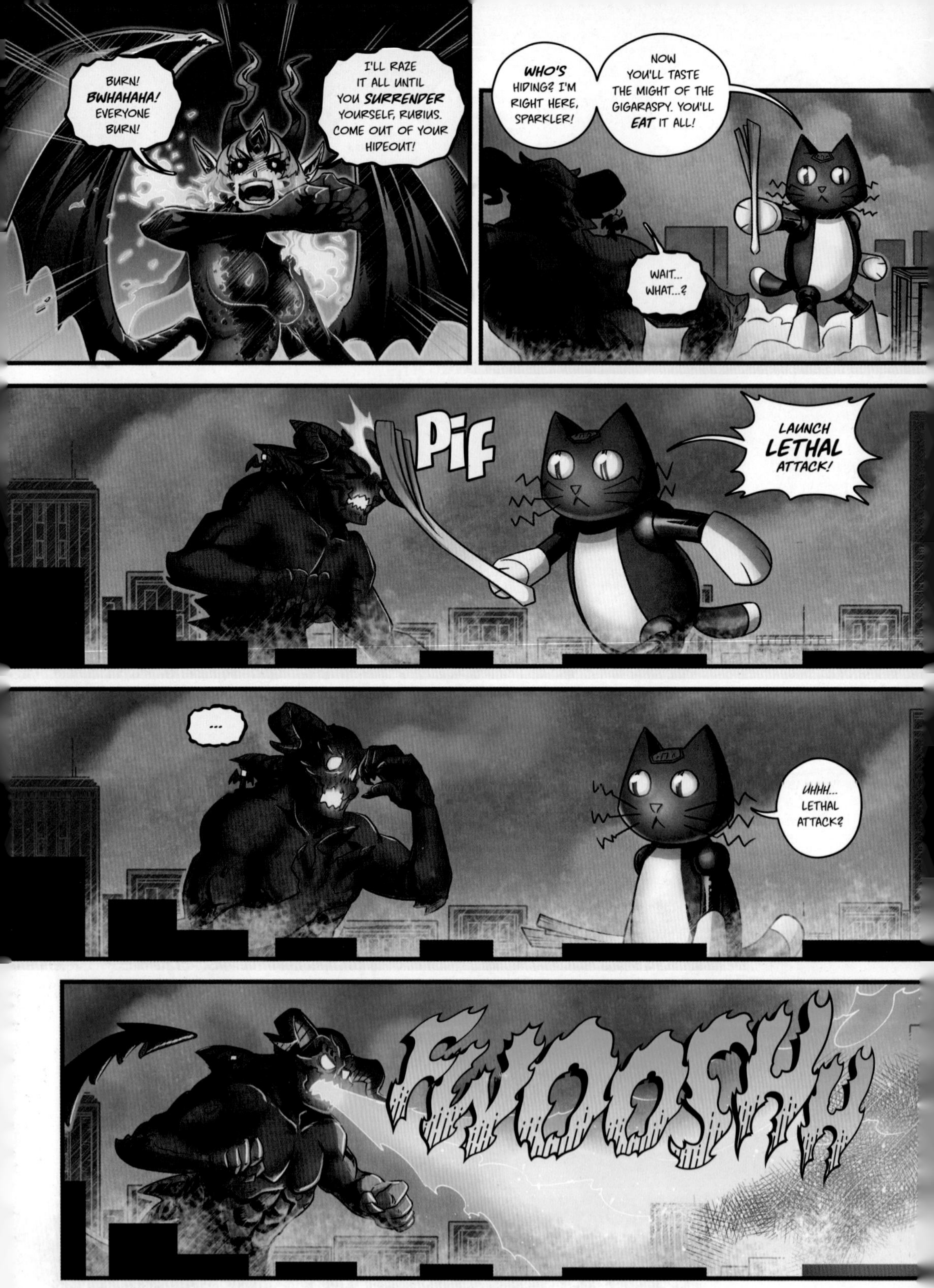

BURN! BWHAHAHA! EVERYONE BURN!
I'LL RAZE IT ALL UNTIL YOU SURRENDER YOURSELF, RUBIUS. COME OUT OF YOUR HIDEOUT!
WHO'S HIDING? I'M RIGHT HERE, SPARKLER!
NOW YOU'LL TASTE THE MIGHT OF THE GIGARASPY. YOU'LL EAT IT ALL!
WAIT... WHAT...?
PIF
LAUNCH LETHAL ATTACK!
...
UHHH... LETHAL ATTACK?
FWOOSH

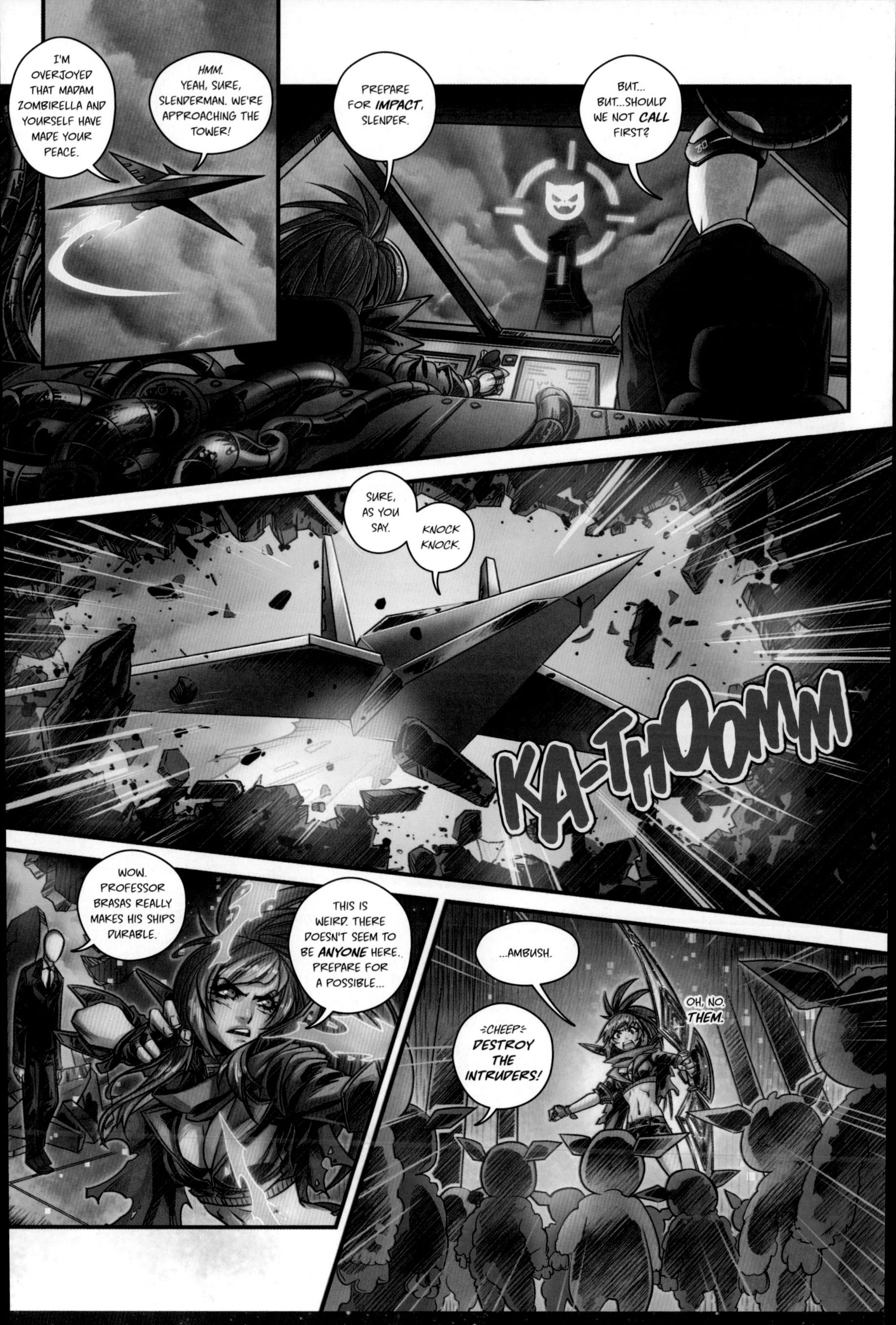
I'M OVERJOYED THAT MADAM ZOMBIRELLA AND YOURSELF HAVE MADE YOUR PEACE.
HMM. YEAH, SURE, SLENDERMAN. WE'RE APPROACHING THE TOWER!
PREPARE FOR IMPACT, SLENDER.
BUT... BUT...SHOULD WE NOT CALL FIRST?
SURE, AS YOU SAY.
KNOCK KNOCK.
KA-THOOMM
WOW. PROFESSOR BRASAS REALLY MAKES HIS SHIPS DURABLE.
THIS IS WEIRD. THERE DOESN'T SEEM TO BE ANYONE HERE.. PREPARE FOR A POSSIBLE...
...AMBUSH.
OH, NO. THEM.
=CHEEP= DESTROY THE INTRUDERS!

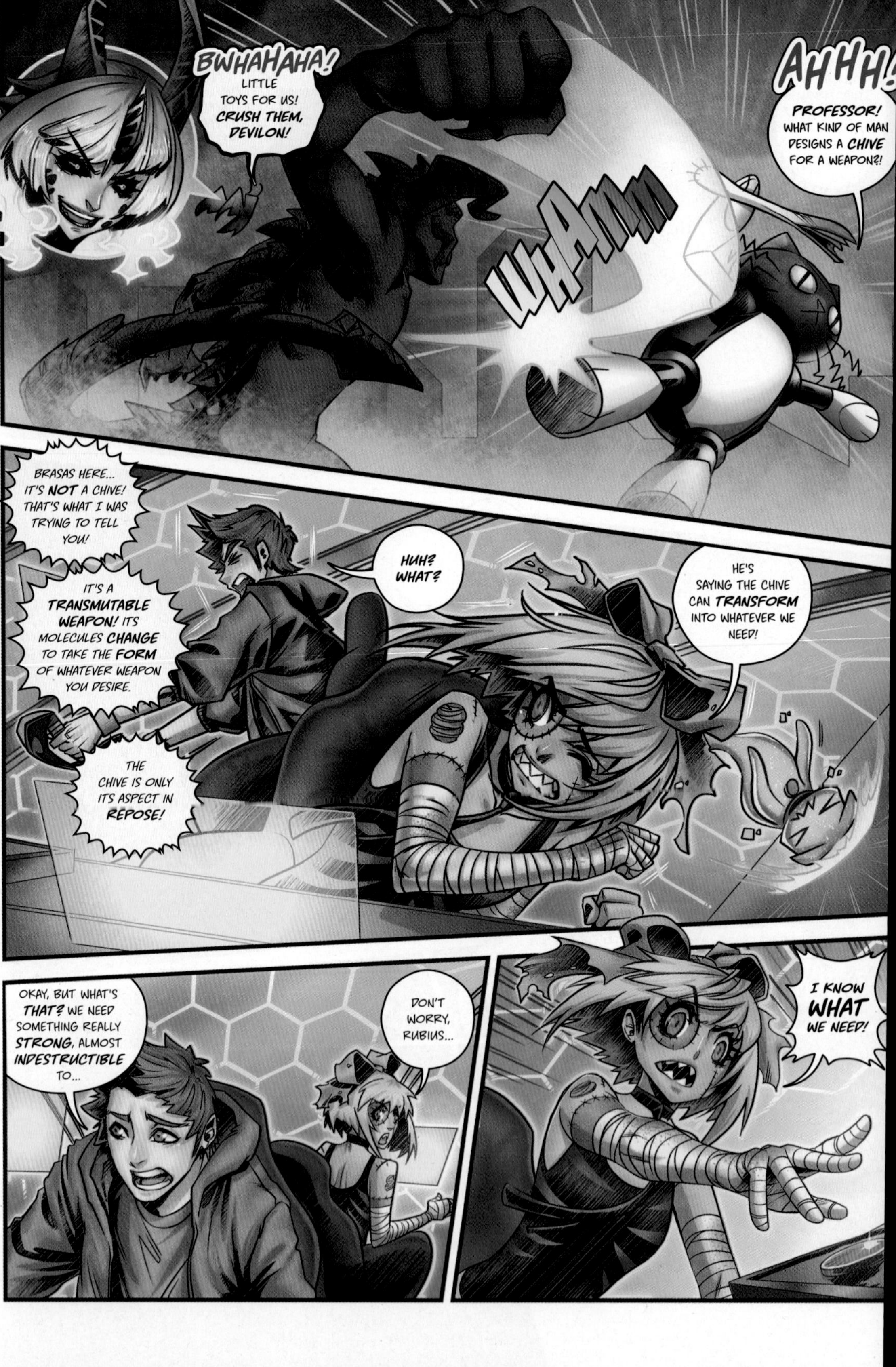
BWHAHAHA!
LITTLE TOYS FOR US! CRUSH THEM, DEVILON!
AHHH!
PROFESSOR! WHAT KIND OF MAN DESIGNS A CHIVE FOR A WEAPON?!
WHAMM
BRASAS HERE... IT'S NOT A CHIVE! THAT'S WHAT I WAS TRYING TO TELL YOU!
IT'S A TRANSMUTABLE WEAPON! ITS MOLECULES CHANGE TO TAKE THE FORM OF WHATEVER WEAPON YOU DESIRE.
THE CHIVE IS ONLY ITS ASPECT IN REPOSE!
HUH? WHAT?
HE'S SAYING THE CHIVE CAN TRANSFORM INTO WHATEVER WE NEED!
OKAY, BUT WHAT'S THAT? WE NEED SOMETHING REALLY STRONG, ALMOST INDESTRUCTIBLE TO...
DON'T WORRY, RUBIUS...
I KNOW WHAT WE NEED!

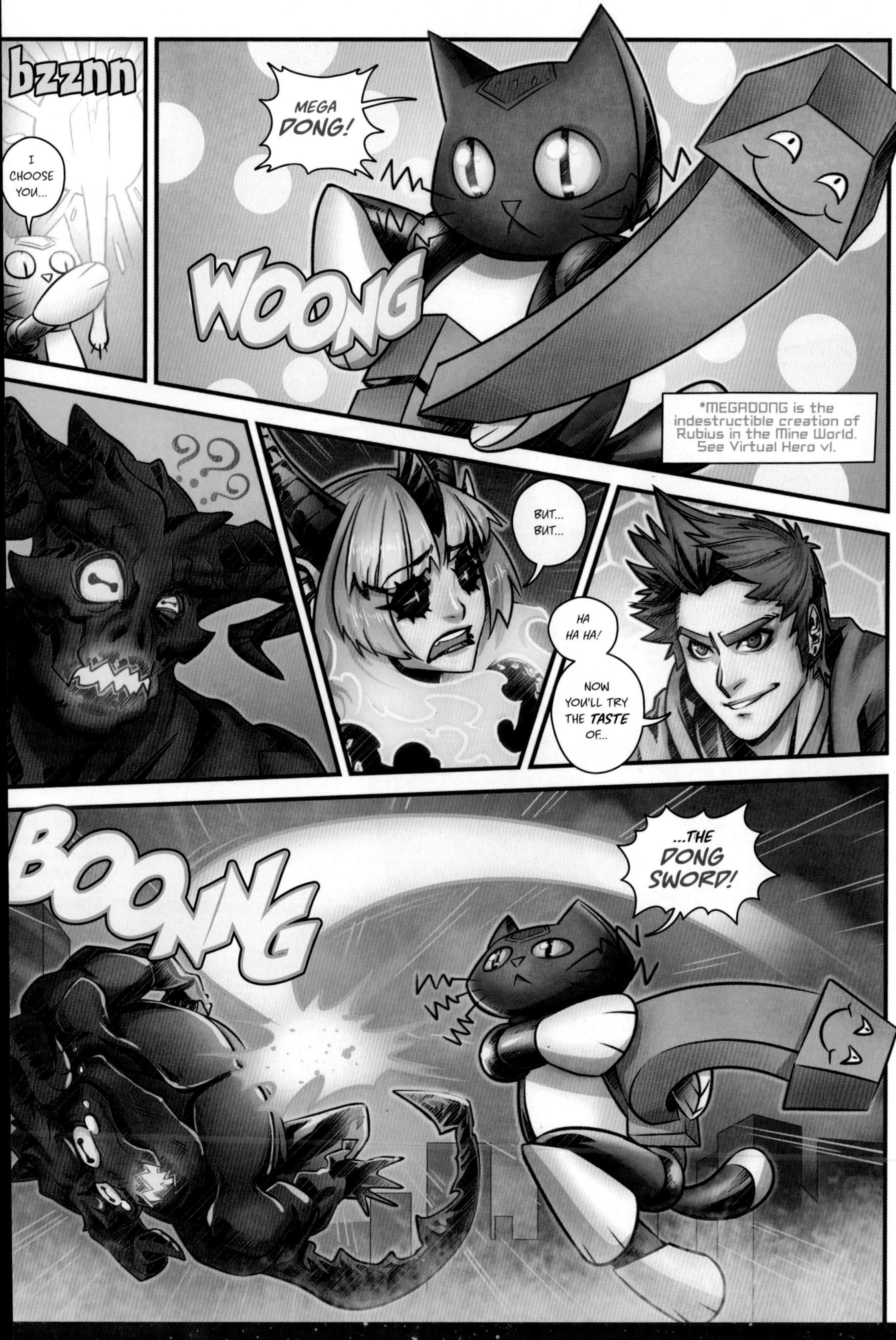
bzznn
I CHOOSE YOU...
MEGA DONG!
WOONG
*MEGADONG is the indestructible creation of Rubius in the Mine World. See Virtual Hero v1.
BUT... BUT...
HA HA HA!
NOW YOU'LL TRY THE TASTE OF...
BOONNG
...THE DONG SWORD!

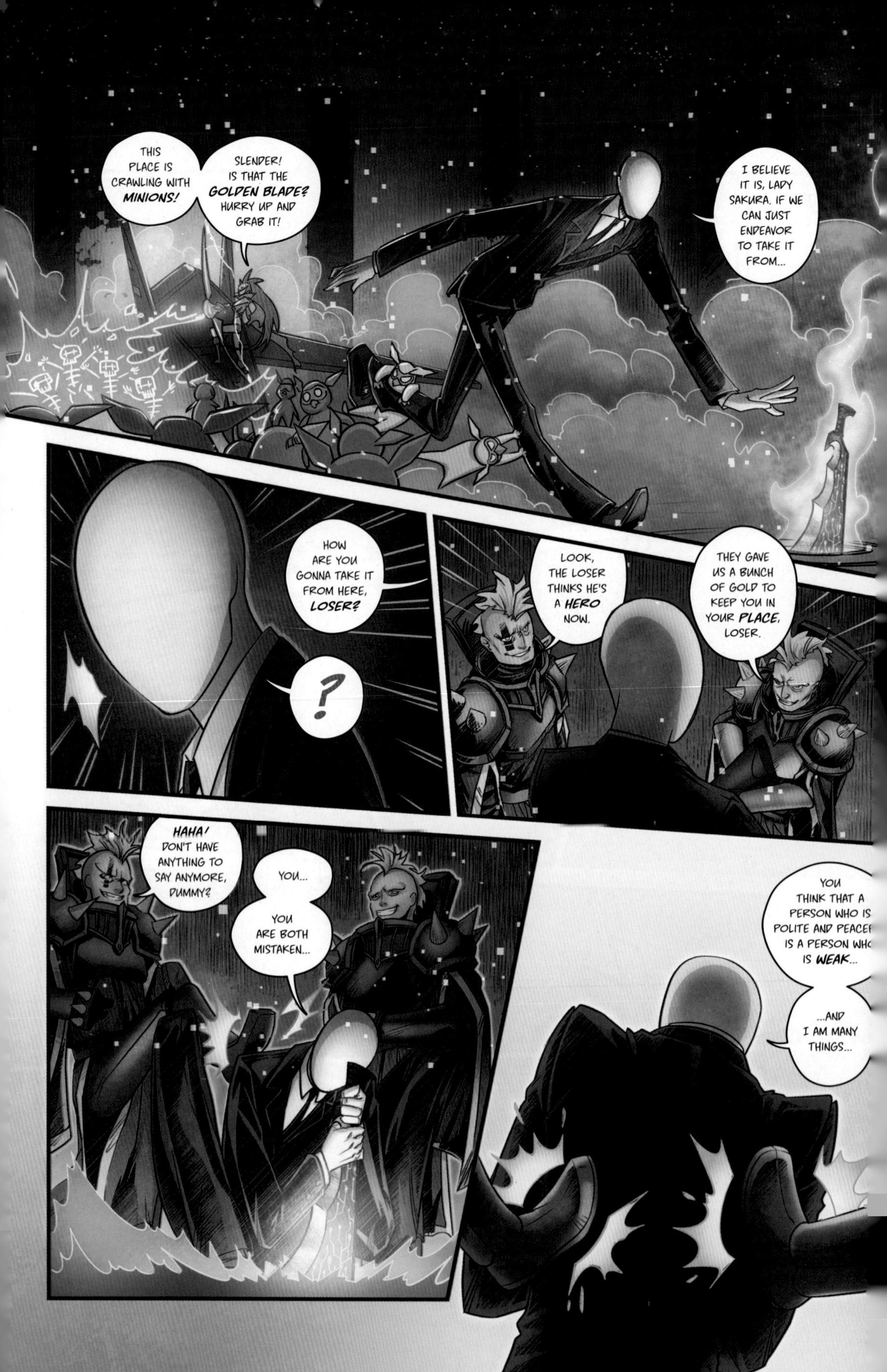
THIS PLACE IS CRAWLING WITH MINIONS!
SLENDER! IS THAT THE GOLDEN BLADE? HURRY UP AND GRAB IT!
I BELIEVE IT IS, LADY SAKURA. IF WE CAN JUST ENDEAVOR TO TAKE IT FROM...
HOW ARE YOU GONNA TAKE IT FROM HERE, LOSER?
?
LOOK, THE LOSER THINKS HE'S A HERO NOW.
THEY GAVE US A BUNCH OF GOLD TO KEEP YOU IN YOUR PLACE, LOSER.
HAHA! DON'T HAVE ANYTHING TO SAY ANYMORE, DUMMY?
YOU...
YOU ARE BOTH MISTAKEN...
YOU THINK THAT A PERSON WHO IS POLITE AND PEACEF IS A PERSON WHO IS WEAK...
...AND I AM MANY THINGS...

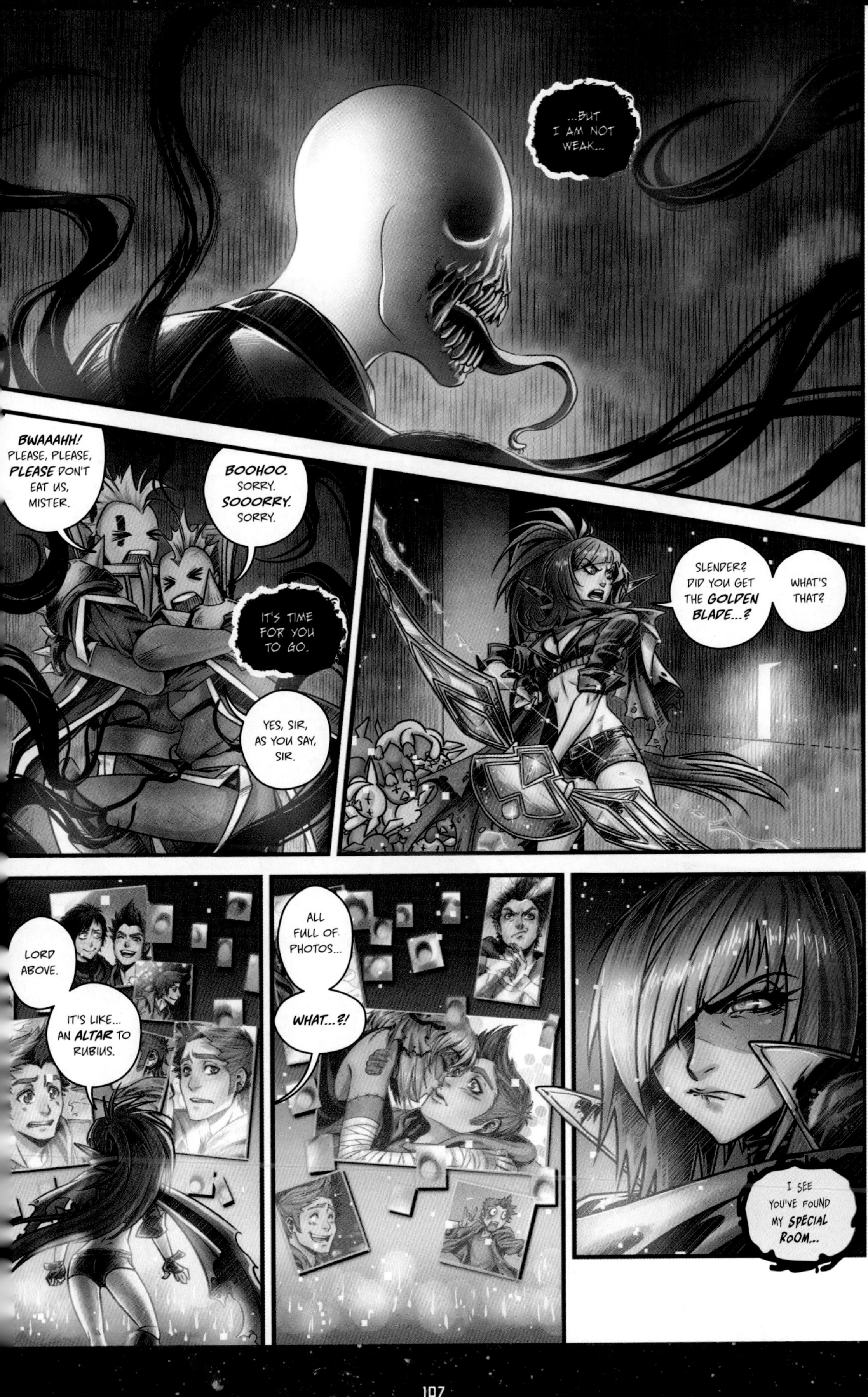
...BUT I AM NOT WEAK...
BWAAAHH! PLEASE, PLEASE, PLEASE DON'T EAT US, MISTER.
BOOHOO. SORRY. SOOORRY. SORRY.
IT'S TIME FOR YOU TO GO.
YES, SIR, AS YOU SAY, SIR.
SLENDER? DID YOU GET THE GOLDEN BLADE...?
WHAT'S THAT?
LORD ABOVE.
IT'S LIKE... AN ALTAR TO RUBIUS.
ALL FULL OF PHOTOS...
WHAT...?!
I SEE YOU'VE FOUND MY SPECIAL ROOM...

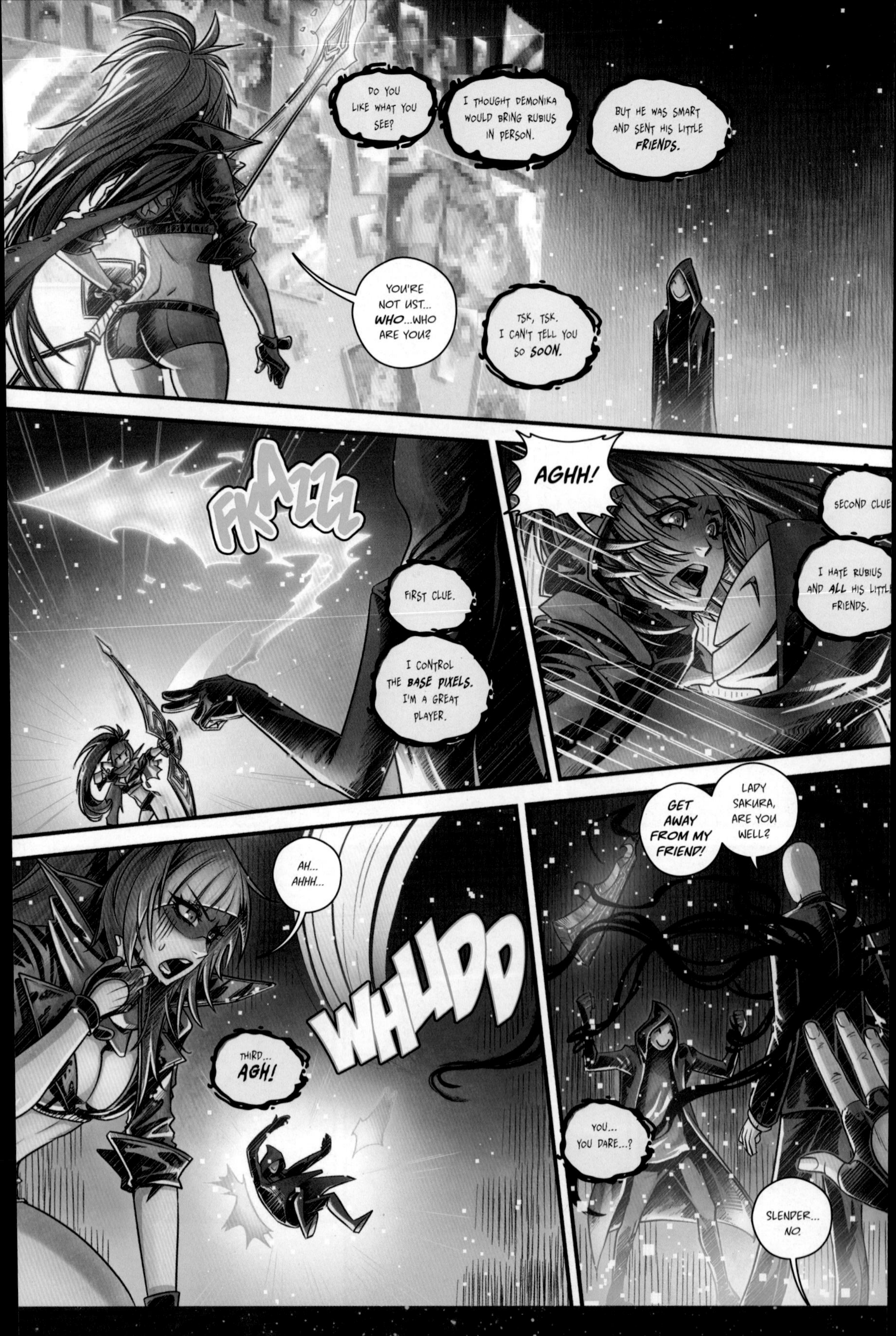

DO YOU LIKE WHAT YOU SEE?
I THOUGHT DEMONIKA WOULD BRING RUBIUS IN PERSON.
BUT HE WAS SMART AND SENT HIS LITTLE FRIENDS.
YOU'RE NOT UST... WHO...WHO ARE YOU?
TSK, TSK. I CAN'T TELL YOU SO SOON.
FKAZZZ
FIRST CLUE.
I CONTROL THE BASE PIXELS. I'M A GREAT PLAYER.
AGHH!
SECOND CLUE.
I HATE RUBIUS AND ALL HIS LITTLE FRIENDS.
AH... AHHH...
WHUDD
THIRD... AGH!
GET AWAY FROM MY FRIEND!
LADY SAKURA, ARE YOU WELL?
YOU... YOU DARE...?
SLENDER... NO.

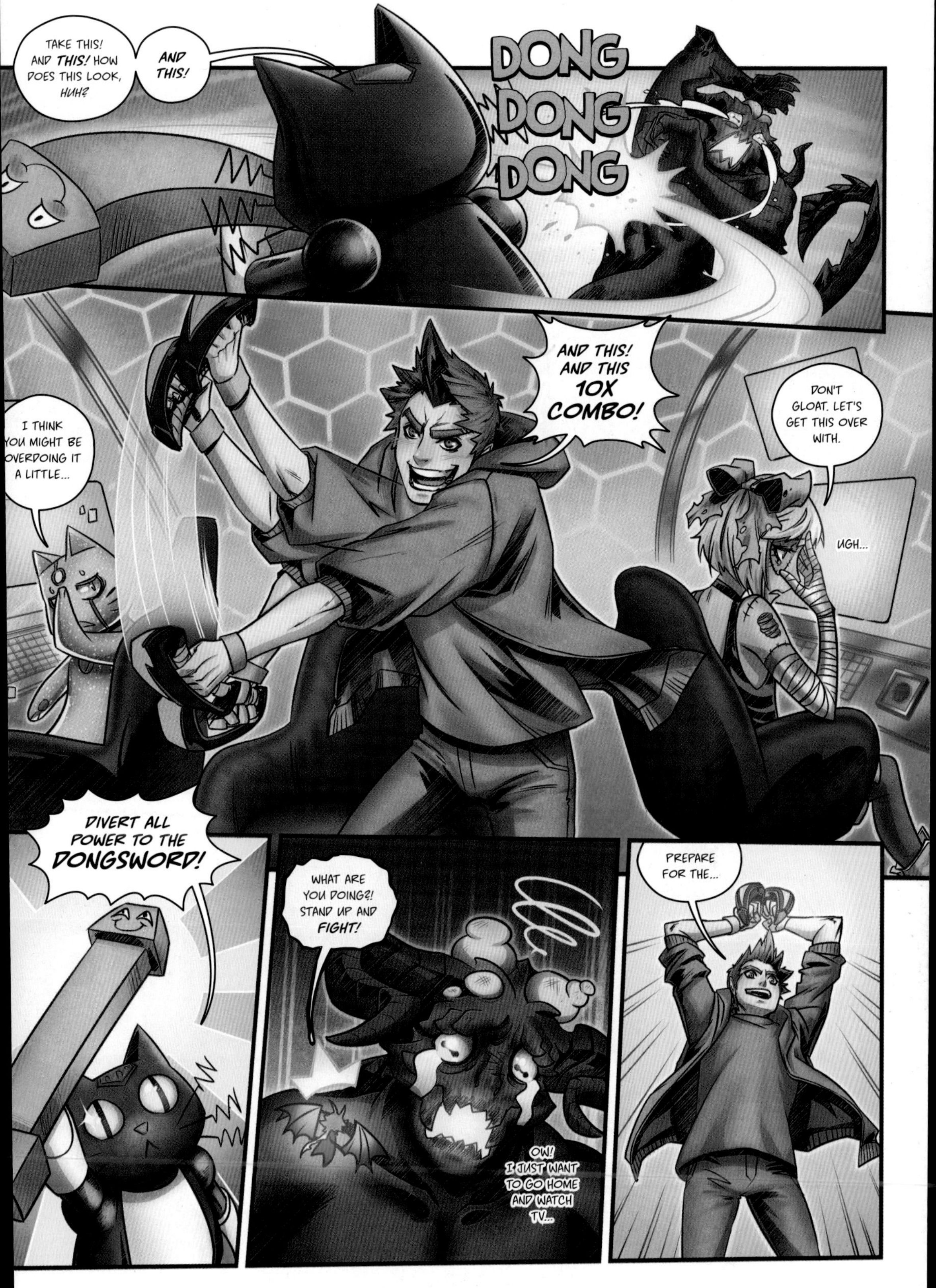
TAKE THIS! AND THIS! HOW DOES THIS LOOK, HUH?
AND THIS!
DONG DONG DONG
I THINK YOU MIGHT BE OVERDOING IT A LITTLE...
AND THIS! AND THIS 10X COMBO!
DON'T GLOAT. LET'S GET THIS OVER WITH.
UGH...
DIVERT ALL POWER TO THE DONGSWORD!
WHAT ARE YOU DOING?! STAND UP AND FIGHT!
OW! I JUST WANT TO GO HOME AND WATCH TV...
PREPARE FOR THE...

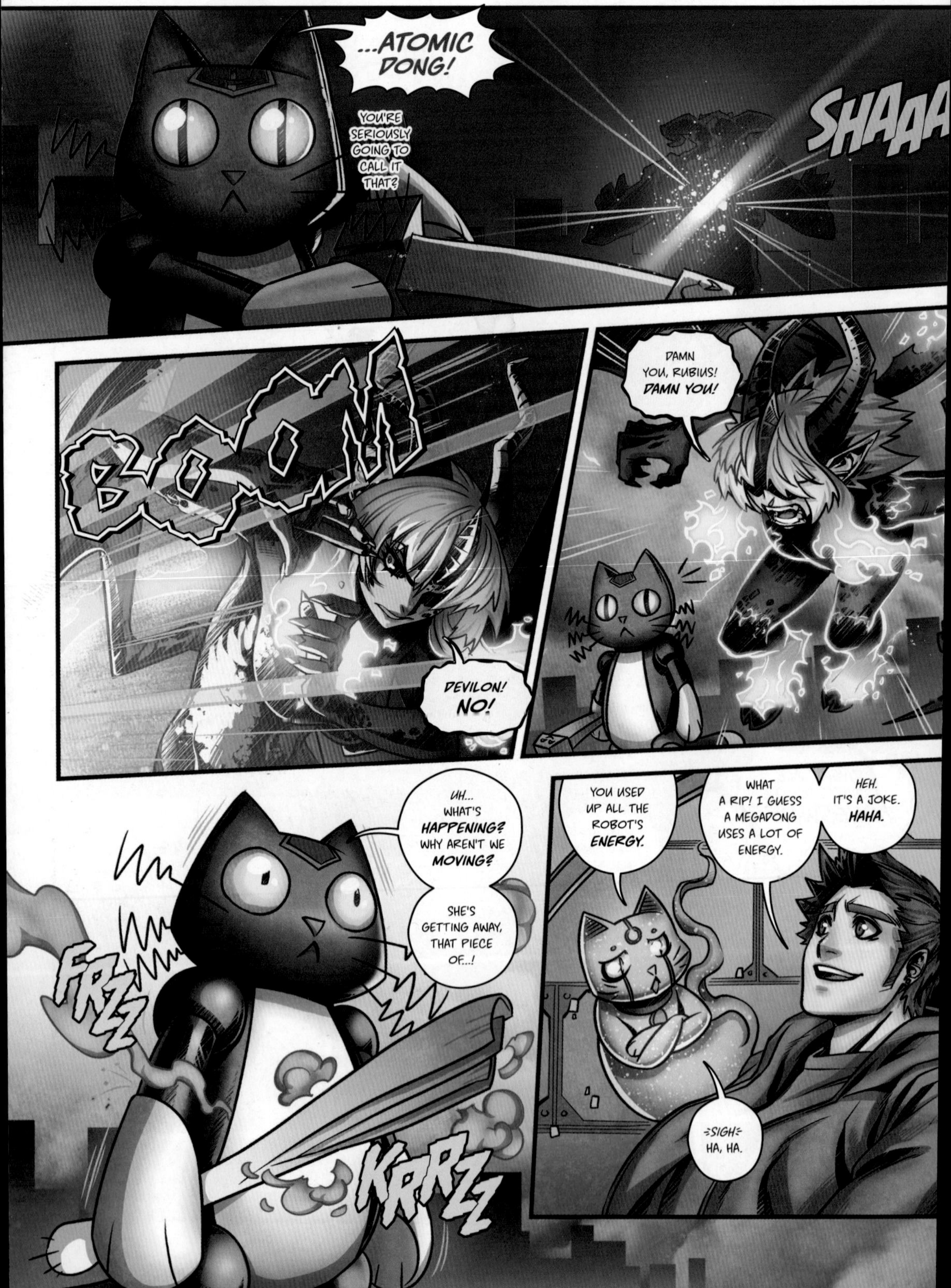

...ATOMIC DONG!
YOU'RE SERIOUSLY GOING TO CALL IT THAT?
SHAAA
BOOM
DEVILON! NO!
DAMN YOU, RUBIUS! DAMN YOU!
UH... WHAT'S HAPPENING? WHY AREN'T WE MOVING?
SHE'S GETTING AWAY, THAT PIECE OF...!
FRZZ
KRRZZ
YOU USED UP ALL THE ROBOT'S ENERGY.
WHAT A RIP! I GUESS A MEGADONG USES A LOT OF ENERGY.
HEH. IT'S A JOKE. HAHA.
=SIGH= HA, HA.

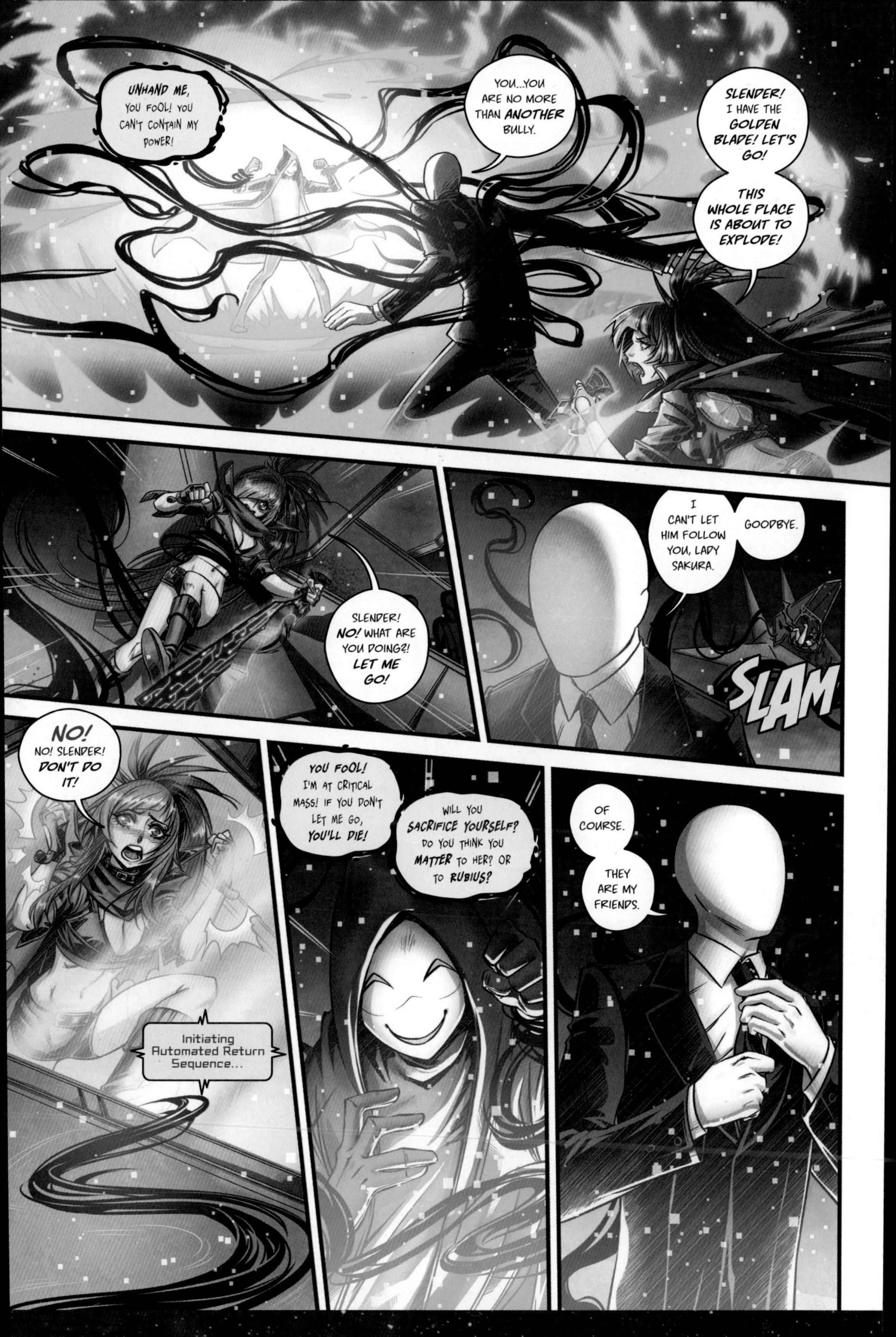
UNHAND ME, YOU FOOL! YOU CAN'T CONTAIN MY POWER!
YOU...YOU ARE NO MORE THAN ANOTHER BULLY.
SLENDER! I HAVE THE GOLDEN BLADE! LET'S GO!
THIS WHOLE PLACE IS ABOUT TO EXPLODE!
SLENDER! NO! WHAT ARE YOU DOING?! LET ME GO!
I CAN'T LET HIM FOLLOW YOU, LADY SAKURA.
GOODBYE.
SLAM
NO! NO! SLENDER! DON'T DO IT!
Initiating Automated Return Sequence...
YOU FOOL! I'M AT CRITICAL MASS! IF YOU DON'T LET ME GO, YOU'LL DIE!
WILL YOU SACRIFICE YOURSELF? DO YOU THINK YOU MATTER TO HER? OR TO RUBIUS?
OF COURSE.
THEY ARE MY FRIENDS.

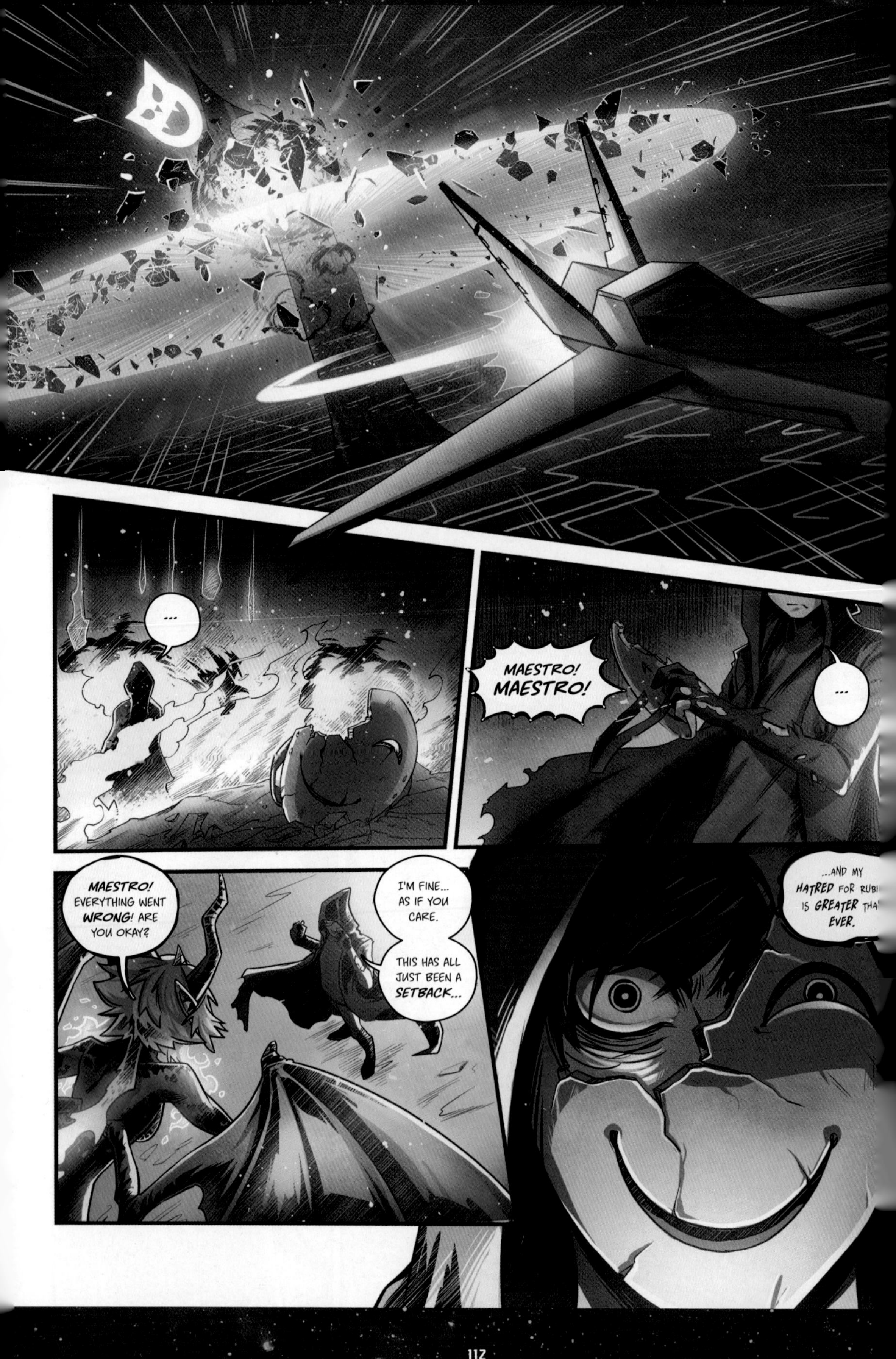
...
MAESTRO! MAESTRO!
...
MAESTRO! EVERYTHING WENT WRONG! ARE YOU OKAY?
I'M FINE... AS IF YOU CARE.
THIS HAS ALL JUST BEEN A SETBACK...
...AND MY HATRED FOR RUBI
IS GREATER THA
EVER.

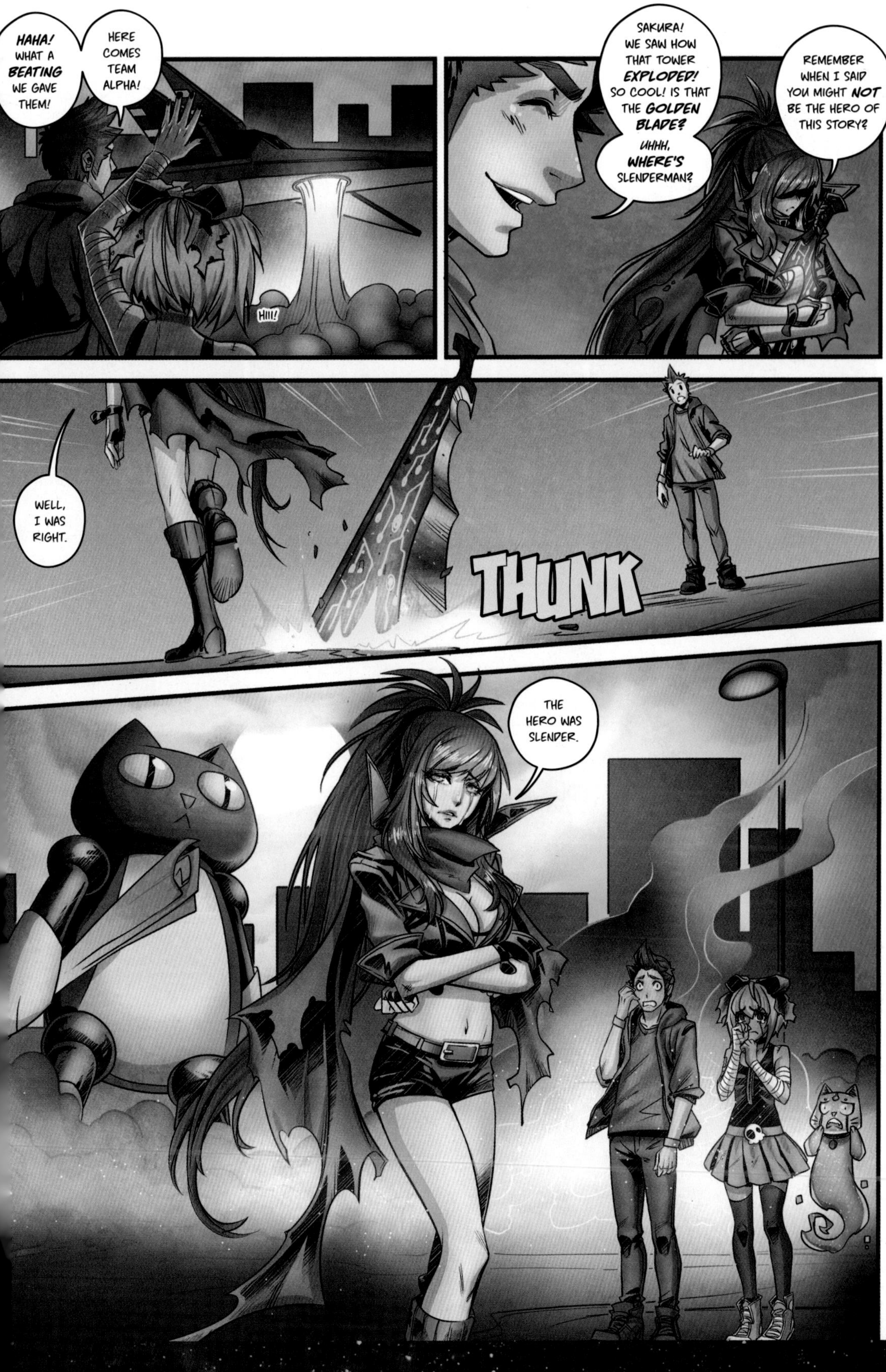

HAHA! WHAT A BEATING WE GAVE THEM!
HERE COMES TEAM ALPHA!
HIII!
SAKURA! WE SAW HOW THAT TOWER EXPLODED! SO COOL! IS THAT THE GOLDEN BLADE?
UHHH, WHERE'S SLENDERMAN?
REMEMBER WHEN I SAID YOU MIGHT NOT BE THE HERO OF THIS STORY?
WELL, I WAS RIGHT.
THUNK
THE HERO WAS SLENDER.

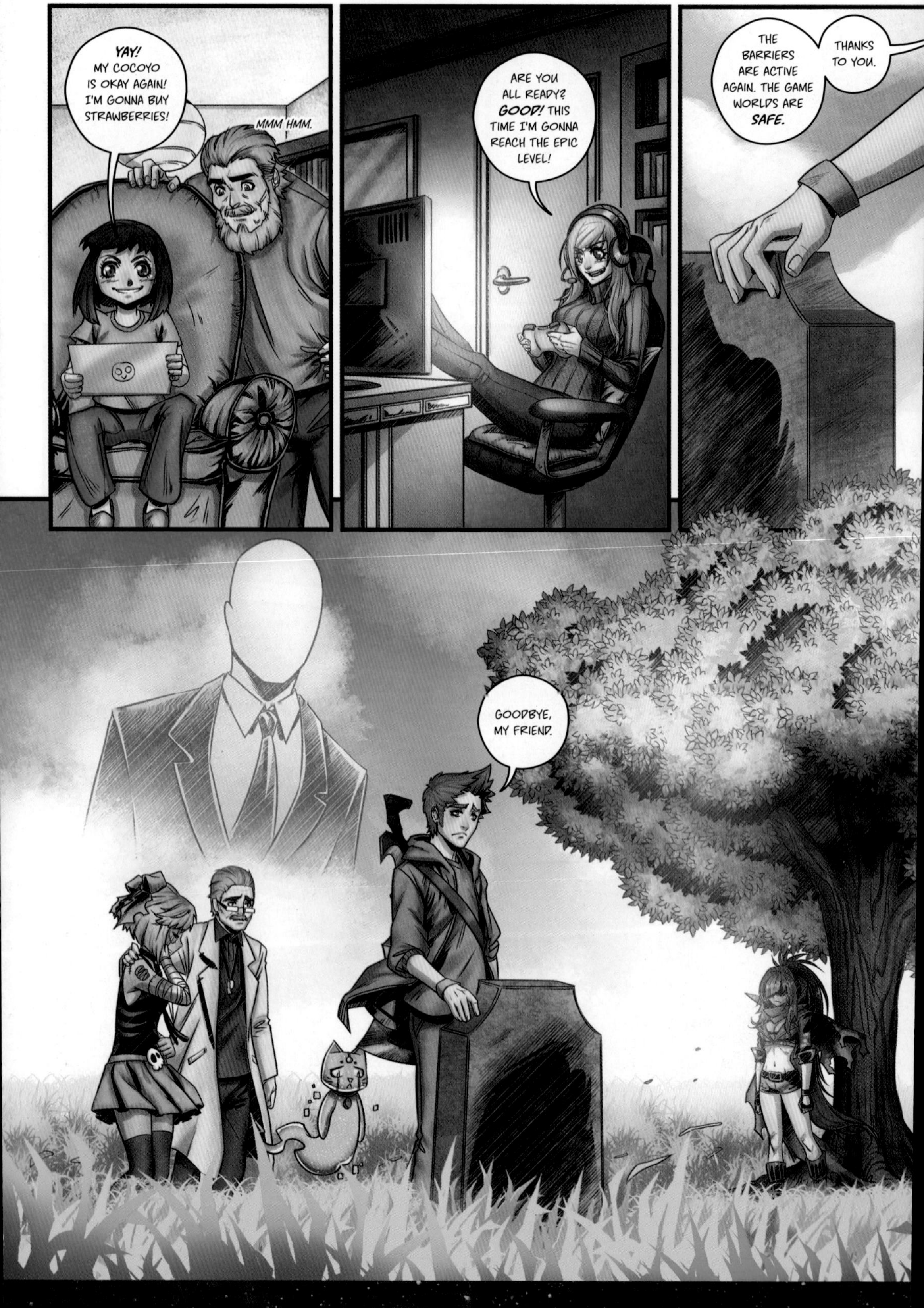
YAY!
MY COCOYO IS OKAY AGAIN! I'M GONNA BUY STRAWBERRIES!
MMM HMM.
ARE YOU ALL READY? GOOD! THIS TIME I'M GONNA REACH THE EPIC LEVEL!
THE BARRIERS ARE ACTIVE AGAIN. THE GAME WORLDS ARE SAFE.
THANKS TO YOU.
GOODBYE, MY FRIEND.

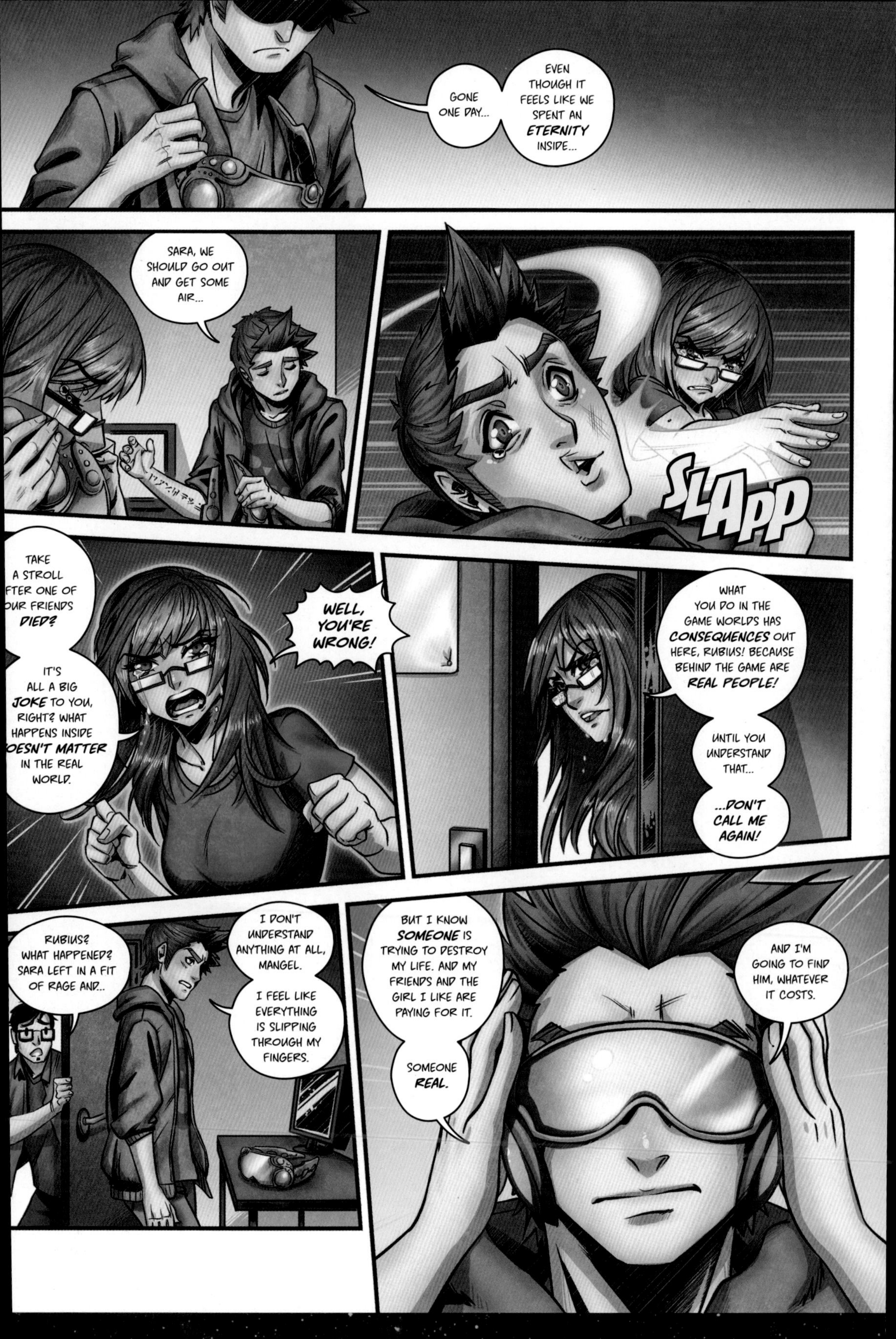
GONE ONE DAY...
EVEN THOUGH IT FEELS LIKE WE SPENT AN ETERNITY INSIDE...
SARA, WE SHOULD GO OUT AND GET SOME AIR...
SLAPP
TAKE A STROLL FTER ONE OF OUR FRIENDS DIED?
IT'S ALL A BIG JOKE TO YOU, RIGHT? WHAT HAPPENS INSIDE OESN'T MATTER IN THE REAL WORLD.
WELL, YOU'RE WRONG!
WHAT YOU DO IN THE GAME WORLDS HAS CONSEQUENCES OUT HERE, RUBIUS! BECAUSE BEHIND THE GAME ARE REAL PEOPLE!
UNTIL YOU UNDERSTAND THAT...
...DON'T CALL ME AGAIN!
RUBIUS? WHAT HAPPENED? SARA LEFT IN A FIT OF RAGE AND...
I DON'T UNDERSTAND ANYTHING AT ALL, MANGEL.
I FEEL LIKE EVERYTHING IS SLIPPING THROUGH MY FINGERS.
BUT I KNOW SOMEONE IS TRYING TO DESTROY MY LIFE. AND MY FRIENDS AND THE GIRL I LIKE ARE PAYING FOR IT.
SOMEONE REAL.
AND I'M GOING TO FIND HIM, WHATEVER IT COSTS.

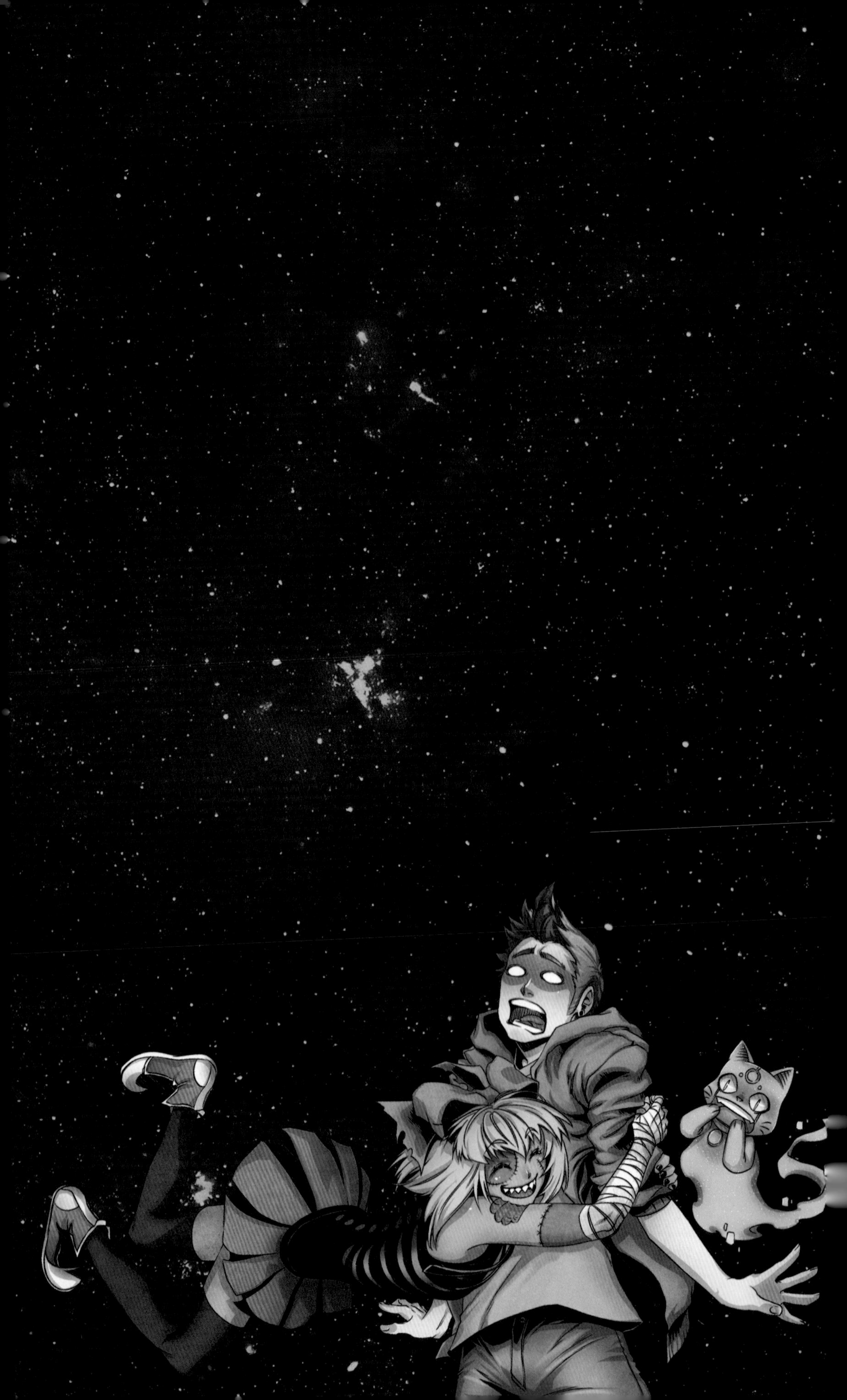

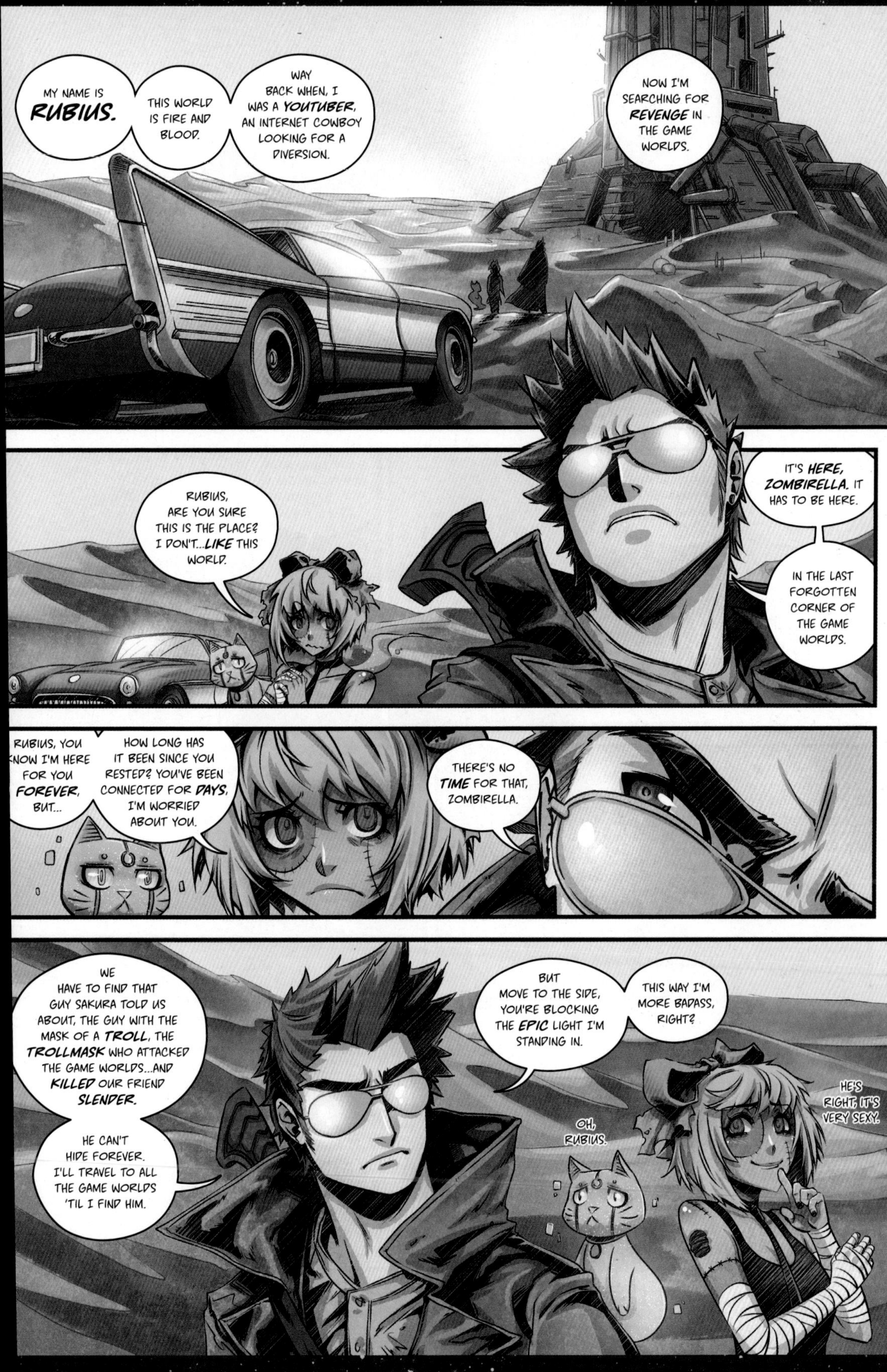
MY NAME IS RUBIUS.
THIS WORLD IS FIRE AND BLOOD.
WAY BACK WHEN, I WAS A YOUTUBER, AN INTERNET COWBOY LOOKING FOR A DIVERSION.
NOW I'M SEARCHING FOR REVENGE IN THE GAME WORLDS.
RUBIUS, ARE YOU SURE THIS IS THE PLACE? I DON'T...LIKE THIS WORLD.
IT'S HERE, ZOMBIRELLA. IT HAS TO BE HERE.
IN THE LAST FORGOTTEN CORNER OF THE GAME WORLDS.
RUBIUS, YOU KNOW I'M HERE FOR YOU FOREVER, BUT...
HOW LONG HAS IT BEEN SINCE YOU RESTED? YOU'VE BEEN CONNECTED FOR DAYS, I'M WORRIED ABOUT YOU.
THERE'S NO TIME FOR THAT, ZOMBIRELLA.
WE HAVE TO FIND THAT GUY SAKURA TOLD US ABOUT, THE GUY WITH THE MASK OF A TROLL, THE TROLLMASK WHO ATTACKED THE GAME WORLDS...AND KILLED OUR FRIEND SLENDER.
HE CAN'T HIDE FOREVER. I'LL TRAVEL TO ALL THE GAME WORLDS 'TIL I FIND HIM.
BUT MOVE TO THE SIDE, YOU'RE BLOCKING THE EPIC LIGHT I'M STANDING IN.
THIS WAY I'M MORE BADASS, RIGHT?
OH, RUBIUS.
HE'S RIGHT, IT'S VERY SEXY.

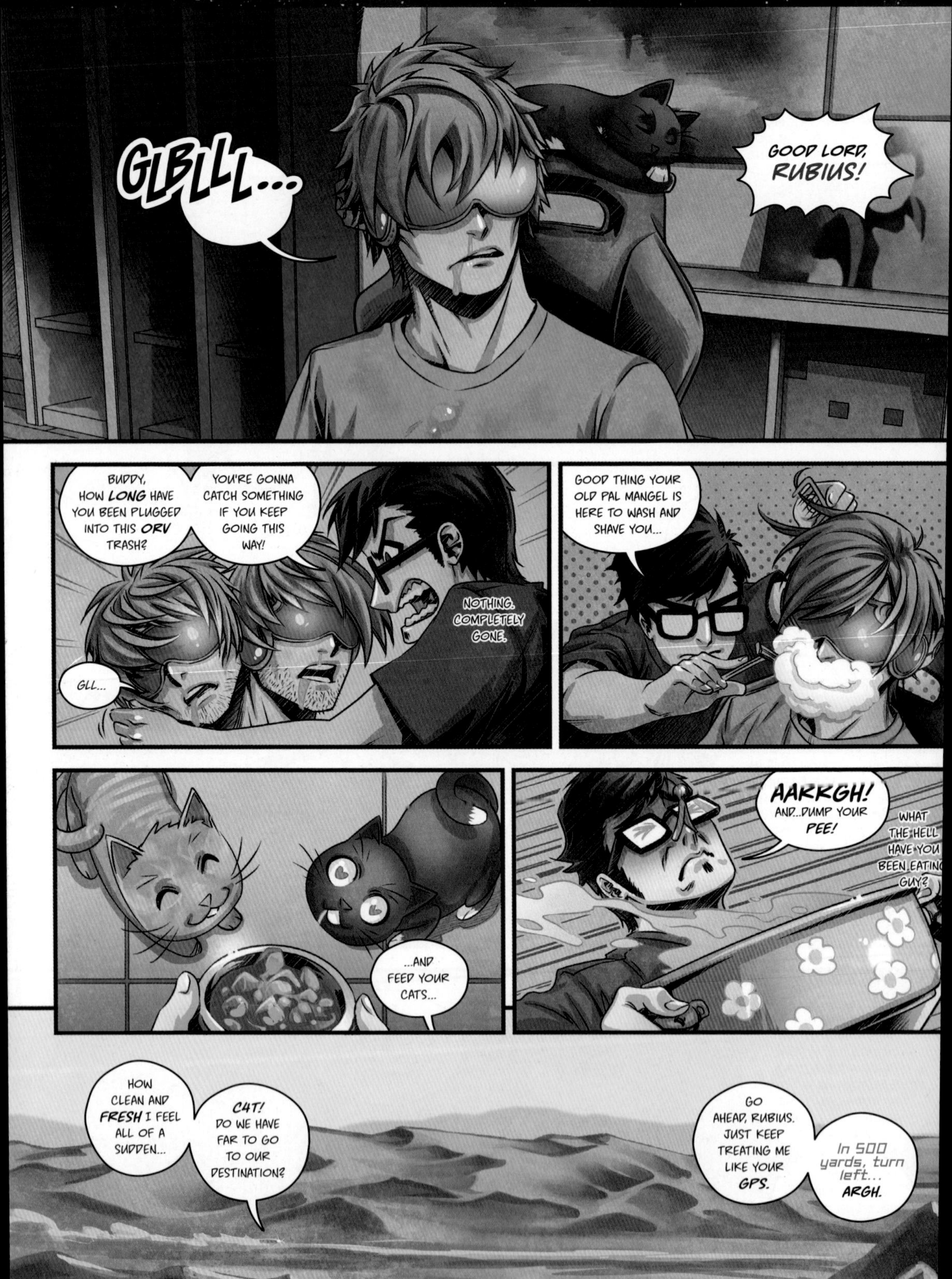

GLBLLL...
GOOD LORD, RUBIUS!
BUDDY, HOW LONG HAVE YOU BEEN PLUGGED INTO THIS ORV TRASH?
YOU'RE GONNA CATCH SOMETHING IF YOU KEEP GOING THIS WAY!
NOTHING. COMPLETELY GONE.
GLL...
GOOD THING YOUR OLD PAL MANGEL IS HERE TO WASH AND SHAVE YOU...
...AND FEED YOUR CATS...
AARKGH!
AND...DUMP YOUR PEE!
WHAT THE HELL HAVE YOU BEEN EATING GUY?
HOW CLEAN AND FRESH I FEEL ALL OF A SUDDEN...
C4T! DO WE HAVE FAR TO GO TO OUR DESTINATION?
GO AHEAD, RUBIUS. JUST KEEP TREATING ME LIKE YOUR GPS.
In 500 yards, turn left... ARGH.

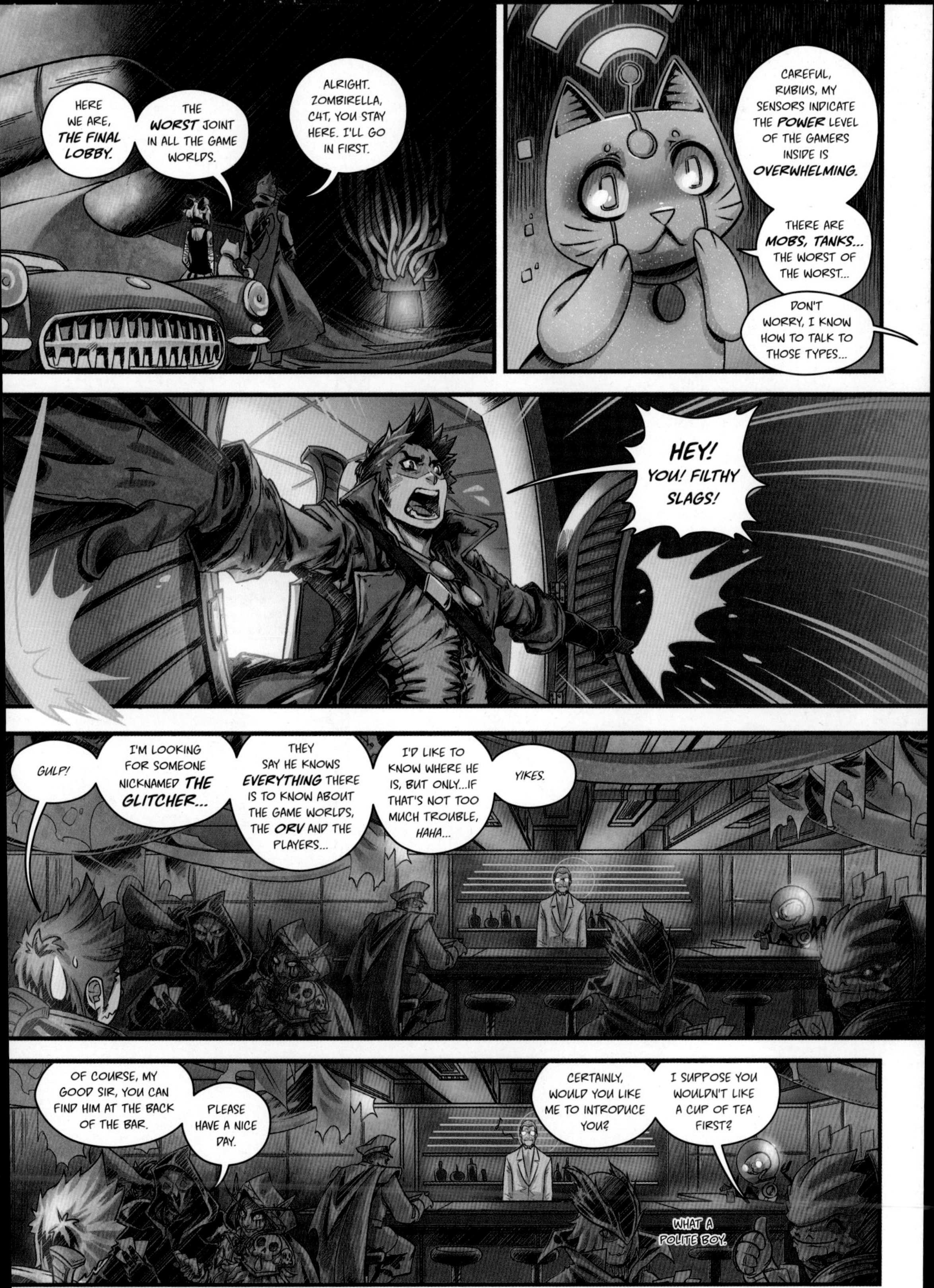
HERE WE ARE, THE FINAL LOBBY.
THE WORST JOINT IN ALL THE GAME WORLDS.
ALRIGHT. ZOMBIRELLA, C4T, YOU STAY HERE. I'LL GO IN FIRST.
CAREFUL, RUBIUS, MY SENSORS INDICATE THE POWER LEVEL OF THE GAMERS INSIDE IS OVERWHELMING.
THERE ARE MOBS, TANKS... THE WORST OF THE WORST...
DON'T WORRY, I KNOW HOW TO TALK TO THOSE TYPES...
HEY! YOU! FILTHY SLAGS!
GULP!
I'M LOOKING FOR SOMEONE NICKNAMED THE GLITCHER...
THEY SAY HE KNOWS EVERYTHING THERE IS TO KNOW ABOUT THE GAME WORLDS, THE ORV AND THE PLAYERS...
I'D LIKE TO KNOW WHERE HE IS, BUT ONLY...IF THAT'S NOT TOO MUCH TROUBLE, HAHA...
YIKES.
OF COURSE, MY GOOD SIR, YOU CAN FIND HIM AT THE BACK OF THE BAR.
PLEASE HAVE A NICE DAY.
CERTAINLY, WOULD YOU LIKE ME TO INTRODUCE YOU?
I SUPPOSE YOU WOULDN'T LIKE A CUP OF TEA FIRST?
WHAT A POLITE BOY.

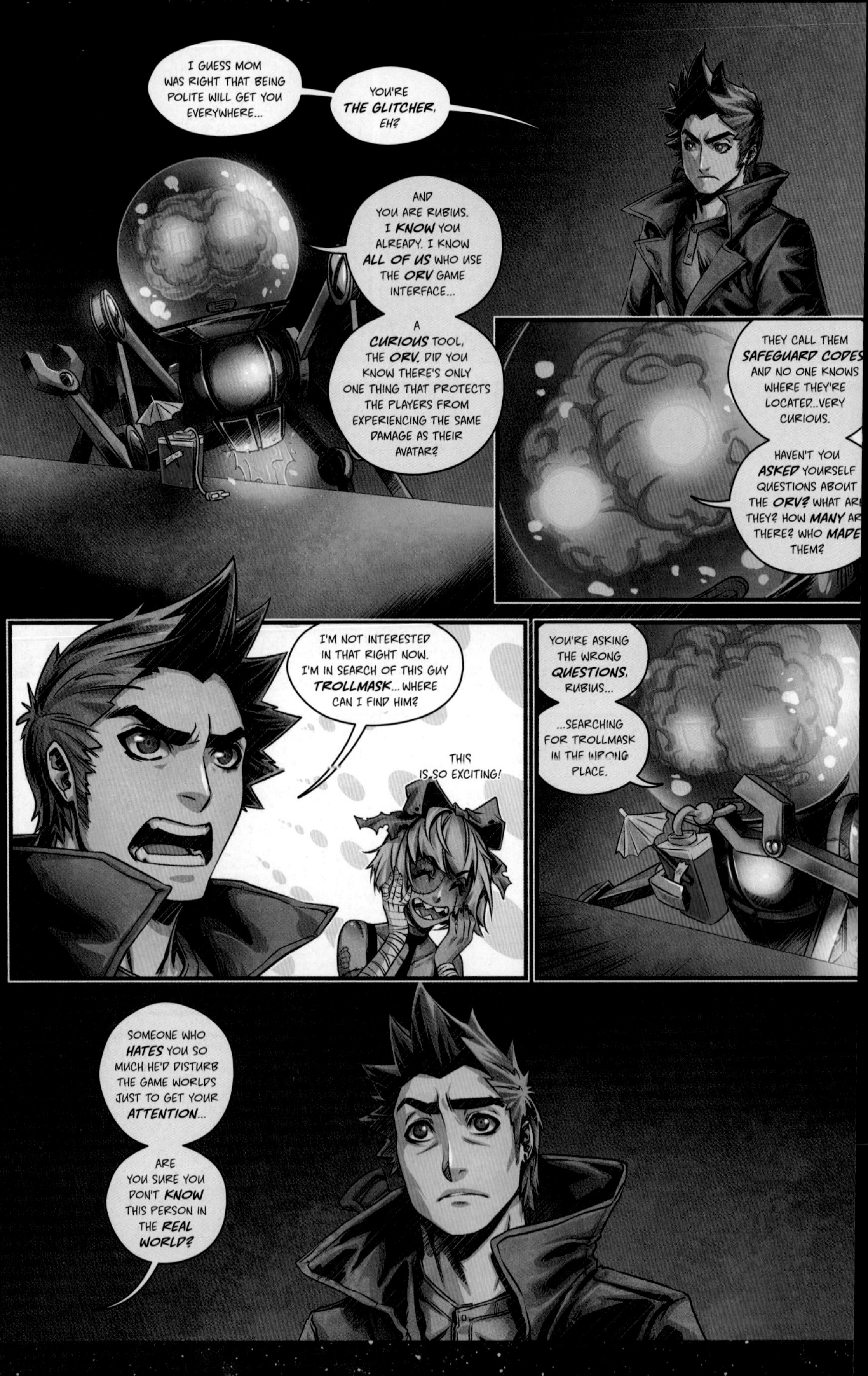
I GUESS MOM WAS RIGHT THAT BEING POLITE WILL GET YOU EVERYWHERE...
YOU'RE THE GLITCHER, EH?
AND YOU ARE RUBIUS. I KNOW YOU ALREADY. I KNOW ALL OF US WHO USE THE ORV GAME INTERFACE...
A CURIOUS TOOL, THE ORV. DID YOU KNOW THERE'S ONLY ONE THING THAT PROTECTS THE PLAYERS FROM EXPERIENCING THE SAME DAMAGE AS THEIR AVATAR?
THEY CALL THEM SAFEGUARD CODES AND NO ONE KNOWS WHERE THEY'RE LOCATED...VERY CURIOUS.
HAVEN'T YOU ASKED YOURSELF QUESTIONS ABOUT THE ORV? WHAT ARE THEY? HOW MANY ARE THERE? WHO MADE THEM?
I'M NOT INTERESTED IN THAT RIGHT NOW. I'M IN SEARCH OF THIS GUY TROLLMASK... WHERE CAN I FIND HIM?
THIS IS SO EXCITING!
YOU'RE ASKING THE WRONG QUESTIONS, RUBIUS...
...SEARCHING FOR TROLLMASK IN THE WRONG PLACE.
SOMEONE WHO HATES YOU SO MUCH HE'D DISTURB THE GAME WORLDS JUST TO GET YOUR ATTENTION...
ARE YOU SURE YOU DON'T KNOW THIS PERSON IN THE REAL WORLD?

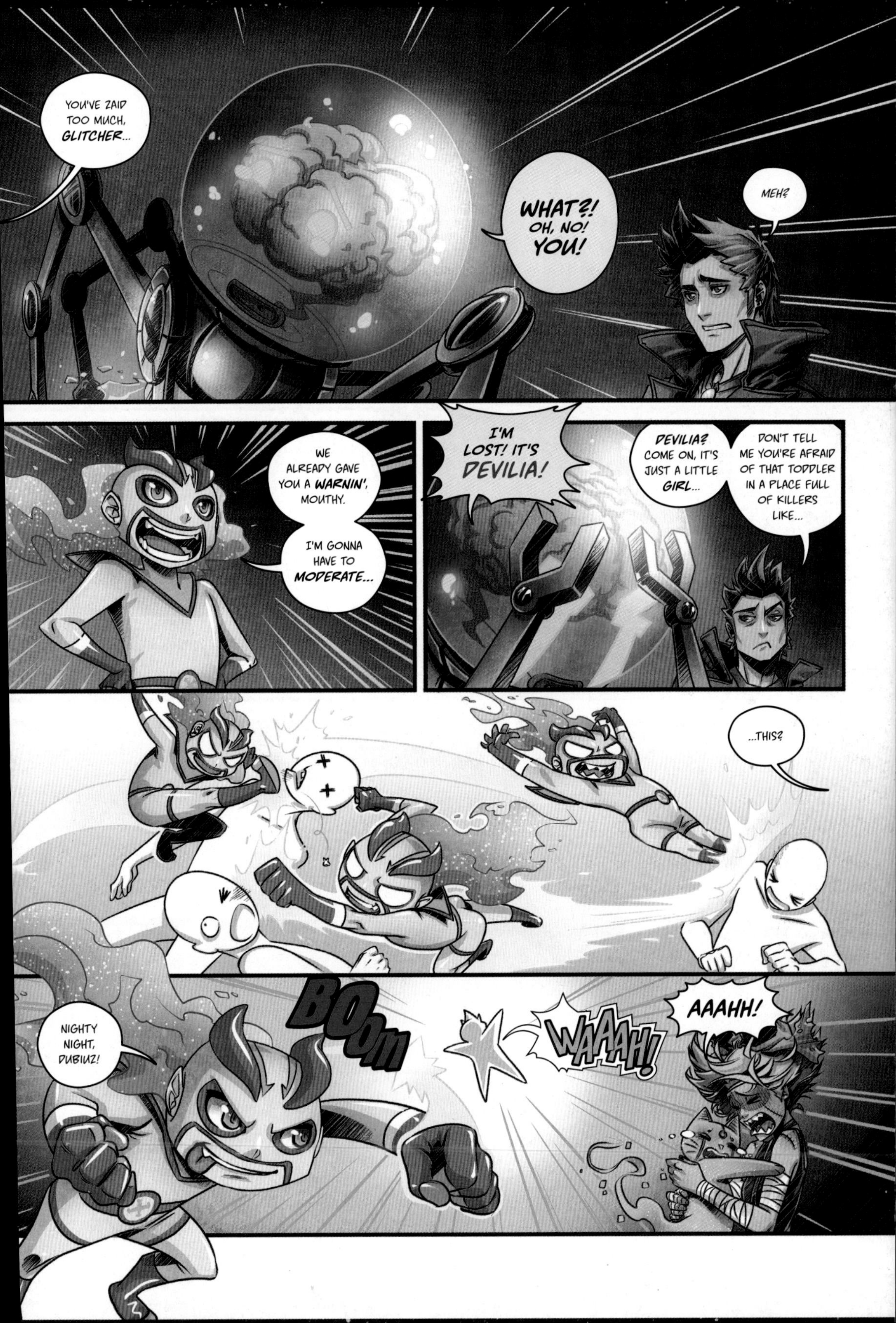
YOU'VE ZAID TOO MUCH, GLITCHER...
WHAT?! OH, NO! YOU!
MEH?
WE ALREADY GAVE YOU A WARNIN', MOUTHY.
I'M GONNA HAVE TO MODERATE...
I'M LOST! IT'S DEVILIA!
DEVILIA? COME ON, IT'S JUST A LITTLE GIRL...
DON'T TELL ME YOU'RE AFRAID OF THAT TODDLER IN A PLACE FULL OF KILLERS LIKE...
...THIS?
NIGHTY NIGHT, DUBIUZ!
BOOM
WAAAH!
AAAHH!

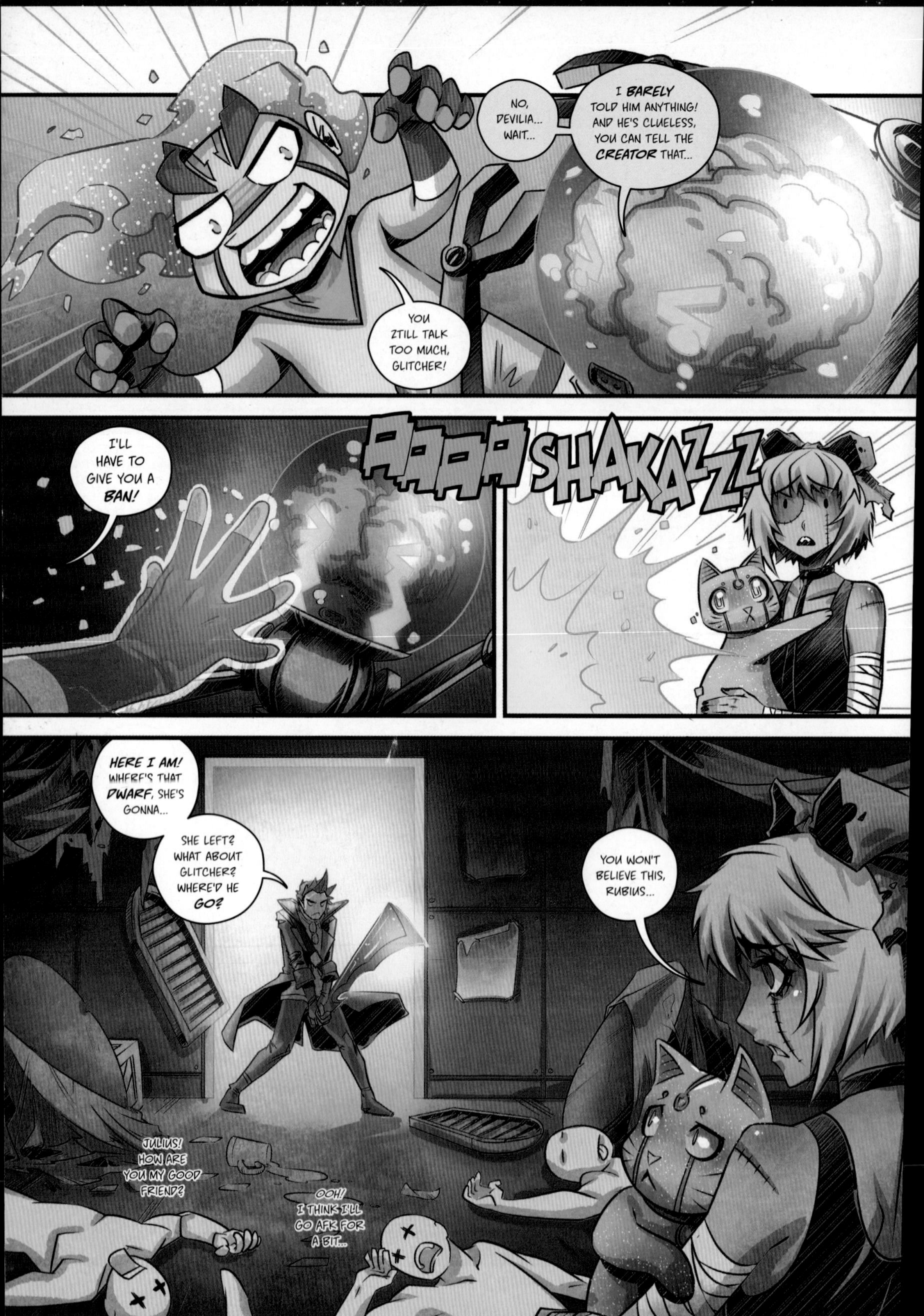
NO, DEVILIA... WAIT...
I BARELY TOLD HIM ANYTHING! AND HE'S CLUELESS, YOU CAN TELL THE CREATOR THAT...
YOU ZTILL TALK TOO MUCH, GLITCHER!
I'LL HAVE TO GIVE YOU A BAN!
SHAKAZZZ
HERE I AM! WHERE'S THAT DWARF, SHE'S GONNA...
SHE LEFT? WHAT ABOUT GLITCHER? WHERE'D HE GO?
YOU WON'T BELIEVE THIS, RUBIUS...
JULIUS! HOW ARE YOU MY GOOD FRIEND?
OOH! I THINK I'LL GO AFK FOR A BIT...

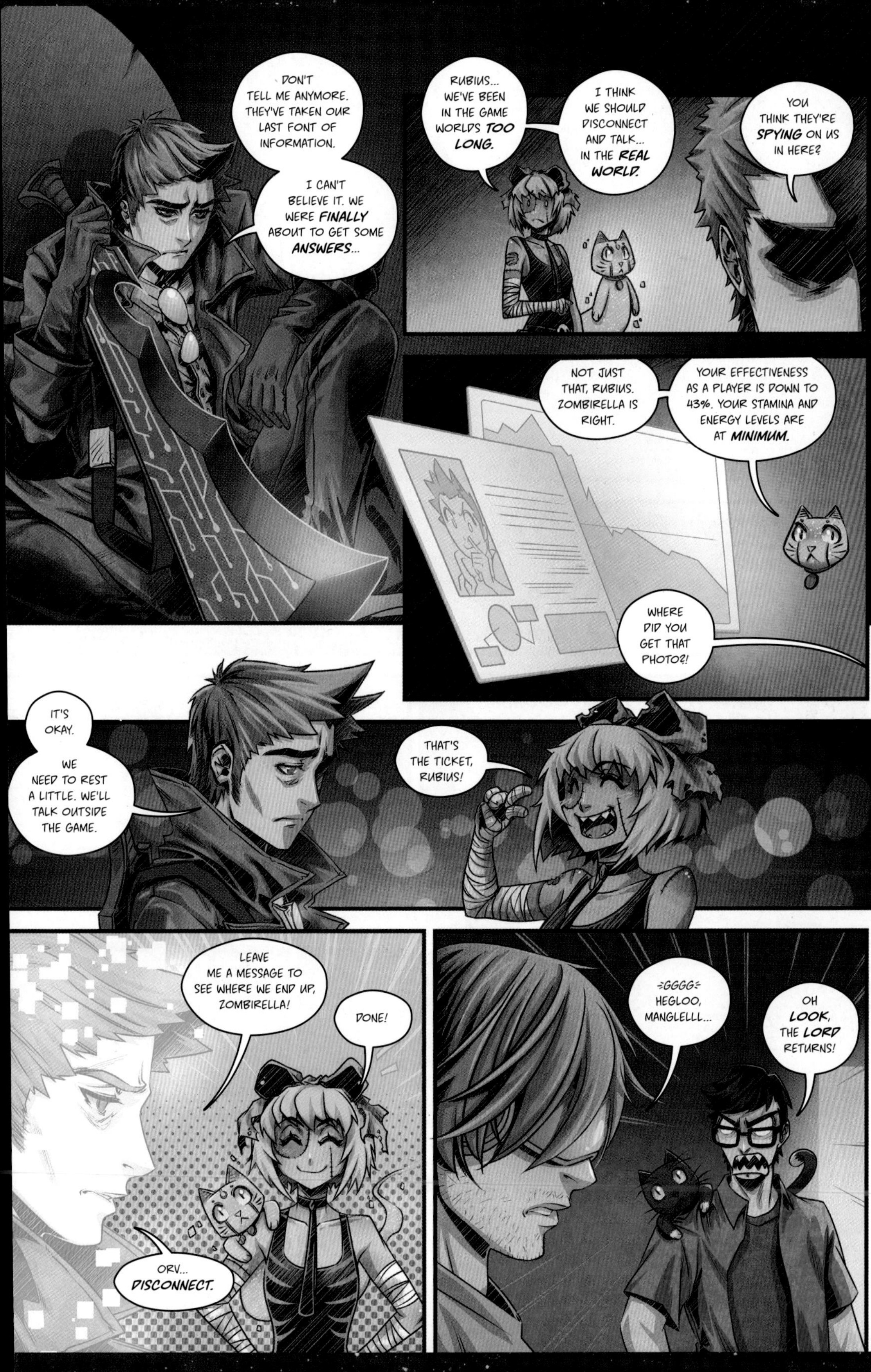
DON'T TELL ME ANYMORE. THEY'VE TAKEN OUR LAST FONT OF INFORMATION.
I CAN'T BELIEVE IT. WE WERE FINALLY ABOUT TO GET SOME ANSWERS...
RUBIUS... WE'VE BEEN IN THE GAME WORLDS TOO LONG.
I THINK WE SHOULD DISCONNECT AND TALK... IN THE REAL WORLD.
YOU THINK THEY'RE SPYING ON US IN HERE?
NOT JUST THAT, RUBIUS. ZOMBIRELLA IS RIGHT.
YOUR EFFECTIVENESS AS A PLAYER IS DOWN TO 43%. YOUR STAMINA AND ENERGY LEVELS ARE AT MINIMUM.
WHERE DID YOU GET THAT PHOTO?!
IT'S OKAY.
WE NEED TO REST A LITTLE. WE'LL TALK OUTSIDE THE GAME.
THAT'S THE TICKET, RUBIUS!
LEAVE ME A MESSAGE TO SEE WHERE WE END UP, ZOMBIRELLA!
DONE!
ORV... DISCONNECT.
=GGGG= HEGLOO, MANGLELLL...
OH LOOK, THE LORD RETURNS!

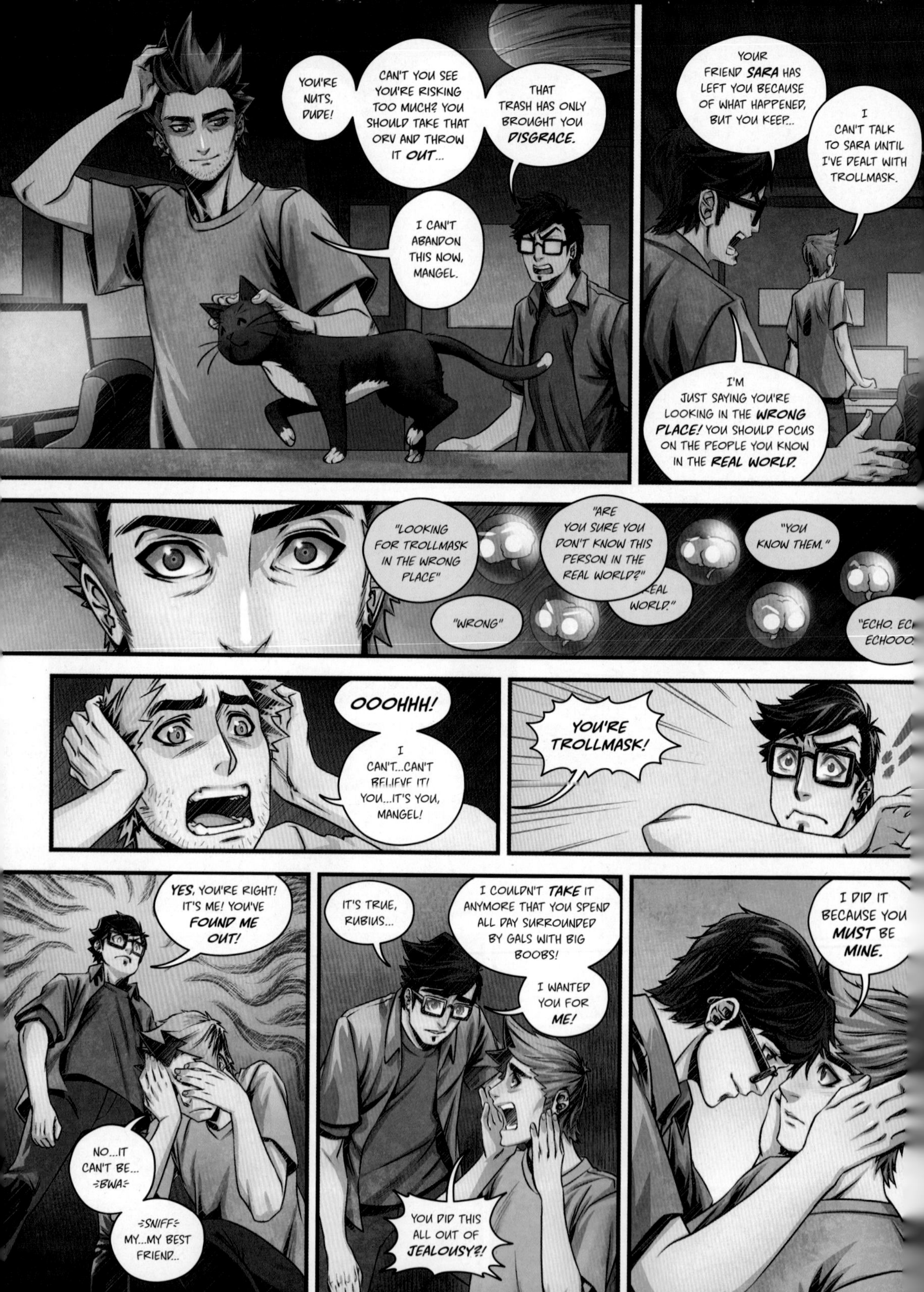
YOU'RE NUTS, DUDE!
CAN'T YOU SEE YOU'RE RISKING TOO MUCH? YOU SHOULD TAKE THAT ORV AND THROW IT OUT...
THAT TRASH HAS ONLY BROUGHT YOU DISGRACE.
I CAN'T ABANDON THIS NOW, MANGEL.
YOUR FRIEND SARA HAS LEFT YOU BECAUSE OF WHAT HAPPENED, BUT YOU KEEP...
I CAN'T TALK TO SARA UNTIL I'VE DEALT WITH TROLLMASK.
I'M JUST SAYING YOU'RE LOOKING IN THE WRONG PLACE! YOU SHOULD FOCUS ON THE PEOPLE YOU KNOW IN THE REAL WORLD.
"LOOKING FOR TROLLMASK IN THE WRONG PLACE"
"WRONG"
"ARE YOU SURE YOU DON'T KNOW THIS PERSON IN THE REAL WORLD?"
EAL WORLD."
"YOU KNOW THEM."
"ECHO. ECH
ECHOOO
OOOHHH!
I CAN'T...CAN'T BELIEVE IT! YOU...IT'S YOU, MANGEL!
YOU'RE TROLLMASK!
YES, YOU'RE RIGHT! IT'S ME! YOU'VE FOUND ME OUT!
NO...IT CAN'T BE... =BWA=
=SNIFF= MY...MY BEST FRIEND...
IT'S TRUE, RUBIUS...
I COULDN'T TAKE IT ANYMORE THAT YOU SPEND ALL DAY SURROUNDED BY GALS WITH BIG BOOBS!
I WANTED YOU FOR ME!
YOU DID THIS ALL OUT OF JEALOUSY?!
I DID IT BECAUSE YOU MUST BE MINE.

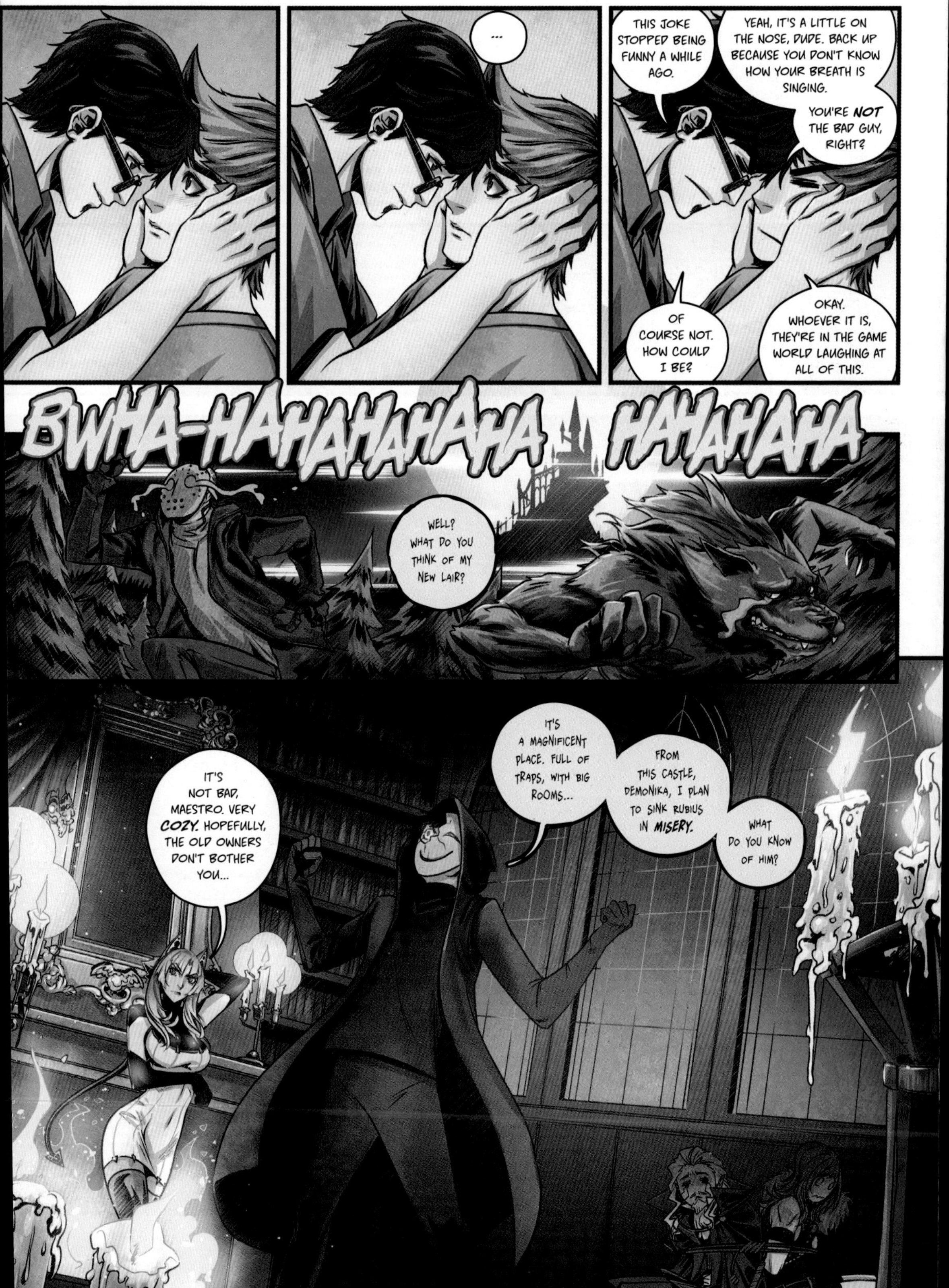
...
THIS JOKE STOPPED BEING FUNNY A WHILE AGO.
YEAH, IT'S A LITTLE ON THE NOSE, DUDE. BACK UP BECAUSE YOU DON'T KNOW HOW YOUR BREATH IS SINGING.
YOU'RE NOT THE BAD GUY, RIGHT?
OF COURSE NOT. HOW COULD I BE?
OKAY. WHOEVER IT IS, THEY'RE IN THE GAME WORLD LAUGHING AT ALL OF THIS.
BWHA-HAHAHAHAHAHA HAHAHAHA
WELL? WHAT DO YOU THINK OF MY NEW LAIR?
IT'S NOT BAD, MAESTRO. VERY COZY. HOPEFULLY, THE OLD OWNERS DON'T BOTHER YOU...
IT'S A MAGNIFICENT PLACE. FULL OF TRAPS, WITH BIG ROOMS...
FROM THIS CASTLE, DEMONIKA, I PLAN TO SINK RUBIUS IN MISERY.
WHAT DO YOU KNOW OF HIM?

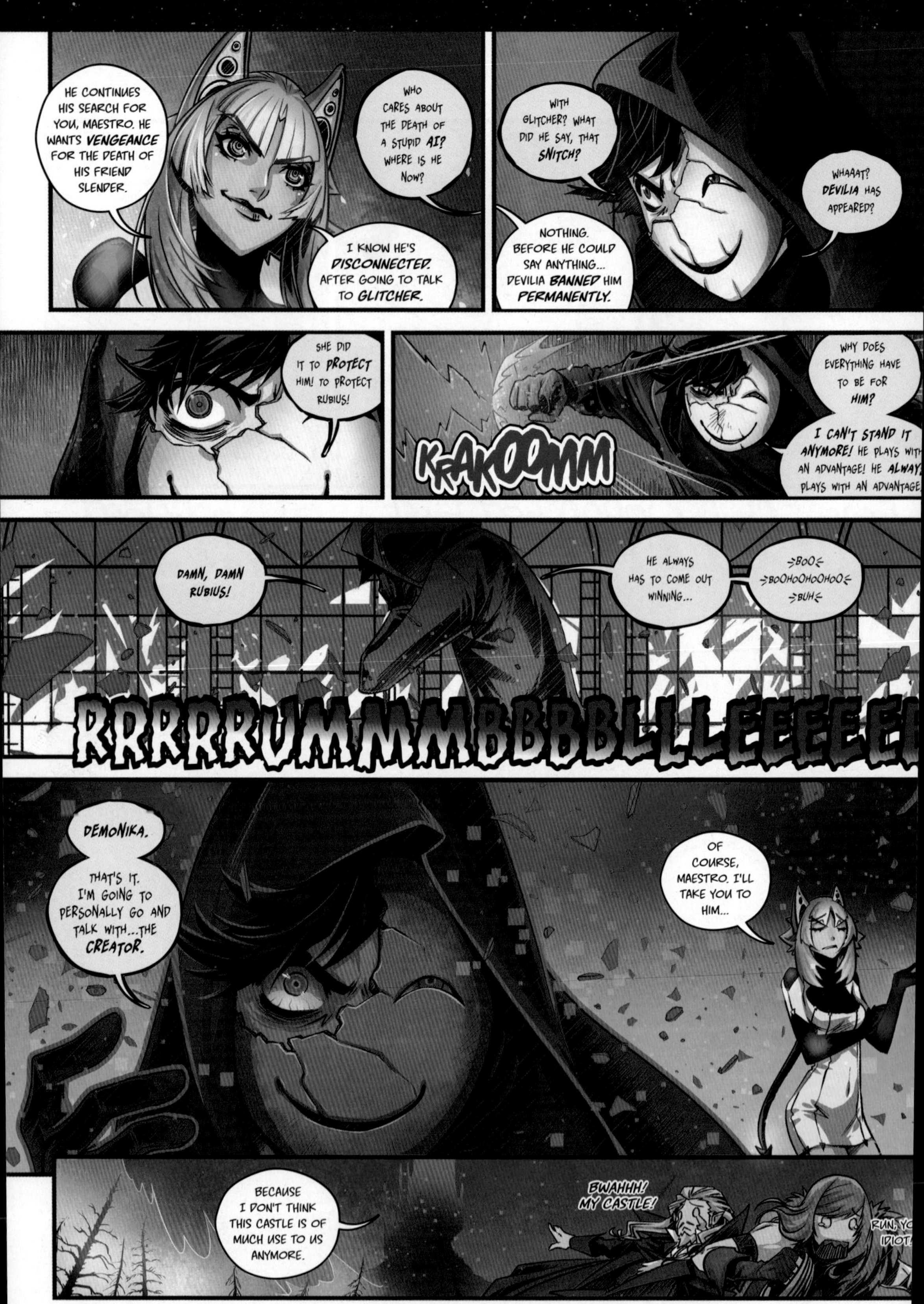
HE CONTINUES HIS SEARCH FOR YOU, MAESTRO. HE WANTS VENGEANCE FOR THE DEATH OF HIS FRIEND SLENDER.
WHO CARES ABOUT THE DEATH OF A STUPID AI? WHERE IS HE NOW?
I KNOW HE'S DISCONNECTED. AFTER GOING TO TALK TO GLITCHER.
WITH GLITCHER? WHAT DID HE SAY, THAT SNITCH?
NOTHING. BEFORE HE COULD SAY ANYTHING... DEVILIA BANNED HIM PERMANENTLY.
WHAAAT? DEVILIA HAS APPEARED?
SHE DID IT TO PROTECT HIM! TO PROTECT RUBIUS!
KRAKOOMM
WHY DOES EVERYTHING HAVE TO BE FOR HIM?
I CAN'T STAND IT ANYMORE! HE PLAYS WITH AN ADVANTAGE! HE ALWAYS PLAYS WITH AN ADVANTAGE!
DAMN, DAMN RUBIUS!
HE ALWAYS HAS TO COME OUT WINNING...
BOO BOOHOOHOOHOO BUH
RRRRRUMMMBBBLLLEEEEEE
DEMONIKA.
THAT'S IT. I'M GOING TO PERSONALLY GO AND TALK WITH...THE CREATOR.
OF COURSE, MAESTRO. I'LL TAKE YOU TO HIM...
BECAUSE I DON'T THINK THIS CASTLE IS OF MUCH USE TO US ANYMORE.
BWAHHH! MY CASTLE!
RUN, YO IDIOT!

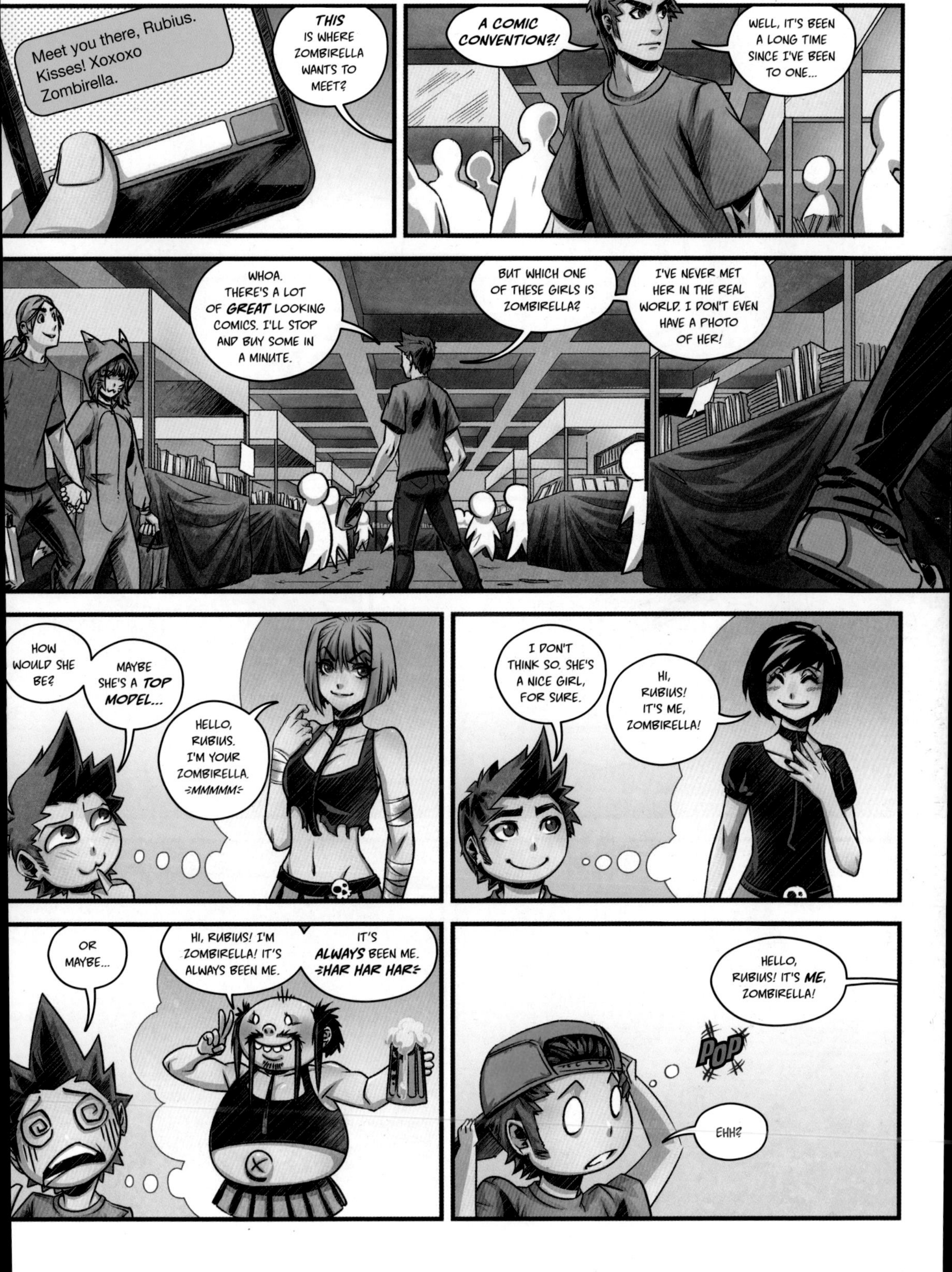
Meet you there, Rubius. Kisses! Xoxoxo Zombirella.
THIS IS WHERE ZOMBIRELLA WANTS TO MEET?
A COMIC CONVENTION?!
WELL, IT'S BEEN A LONG TIME SINCE I'VE BEEN TO ONE...
WHOA. THERE'S A LOT OF GREAT LOOKING COMICS. I'LL STOP AND BUY SOME IN A MINUTE.
BUT WHICH ONE OF THESE GIRLS IS ZOMBIRELLA?
I'VE NEVER MET HER IN THE REAL WORLD. I DON'T EVEN HAVE A PHOTO OF HER!
HOW WOULD SHE BE?
MAYBE SHE'S A TOP MODEL...
HELLO, RUBIUS. I'M YOUR ZOMBIRELLA. =MMMMM=
I DON'T THINK SO. SHE'S A NICE GIRL, FOR SURE.
HI, RUBIUS! IT'S ME, ZOMBIRELLA!
OR MAYBE...
HI, RUBIUS! I'M ZOMBIRELLA! IT'S ALWAYS BEEN ME.
IT'S ALWAYS BEEN ME. =HAR HAR HAR=
HELLO, RUBIUS! IT'S ME, ZOMBIRELLA!
POP
EHH?

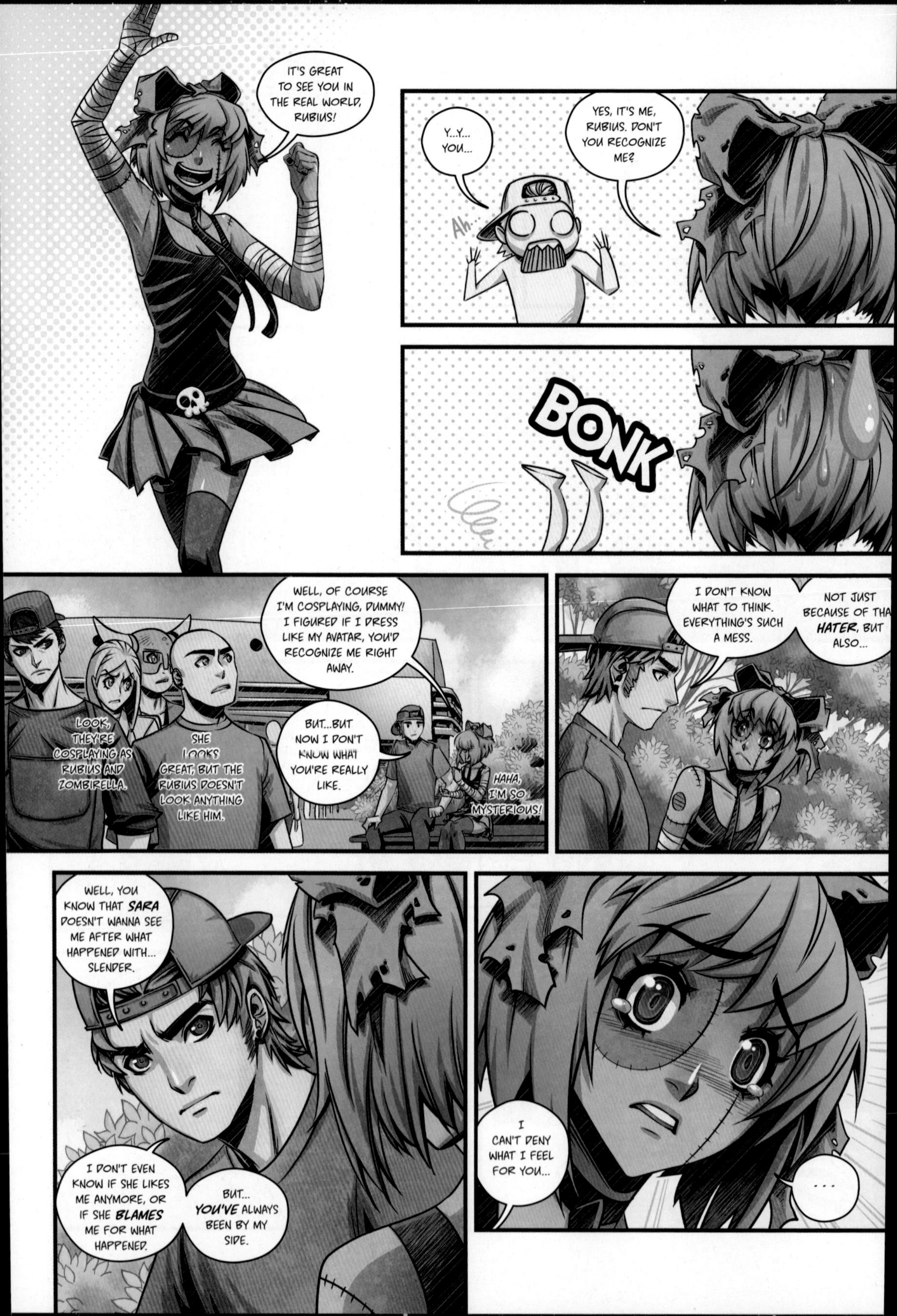
IT'S GREAT TO SEE YOU IN THE REAL WORLD, RUBIUS!
Y...Y... YOU...
AH...
YES, IT'S ME, RUBIUS. DON'T YOU RECOGNIZE ME?
BONK
WELL, OF COURSE I'M COSPLAYING, DUMMY! I FIGURED IF I DRESS LIKE MY AVATAR, YOU'D RECOGNIZE ME RIGHT AWAY.
LOOK, THEY'RE COSPLAYING AS RUBIUS AND ZOMBIRELLA.
SHE LOOKS GREAT, BUT THE RUBIUS DOESN'T LOOK ANYTHING LIKE HIM.
BUT...BUT NOW I DON'T KNOW WHAT YOU'RE REALLY LIKE.
HAHA, I'M SO MYSTERIOUS!
I DON'T KNOW WHAT TO THINK. EVERYTHING'S SUCH A MESS.
NOT JUST BECAUSE OF THAT HATER, BUT ALSO...
WELL, YOU KNOW THAT SARA DOESN'T WANNA SEE ME AFTER WHAT HAPPENED WITH... SLENDER.
I DON'T EVEN KNOW IF SHE LIKES ME ANYMORE, OR IF SHE BLAMES ME FOR WHAT HAPPENED.
BUT... YOU'VE ALWAYS BEEN BY MY SIDE.
I CAN'T DENY WHAT I FEEL FOR YOU...
...

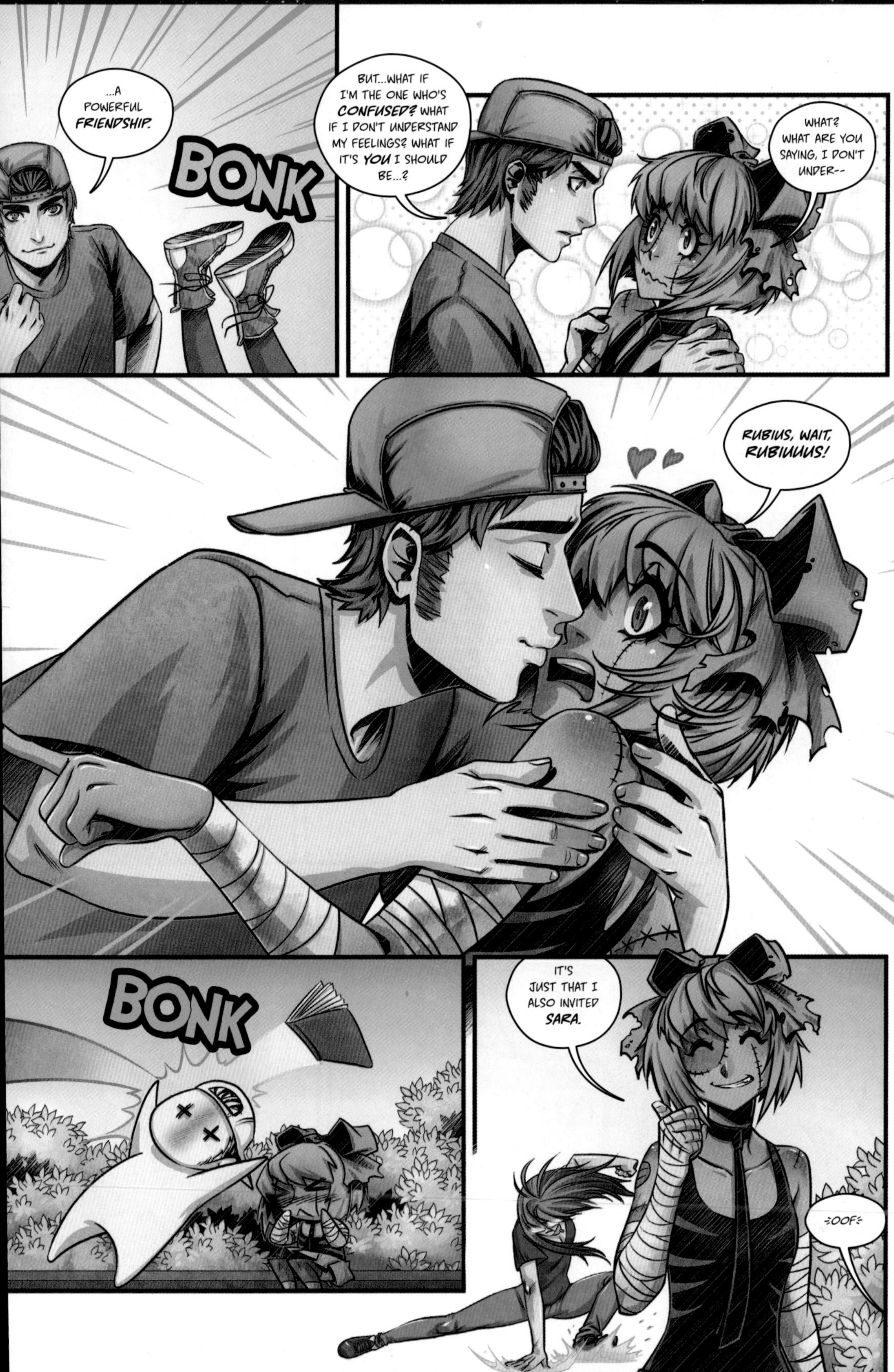
...A POWERFUL FRIENDSHIP.
BONK
BUT...WHAT IF I'M THE ONE WHO'S CONFUSED? WHAT IF I DON'T UNDERSTAND MY FEELINGS? WHAT IF IT'S YOU I SHOULD BE...?
WHAT? WHAT ARE YOU SAYING, I DON'T UNDER--
RUBIUS, WAIT, RUBIUUUS!
BONK
IT'S JUST THAT I ALSO INVITED SARA.
OOF

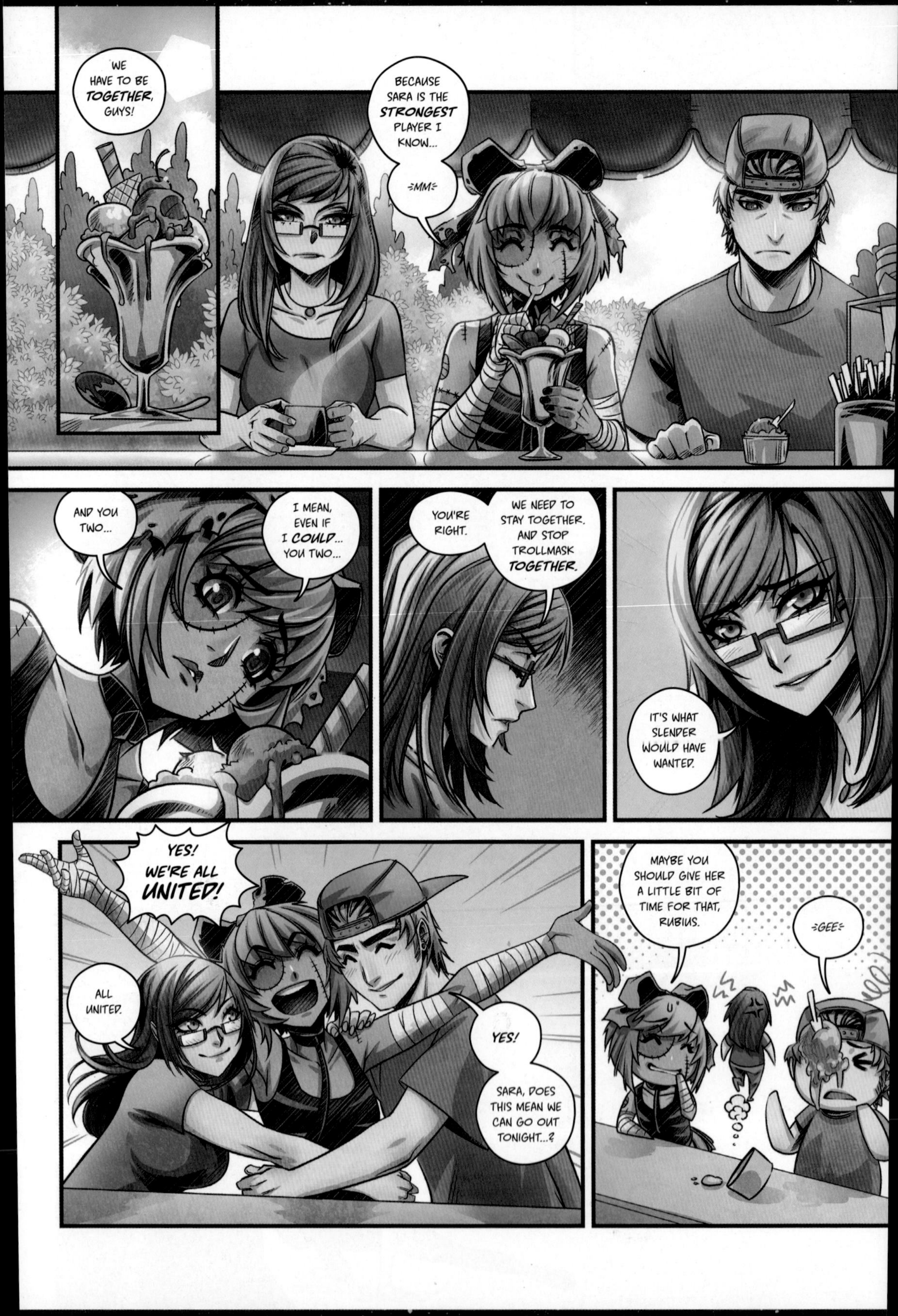
WE HAVE TO BE TOGETHER, GUYS!
BECAUSE SARA IS THE STRONGEST PLAYER I KNOW...
=MM=
AND YOU TWO...
I MEAN, EVEN IF I COULD... YOU TWO...
YOU'RE RIGHT.
WE NEED TO STAY TOGETHER. AND STOP TROLLMASK TOGETHER.
IT'S WHAT SLENDER WOULD HAVE WANTED.
YES! WE'RE ALL UNITED!
ALL UNITED.
YES!
SARA, DOES THIS MEAN WE CAN GO OUT TONIGHT...?
MAYBE YOU SHOULD GIVE HER A LITTLE BIT OF TIME FOR THAT, RUBIUS.
=GEE=

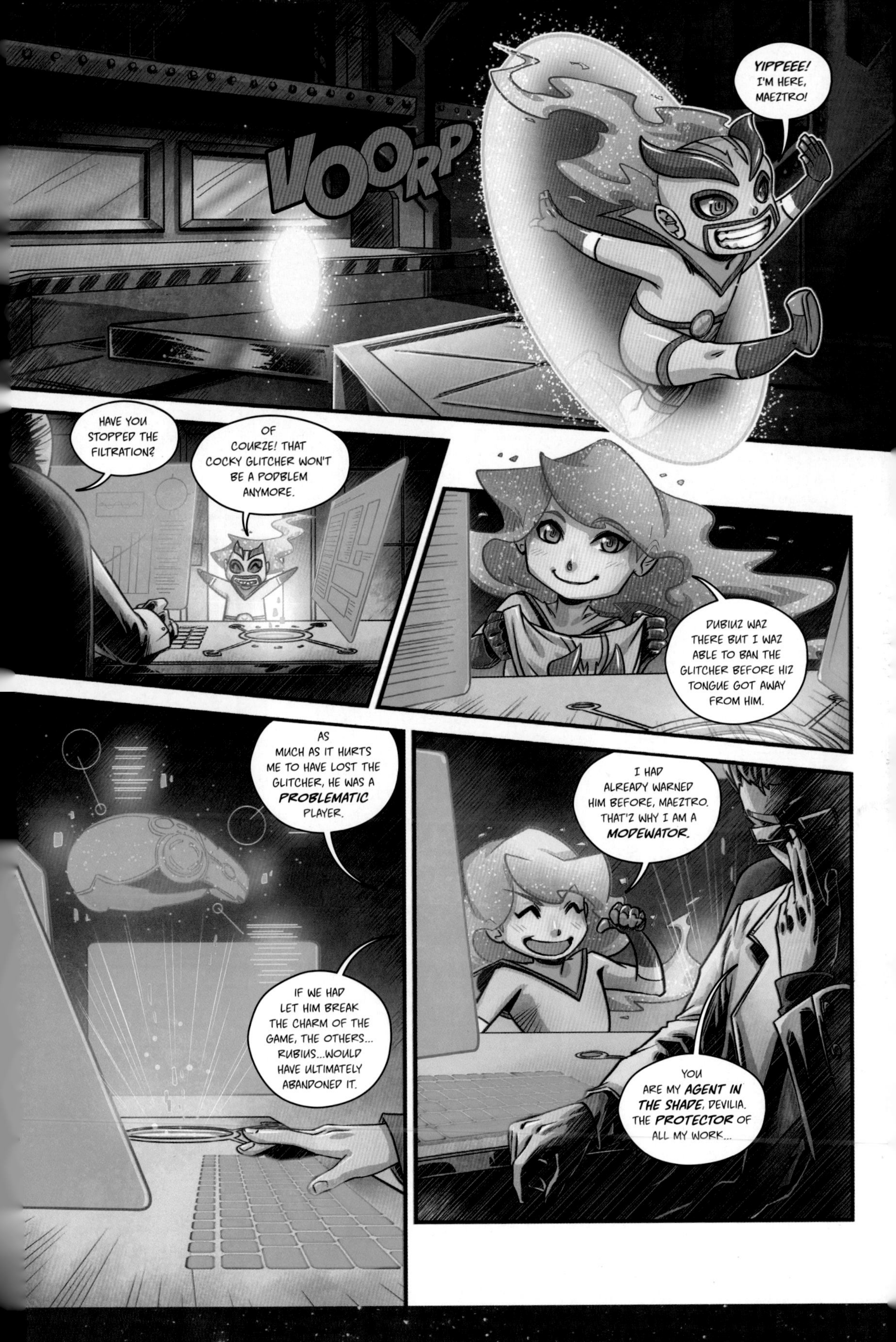
VOORP
YIPPEEE! I'M HERE, MAEZTRO!
HAVE YOU STOPPED THE FILTRATION?
OF COURZE! THAT COCKY GLITCHER WON'T BE A PODBLEM ANYMORE.
DUBIUZ WAZ THERE BUT I WAZ ABLE TO BAN THE GLITCHER BEFORE HIZ TONGUE GOT AWAY FROM HIM.
AS MUCH AS IT HURTS ME TO HAVE LOST THE GLITCHER, HE WAS A PROBLEMATIC PLAYER.
IF WE HAD LET HIM BREAK THE CHARM OF THE GAME, THE OTHERS... RUBIUS...WOULD HAVE ULTIMATELY ABANDONED IT.
I HAD ALREADY WARNED HIM BEFORE, MAEZTRO. THAT'Z WHY I AM A MODEWATOR.
YOU ARE MY AGENT IN THE SHADE, DEVILIA. THE PROTECTOR OF ALL MY WORK...

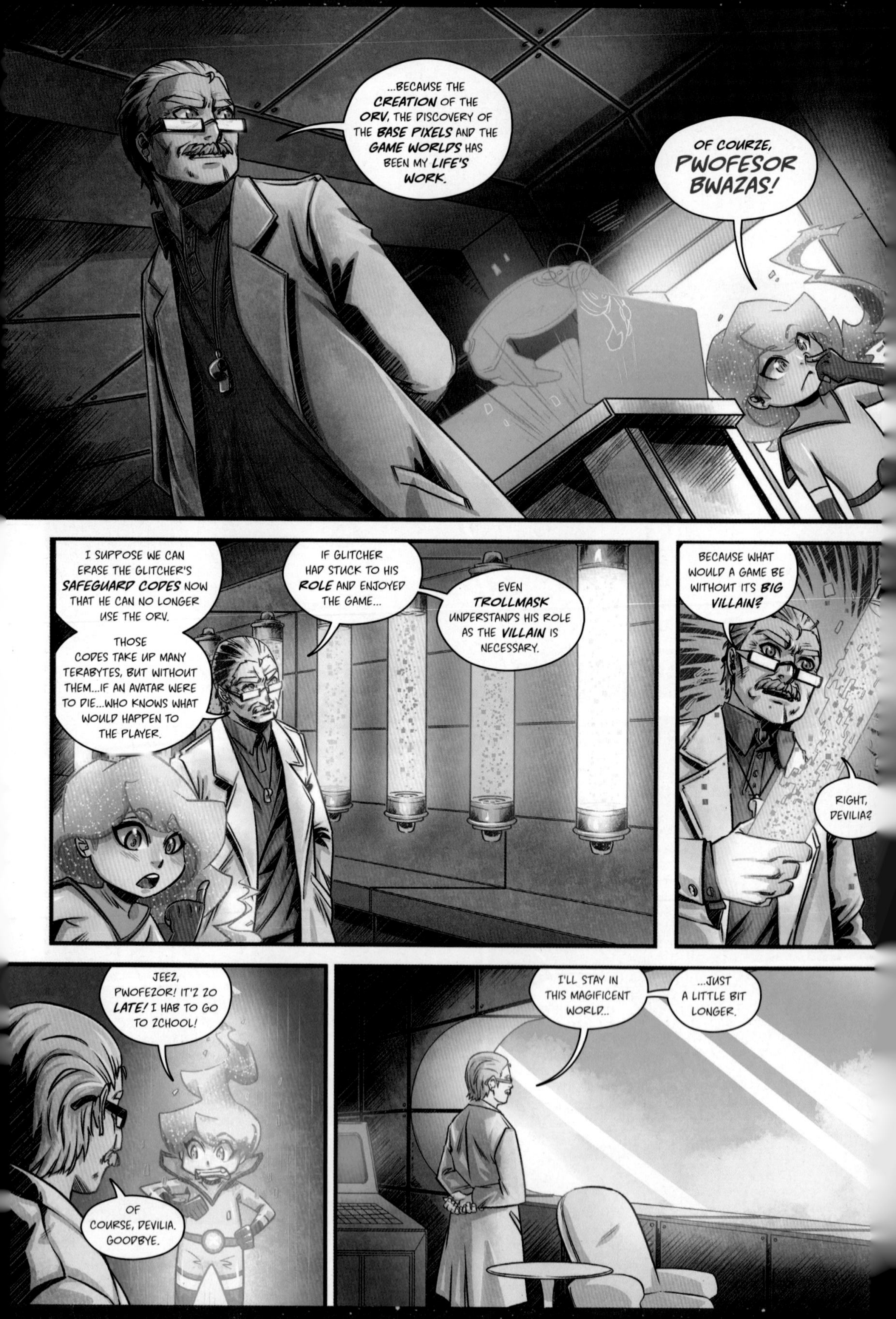
...BECAUSE THE CREATION OF THE ORV, THE DISCOVERY OF THE BASE PIXELS AND THE GAME WORLDS HAS BEEN MY LIFE'S WORK.
OF COURZE, PWOFESOR BWAZAS!
I SUPPOSE WE CAN ERASE THE GLITCHER'S SAFEGUARD CODES NOW THAT HE CAN NO LONGER USE THE ORV.
THOSE CODES TAKE UP MANY TERABYTES, BUT WITHOUT THEM...IF AN AVATAR WERE TO DIE...WHO KNOWS WHAT WOULD HAPPEN TO THE PLAYER.
IF GLITCHER HAD STUCK TO HIS ROLE AND ENJOYED THE GAME...
EVEN TROLLMASK UNDERSTANDS HIS ROLE AS THE VILLAIN IS NECESSARY.
BECAUSE WHAT WOULD A GAME BE WITHOUT ITS BIG VILLAIN?
RIGHT, DEVILIA?
JEEZ, PWOFEZOR! IT'Z ZO LATE! I HAB TO GO TO ZCHOOL!
OF COURSE, DEVILIA. GOODBYE.
I'LL STAY IN THIS MAGIFICENT WORLD...
...JUST A LITTLE BIT LONGER.

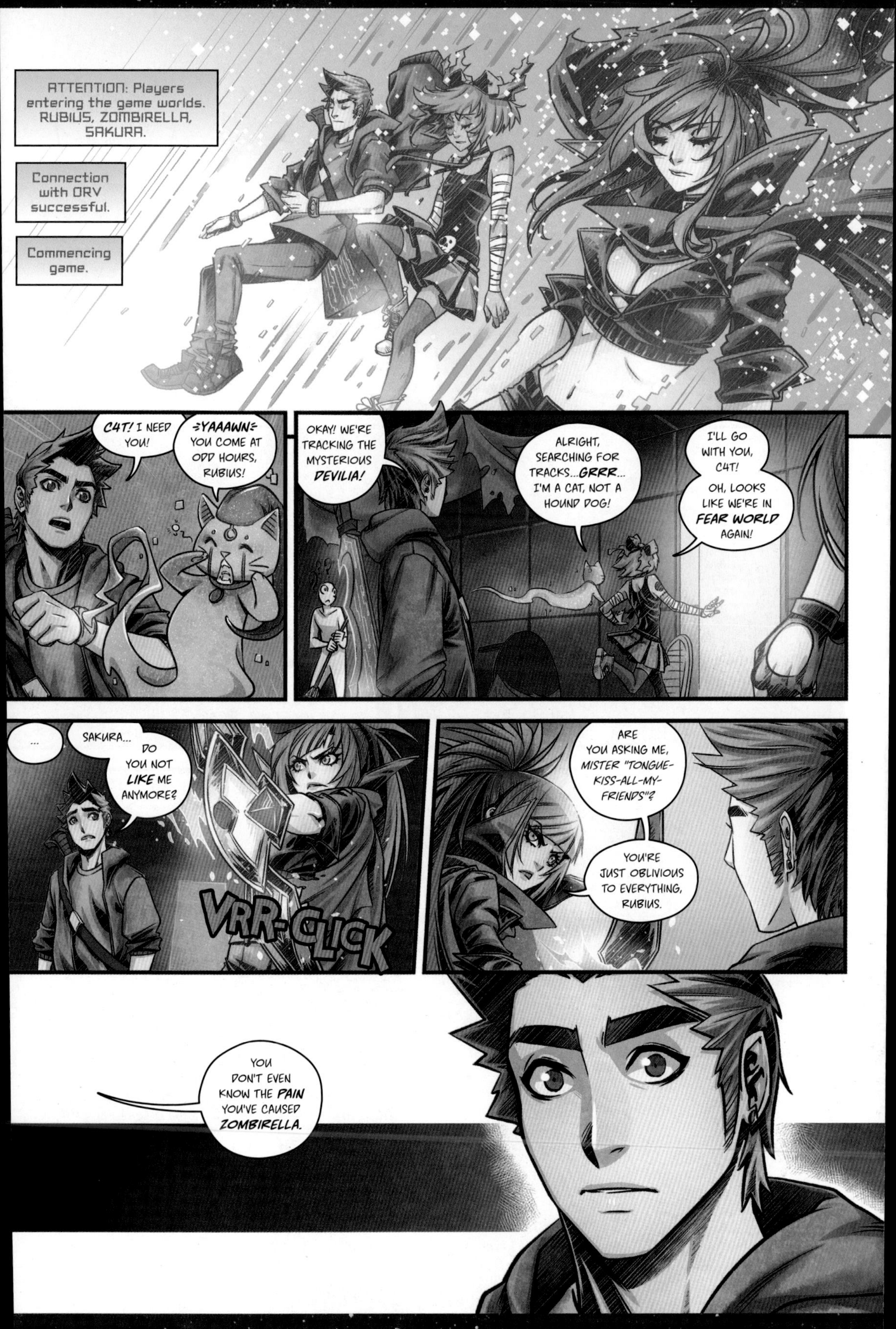
ATTENTION: Players entering the game worlds. RUBIUS, ZOMBIRELLA, SAKURA.
Connection with ORV successful.
Commencing game.
C4T! I NEED YOU!
=YAAAWN= YOU COME AT ODD HOURS, RUBIUS!
OKAY! WE'RE TRACKING THE MYSTERIOUS DEVILIA!
ALRIGHT, SEARCHING FOR TRACKS...GRRR... I'M A CAT, NOT A HOUND DOG!
I'LL GO WITH YOU, C4T!
OH, LOOKS LIKE WE'RE IN FEAR WORLD AGAIN!
...
SAKURA... DO YOU NOT LIKE ME ANYMORE?
VRR-CLICK
ARE YOU ASKING ME, MISTER "TONGUE-KISS-ALL-MY-FRIENDS"?
YOU'RE JUST OBLIVIOUS TO EVERYTHING, RUBIUS.
YOU DON'T EVEN KNOW THE PAIN YOU'VE CAUSED ZOMBIRELLA.

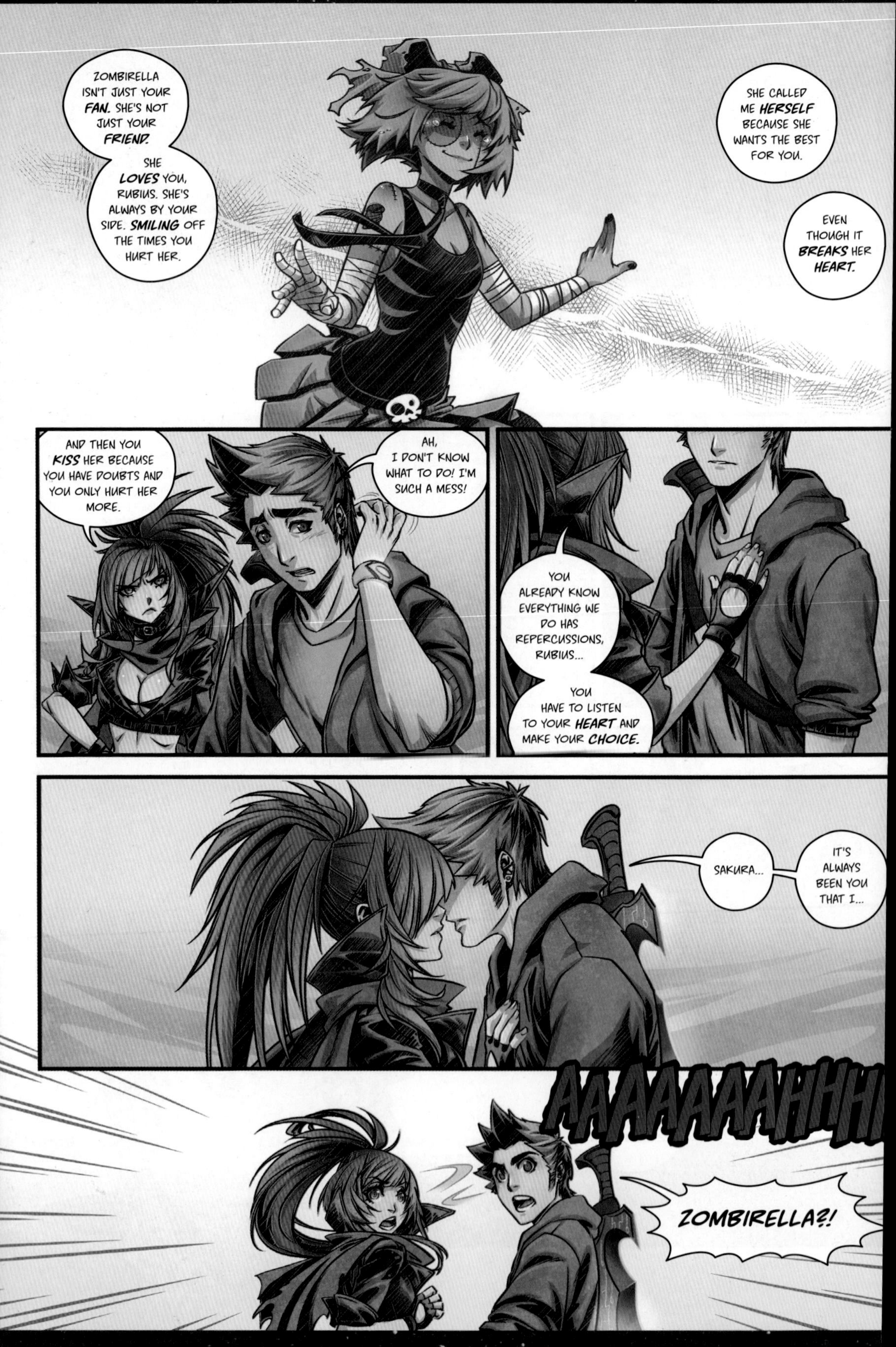
ZOMBIRELLA ISN'T JUST YOUR FAN. SHE'S NOT JUST YOUR FRIEND.
SHE LOVES YOU, RUBIUS. SHE'S ALWAYS BY YOUR SIDE. SMILING OFF THE TIMES YOU HURT HER.
SHE CALLED ME HERSELF BECAUSE SHE WANTS THE BEST FOR YOU.
EVEN THOUGH IT BREAKS HER HEART.
AND THEN YOU KISS HER BECAUSE YOU HAVE DOUBTS AND YOU ONLY HURT HER MORE.
AH, I DON'T KNOW WHAT TO DO! I'M SUCH A MESS!
YOU ALREADY KNOW EVERYTHING WE DO HAS REPERCUSSIONS, RUBIUS...
YOU HAVE TO LISTEN TO YOUR HEART AND MAKE YOUR CHOICE.
SAKURA...
IT'S ALWAYS BEEN YOU THAT I...
AAAAAAAAHHH
ZOMBIRELLA?!

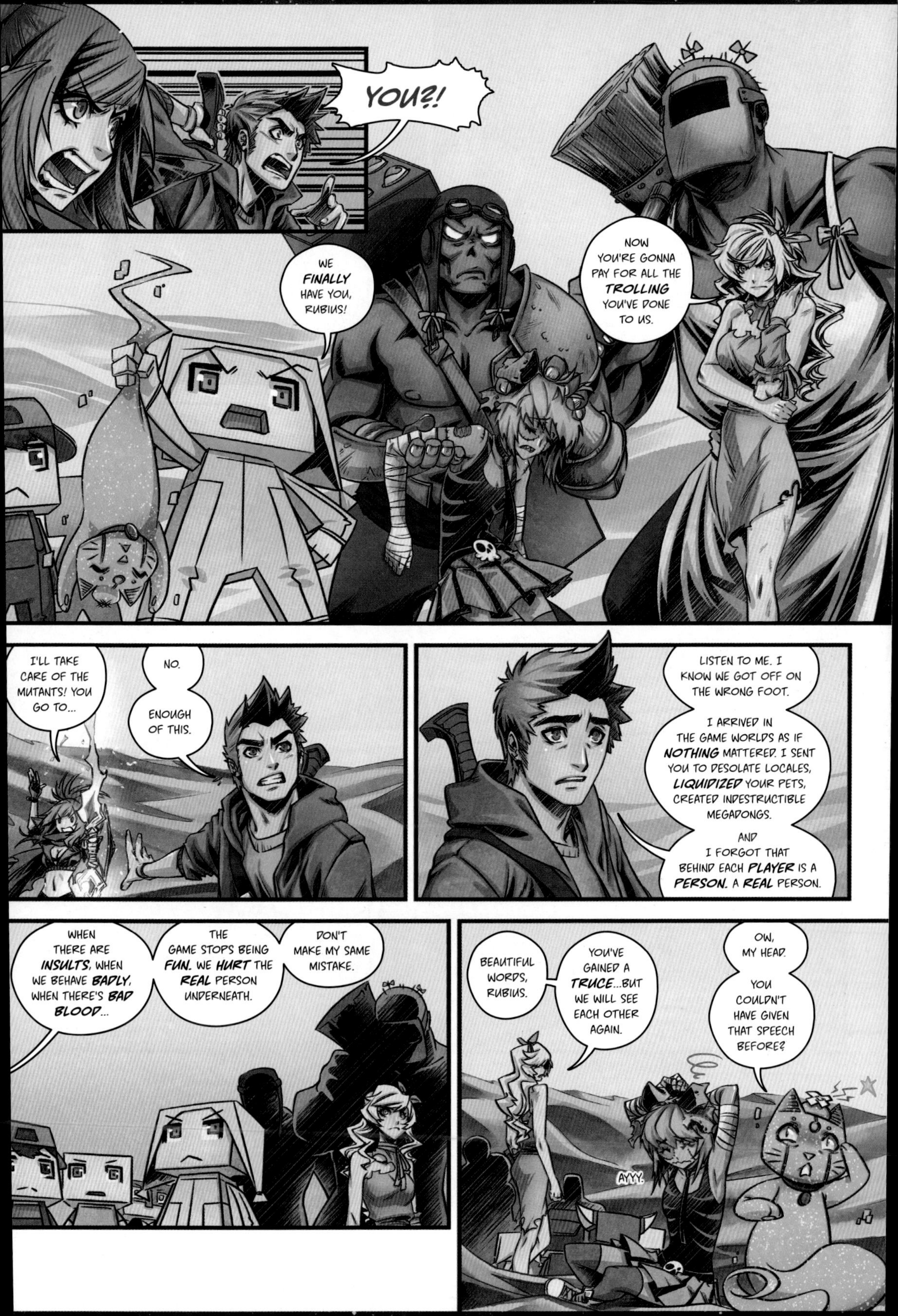
YOU?!
WE FINALLY HAVE YOU, RUBIUS!
NOW YOU'RE GONNA PAY FOR ALL THE TROLLING YOU'VE DONE TO US.
I'LL TAKE CARE OF THE MUTANTS! YOU GO TO...
NO.
ENOUGH OF THIS.
LISTEN TO ME. I KNOW WE GOT OFF ON THE WRONG FOOT.
I ARRIVED IN THE GAME WORLDS AS IF NOTHING MATTERED. I SENT YOU TO DESOLATE LOCALES, LIQUIDIZED YOUR PETS, CREATED INDESTRUCTIBLE MEGADONGS.
AND I FORGOT THAT BEHIND EACH PLAYER IS A PERSON. A REAL PERSON.
WHEN THERE ARE INSULTS, WHEN WE BEHAVE BADLY, WHEN THERE'S BAD BLOOD...
THE GAME STOPS BEING FUN. WE HURT THE REAL PERSON UNDERNEATH.
DON'T MAKE MY SAME MISTAKE.
BEAUTIFUL WORDS, RUBIUS.
YOU'VE GAINED A TRUCE...BUT WE WILL SEE EACH OTHER AGAIN.
OW, MY HEAD.
YOU COULDN'T HAVE GIVEN THAT SPEECH BEFORE?
AYYY.

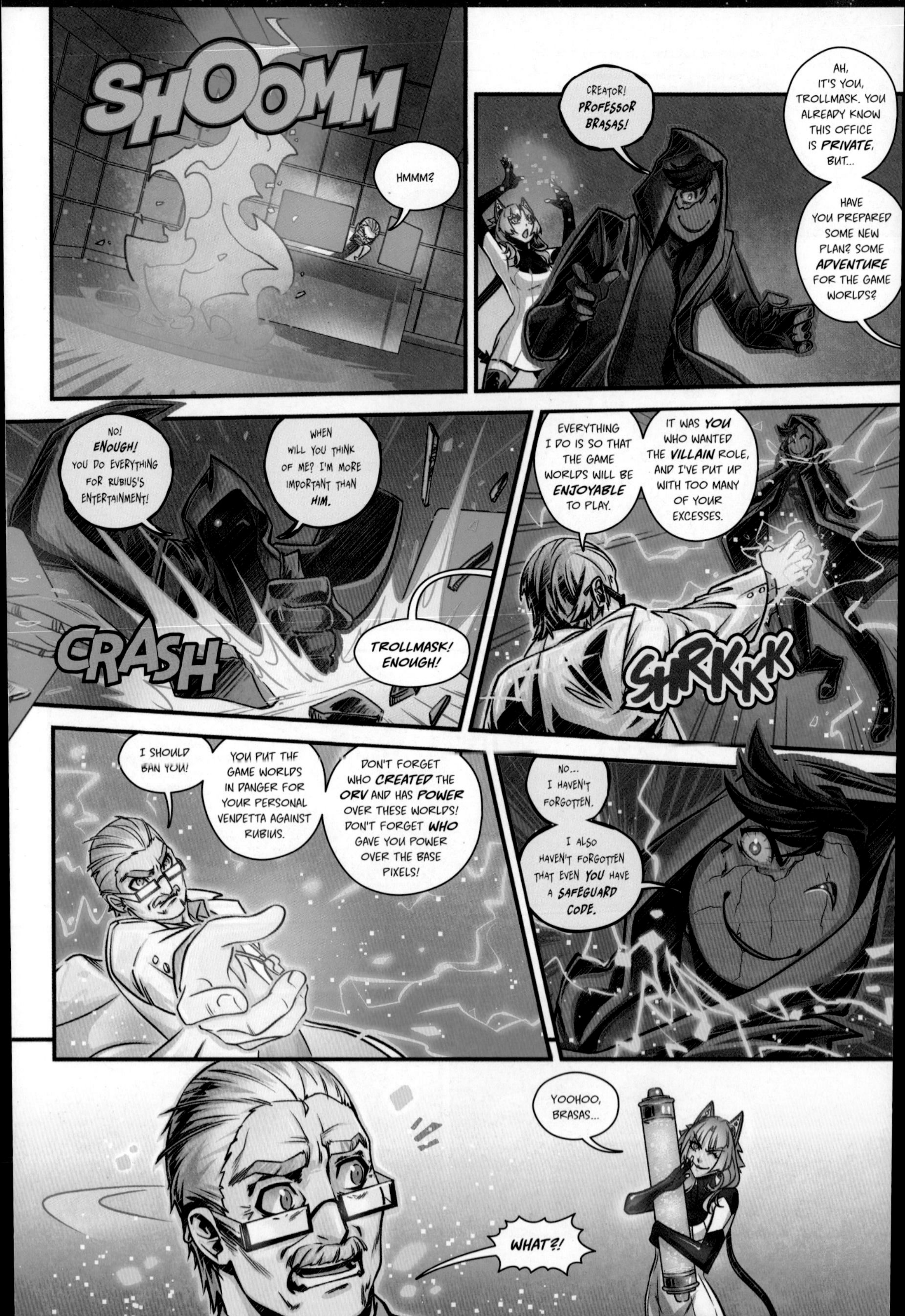
SHOOMM
HMMM?
CREATOR! PROFESSOR BRASAS!
AH, IT'S YOU, TROLLMASK. YOU ALREADY KNOW THIS OFFICE IS PRIVATE, BUT...
HAVE YOU PREPARED SOME NEW PLAN? SOME ADVENTURE FOR THE GAME WORLDS?
NO! ENOUGH! YOU DO EVERYTHING FOR RUBIUS'S ENTERTAINMENT!
WHEN WILL YOU THINK OF ME? I'M MORE IMPORTANT THAN HIM.
CRASH
TROLLMASK! ENOUGH!
EVERYTHING I DO IS SO THAT THE GAME WORLDS WILL BE ENJOYABLE TO PLAY.
IT WAS YOU WHO WANTED THE VILLAIN ROLE, AND I'VE PUT UP WITH TOO MANY OF YOUR EXCESSES.
SHRKKK
I SHOULD BAN YOU!
YOU PUT THE GAME WORLDS IN DANGER FOR YOUR PERSONAL VENDETTA AGAINST RUBIUS.
DON'T FORGET WHO CREATED THE ORV AND HAS POWER OVER THESE WORLDS! DON'T FORGET WHO GAVE YOU POWER OVER THE BASE PIXELS!
NO... I HAVEN'T FORGOTTEN.
I ALSO HAVEN'T FORGOTTEN THAT EVEN YOU HAVE A SAFEGUARD CODE.
YOOHOO, BRASAS...
WHAT?!

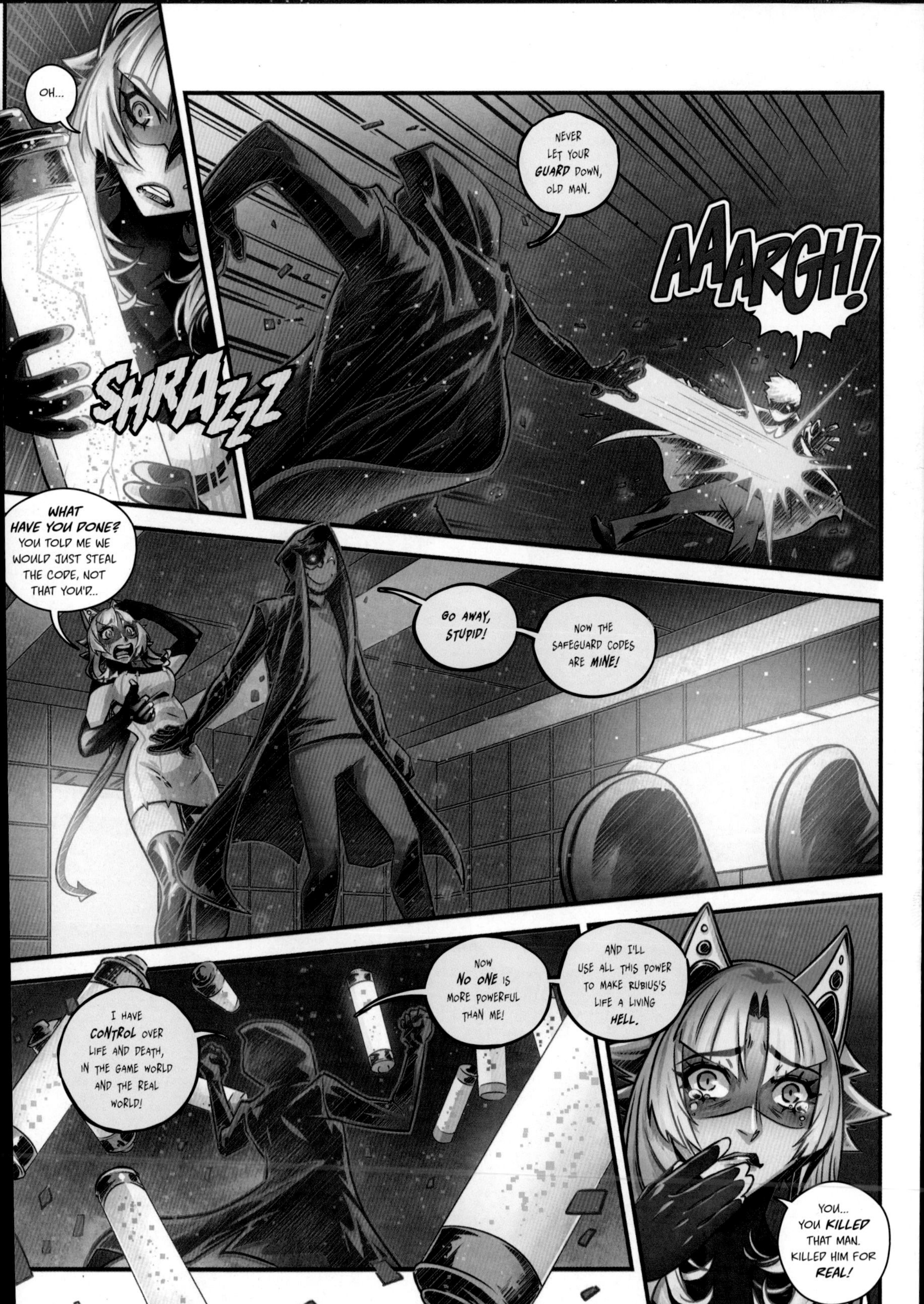
OH...
NEVER LET YOUR GUARD DOWN, OLD MAN.
AAARGH!
SHRAZZZ
WHAT HAVE YOU DONE? YOU TOLD ME WE WOULD JUST STEAL THE CODE, NOT THAT YOU'D...
GO AWAY, STUPID!
NOW THE SAFEGUARD CODES ARE MINE!
I HAVE CONTROL OVER LIFE AND DEATH, IN THE GAME WORLD AND THE REAL WORLD!
NOW NO ONE IS MORE POWERFUL THAN ME!
AND I'LL USE ALL THIS POWER TO MAKE RUBIUS'S LIFE A LIVING HELL.
YOU... YOU KILLED THAT MAN. KILLED HIM FOR REAL!

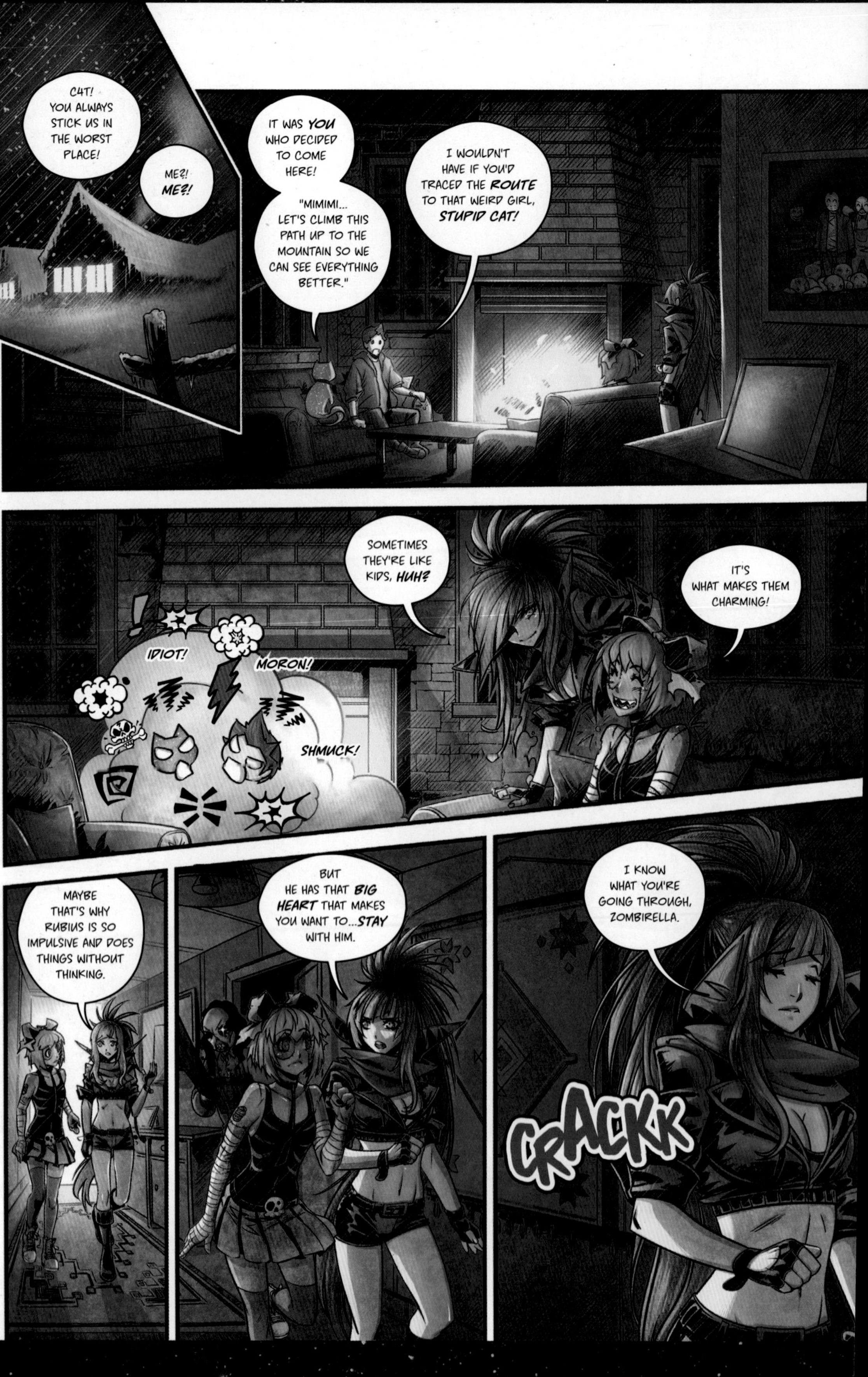
C4T! YOU ALWAYS STICK US IN THE WORST PLACE!
ME?! ME?!
IT WAS YOU WHO DECIDED TO COME HERE!
"MIMIMI... LET'S CLIMB THIS PATH UP TO THE MOUNTAIN SO WE CAN SEE EVERYTHING BETTER."
I WOULDN'T HAVE IF YOU'D TRACED THE ROUTE TO THAT WEIRD GIRL, STUPID CAT!
IDIOT!
MORON!
SHMUCK!
SOMETIMES THEY'RE LIKE KIDS, HUH?
IT'S WHAT MAKES THEM CHARMING!
MAYBE THAT'S WHY RUBIUS IS SO IMPULSIVE AND DOES THINGS WITHOUT THINKING.
BUT HE HAS THAT BIG HEART THAT MAKES YOU WANT TO...STAY WITH HIM.
I KNOW WHAT YOU'RE GOING THROUGH, ZOMBIRELLA.
CRACKK

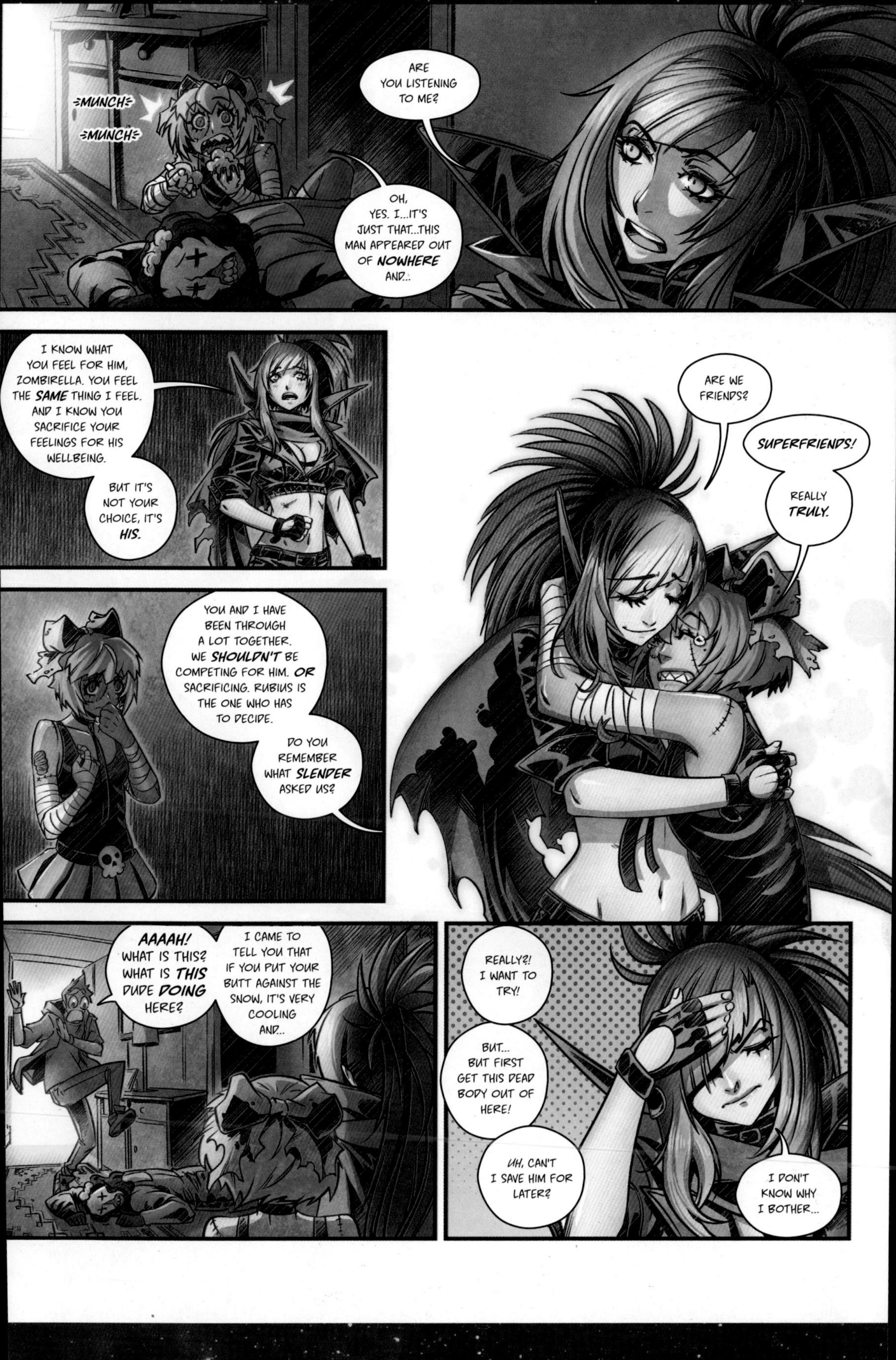

=MUNCH=
=MUNCH=
ARE YOU LISTENING TO ME?
OH, YES. I...IT'S JUST THAT...THIS MAN APPEARED OUT OF NOWHERE AND...
I KNOW WHAT YOU FEEL FOR HIM, ZOMBIRELLA. YOU FEEL THE SAME THING I FEEL. AND I KNOW YOU SACRIFICE YOUR FEELINGS FOR HIS WELLBEING.
BUT IT'S NOT YOUR CHOICE, IT'S HIS.
YOU AND I HAVE BEEN THROUGH A LOT TOGETHER. WE SHOULDN'T BE COMPETING FOR HIM. OR SACRIFICING. RUBIUS IS THE ONE WHO HAS TO DECIDE.
DO YOU REMEMBER WHAT SLENDER ASKED US?
ARE WE FRIENDS?
SUPERFRIENDS!
REALLY TRULY.
AAAAH! WHAT IS THIS? WHAT IS THIS DUDE DOING HERE?
I CAME TO TELL YOU THAT IF YOU PUT YOUR BUTT AGAINST THE SNOW, IT'S VERY COOLING AND...
REALLY?! I WANT TO TRY!
BUT... BUT FIRST GET THIS DEAD BODY OUT OF HERE!
UH, CAN'T I SAVE HIM FOR LATER?
I DON'T KNOW WHY I BOTHER...

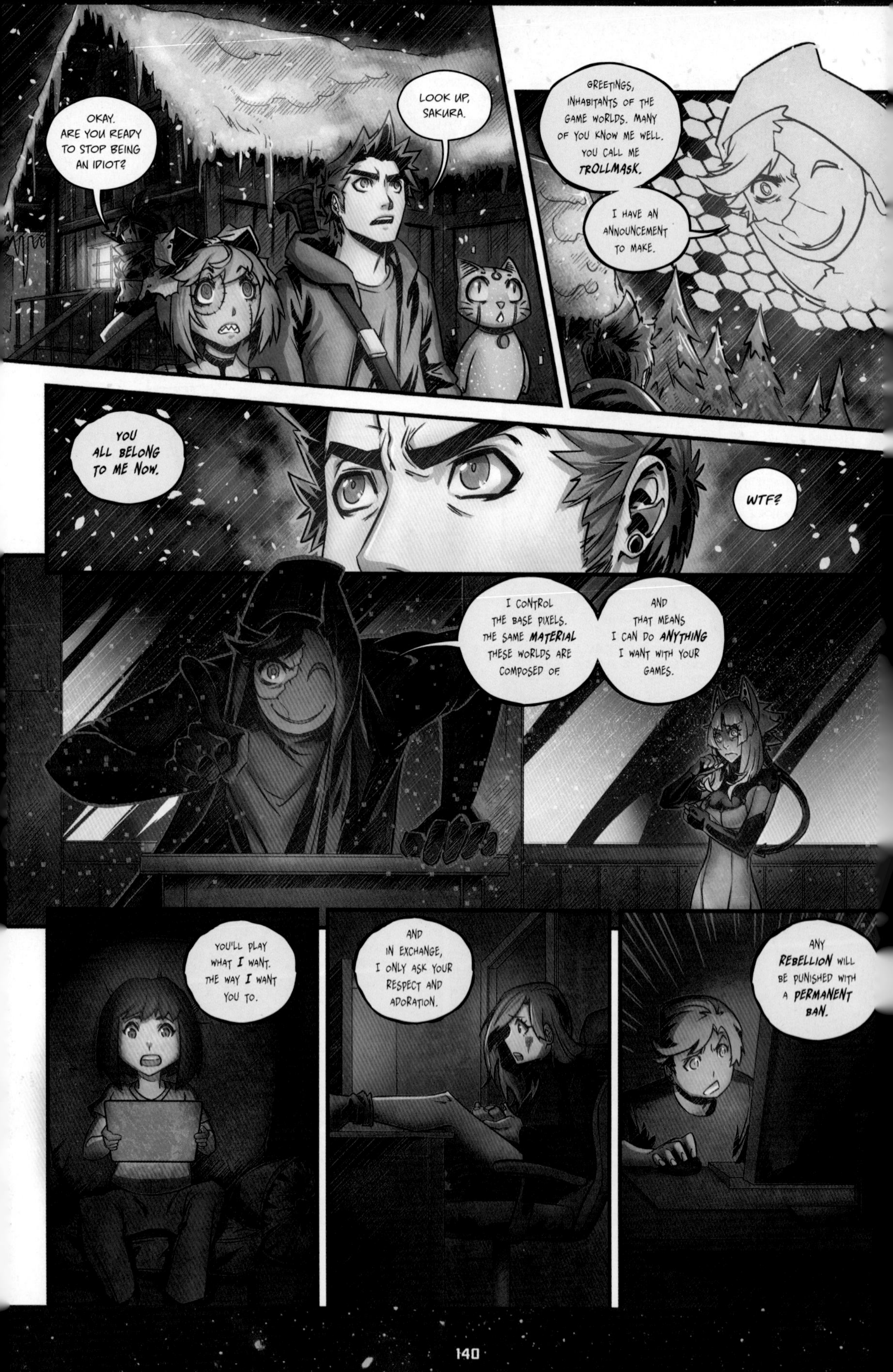
OKAY. ARE YOU READY TO STOP BEING AN IDIOT?
LOOK UP, SAKURA.
GREETINGS, INHABITANTS OF THE GAME WORLDS. MANY OF YOU KNOW ME WELL. YOU CALL ME TROLLMASK.
I HAVE AN ANNOUNCEMENT TO MAKE.
YOU ALL BELONG TO ME NOW.
WTF?
I CONTROL THE BASE PIXELS. THE SAME MATERIAL THESE WORLDS ARE COMPOSED OF.
AND THAT MEANS I CAN DO ANYTHING I WANT WITH YOUR GAMES.
YOU'LL PLAY WHAT I WANT. THE WAY I WANT YOU TO.
AND IN EXCHANGE, I ONLY ASK YOUR RESPECT AND ADORATION.
ANY REBELLION WILL BE PUNISHED WITH A PERMANENT BAN.

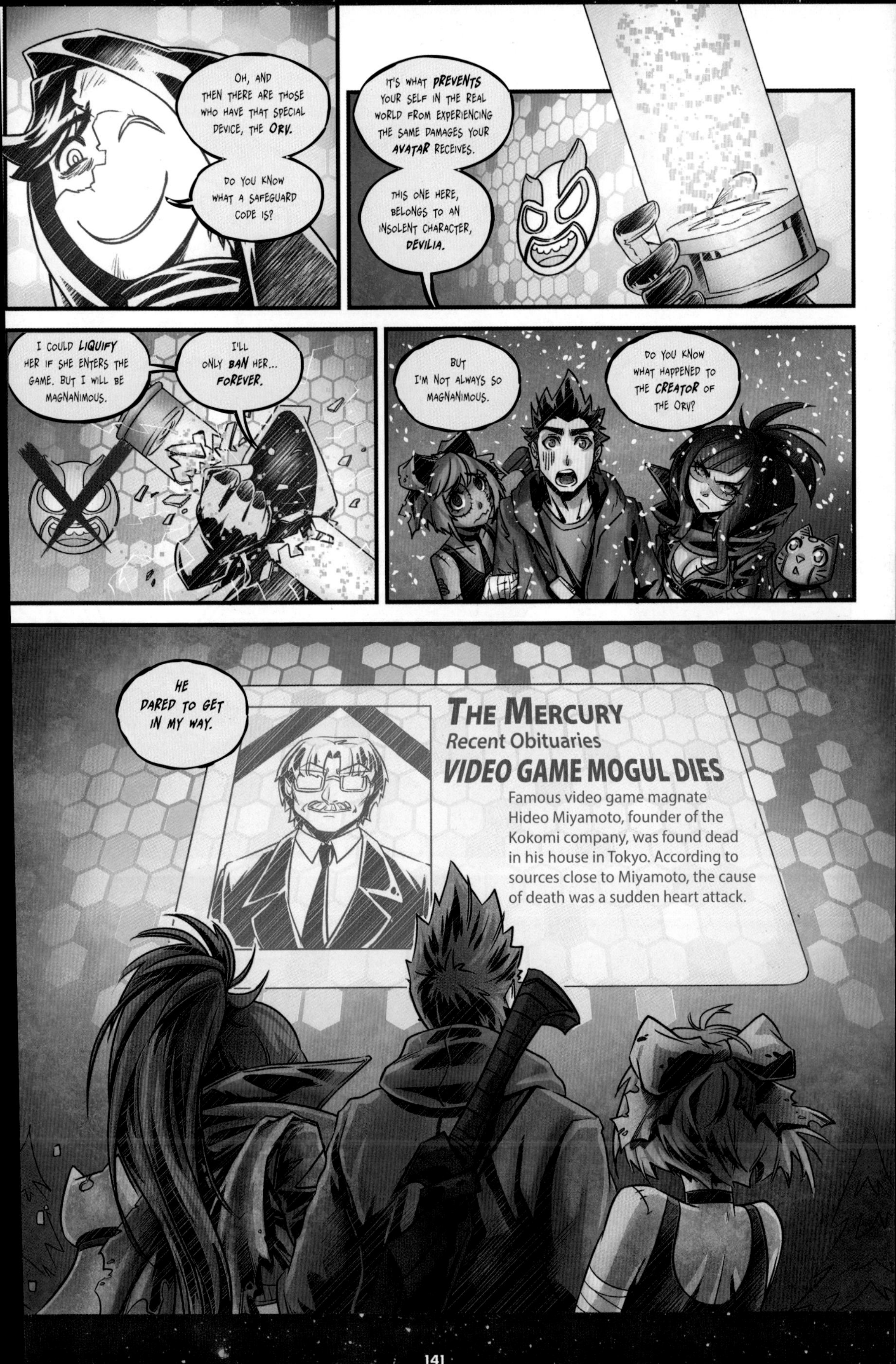
OH, AND THEN THERE ARE THOSE WHO HAVE THAT SPECIAL DEVICE, THE ORV.
DO YOU KNOW WHAT A SAFEGUARD CODE IS?
IT'S WHAT PREVENTS YOUR SELF IN THE REAL WORLD FROM EXPERIENCING THE SAME DAMAGES YOUR AVATAR RECEIVES.
THIS ONE HERE, BELONGS TO AN INSOLENT CHARACTER, DEVILIA.
I COULD LIQUIFY HER IF SHE ENTERS THE GAME. BUT I WILL BE MAGNANIMOUS.
I'LL ONLY BAN HER... FOREVER.
BUT I'M NOT ALWAYS SO MAGNANIMOUS.
DO YOU KNOW WHAT HAPPENED TO THE CREATOR OF THE ORV?
HE DARED TO GET IN MY WAY.
THE MERCURY
Recent Obituaries
VIDEO GAME MOGUL DIES
Famous video game magnate Hideo Miyamoto, founder of the Kokomi company, was found dead in his house in Tokyo. According to sources close to Miyamoto, the cause of death was a sudden heart attack.

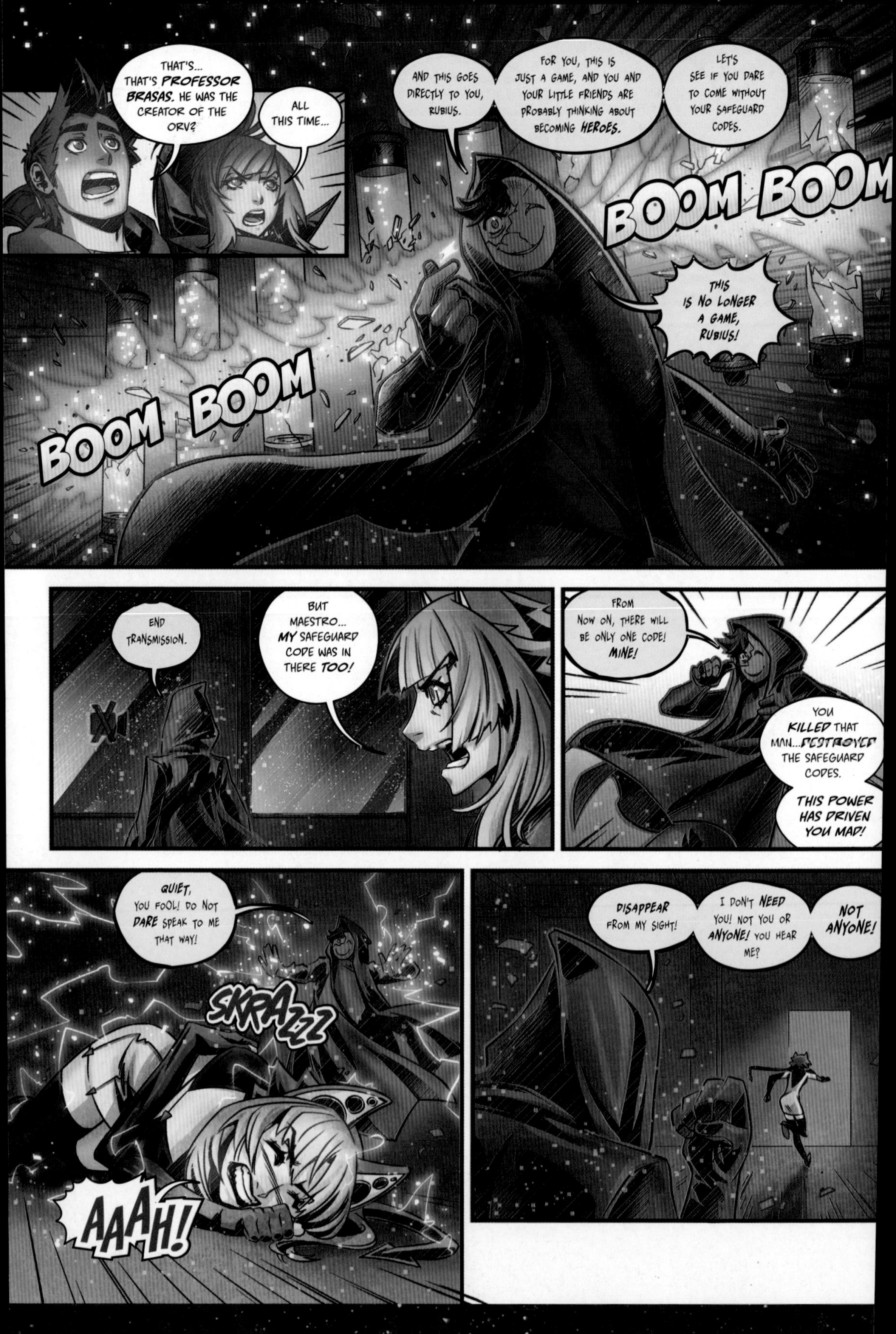

THAT'S... THAT'S **PROFESSOR BRASAS.** HE WAS THE CREATOR OF THE ORV?
ALL THIS TIME...
AND THIS GOES DIRECTLY TO YOU, RUBIUS.
FOR YOU, THIS IS JUST A GAME, AND YOU AND YOUR LITTLE FRIENDS ARE PROBABLY THINKING ABOUT BECOMING **HEROES.**
LET'S SEE IF YOU DARE TO COME WITHOUT YOUR SAFEGUARD CODES.
BOOM BOOM
THIS IS NO LONGER A GAME, RUBIUS!
BOOM BOOM
END TRANSMISSION.
BUT MAESTRO... **MY** SAFEGUARD CODE WAS IN THERE **TOO!**
FROM NOW ON, THERE WILL BE ONLY ONE CODE! **MINE!**
YOU **KILLED** THAT MAN...**DESTROYED** THE SAFEGUARD CODES.
THIS POWER HAS DRIVEN YOU MAD!
QUIET, YOU FOOL! DO NOT **DARE** SPEAK TO ME THAT WAY!
SKRAZZZ
AAAH!
DISAPPEAR FROM MY SIGHT!
I DON'T **NEED** YOU! NOT YOU OR **ANYONE!** YOU HEAR ME?
NOT ANYONE!

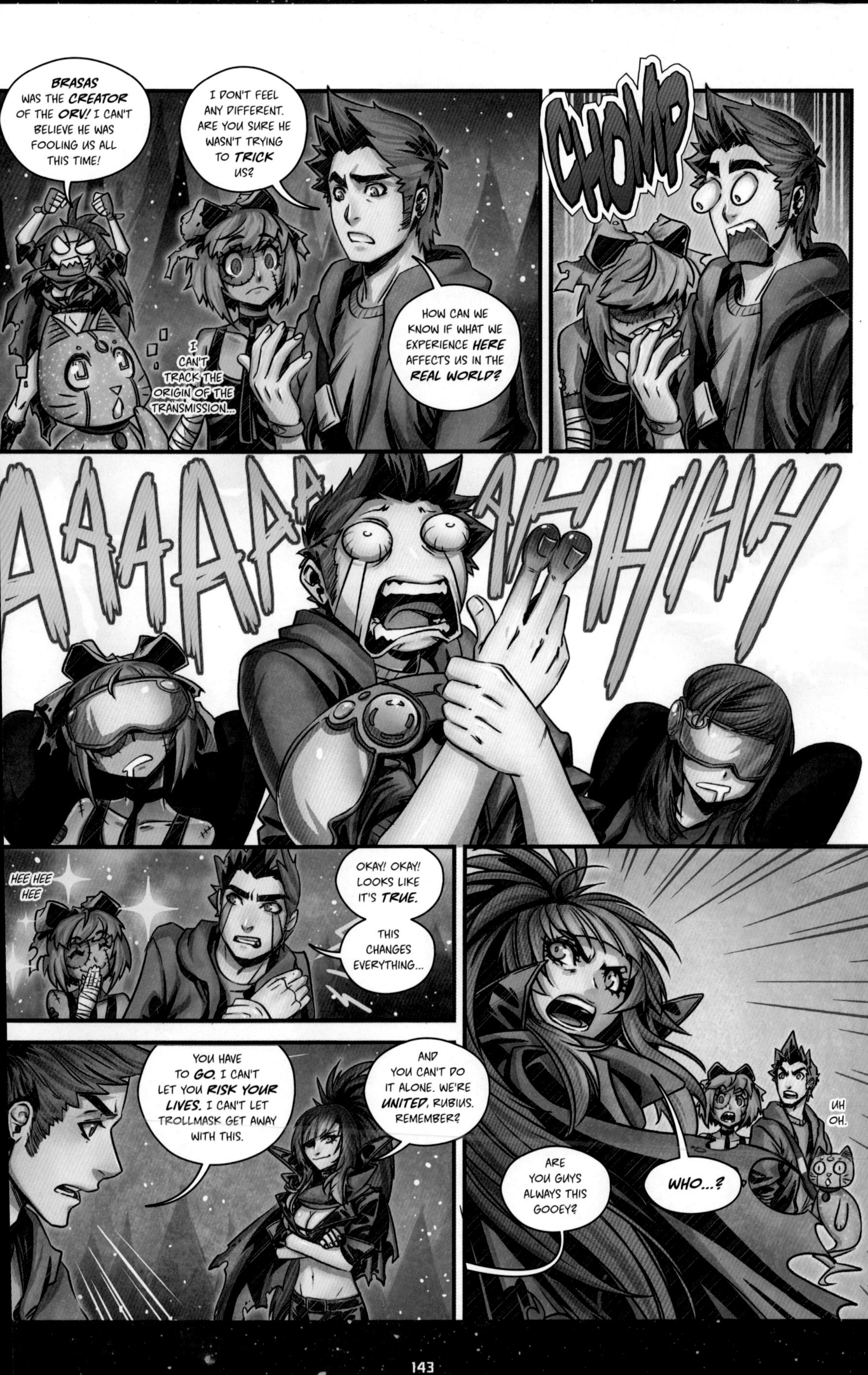
BRASAS WAS THE CREATOR OF THE ORV! I CAN'T BELIEVE HE WAS FOOLING US ALL THIS TIME!
I DON'T FEEL ANY DIFFERENT. ARE YOU SURE HE WASN'T TRYING TO TRICK US?
I CAN'T TRACK THE ORIGIN OF THE TRANSMISSION...
HOW CAN WE KNOW IF WHAT WE EXPERIENCE HERE AFFECTS US IN THE REAL WORLD?
CHOMP
AAAAAAHHHH
HEE HEE HEE
OKAY! OKAY! LOOKS LIKE IT'S TRUE.
THIS CHANGES EVERYTHING...
YOU HAVE TO GO. I CAN'T LET YOU RISK YOUR LIVES. I CAN'T LET TROLLMASK GET AWAY WITH THIS.
AND YOU CAN'T DO IT ALONE. WE'RE UNITED, RUBIUS. REMEMBER?
ARE YOU GUYS ALWAYS THIS GOOEY?
WHO...?
UH OH.

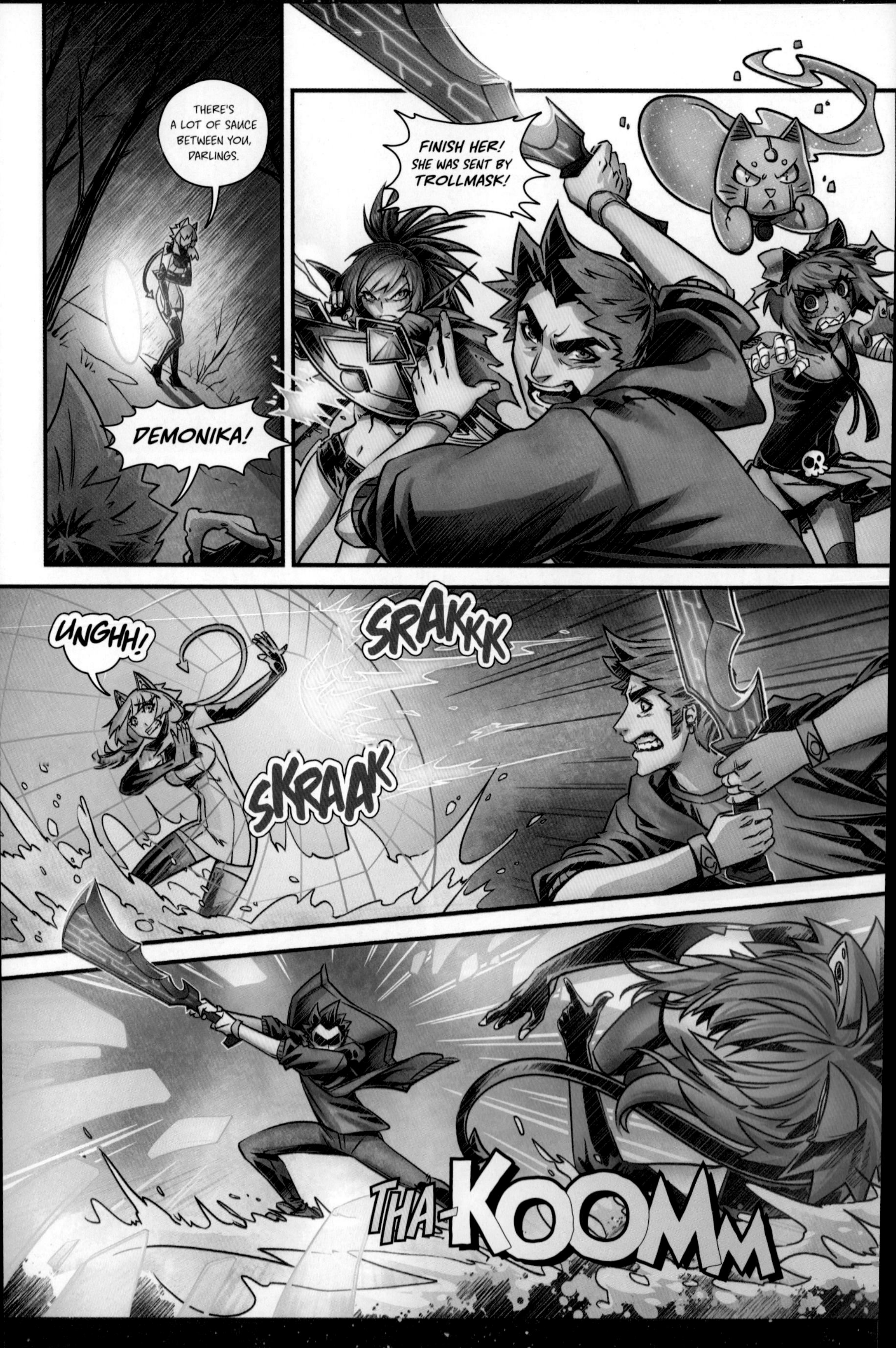
THERE'S A LOT OF SAUCE BETWEEN YOU, DARLINGS.
DEMONIKA!
FINISH HER! SHE WAS SENT BY TROLLMASK!
UNGHH!
SRAKKK
SKRAAK
THA-KOOMM

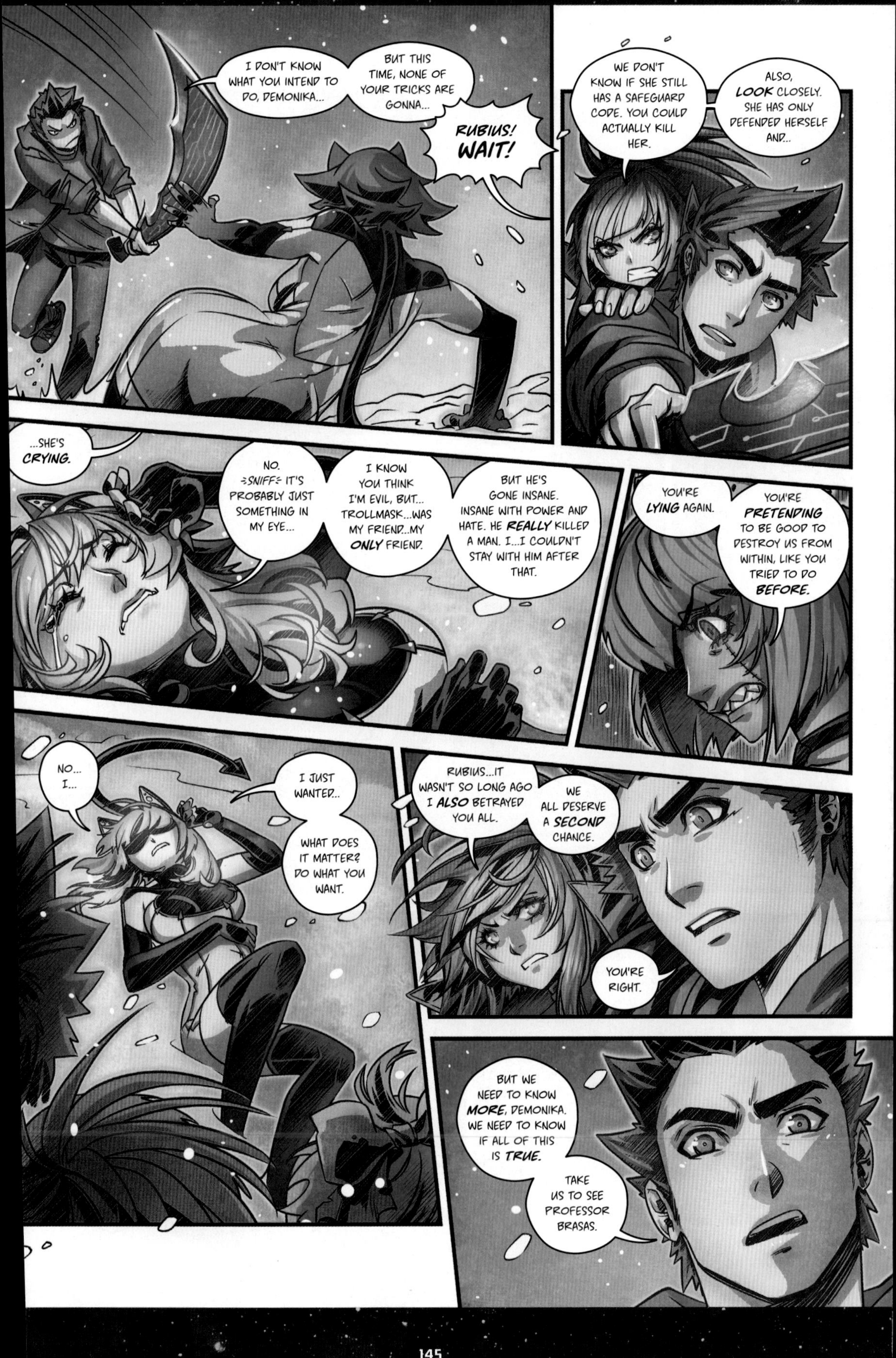
I DON'T KNOW WHAT YOU INTEND TO DO, DEMONIKA...
BUT THIS TIME, NONE OF YOUR TRICKS ARE GONNA...
RUBIUS! WAIT!
WE DON'T KNOW IF SHE STILL HAS A SAFEGUARD CODE. YOU COULD ACTUALLY KILL HER.
ALSO, LOOK CLOSELY. SHE HAS ONLY DEFENDED HERSELF AND...
...SHE'S CRYING.
NO. =SNIFF= IT'S PROBABLY JUST SOMETHING IN MY EYE...
I KNOW YOU THINK I'M EVIL, BUT... TROLLMASK...WAS MY FRIEND...MY ONLY FRIEND.
BUT HE'S GONE INSANE. INSANE WITH POWER AND HATE. HE REALLY KILLED A MAN. I...I COULDN'T STAY WITH HIM AFTER THAT.
YOU'RE LYING AGAIN.
YOU'RE PRETENDING TO BE GOOD TO DESTROY US FROM WITHIN, LIKE YOU TRIED TO DO BEFORE.
NO... I...
I JUST WANTED...
WHAT DOES IT MATTER? DO WHAT YOU WANT.
RUBIUS...IT WASN'T SO LONG AGO I ALSO BETRAYED YOU ALL.
WE ALL DESERVE A SECOND CHANCE.
YOU'RE RIGHT.
BUT WE NEED TO KNOW MORE, DEMONIKA. WE NEED TO KNOW IF ALL OF THIS IS TRUE.
TAKE US TO SEE PROFESSOR BRASAS.

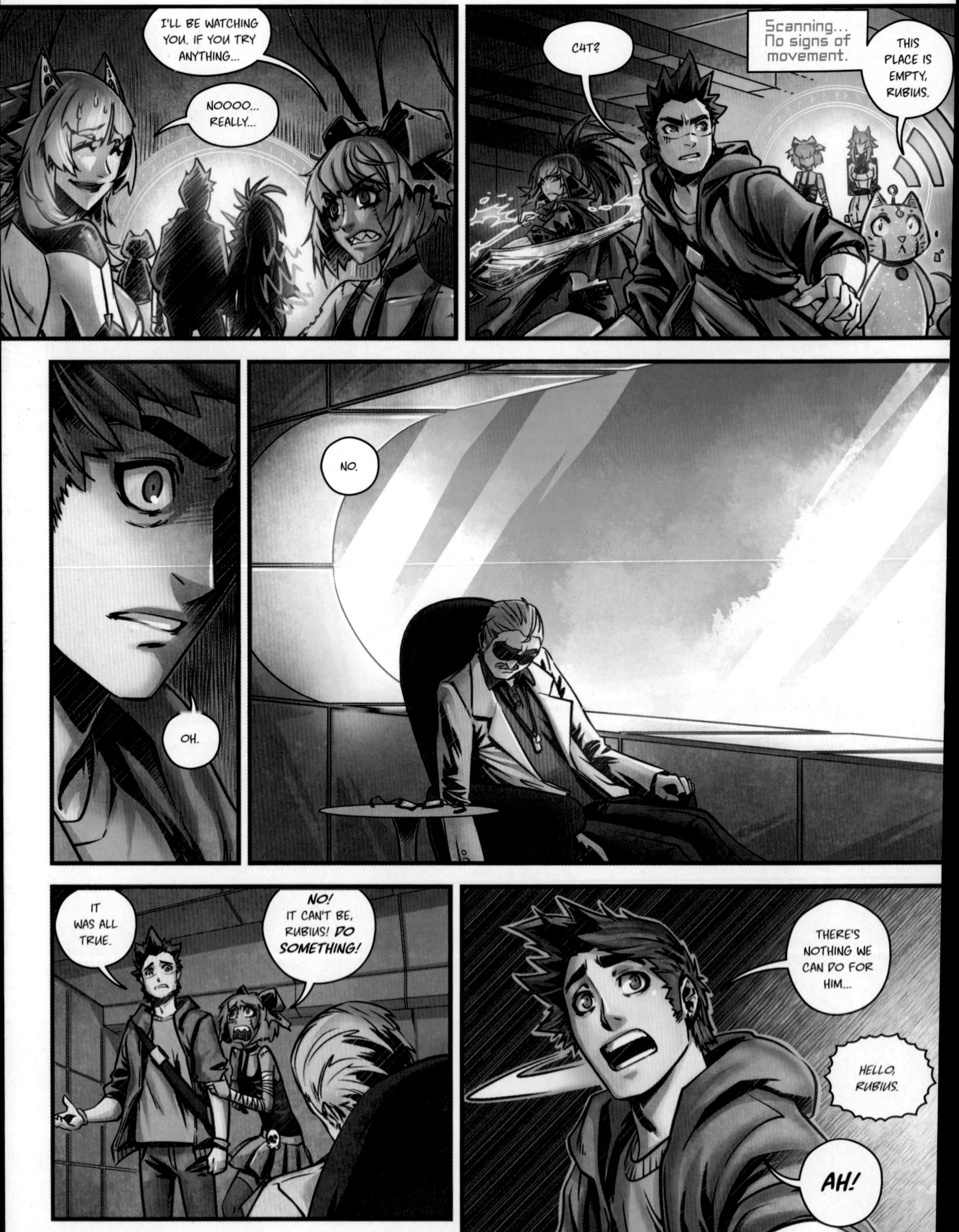
I'LL BE WATCHING YOU. IF YOU TRY ANYTHING...
NOOOO... REALLY...
C4T?
Scanning... No signs of movement.
THIS PLACE IS EMPTY, RUBIUS.
NO.
OH.
IT WAS ALL TRUE.
NO! IT CAN'T BE, RUBIUS! DO SOMETHING!
THERE'S NOTHING WE CAN DO FOR HIM...
HELLO, RUBIUS.
AH!

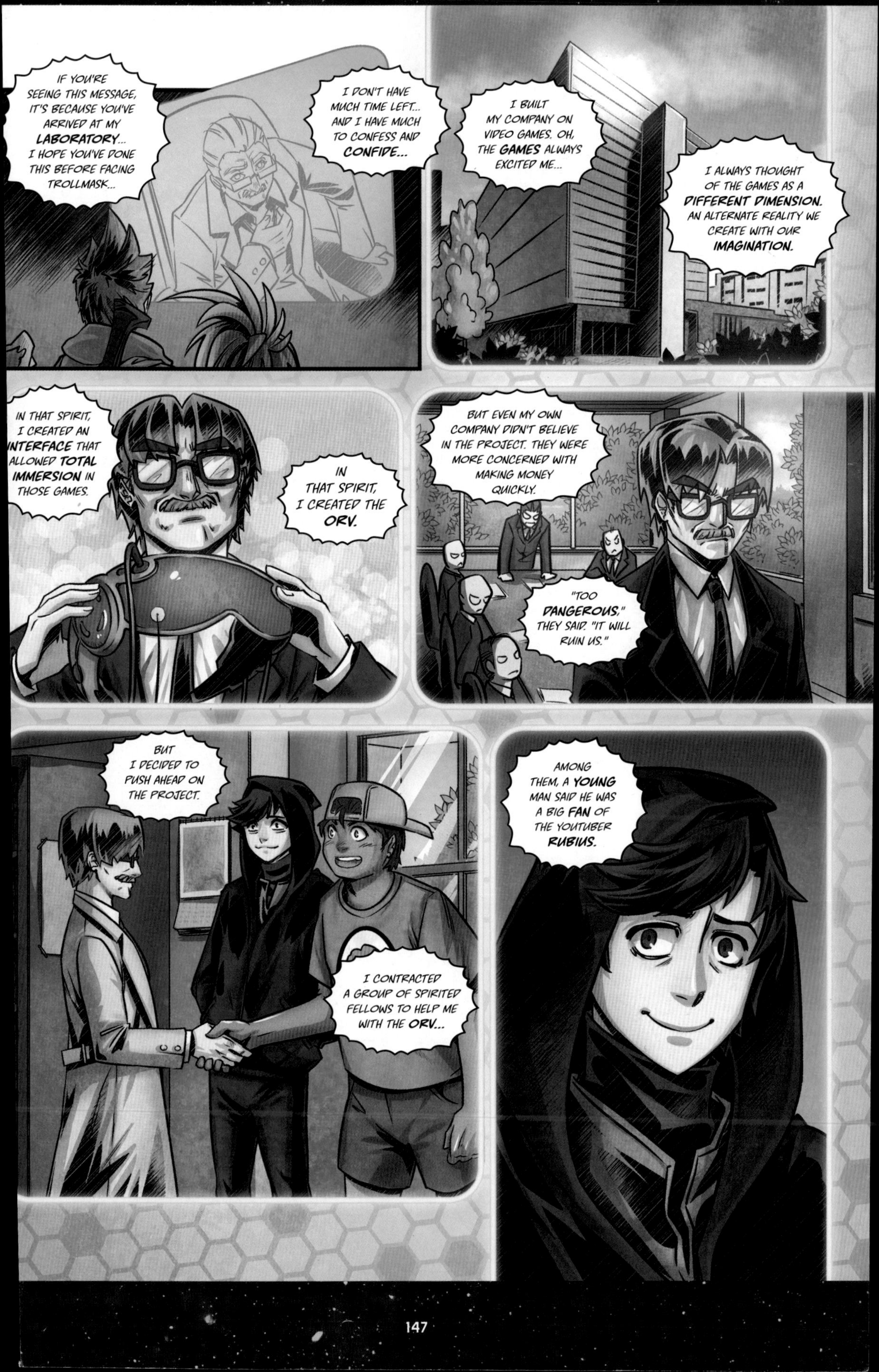

IF YOU'RE SEEING THIS MESSAGE, IT'S BECAUSE YOU'VE ARRIVED AT MY LABORATORY... I HOPE YOU'VE DONE THIS BEFORE FACING TROLLMASK...
I DON'T HAVE MUCH TIME LEFT... AND I HAVE MUCH TO CONFESS AND CONFIDE...
I BUILT MY COMPANY ON VIDEO GAMES. OH, THE GAMES ALWAYS EXCITED ME...
I ALWAYS THOUGHT OF THE GAMES AS A DIFFERENT DIMENSION. AN ALTERNATE REALITY WE CREATE WITH OUR IMAGINATION.
IN THAT SPIRIT, I CREATED AN INTERFACE THAT ALLOWED TOTAL IMMERSION IN THOSE GAMES.
IN THAT SPIRIT, I CREATED THE ORV.
BUT EVEN MY OWN COMPANY DIDN'T BELIEVE IN THE PROJECT. THEY WERE MORE CONCERNED WITH MAKING MONEY QUICKLY.
"TOO DANGEROUS," THEY SAID. "IT WILL RUIN US."
BUT I DECIDED TO PUSH AHEAD ON THE PROJECT.
I CONTRACTED A GROUP OF SPIRITED FELLOWS TO HELP ME WITH THE ORV...
AMONG THEM, A YOUNG MAN SAID HE WAS A BIG FAN OF THE YOUTUBER RUBIUS.

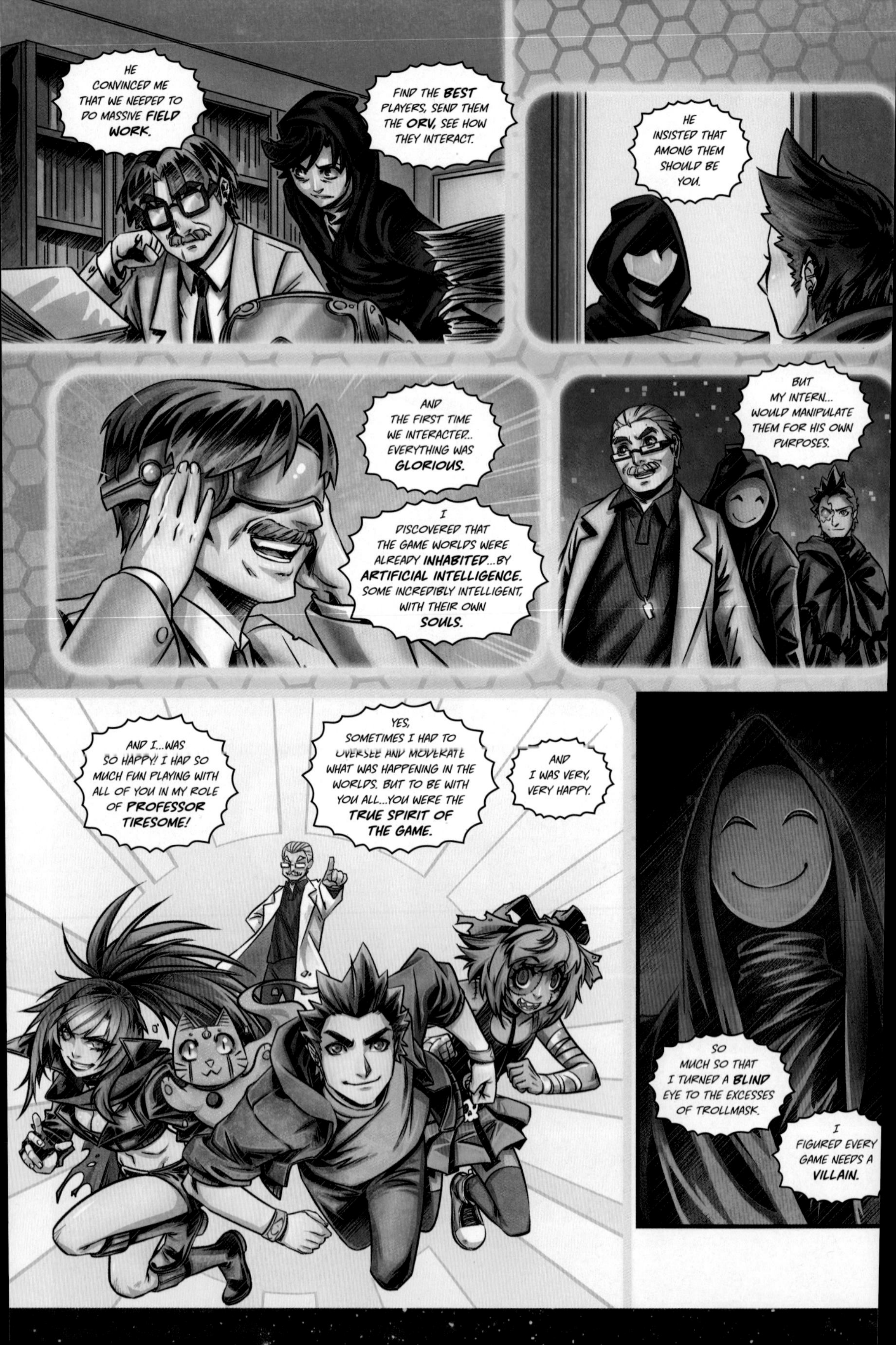
HE CONVINCED ME THAT WE NEEDED TO DO MASSIVE **FIELD WORK.**
FIND THE **BEST** PLAYERS, SEND THEM THE **ORV,** SEE HOW THEY INTERACT.
HE INSISTED THAT AMONG THEM SHOULD BE YOU.
AND THE FIRST TIME WE INTERACTED... EVERYTHING WAS **GLORIOUS.**
I DISCOVERED THAT THE GAME WORLDS WERE ALREADY **INHABITED**...BY **ARTIFICIAL INTELLIGENCE.** SOME INCREDIBLY INTELLIGENT, WITH THEIR OWN **SOULS.**
BUT MY INTERN... WOULD MANIPULATE THEM FOR HIS OWN PURPOSES.
AND I...WAS SO HAPPY! I HAD SO MUCH FUN PLAYING WITH ALL OF YOU IN MY ROLE OF **PROFESSOR TIRESOME!**
YES, SOMETIMES I HAD TO OVERSEE AND MODERATE WHAT WAS HAPPENING IN THE WORLDS. BUT TO BE WITH YOU ALL...YOU WERE THE **TRUE SPIRIT OF THE GAME.**
AND I WAS VERY, VERY HAPPY.
SO MUCH SO THAT I TURNED A **BLIND** EYE TO THE EXCESSES OF TROLLMASK.
I FIGURED EVERY GAME NEEDS A **VILLAIN.**

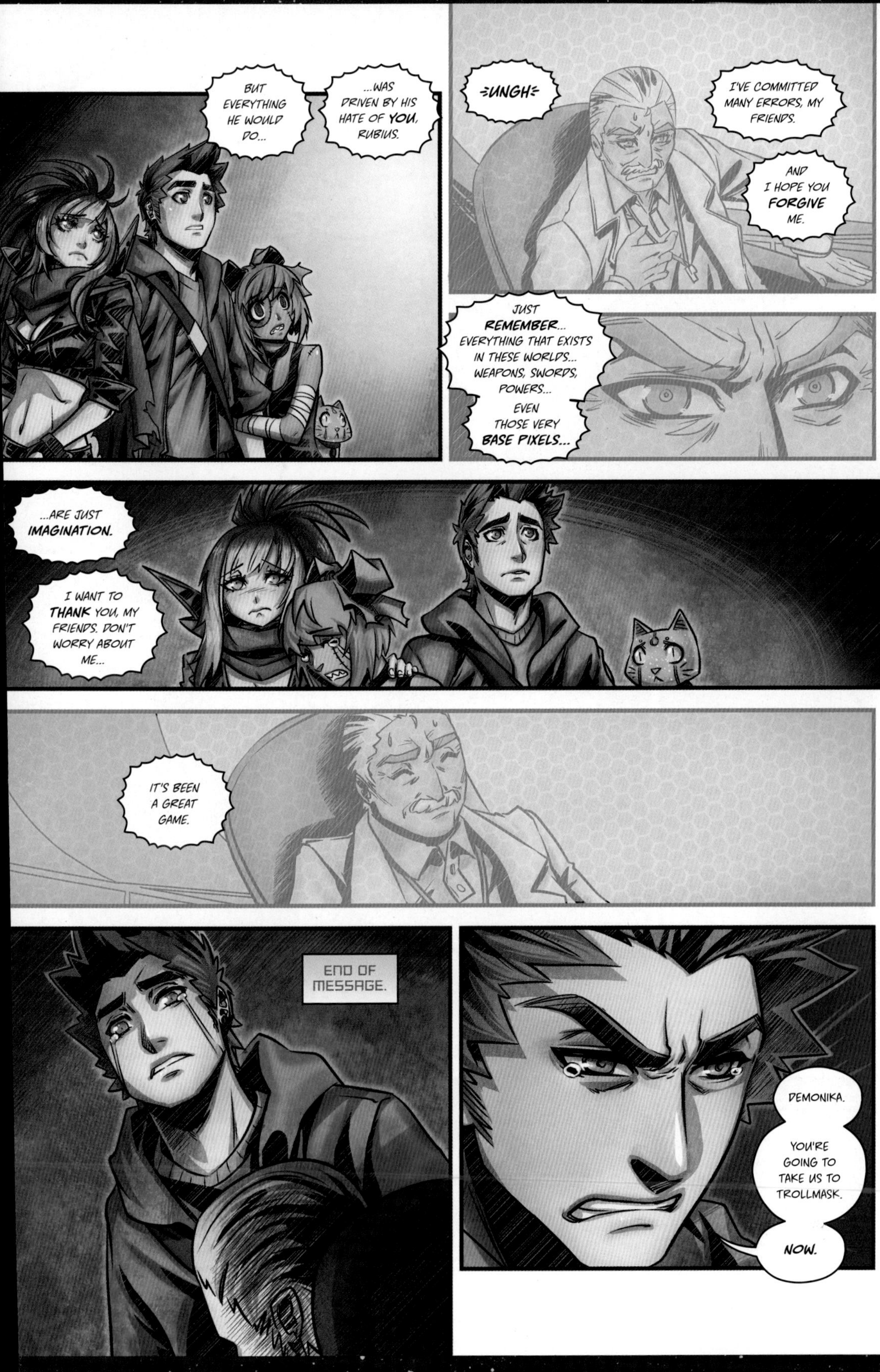

BUT EVERYTHING HE WOULD DO...
...WAS DRIVEN BY HIS HATE OF YOU, RUBIUS.
UNGH
I'VE COMMITTED MANY ERRORS, MY FRIENDS.
AND I HOPE YOU FORGIVE ME.
JUST REMEMBER... EVERYTHING THAT EXISTS IN THESE WORLDS... WEAPONS, SWORDS, POWERS...
EVEN THOSE VERY BASE PIXELS...
...ARE JUST IMAGINATION.
I WANT TO THANK YOU, MY FRIENDS. DON'T WORRY ABOUT ME...
IT'S BEEN A GREAT GAME.
END OF MESSAGE.
DEMONIKA.
YOU'RE GOING TO TAKE US TO TROLLMASK.
NOW.

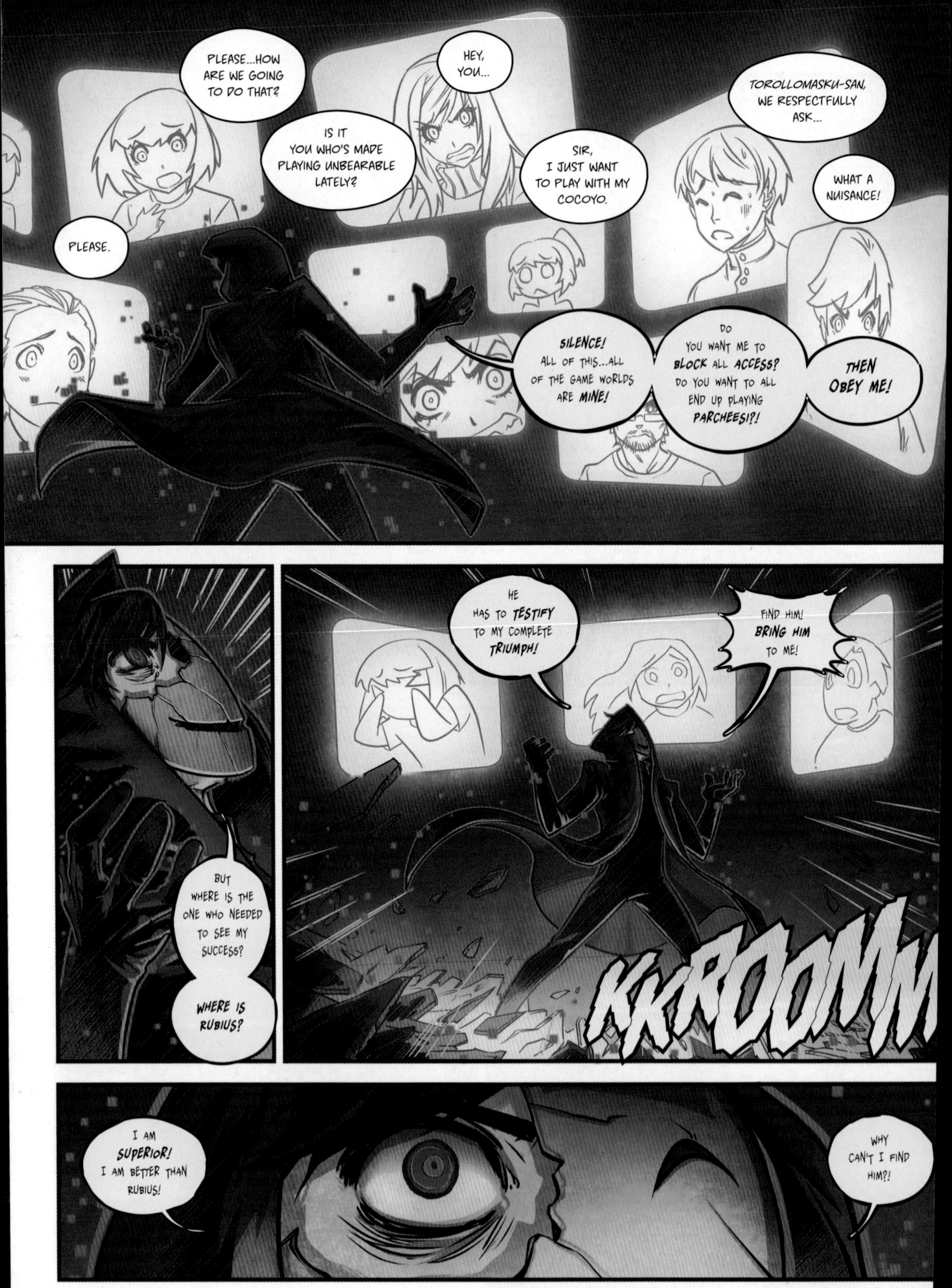
PLEASE...HOW ARE WE GOING TO DO THAT?
HEY, YOU...
IS IT YOU WHO'S MADE PLAYING UNBEARABLE LATELY?
SIR, I JUST WANT TO PLAY WITH MY COCOYO.
TOROLLOMASKU-SAN, WE RESPECTFULLY ASK...
WHAT A NUISANCE!
PLEASE.
SILENCE! ALL OF THIS...ALL OF THE GAME WORLDS ARE MINE!
DO YOU WANT ME TO BLOCK ALL ACCESS? DO YOU WANT TO ALL END UP PLAYING PARCHEESI?!
THEN OBEY ME!
BUT WHERE IS THE ONE WHO NEEDED TO SEE MY SUCCESS?
WHERE IS RUBIUS?
HE HAS TO TESTIFY TO MY COMPLETE TRIUMPH!
FIND HIM! BRING HIM TO ME!
KKROOMM
I AM SUPERIOR! I AM BETTER THAN RUBIUS!
WHY CAN'T I FIND HIM?!

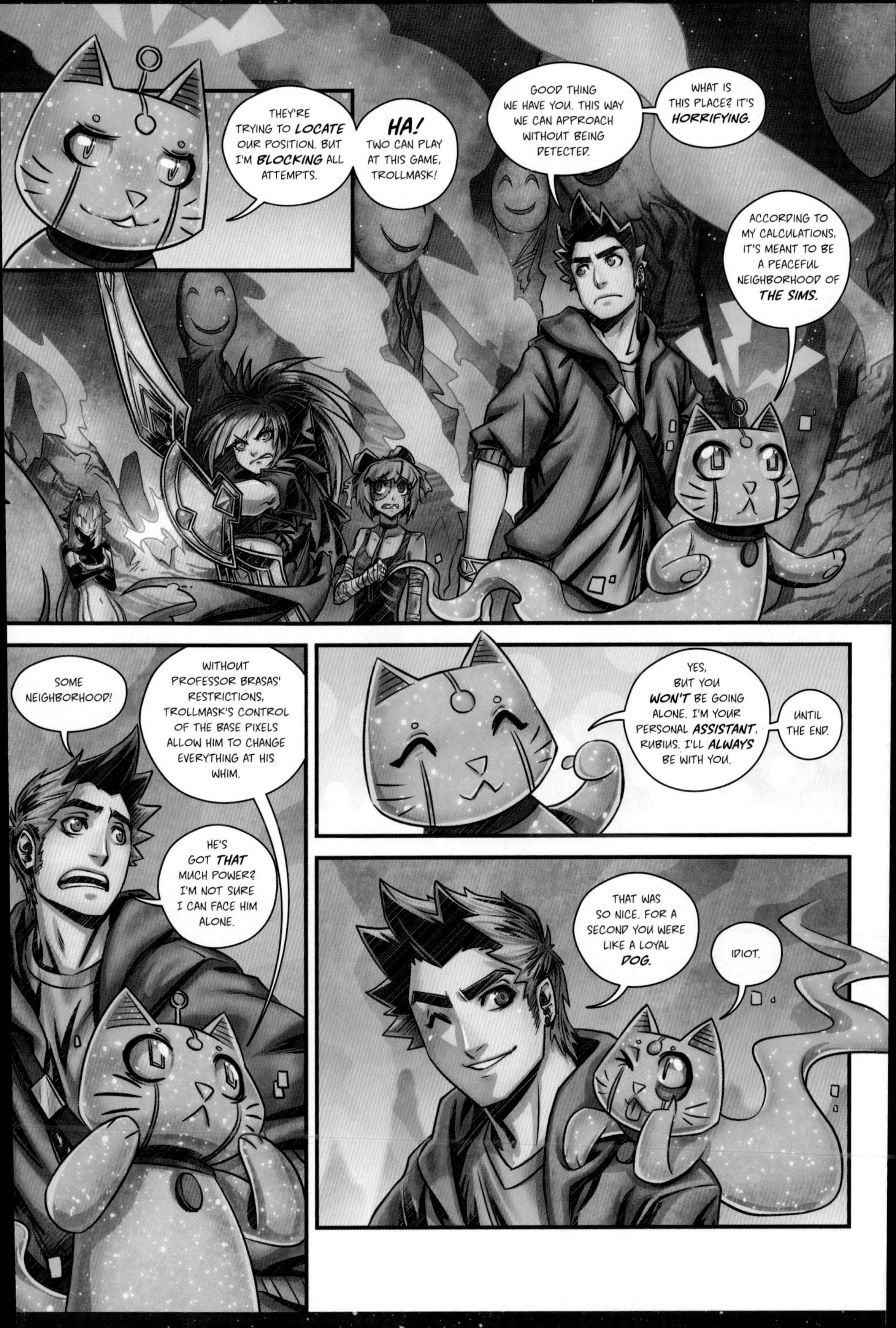
THEY'RE TRYING TO LOCATE OUR POSITION. BUT I'M BLOCKING ALL ATTEMPTS.
HA! TWO CAN PLAY AT THIS GAME, TROLLMASK!
GOOD THING WE HAVE YOU. THIS WAY WE CAN APPROACH WITHOUT BEING DETECTED.
WHAT IS THIS PLACE? IT'S HORRIFYING.
ACCORDING TO MY CALCULATIONS, IT'S MEANT TO BE A PEACEFUL NEIGHBORHOOD OF THE SIMS.
SOME NEIGHBORHOOD!
WITHOUT PROFESSOR BRASAS' RESTRICTIONS, TROLLMASK'S CONTROL OF THE BASE PIXELS ALLOW HIM TO CHANGE EVERYTHING AT HIS WHIM.
HE'S GOT THAT MUCH POWER? I'M NOT SURE I CAN FACE HIM ALONE.
YES, BUT YOU WON'T BE GOING ALONE. I'M YOUR PERSONAL ASSISTANT, RUBIUS. I'LL ALWAYS BE WITH YOU.
UNTIL THE END.
THAT WAS SO NICE. FOR A SECOND YOU WERE LIKE A LOYAL DOG.
IDIOT.

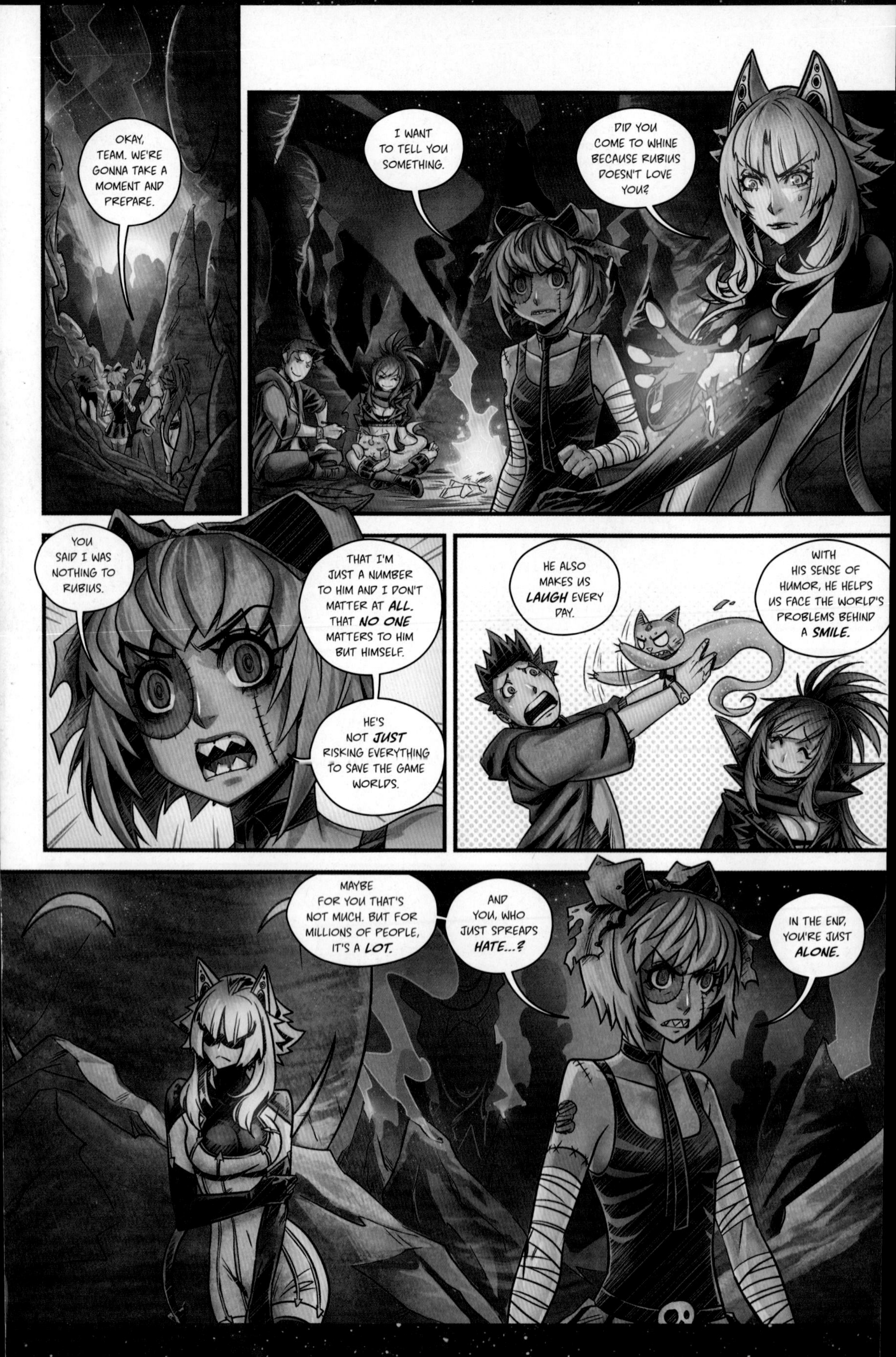
OKAY, TEAM. WE'RE GONNA TAKE A MOMENT AND PREPARE.
I WANT TO TELL YOU SOMETHING.
DID YOU COME TO WHINE BECAUSE RUBIUS DOESN'T LOVE YOU?
YOU SAID I WAS NOTHING TO RUBIUS.
THAT I'M JUST A NUMBER TO HIM AND I DON'T MATTER AT ALL. THAT NO ONE MATTERS TO HIM BUT HIMSELF.
HE'S NOT JUST RISKING EVERYTHING TO SAVE THE GAME WORLDS.
HE ALSO MAKES US LAUGH EVERY DAY.
WITH HIS SENSE OF HUMOR, HE HELPS US FACE THE WORLD'S PROBLEMS BEHIND A SMILE.
MAYBE FOR YOU THAT'S NOT MUCH. BUT FOR MILLIONS OF PEOPLE, IT'S A LOT.
AND YOU, WHO JUST SPREADS HATE...?
IN THE END, YOU'RE JUST ALONE.

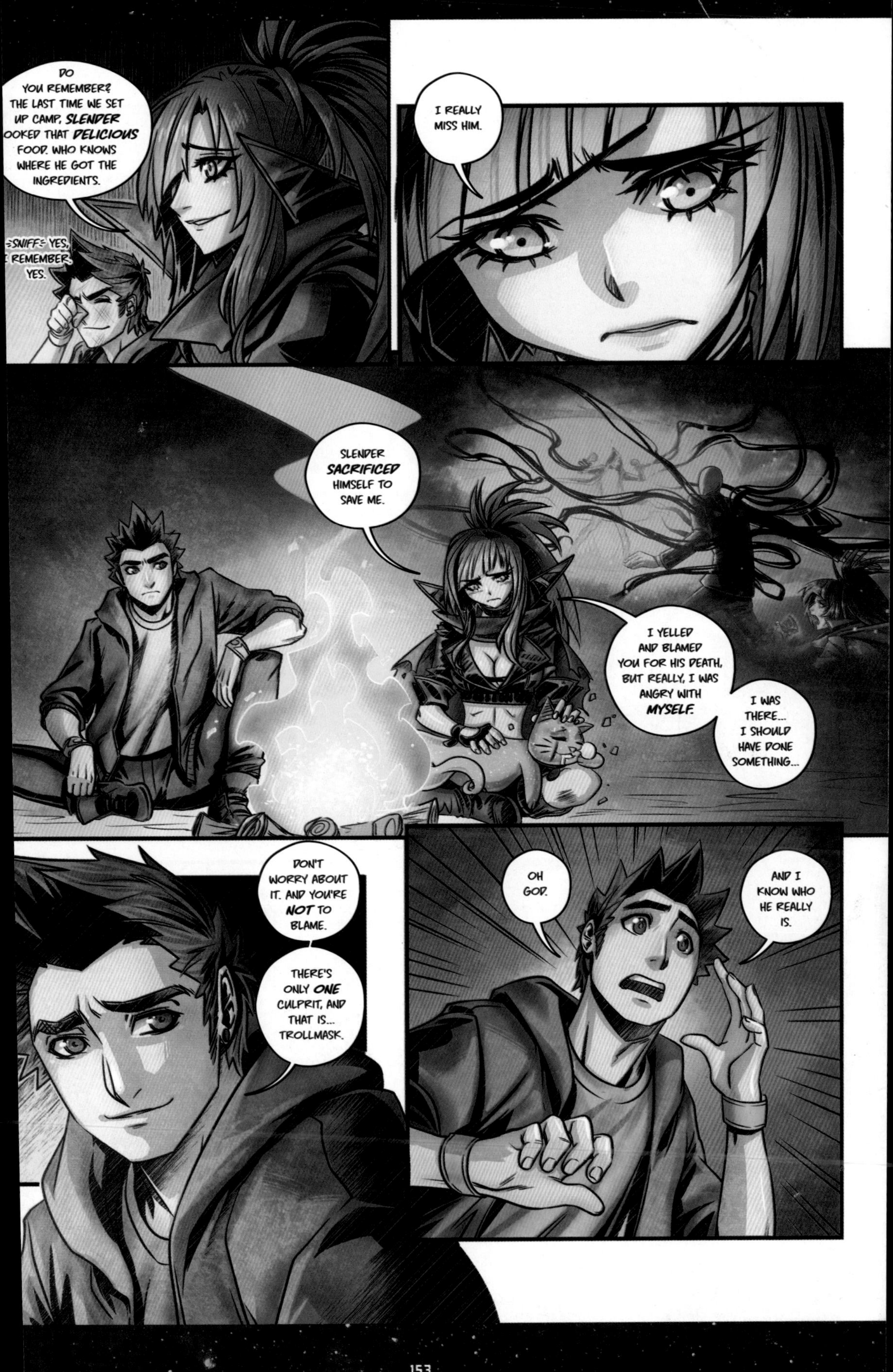

DO YOU REMEMBER? THE LAST TIME WE SET UP CAMP, SLENDER OOKED THAT DELICIOUS FOOD. WHO KNOWS WHERE HE GOT THE INGREDIENTS.
=SNIFF= YES, I REMEMBER. YES.
I REALLY MISS HIM.
SLENDER SACRIFICED HIMSELF TO SAVE ME.
I YELLED AND BLAMED YOU FOR HIS DEATH, BUT REALLY, I WAS ANGRY WITH MYSELF.
I WAS THERE... I SHOULD HAVE DONE SOMETHING...
DON'T WORRY ABOUT IT. AND YOU'RE NOT TO BLAME.
THERE'S ONLY ONE CULPRIT, AND THAT IS... TROLLMASK.
OH GOD.
AND I KNOW WHO HE REALLY IS.

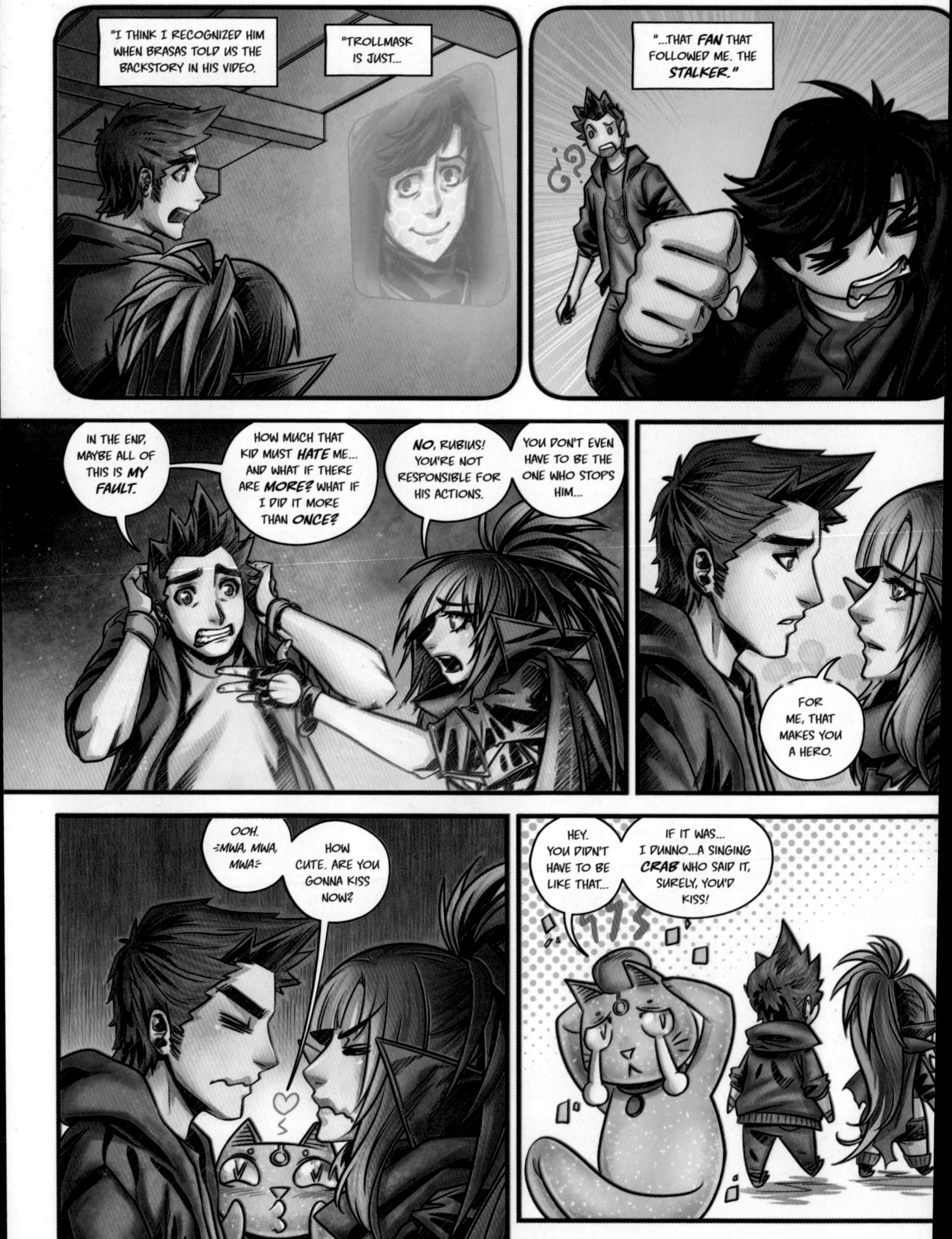
"I THINK I RECOGNIZED HIM WHEN BRASAS TOLD US THE BACKSTORY IN HIS VIDEO.
"TROLLMASK IS JUST...
"...THAT FAN THAT FOLLOWED ME. THE STALKER."
¿?
IN THE END, MAYBE ALL OF THIS IS MY FAULT.
HOW MUCH THAT KID MUST HATE ME... AND WHAT IF THERE ARE MORE? WHAT IF I DID IT MORE THAN ONCE?
NO, RUBIUS! YOU'RE NOT RESPONSIBLE FOR HIS ACTIONS.
YOU DON'T EVEN HAVE TO BE THE ONE WHO STOPS HIM...
FOR ME, THAT MAKES YOU A HERO.
OOH. =MWA, MWA, MWA=
HOW CUTE. ARE YOU GONNA KISS NOW?
HEY. YOU DIDN'T HAVE TO BE LIKE THAT...
IF IT WAS... I DUNNO...A SINGING CRAB WHO SAID IT, SURELY, YOU'D KISS!

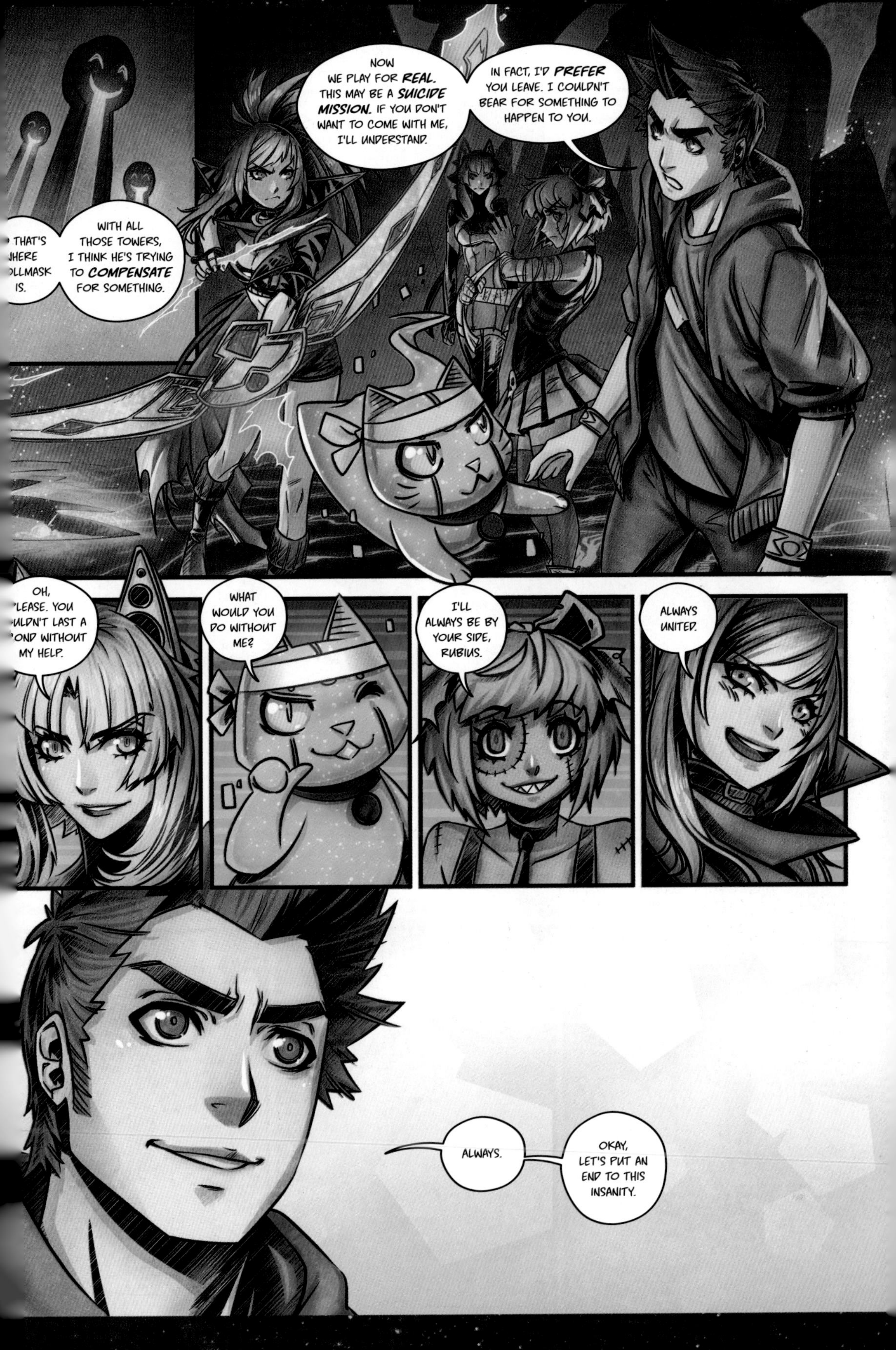
THAT'S HERE LLMASK IS.
WITH ALL THOSE TOWERS, I THINK HE'S TRYING TO COMPENSATE FOR SOMETHING.
NOW WE PLAY FOR REAL. THIS MAY BE A SUICIDE MISSION. IF YOU DON'T WANT TO COME WITH ME, I'LL UNDERSTAND.
IN FACT, I'D PREFER YOU LEAVE. I COULDN'T BEAR FOR SOMETHING TO HAPPEN TO YOU.
OH, PLEASE. YOU ULDN'T LAST A OND WITHOUT MY HELP.
WHAT WOULD YOU DO WITHOUT ME?
I'LL ALWAYS BE BY YOUR SIDE, RUBIUS.
ALWAYS UNITED.
ALWAYS.
OKAY, LET'S PUT AN END TO THIS INSANITY.

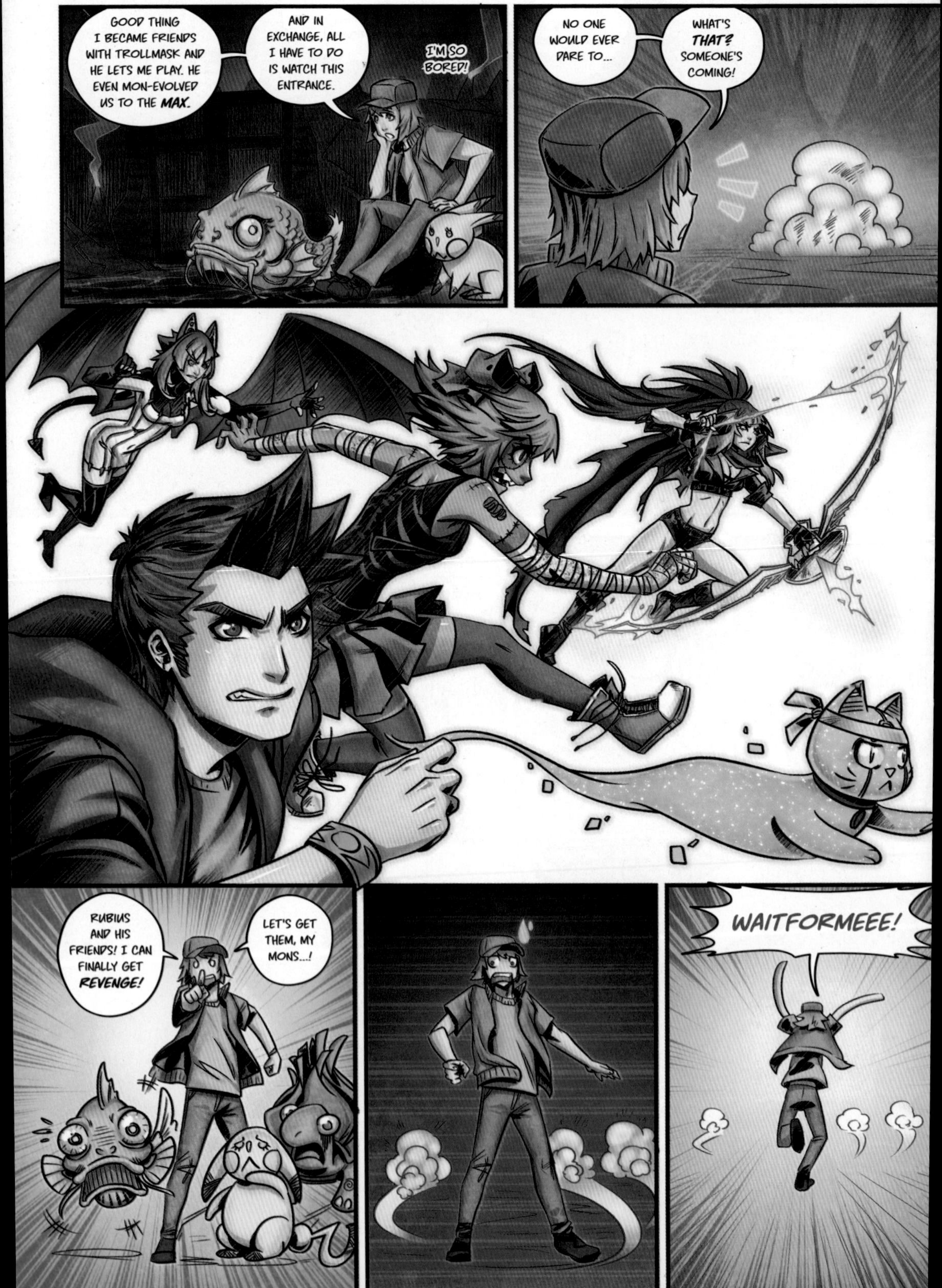
GOOD THING I BECAME FRIENDS WITH TROLLMASK AND HE LETS ME PLAY. HE EVEN MON-EVOLVED US TO THE MAX.
AND IN EXCHANGE, ALL I HAVE TO DO IS WATCH THIS ENTRANCE.
I'M SO BORED!
NO ONE WOULD EVER DARE TO...
WHAT'S THAT? SOMEONE'S COMING!
RUBIUS AND HIS FRIENDS! I CAN FINALLY GET REVENGE!
LET'S GET THEM, MY MONS...!
WAITFORMEEE!

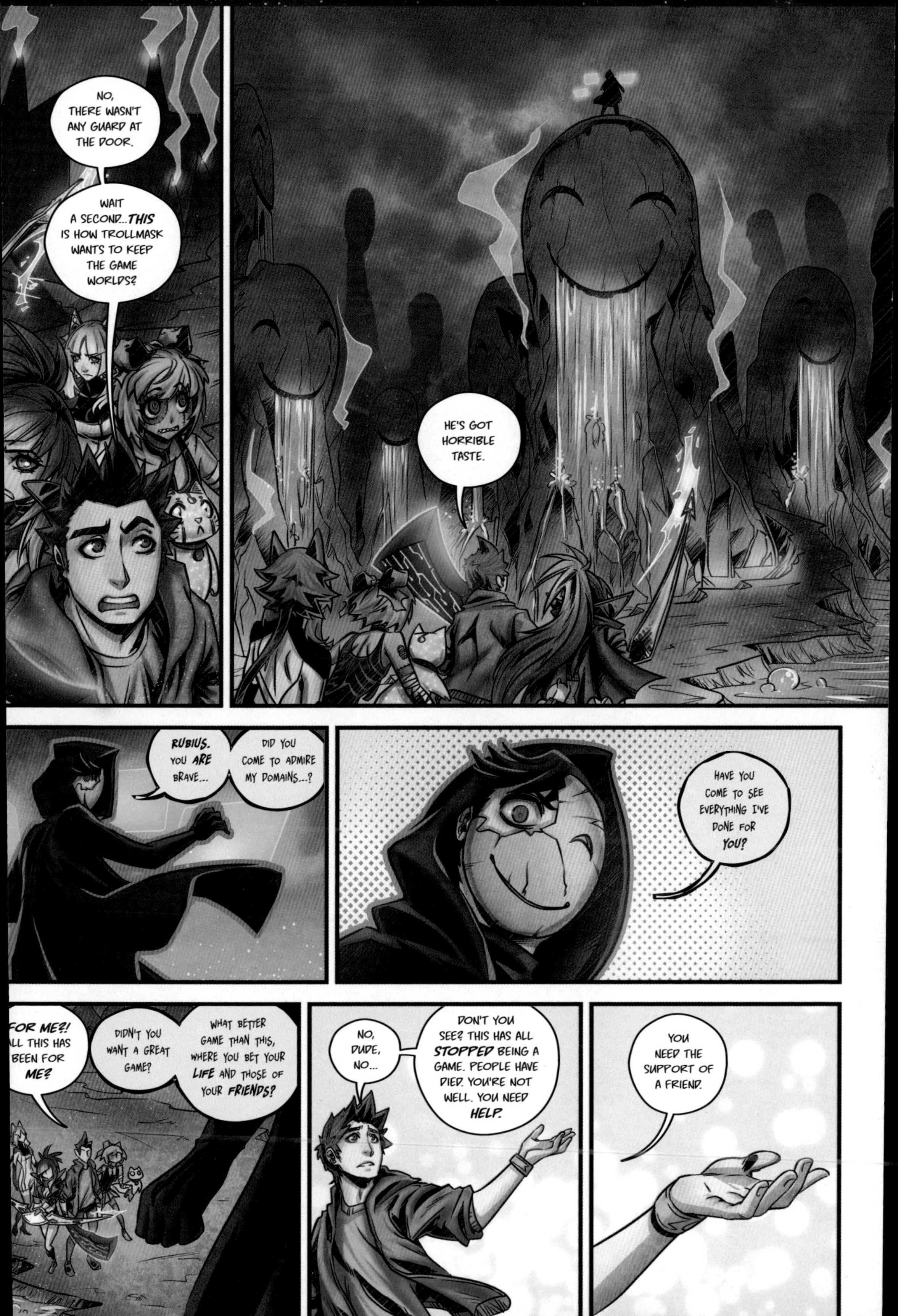

NO, THERE WASN'T ANY GUARD AT THE DOOR.
WAIT A SECOND...THIS IS HOW TROLLMASK WANTS TO KEEP THE GAME WORLDS?
HE'S GOT HORRIBLE TASTE.
RUBIUS. YOU ARE BRAVE...
DID YOU COME TO ADMIRE MY DOMAINS...?
HAVE YOU COME TO SEE EVERYTHING I'VE DONE FOR YOU?
FOR ME?! ALL THIS HAS BEEN FOR ME?
DIDN'T YOU WANT A GREAT GAME?
WHAT BETTER GAME THAN THIS, WHERE YOU BET YOUR LIFE AND THOSE OF YOUR FRIENDS?
NO, DUDE, NO...
DON'T YOU SEE? THIS HAS ALL STOPPED BEING A GAME. PEOPLE HAVE DIED. YOU'RE NOT WELL. YOU NEED HELP.
YOU NEED THE SUPPORT OF A FRIEND.

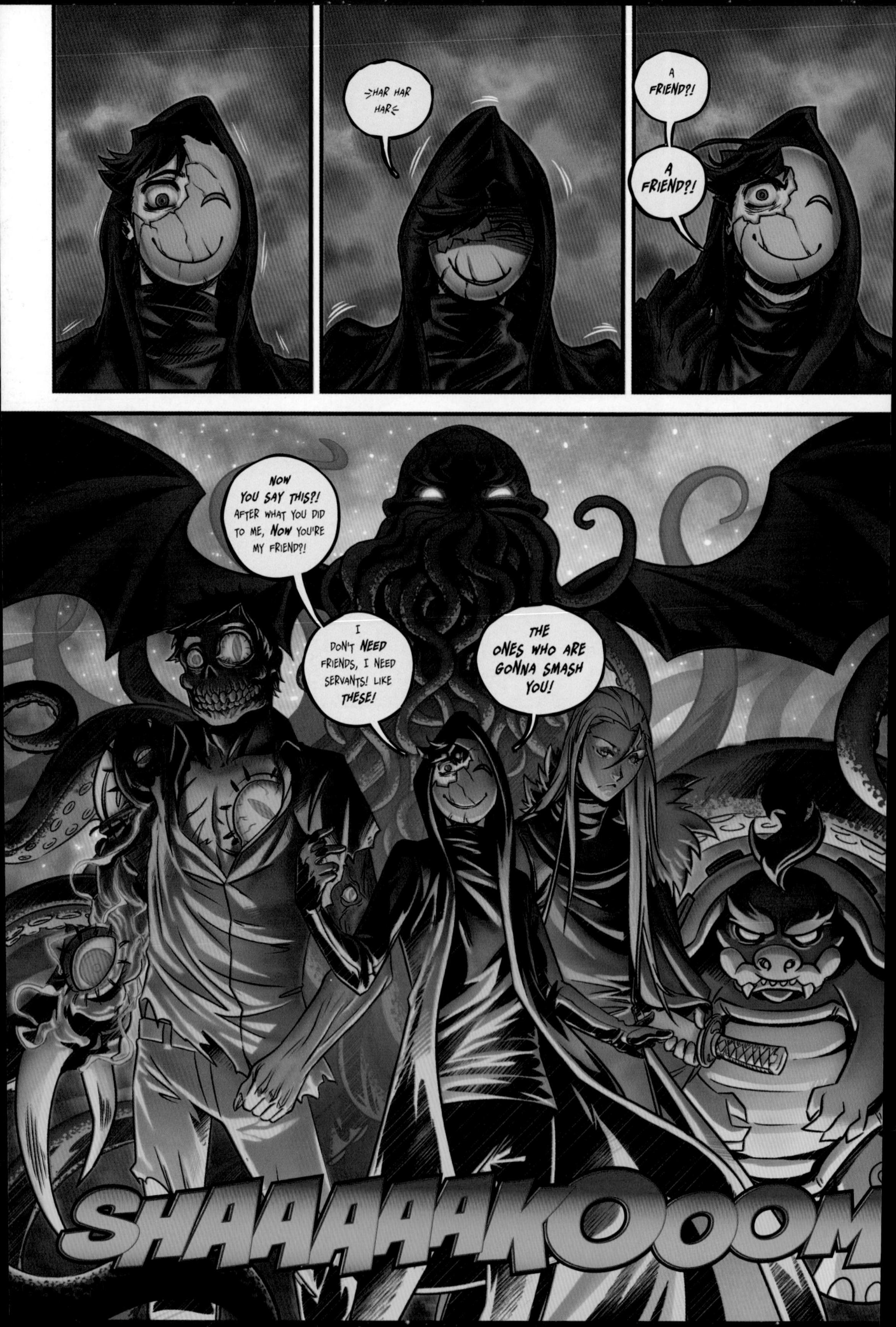

≶HAR HAR HAR≷
A FRIEND?!
A FRIEND?!
NOW YOU SAY THIS?! AFTER WHAT YOU DID TO ME, NOW YOU'RE MY FRIEND?!
I DON'T NEED FRIENDS, I NEED SERVANTS! LIKE THESE!
THE ONES WHO ARE GONNA SMASH YOU!
SHAAAAAKOOOOM

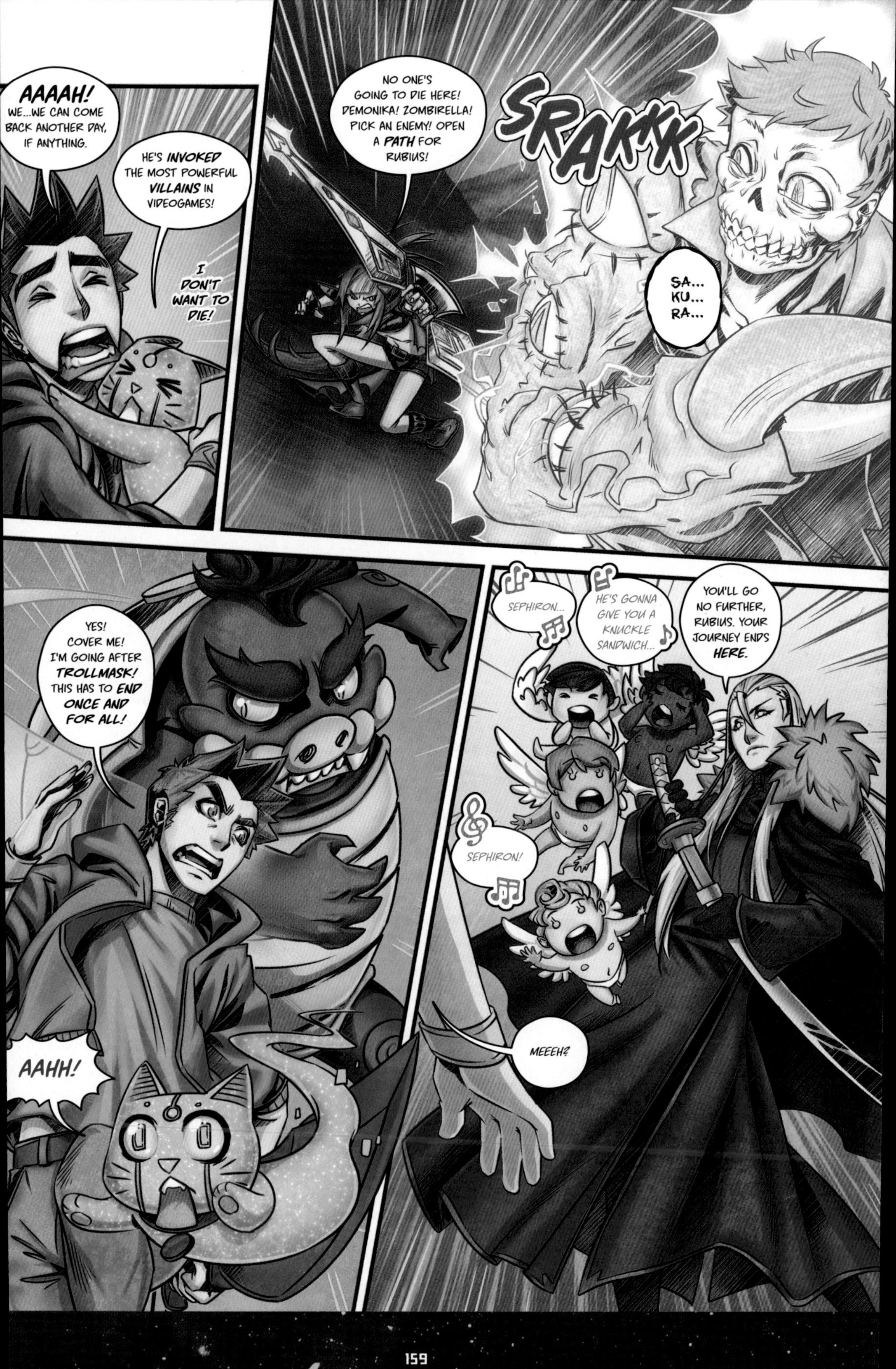
AAAAH! WE...WE CAN COME BACK ANOTHER DAY, IF ANYTHING.
HE'S INVOKED THE MOST POWERFUL VILLAINS IN VIDEOGAMES!
I DON'T WANT TO DIE!
NO ONE'S GOING TO DIE HERE! DEMONIKA! ZOMBIRELLA! PICK AN ENEMY! OPEN A PATH FOR RUBIUS!
SRAKKK
SA... KU... RA...
YES! COVER ME! I'M GOING AFTER TROLLMASK! THIS HAS TO END ONCE AND FOR ALL!
AAHH!
SEPHIRON...
HE'S GONNA GIVE YOU A KNUCKLE SANDWICH...
YOU'LL GO NO FURTHER, RUBIUS. YOUR JOURNEY ENDS HERE.
SEPHIRON!
MEEEH?

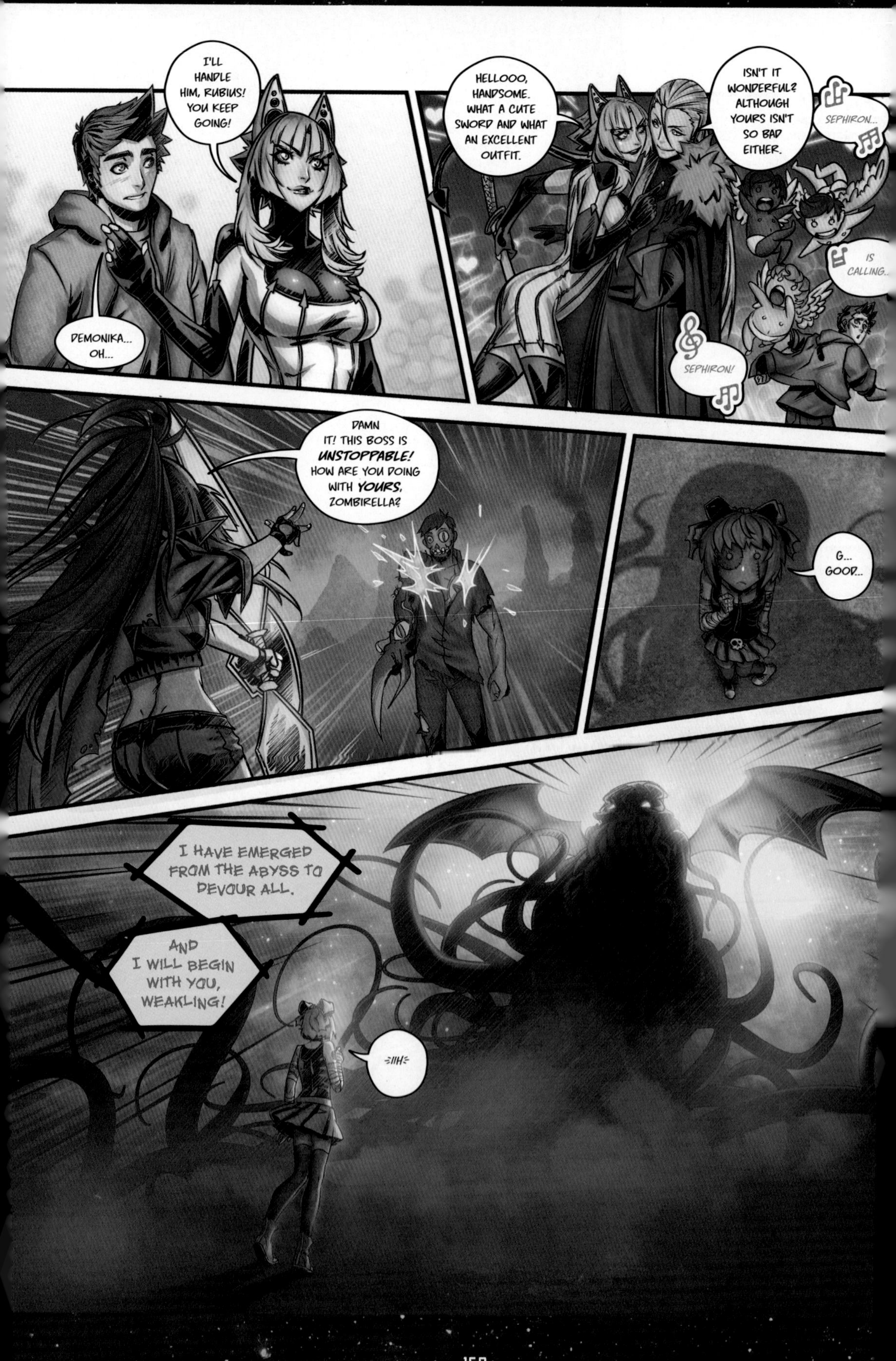

I'LL HANDLE HIM, RUBIUS! YOU KEEP GOING!
DEMONIKA... OH...
HELLOOO, HANDSOME. WHAT A CUTE SWORD AND WHAT AN EXCELLENT OUTFIT.
ISN'T IT WONDERFUL? ALTHOUGH YOURS ISN'T SO BAD EITHER.
SEPHIRON...
IS CALLING...
SEPHIRON!
DAMN IT! THIS BOSS IS UNSTOPPABLE! HOW ARE YOU DOING WITH YOURS, ZOMBIRELLA?
G... GOOD...
I HAVE EMERGED FROM THE ABYSS TO DEVOUR ALL.
AND I WILL BEGIN WITH YOU, WEAKLING!
IIH

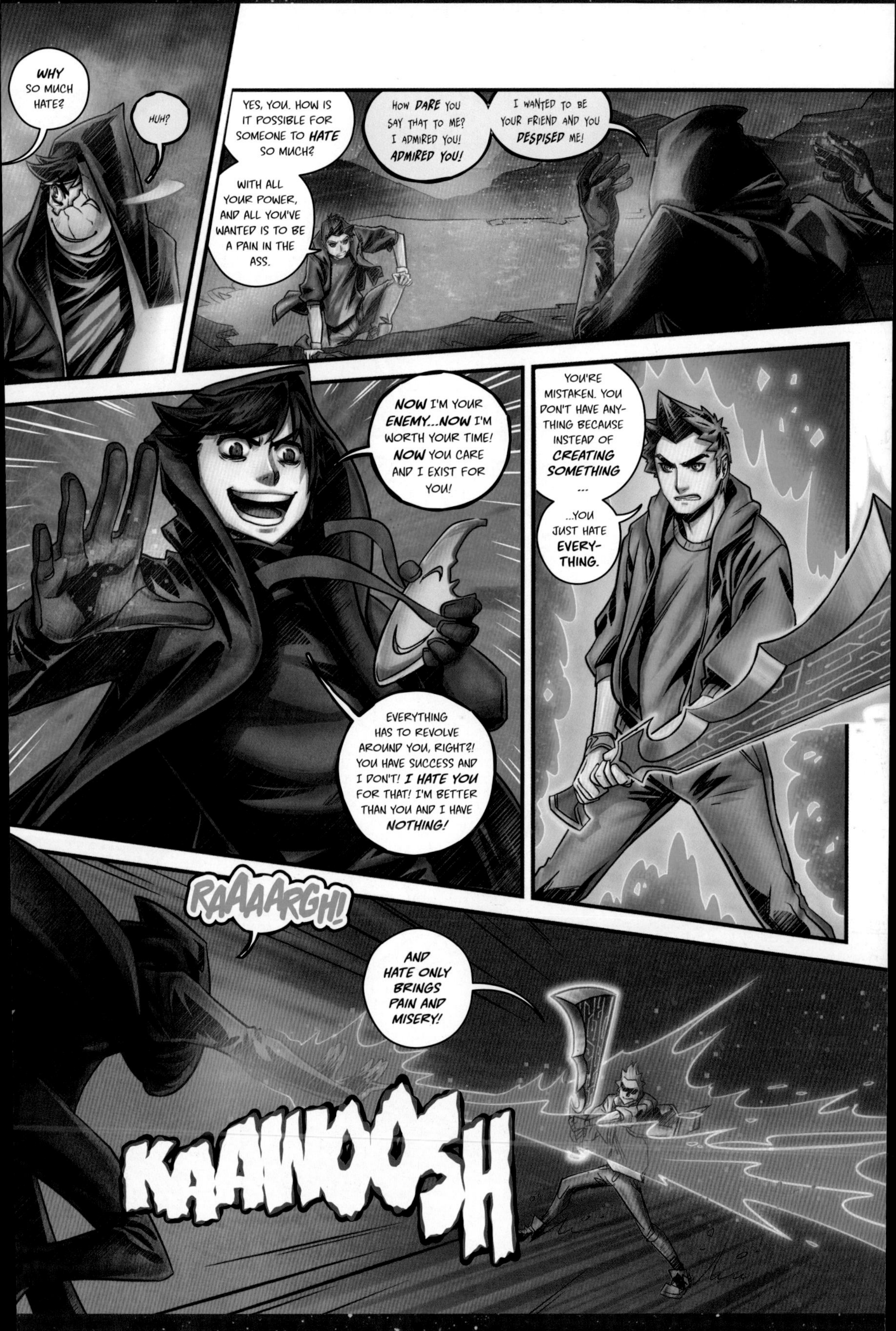

WHY SO MUCH HATE?
HUH?
YES, YOU. HOW IS IT POSSIBLE FOR SOMEONE TO HATE SO MUCH?
WITH ALL YOUR POWER, AND ALL YOU'VE WANTED IS TO BE A PAIN IN THE ASS.
HOW DARE YOU SAY THAT TO ME? I ADMIRED YOU! ADMIRED YOU!
I WANTED TO BE YOUR FRIEND AND YOU DESPISED ME!
NOW I'M YOUR ENEMY...NOW I'M WORTH YOUR TIME! NOW YOU CARE AND I EXIST FOR YOU!
EVERYTHING HAS TO REVOLVE AROUND YOU, RIGHT?! YOU HAVE SUCCESS AND I DON'T! I HATE YOU FOR THAT! I'M BETTER THAN YOU AND I HAVE NOTHING!
YOU'RE MISTAKEN. YOU DON'T HAVE ANYTHING BECAUSE INSTEAD OF CREATING SOMETHING...
...YOU JUST HATE EVERYTHING.
RAAAARGH!
AND HATE ONLY BRINGS PAIN AND MISERY!
KAAWOOSH

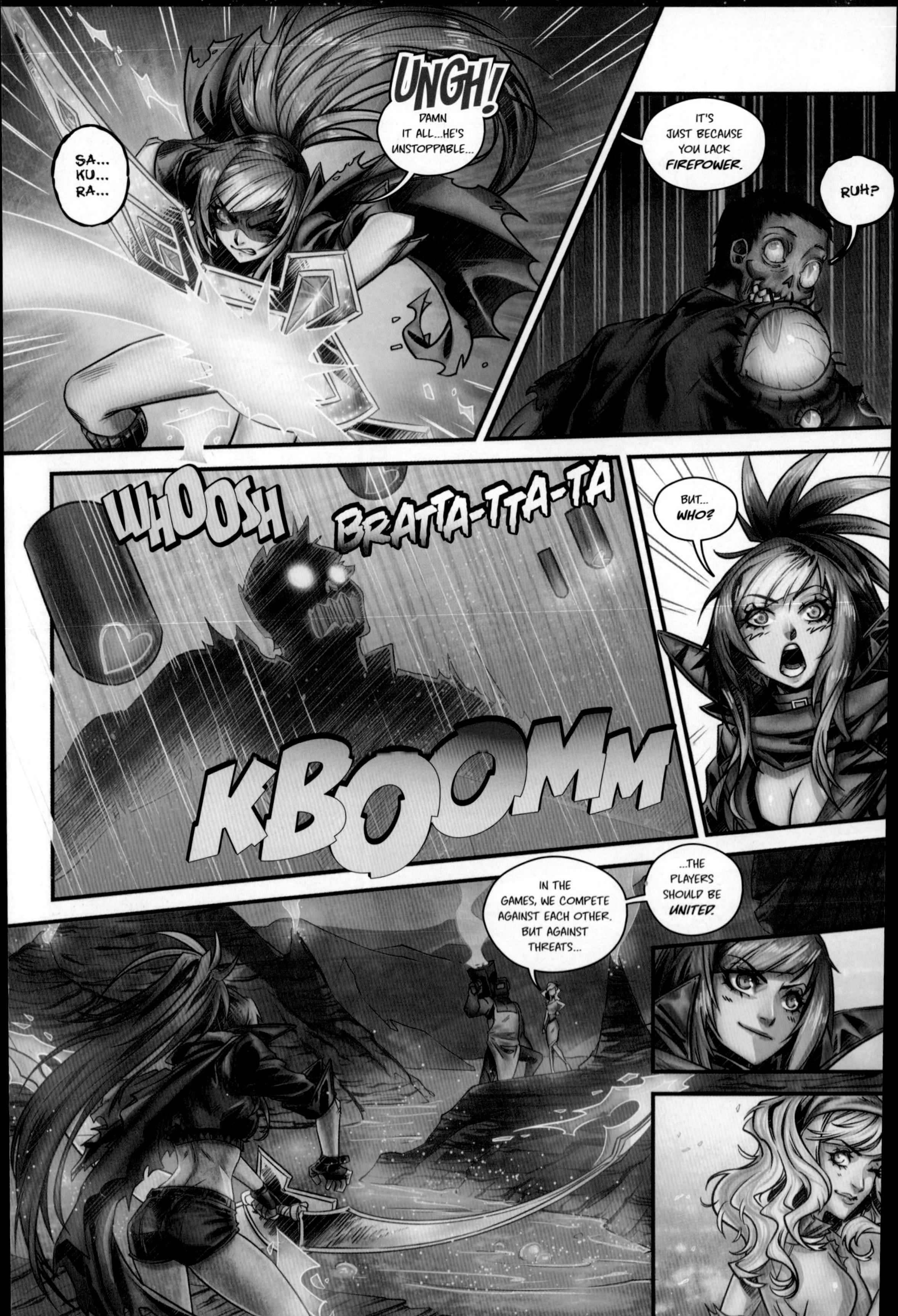
SA... KU... RA...
UNGH!
DAMN IT ALL...HE'S UNSTOPPABLE...
IT'S JUST BECAUSE YOU LACK FIREPOWER.
RUH?
WHOOSH
BRATTA-TTA-TA
KBOOMM
BUT... WHO?
IN THE GAMES, WE COMPETE AGAINST EACH OTHER. BUT AGAINST THREATS...
...THE PLAYERS SHOULD BE UNITED.

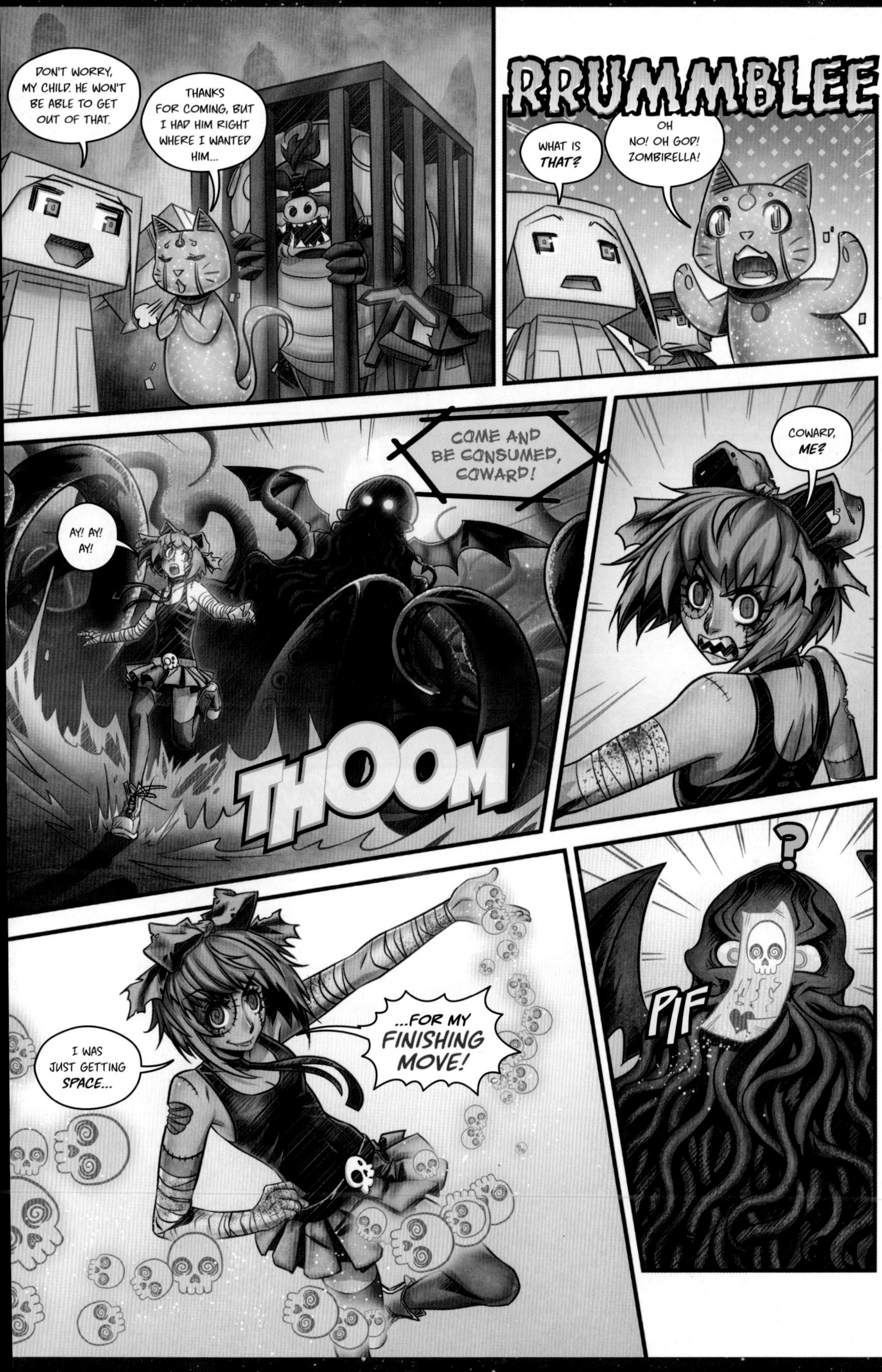

DON'T WORRY, MY CHILD. HE WON'T BE ABLE TO GET OUT OF THAT.
THANKS FOR COMING, BUT I HAD HIM RIGHT WHERE I WANTED HIM...
RRUMMBLEE
WHAT IS THAT?
OH NO! OH GOD! ZOMBIRELLA!
COME AND BE CONSUMED, COWARD!
AY! AY! AY!
THOOM
COWARD, ME?
I WAS JUST GETTING SPACE...
...FOR MY FINISHING MOVE!
?
PIF

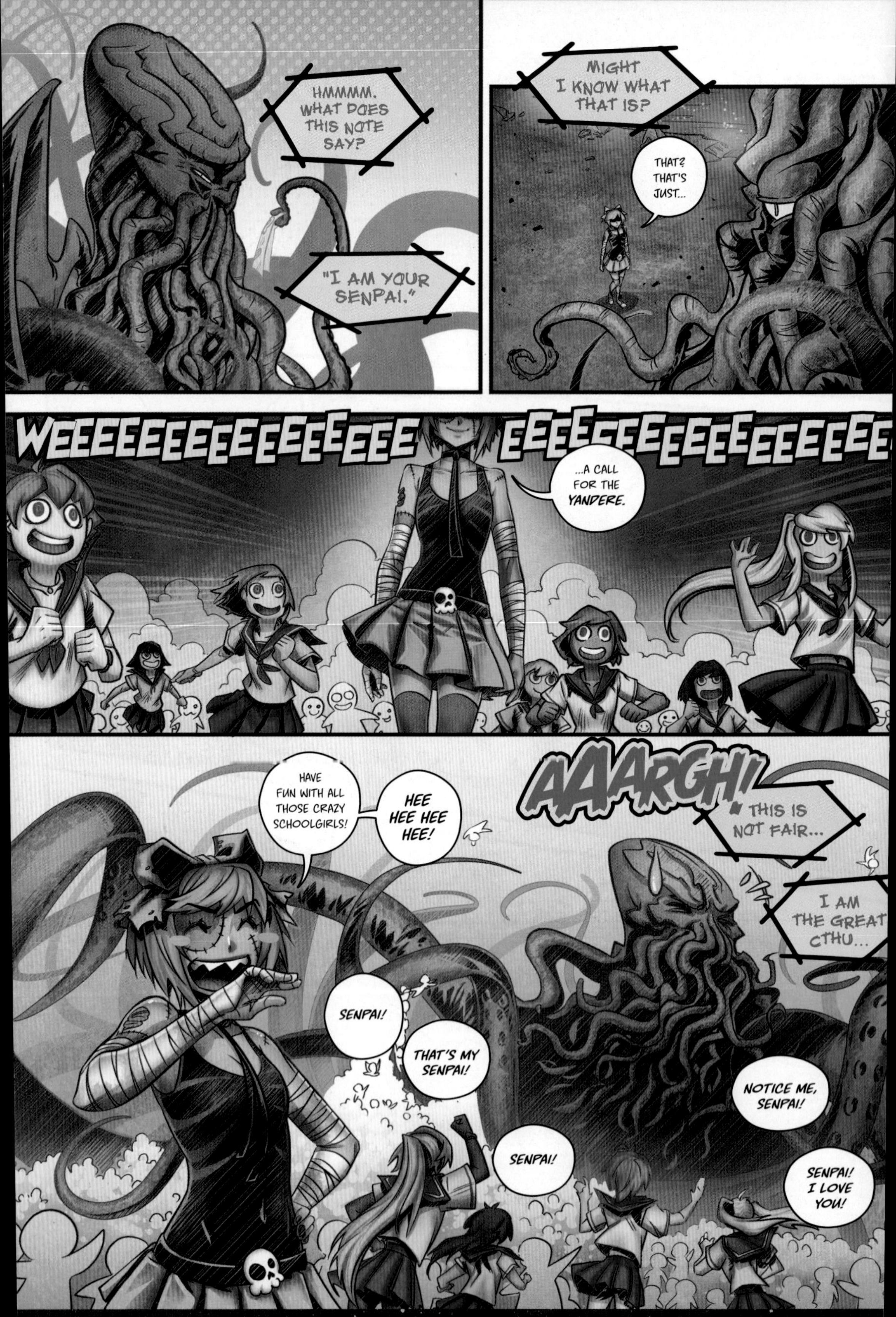

HMMMM. WHAT DOES THIS NOTE SAY?
"I AM YOUR SENPAI."
MIGHT I KNOW WHAT THAT IS?
THAT? THAT'S JUST...
WEEEEEEEEEEEEEEEE EEEEEEEEEEEEEEEEE
...A CALL FOR THE YANDERE.
HAVE FUN WITH ALL THOSE CRAZY SCHOOLGIRLS!
HEE HEE HEE HEE!
AAARGH!
THIS IS NOT FAIR...
I AM THE GREAT CTHU...
SENPAI!
THAT'S MY SENPAI!
NOTICE ME, SENPAI!
SENPAI!
SENPAI! I LOVE YOU!

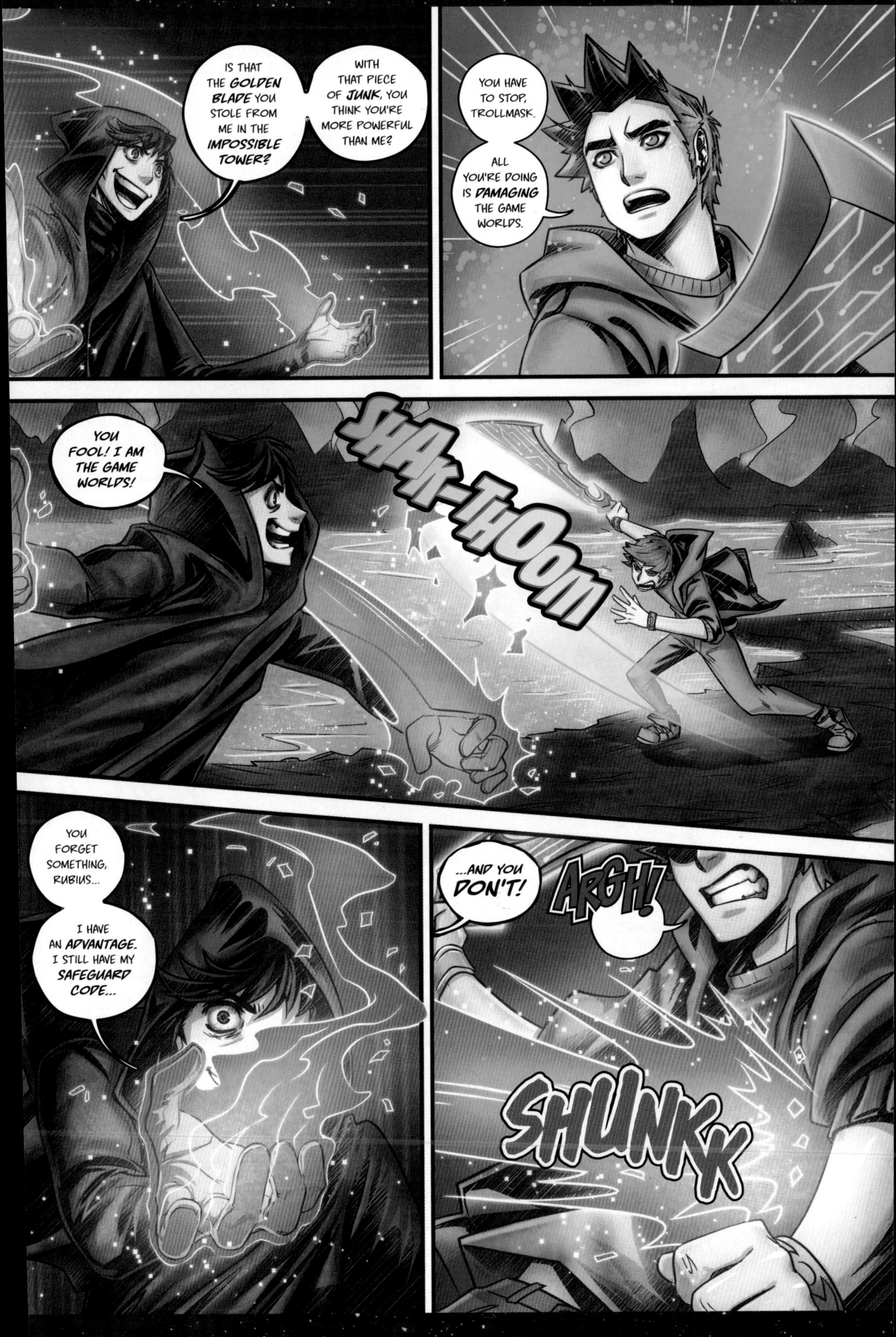
IS THAT THE GOLDEN BLADE YOU STOLE FROM ME IN THE IMPOSSIBLE TOWER?
WITH THAT PIECE OF JUNK, YOU THINK YOU'RE MORE POWERFUL THAN ME?
YOU HAVE TO STOP, TROLLMASK.
ALL YOU'RE DOING IS DAMAGING THE GAME WORLDS.
YOU FOOL! I AM THE GAME WORLDS!
SHAK-THOOOM
YOU FORGET SOMETHING, RUBIUS...
I HAVE AN ADVANTAGE. I STILL HAVE MY SAFEGUARD CODE...
...AND YOU DON'T!
ARGH!
SHUNKK

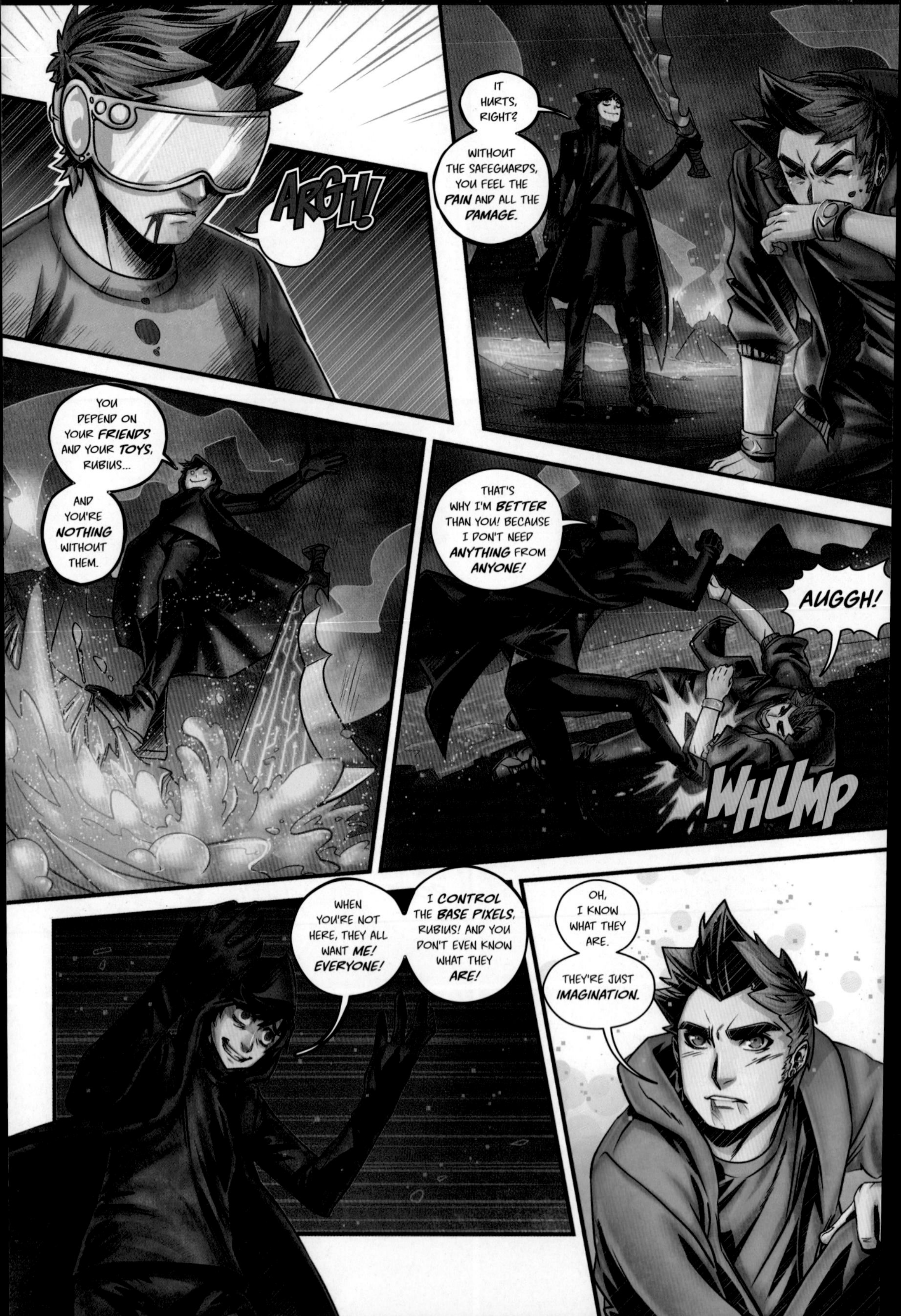
ARGH!
IT HURTS, RIGHT?
WITHOUT THE SAFEGUARDS, YOU FEEL THE PAIN AND ALL THE DAMAGE.
YOU DEPEND ON YOUR FRIENDS AND YOUR TOYS, RUBIUS...
AND YOU'RE NOTHING WITHOUT THEM.
THAT'S WHY I'M BETTER THAN YOU! BECAUSE I DON'T NEED ANYTHING FROM ANYONE!
AUGGH!
WHUMP
WHEN YOU'RE NOT HERE, THEY ALL WANT ME! EVERYONE!
I CONTROL THE BASE PIXELS, RUBIUS! AND YOU DON'T EVEN KNOW WHAT THEY ARE!
OH, I KNOW WHAT THEY ARE.
THEY'RE JUST IMAGINATION.

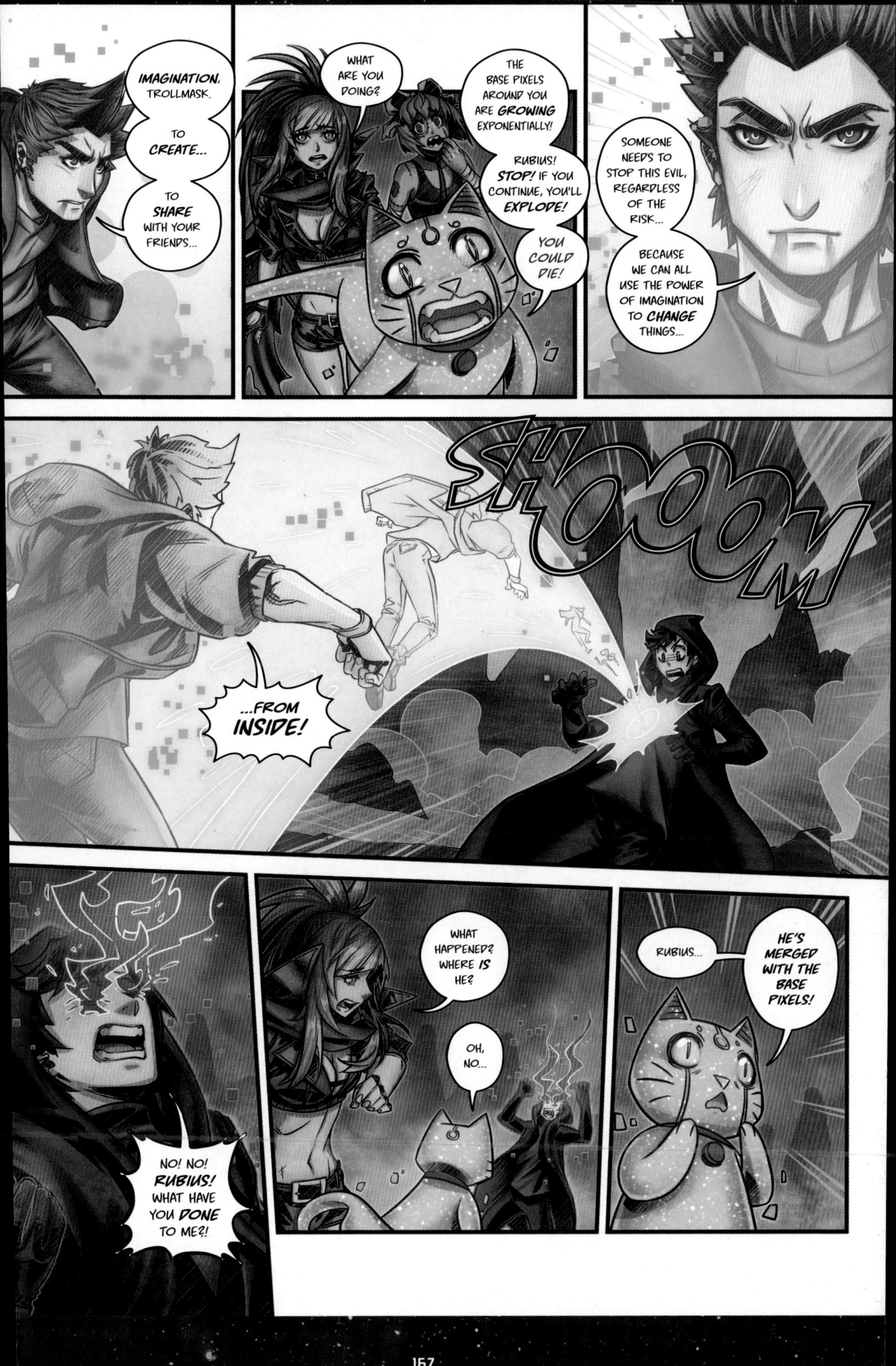
IMAGINATION, TROLLMASK.
TO CREATE...
TO SHARE WITH YOUR FRIENDS...
WHAT ARE YOU DOING?
THE BASE PIXELS AROUND YOU ARE GROWING EXPONENTIALLY!
RUBIUS! STOP! IF YOU CONTINUE, YOU'LL EXPLODE!
YOU COULD DIE!
SOMEONE NEEDS TO STOP THIS EVIL, REGARDLESS OF THE RISK...
BECAUSE WE CAN ALL USE THE POWER OF IMAGINATION TO CHANGE THINGS...
SHOOOOM
...FROM INSIDE!
NO! NO! RUBIUS! WHAT HAVE YOU DONE TO ME?!
WHAT HAPPENED? WHERE IS HE?
OH, NO...
RUBIUS...
HE'S MERGED WITH THE BASE PIXELS!

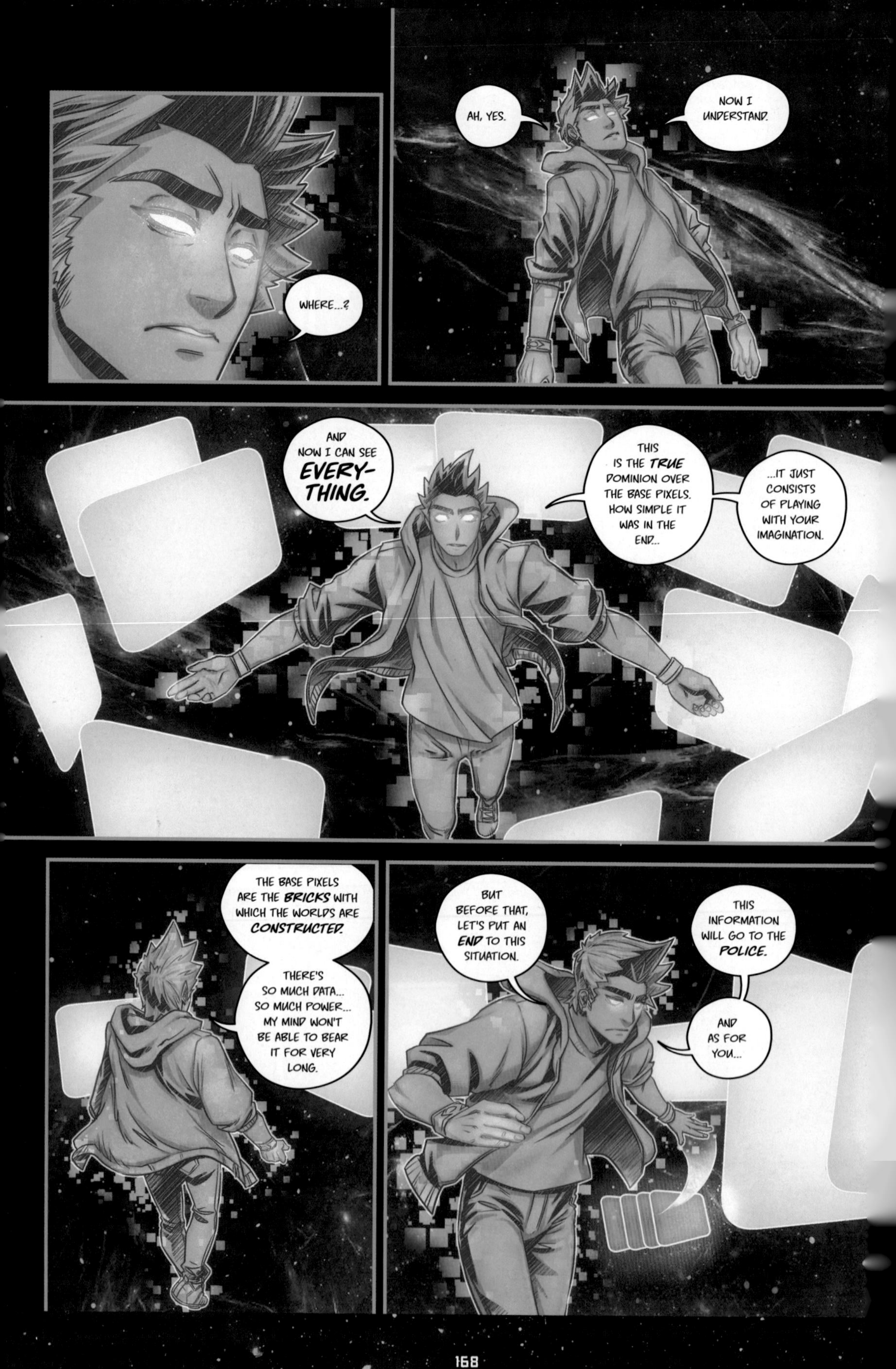
WHERE...?
AH, YES.
NOW I UNDERSTAND.
AND NOW I CAN SEE EVERY-THING.
THIS IS THE TRUE DOMINION OVER THE BASE PIXELS. HOW SIMPLE IT WAS IN THE END...
...IT JUST CONSISTS OF PLAYING WITH YOUR IMAGINATION.
THE BASE PIXELS ARE THE BRICKS WITH WHICH THE WORLDS ARE CONSTRUCTED.
THERE'S SO MUCH DATA... SO MUCH POWER... MY MIND WON'T BE ABLE TO BEAR IT FOR VERY LONG.
BUT BEFORE THAT, LET'S PUT AN END TO THIS SITUATION.
THIS INFORMATION WILL GO TO THE POLICE.
AND AS FOR YOU...

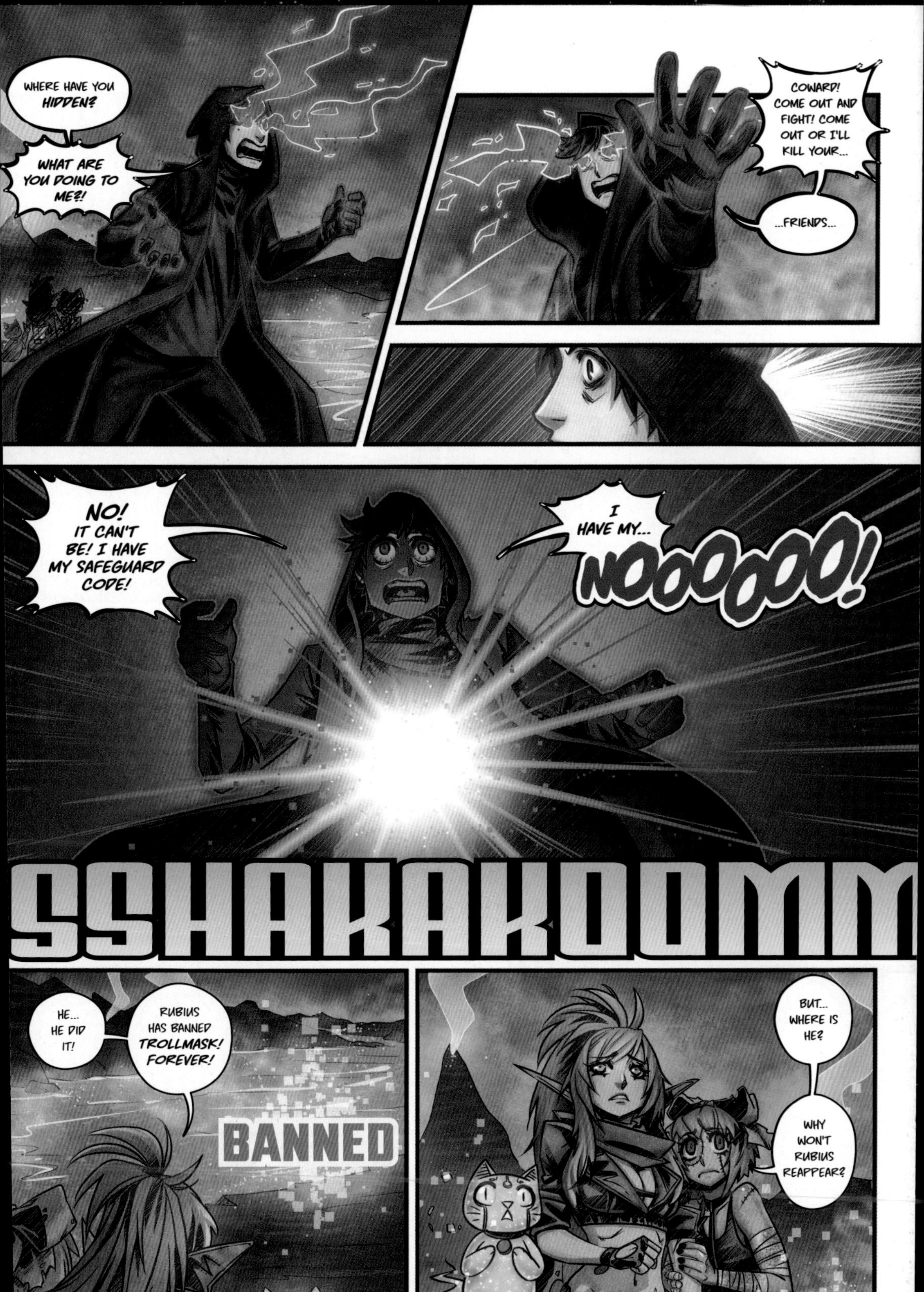

WHERE HAVE YOU HIDDEN?
WHAT ARE YOU DOING TO ME?!
COWARD! COME OUT AND FIGHT! COME OUT OR I'LL KILL YOUR...
...FRIENDS...
NO! IT CAN'T BE! I HAVE MY SAFEGUARD CODE!
I HAVE MY...
NOOOOOO!
SSHAKAKOOMM
HE... HE DID IT!
RUBIUS HAS BANNED TROLLMASK! FOREVER!
BANNED
BUT... WHERE IS HE?
WHY WON'T RUBIUS REAPPEAR?

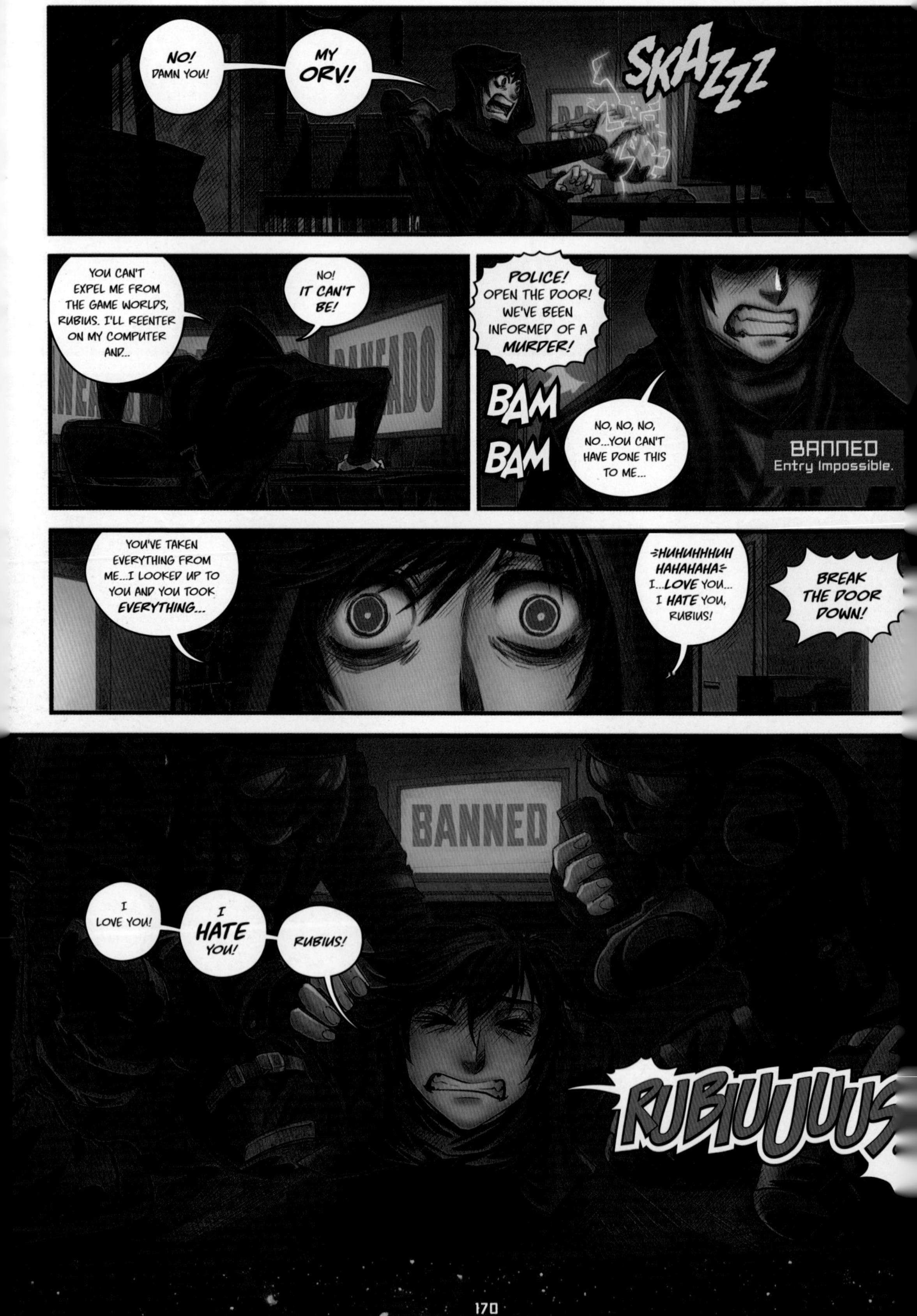
NO! DAMN YOU!
MY ORV!
SKAZZZ
YOU CAN'T EXPEL ME FROM THE GAME WORLDS, RUBIUS. I'LL REENTER ON MY COMPUTER AND...
NO! IT CAN'T BE!
POLICE! OPEN THE DOOR! WE'VE BEEN INFORMED OF A MURDER!
BAM
BAM
NO, NO, NO, NO...YOU CAN'T HAVE DONE THIS TO ME...
BANNED
Entry Impossible.
YOU'VE TAKEN EVERYTHING FROM ME...I LOOKED UP TO YOU AND YOU TOOK EVERYTHING...
HUHUHHHHUH HAHAHAHA I...LOVE YOU... I HATE YOU, RUBIUS!
BREAK THE DOOR DOWN!
BANNED
I LOVE YOU!
I HATE YOU!
RUBIUS!
RUBIUUUUS

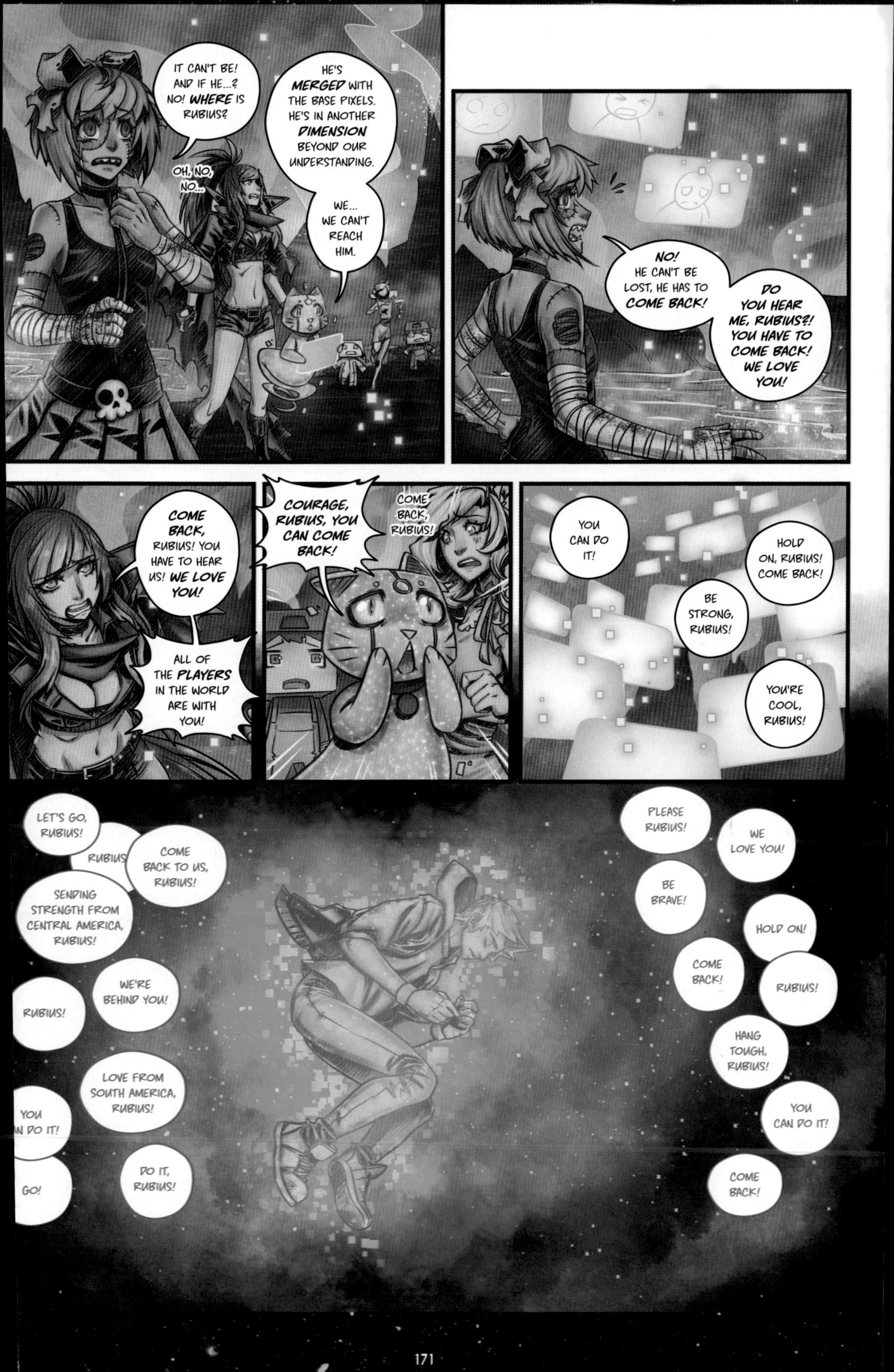

IT CAN'T BE! AND IF HE...? NO! WHERE IS RUBIUS?
HE'S MERGED WITH THE BASE PIXELS. HE'S IN ANOTHER DIMENSION BEYOND OUR UNDERSTANDING.
OH, NO, NO...
WE... WE CAN'T REACH HIM.
NO! HE CAN'T BE LOST, HE HAS TO COME BACK!
DO YOU HEAR ME, RUBIUS?! YOU HAVE TO COME BACK! WE LOVE YOU!
COME BACK, RUBIUS! YOU HAVE TO HEAR US! WE LOVE YOU!
ALL OF THE PLAYERS IN THE WORLD ARE WITH YOU!
COURAGE, RUBIUS, YOU CAN COME BACK!
COME BACK, RUBIUS!
YOU CAN DO IT!
HOLD ON, RUBIUS! COME BACK!
BE STRONG, RUBIUS!
YOU'RE COOL, RUBIUS!
LET'S GO, RUBIUS!
RUBIUS
COME BACK TO US, RUBIUS!
SENDING STRENGTH FROM CENTRAL AMERICA, RUBIUS!
WE'RE BEHIND YOU!
RUBIUS!
LOVE FROM SOUTH AMERICA, RUBIUS!
DO IT, RUBIUS!
GO!
PLEASE RUBIUS!
WE LOVE YOU!
BE BRAVE!
HOLD ON!
COME BACK!
RUBIUS!
HANG TOUGH, RUBIUS!
YOU CAN DO IT!
COME BACK!

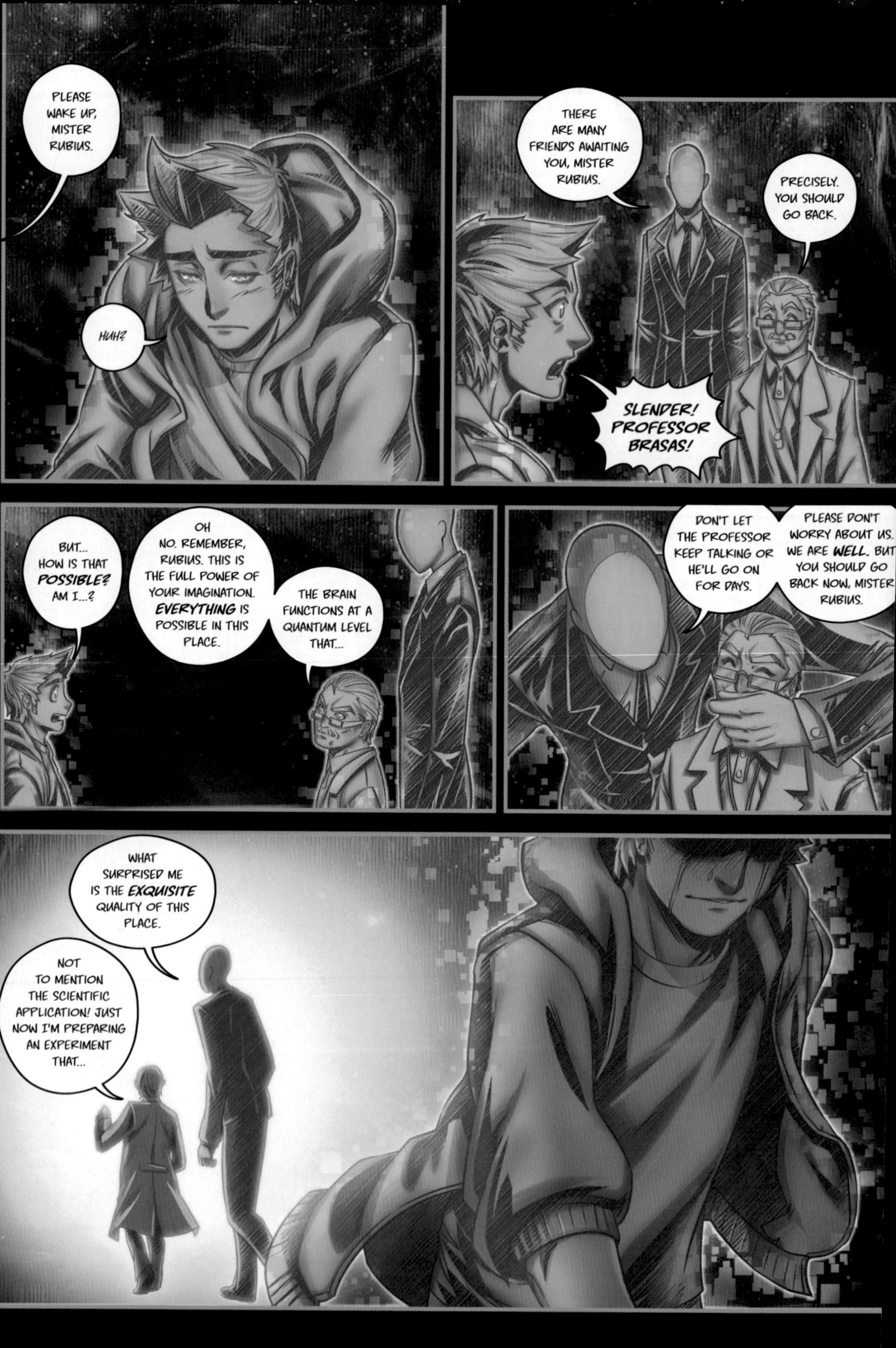

PLEASE WAKE UP, MISTER RUBIUS.
HUH?
THERE ARE MANY FRIENDS AWAITING YOU, MISTER RUBIUS.
PRECISELY. YOU SHOULD GO BACK.
SLENDER! PROFESSOR BRASAS!
BUT... HOW IS THAT POSSIBLE? AM I...?
OH NO. REMEMBER, RUBIUS. THIS IS THE FULL POWER OF YOUR IMAGINATION. EVERYTHING IS POSSIBLE IN THIS PLACE.
THE BRAIN FUNCTIONS AT A QUANTUM LEVEL THAT...
DON'T LET THE PROFESSOR KEEP TALKING OR HE'LL GO ON FOR DAYS.
PLEASE DON'T WORRY ABOUT US. WE ARE WELL. BUT YOU SHOULD GO BACK NOW, MISTER RUBIUS.
WHAT SURPRISED ME IS THE EXQUISITE QUALITY OF THIS PLACE.
NOT TO MENTION THE SCIENTIFIC APPLICATION! JUST NOW I'M PREPARING AN EXPERIMENT THAT...

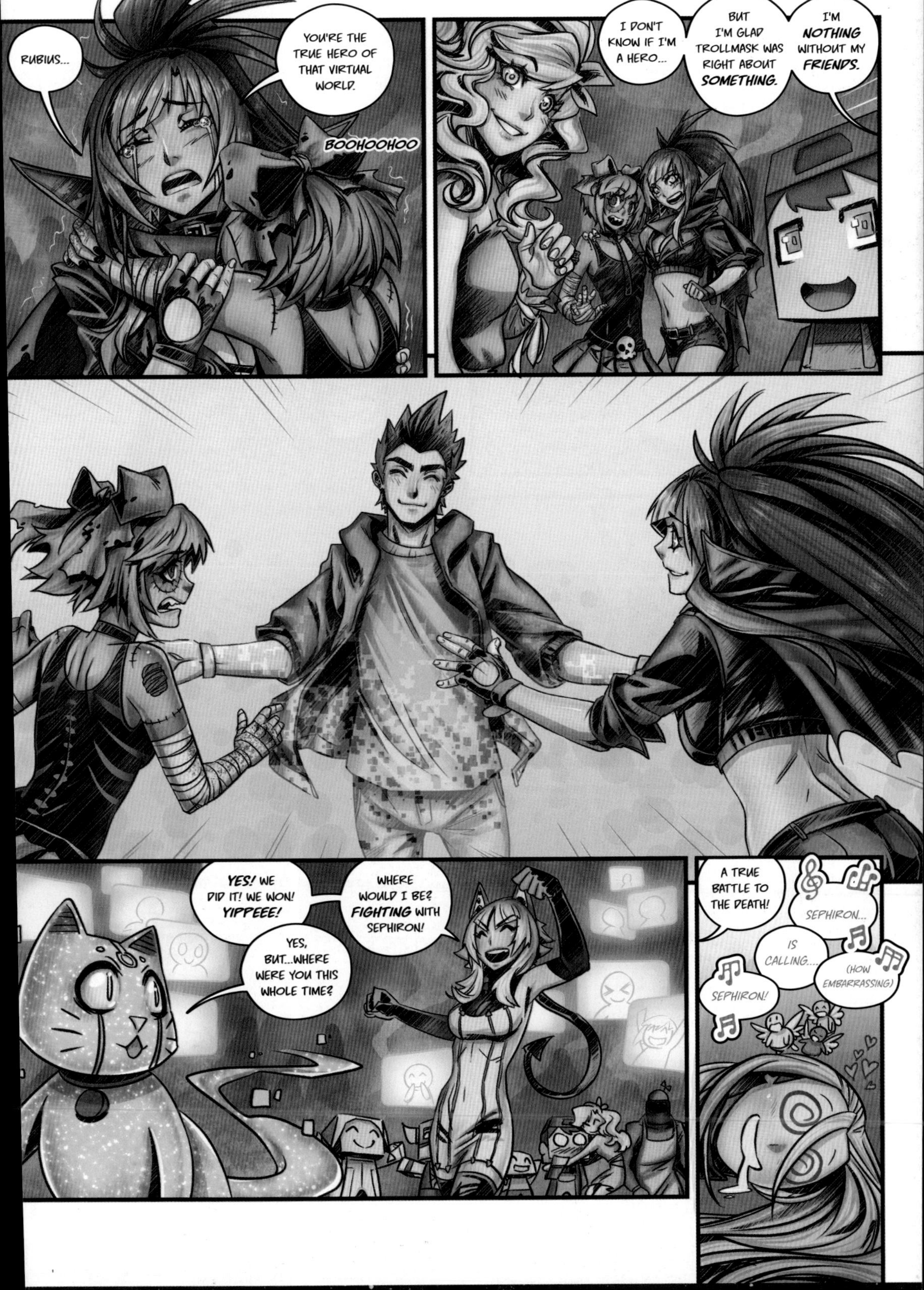
RUBIUS...
YOU'RE THE TRUE HERO OF THAT VIRTUAL WORLD.
BOOHOOHOO
I DON'T KNOW IF I'M A HERO...
BUT I'M GLAD TROLLMASK WAS RIGHT ABOUT SOMETHING.
I'M NOTHING WITHOUT MY FRIENDS.
YES! WE DID IT! WE WON! YIPPEEE!
YES, BUT...WHERE WERE YOU THIS WHOLE TIME?
WHERE WOULD I BE? FIGHTING WITH SEPHIRON!
A TRUE BATTLE TO THE DEATH!
SEPHIRON...
IS CALLING....
SEPHIRON!
(HOW EMBARRASSING)

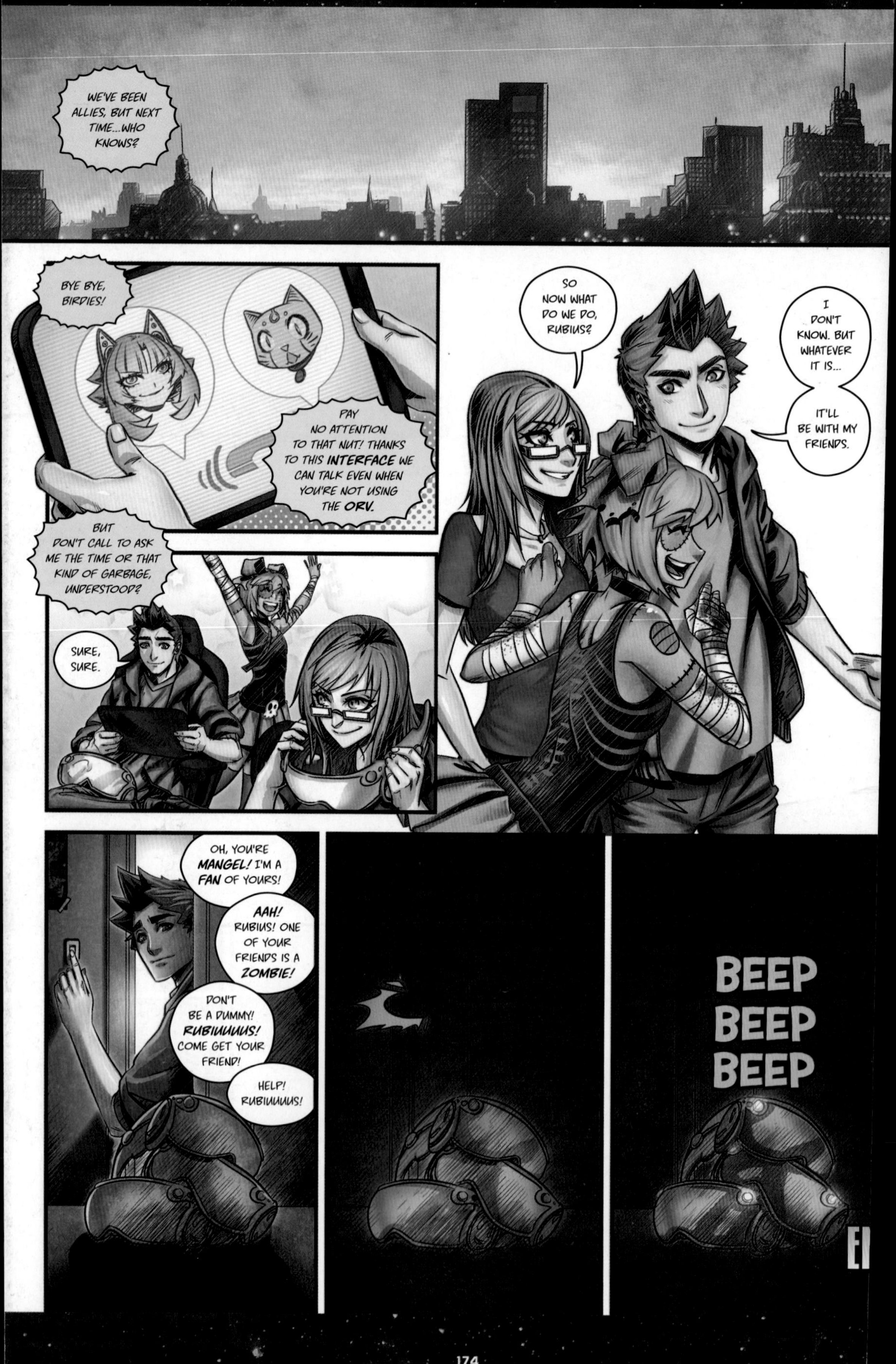
WE'VE BEEN ALLIES, BUT NEXT TIME...WHO KNOWS?
BYE BYE, BIRDIES!
PAY NO ATTENTION TO THAT NUT! THANKS TO THIS INTERFACE WE CAN TALK EVEN WHEN YOU'RE NOT USING THE ORV.
BUT DON'T CALL TO ASK ME THE TIME OR THAT KIND OF GARBAGE, UNDERSTOOD?
SURE, SURE.
SO NOW WHAT DO WE DO, RUBIUS?
I DON'T KNOW. BUT WHATEVER IT IS...
IT'LL BE WITH MY FRIENDS.
OH, YOU'RE MANGEL! I'M A FAN OF YOURS!
AAH! RUBIUS! ONE OF YOUR FRIENDS IS A ZOMBIE!
DON'T BE A DUMMY! RUBIUUUUS! COME GET YOUR FRIEND!
HELP! RUBIUUUUS!
BEEP
BEEP
BEEP

Thank you all for making this
beautiful adventure possible.

Without you, the readers and my
subscribers, I could not have fulfilled
my dream of creating a comic.

Nor could I have done it without the help
of El Torres and Lolita Aldea, who have
shaped this entire story in incredible ways.

This is the end of the Virtual Hero
trilogy, but there may be a little
surprise for all the fans, a surprise
that you will discover shortly.

Thank you.

RUBIUS

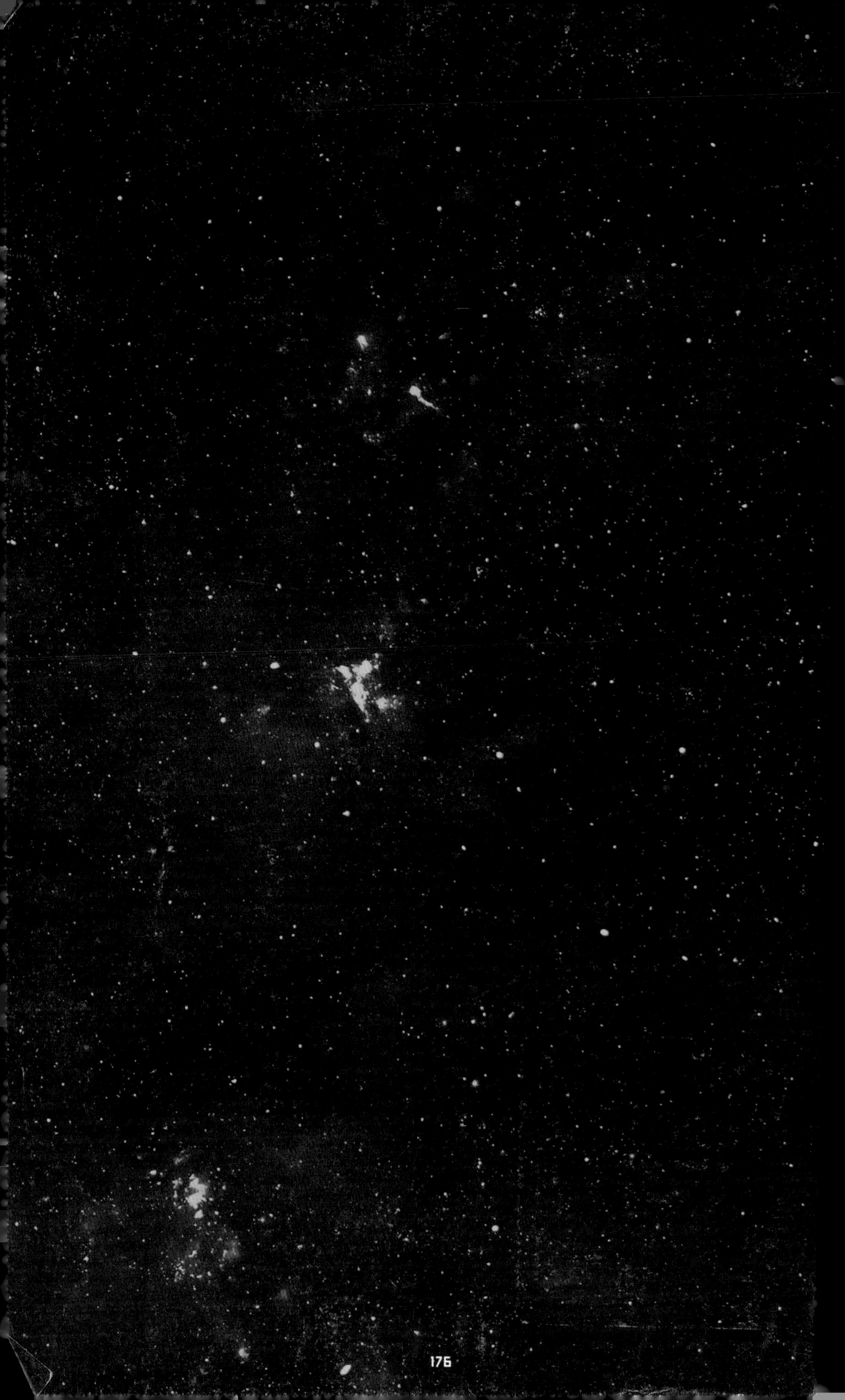